Falling Bodies

Falling Bodies
By Sue Kaufman

HAMISH HAMILTON

LONDON

First published in Great Britain 1974
by Hamish Hamilton Ltd.,
90 Great Russell Street, London WC1

Copyright © 1974 by Sue Kaufman

SBN 241 89069 1

Grateful acknowledgment is given for permission to reprint
the following: Seven lines from *The Age of Anxiety* by
W. H. Auden. Reprinted by permission of Faber & Faber Ltd.
One line from "Spring is like a perhaps hand" from *Complete
Poems 1913-1962* by E. E. Cummings. Reprinted by permission
of MacGibbon & Kee Ltd.

Printed in Great Britain by Compton Printing Limited,
Aylesbury, Bucks.

for my father

Contents

ROSETTA: We must try to get on
Though mobs run amok and markets fall,
Though lights burn late at police stations,
Though passports expire and ports are watched,
Though thousands tumble.

. . . .

QUANT: I must go away
With my terrors until I have taught them to sing.

THE AGE OF ANXIETY

W. H. AUDEN

Falling Bodies

Emma Half-Awake

"Let's take five. Want a smoke?"

"Not just now. Only . . . could you move over a teensy bit?"

"Could if I have to. Okay—teensy like you said. Listen, sweetheart. Tell me something. There's something I've gotta know. What's going to happen. When you get back up there I mean."

"You asked me that last night. And please don't start that whole . . ."

"Now I'm asking again. I *know* you, remember. And I know those bastards and how they operate. All those Harvard faggots and sneaky professors who slip it to you with a little private tutoring. Horny geniuses. Big deal. Big big deal. But I'll tell you one thing, baby. None of them could make you feel like this. Could they, Em baby. Could they. Dammit Emma— answer me."

"No. They couldn't. And you know it too."

"Only one thing I know. How I feel. Now. And always will. No matter where we are. No matter what."

"Burt. Sweetie. We've only got three more nights. Don't spoil things. I hate when you start piling it on, hamming it up. And you talk like we'll never see each oth . . . Oh God. Burt. What was *that*?"

"Just the wind in the trees. Just the wind in the sweet old grass.—'Piling it on.' You know what you can do with *that*. But never mind. We're wasting time. Let's get out on that grass. Be more room to . . ."

"No. I'm not getting out of this car. That grass is too high. And sharp. And remember last week when those boys chased us up the back roads for miles? Can you *imagine* what would've happened if we hadn't been in the car when they drove up?"

"I don't have to imagine. I know. I'd have beat the bijeezuz out of them. Just like I would've if you'd let me stop the car. But you were too scared. Like now. What's bugging you, baby? What's got you so scared?"

"I'm not 'bugged.' Or 'scared.' It's just that we're off in the middle of noplace here. And there are a lot of crazy people running around."

"Oh no. Now don't *you* start."

"Start what."

"Start that business. Start carrying on. People are crazy. People are bad. *Things* are bad. Shit, sweetheart. You don't really believe that. You know better than that."

"You're damned right I do. And I don't 'carry on.' "

"Sometimes you do. You sure as hell do. But as long as I'm around I'll snap you out of it. Fast."

"Fascinating. How."

" 'Fascinating. How.' You must be *kidding* trying to pull that tight-assed Radcliffe routine on *me*. This is Burt. Remember? Burt. . . . Ye-es. I see you remember. How. Like that, Emma baby. Like that. . . . Now what've you got to say for yourself? Not much, I see. Not much. . . . Me either. Except to say that this is what it's all about. Piling it on. Yeah. Hamming it up. It's *this* that makes the world go round."

A Vanishing Breed

"Em. Have you *seen* this?"

Emma laughed. "It was the first thing I saw when I came home from the hospital. But I don't understand. Haven't *you* seen it before now?"

"I have, but it seems to have mushroomed overnight. It's taking over the whole damned wall. What is it? What's it supposed to be? Some sort of computer?"

"No. I asked and he said no."

"Maybe a bank of consoles like the ones they had in Mission Control? Remember how he was always more interested in the shots of Houston than the live shots from the spacecraft or moon?"

"I remember. And I asked that too. He got *very* annoyed and said that if he was going to do anything that dumb and archaic—yes, archaic—he would have made it look exactly what it was supposed to be. He said this was just what it looked like: a bunch of old electrical equipment and parts."

"Yes. Well. It certainly is that— Does it do anything? Work in some way?"

". . . do? Work?"

"*You* know. Light up or buzz or ring bells."

More laughter from Emma. "No. That's all we'd need. He promised none of those wires were hooked up to any outlets or batteries. Which is a relief. I mean it could have been a terrific fire hazard otherwise."

From the sound Harold made it was clear he would have far preferred the fire hazard.

They were standing side-by-side in the doorway of their son, Benjy's, room—Emma Sohier, pale and frail from a recent illness, still in pajamas and robe, Harold Sohier, stocky and pink, fully dressed for work, dispatch case in hand. It was eight twenty-three on a hot October morning. Benjy had left for school at eight. Harold, just now leaving, had passed Benjy's room and stopped in his tracks and called Emma to come. In spite of feeling dizzy, Emma had come, and now they stood in depressed silence considering what had stopped Harold cold—a left-hand wall covered with strip shelves from ceiling to floor, except for a center space filled by a maple desk and chair. A carpenter had built the shelves when they'd first moved in the year before, and up until a month ago the shelves had held the accumulations of eleven years, the possessions of a perfectly ordinary eleven-year-old boy who obviously couldn't throw anything away. A boy with just as striking a passion for neatness and a wry sense of chronology. Rows of books beginning with Mother Goose and Dr. Seuss, working up through the mysteries of Danny Dunn and a complete collection of Charlie Brown paperbacks; a regimental lineup of toys and boxed games starting out with thread-bare stuffed animals and nested alphabet blocks, progressing through Lincoln Logs and Tinker Toys to a telescope and advanced chemistry set; records packed like Necco wafers, ranging from albums where Cyril Ritchard read Beatrix Potter and Giselle MacKenzie sang *Babar,* to the recordings of rock groups with names like the Freak Outs and Mothering Five, and the sound tracks of X-rated movies he hadn't been able to see.

Now, with the exception of the shelf above the desk, which still held reference books needed for homework—dictionaries, textbooks, desk encyclopedias—all these long-treasured objects had been banished to a large walk-in closet on the opposite side of the room, and in their place was "a bunch of old electrical equipment and parts." Indeed. There were small motors, generators, fan belts and adapters. There were condensers and fuses and rheostats and plugs. There were switches and sockets and mixers and sprockets and trimmers and dimmers and triodes and grids. There were grommets, transformers, repeaters and starters, there were junction boxes and gauges and taps. There were locking devices and grounding devices . . . and devices only an electrician could name. Interconnecting all the separate pieces, criss-crossing and looping like vines from object to object and shelf to shelf, was a thick tangle of wires and filaments which gave the shelves a con-tiguous look, made them seem one scrummy mass. And overlaying all was a fine powdering of dust, that turned pink copper gray and formed linty feathers in corners and coils.

Focused on this dust, Emma was thinking of a terrible row she'd heard it had caused, but guessed that Harold had focused on the tangled wires—which he probably saw as some manifest symbol of their son's twisted mind. So, though she felt far from bright, she was about to say something cheerful and bright, when Harold said, "Where's he get all that stuff, Em. You have any idea?"

"I do because I asked. He buys some with his allowance in hardware and electric supply stores, and some are parts of broken appliances—old toasters and Mixmasters and clock radios—we've thrown out over the years. Seems he's been salvaging things from our garbage cans since he was a baby, so he's obviously been planning this little project for quite some time."

"Project, hell. Nice fancy word. And we never had anything with a fan belt like the one up there on the next-to-top shelf. Or owned a sewing machine—and look at that treadle on the shelf above the books. Where d'you suppose he gets things like *that?*"

Emma, who had been feeling weaker by the minute, leaned against the doorframe and took a deep breath: "I believe he picks them up off the ground or fishes them out of trash cans on the street."

"What?"

"I said I believe he picks them up off the ground or fishes them out of trash cans on the street."

"Oh my God. That's dis*gust*ing. And dangerous. Those things are probably loaded with bacteria—he could get some lousy infection or some kind of contact dermatitis. To say nothing of getting an allergy from that dust. Just take a look at all that goddamn dust."

Emma, who had looked long enough at the dust, now looked intently at Harold instead. "He told me he washes each piece he gets off the street with formaldehyde. I believe his science teacher gave him the formaldehyde. As for the dust . . . he won't let anyone touch it." She laughed. "Just ask poor Maria."

"Jesus, Em. How can you laugh. This is serious and I'm worried sick. That stuff my mother wrote you was right, only 'apathetic' was putting it mildly. 'Disturbed' is more like it. He's turning into some kind of 'disturbed' child. You probably haven't been home long enough or been feeling well enough to notice how quiet he's gotten, or how he's dropped all his friends. Or maybe it's just the reverse. Point is, this place used to be crawling with kids, and nobody shows or calls anymore. Maybe he had some godawful kind of traumatizing experience at camp and is trying to tell us something by building this . . . this thing."

"Harold, darling," she finally said with dangerous sweetness. "I'm sure it's nothing serious. It's just some sort of collector phase—like that time he was collecting rocks and pebbles and his room looked like a quarry for months?"

"He was eight then, and that was normal for eight. Christ. Other boys his age are collecting centerfolds from *Playboy* and *Screw*. That's the sort of phase that's normal for an eleven-year-old boy."

"I don't agree. You're rushing things. And when you think of the phases *some* eleven-year-olds are in—and I mean the drug scene, not centerfolds—we've got a lot to be grateful for. Anyway, we can talk about it tonight. Going by Benjy's clock you're late for your car. Hadn't you better go?"

Acknowledging he had, Harold quickly kissed her cheek and rushed off down the hall, leaving the aftermath of some awful new after shave in his wake. Sniffing—when had he gotten that and why?—Emma queasily swallowed, and as the front door slammed started for the kitchen with a wobbly gait.

The kitchen was spotless and deserted. From behind Maria's closed door came the soft chitter of the Spanish-speaking station she played whenever she was in her room. The half-full pot of coffee she'd asked Maria to leave warming was gone from the stove, the pot stood upended and Brillo shiny in the dish-drying rack. The language barrier, she told herself, and wondering why the language barrier never seemed to operate in the matter of the *Daily News* or prime-time TV, went to put a light under the kettle. She was measuring instant coffee into a cup, when a voice in back of her softly said, "*Señora?*"—making her scatter brown powder everywhere.

It was Maria, standing right smack in back of her, her usually sallow face flushed with excitement, searching for something in the pockets of her uniform. Small, sturdy, the curling ends of her short black hair almost quivering with impatience, she finally pulled a scrap of paper from one of the pockets, and held it out with a shy smile: "You know O'Dwyer, *señora?*"

"You mean Paul? The senator?" said Emma, reluctantly taking the slip of paper—a news clipping yellow and fuzzy with age.

"No, Bill. The onetime mayor of New York."

"William O'Dwyer?"

"*Sí.*" The black eyes shone with pride.

"Well, I know who he is. Was. I mean, isn't he dead?"

". . . *qué?*"

"Nothing, Maria. Nothing," Emma said hastily, and blinked down at what appeared to be an ancient newsphoto of, yes, William O'Dwyer

—and Carmine De Sapio. "That's him all right," she said, and as the kettle began singing, handed back the clipping and went to the stove.

"I work for the cousin of his wife," said Maria, watching her bring back the kettle and add boiling water to whatever powder had landed in the cup.

"You mean his *ex*-wife? Sloane Simpson O'Dwyer?" said Emma, distractedly stirring, wishing she would go a*way*.

"I no know her name. The cousin name is Spratt. Mrs. Lewis T. Spratt. I work for the Spratt one month in Acapulco where they have the gorgeous villa, then come with them to this country to Houston where they live most the time."

"Grand, Maria. Lovely. How nice."

"Was more than nice. Was benediction to work for people like that."

"I'll bet," Emma murmured inaudibly, spooning sugar into the cup with a lavish hand.

"I stay with them seven month in Houston, and Mr. Lewis T. is working on my permanent citizer—he very big in the *gobierno*—when he die, tlick tlack, just like that. Mrs. Lewis T. then decide to go live in France, and because she cannot take me with, she send me to work some friend Mrs. Larrabee in Wilmington, Delaware. Mrs. Lewis T. is wunnerful lady and only mean to help me finish getting my citizer, but I hate being ship off like the cow to the *hacienda*, and I more than hate Mrs. Larrabee who was terrible person, mean and cruel. So I give up my chance for the citizer and go back to my *madre* and Carlos in Santa Marta, Colombia, where I remain until the month ago."

"Colombia? Funny. I thought you were from Mexico like your aunt, Maria." Emma picked up her coffee, ready to escape.

"What is funny? And why all the Americanos think every *hispano* come this country from Puerto Rico or Mexico? True, my aunt Constanza work long time in Mexico before she go to Albuquerque and work for your mother, but Constanza come from Colombia like I."

"My mother-in-law, not my mother," Emma said with asperity and headed for the door.

"Oh. *Suegra*. Mother-in-law. Was wunnerful person."

"My mother-in-law? . . . Ah, yes. That she is, Maria, that she is."

"No. Mrs. Lewis T. Spratt. She very *aristocrática*. Very refine. The true lady. In all way. She run a beautiful house, very fancy, very gay. They give many party and I cook lovely thing. They love best my pork roast— You give the party soon, *Señora* Soller?"

Señora Soller stopped at the door. They were in fact giving a party soon. They were giving a party in two weeks. A very small dinner party, to be sure—an inspiration of Harold's, who had suggested that seeing some old friends might cheer her up—but, small or not, she had already asked a woman named Cora Matthews to come and do the cooking. Now she saw she had created a touchy situation, but one she wasn't up to handling at the moment. "Well, we do give parties, Maria, but probably won't for a while," she lied. "At least not until I've got my strength back. . . . I'm really still not myself."

"Yes, is true, *señora*. You not looking very good today. In fack you look just terrible. You look much better when you first come from hospital. I think is good idea you go lie down."

Hardly needing any urging, Emma said that *did* sound like a good idea, and fled up front to her room, sloshing coffee everywhere. Shutting the door, she carried the oversugared coffee into her bathroom and poured it down the sink; more red blood cells, not dextrose, was what her poor old anemic body required. Dizzy and short of breath from the same anemia (as well as from a more sinister cause), she went out and sat down on Harold's side of their king-sized bed, a spot that had become her place of reckoning in the twelve days she'd been home from the hospital. Just so, it became that now as she glared at the block of lucite sitting between the phone and opaline lamp on the bedside bachelor's chest.

Embedded in the plastic was a colored Polaroid snapshot of her *suegra*, Elsie Sohier, taken by Harold in their old apartment last Thanksgiving, just before they'd moved. Thin-nosed and thin-lipped and jutty of jaw, wearing a velvet beret that hid her wispy gray hair (which she hadn't had time to have "done" before leaving Albuquerque, she'd explained, even keeping the hat on during the long Thanksgiving dinner), Harold's mother was the spitting image of Holbein's *Erasmus*—a painting Emma had once loved.

Emma no longer loved the painting and had never loved her mother-in-law, an aggressive old battle-ax who had made too many inroads and incursions into her life. (Maria Nonez being the latest example of this, for it was none other than her mother-in-law who had installed the strange young woman in her kitchen and her life, while she'd been in the hospital.) An eccentric old witch, who fourteen years ago had astonished everyone by taking her life savings—a considerable sum for a retired Brooklyn schoolteacher—and by going off to Albuquerque, where she bought a small farm, which she'd quickly parlayed into a booming, dude-ranch-style motel. A tough old bird who had never squandered much time or affection on Harold, her only child—who not only seemed oblivious to her coldness, but went around describing her to everyone as a Great Old Girl.

But then . . . Harold did that. Was given to that sort of thing. For someone who had been one of the most exacting editors in New York, Harold was given to peculiar lapses from time to time. In the twelve days since she'd been home, she'd overheard him talking on the phone several times, saying to someone who'd obviously just asked after her, "Emma? Oh, she's just fine. Just great. Doing beautifully. In fact, considering the rough year she's just been through, she's doing fant*asti*cally well!"—and sitting in a nearby room, she hadn't known whether to burst out laughing or leap up and slam the door shut.

Rough year. Rough year. She had just been through a year of absolute hell. A year which had begun last October, when they'd learned they had six weeks to move, and she'd had to abandon her storefront tutoring project for Knickerbocker House, find them an apartment, get them moved, furnish the new apartment. A year when, no sooner was that over and she was back at work, she was informed that her mother had a widely metastasized carcinoma of the pancreas, and had to spend the next two months watching her mother slowly die, and the two months following that settling her mother's affairs—selling the old Connecticut house and her mother's antiques and paintings to meet the staggering bills, cover the obscene cost of a "terminal illness." A year when, once *that* nightmare was over, she had a brief respite, an illusory breathing spell, during which she again returned to work, got Benjy off to camp, and finally began a much-needed vacation with Harold in Vinyard Haven . . . where she suddenly came down with a fever no one could diagnose. A fever that finally sent her back to New York, into the hospital, where she was told she had a Fever of Unknown Origin, or what they took to calling a FUO, and where she remained a month—the fever finally vanishing just as suddenly and mysteriously as it had come, leaving her weak and anemic and ten pounds lighter, a wraithlike version of her former vital self. "It's going to take at least a month for you to get back to yourself, Emma," her doctor, Martin Tepp, had warned when she was discharged from the hospital. "A lot will depend on you. I mean if you're sensible and patient and take your iron pills and get a lot of rest, it might take as little as three weeks for you to snap back. On the other hand, it could take as much as five or six weeks if you push and try to rush things—if you overdo."

On that bright October morning, the last thing in the world Emma planned to do was Overdo. Hard as it was going to be. And it was going to be hard. For one thing, it was going to be more than hard for her to sit around the house doing nothing, feeling useless, a sitting duck for things like Minda Wolfe's calls or the strange attacks of dizziness and anxiety (one of which she'd been fighting all morning)—trapped with a total stranger to boot. And though on that score, thanks to her mother-in-law, there was little chance she was going to Overdo around the house, she really didn't see how she was going to take two or three more weeks of sitting around, convalescing—while being cooped up with that peculiar young woman. That . . . maid.

She hated having servants. Maids. Housekeepers. Whatever you wanted to call them, it made her uneasy to have people hovering around, waiting on her, serving her, and they had certainly never *ever* had a full-time person or maid working for them. While domestic arrangements had never been her forte, she had managed to run a household for fourteen years in her own casual, slapdash way, using only occasional part-time help—but it had produced a life style that had worked for them, suited them all. And at the beginning of her hospitalization, sick as she'd been, she had still managed to keep her household running from her hospital bed with the same arrangements. Then the second week everything had suddenly broken down—Millie Brundage, their long-time, sixty-year-old sitter actually breaking her hip (in her own apartment, thank God), their cleaning woman mysteriously quitting—and poor Harold, who had been coping heroically until then, pushed the panic button and called his mother in Albuquerque. Rallying, Elsie had immediately flown to New York and commandeered their household and contacted every employment agency in town. But as the days passed, and none of the agencies returned her calls, Elsie made an interesting discovery during one of her daily long-distance conversations with Constanza Vallejo, the excellent manageress of her motel: Constanza, it seemed, had a niece named Maria Nonez, who was about to start a six-week job in Santa Fe, but who might be persuaded to defect . . . if it were made worth her while. Rallying again, Elsie not only made it worth her while, by guaranteeing seven weeks of employment at $130 a week—but after staying long enough to (as she put it) "break in" Maria Nonez, Elsie had paid the seven weeks' salary herself. In advance. In cash.

A surprisingly handsome gesture, considering whence it came. A positively dazzling burst of maternal munificence or, as it turned out, grand-maternal munificence, since Elsie immediately canceled any element of surprise by explaining it was all being done for the sake of her "darling grandson"—who she said was left alone too much.

Which was actually only one of the things she said. On the day she left for Albuquerque, having never visited Emma in the hospital ("They have no idea what you've got, Emma dear, and I frankly have too much of an investment at stake to risk catching what you've got and getting sick myself," she had explained over the phone), Elsie sent her a letter, via Harold, by hand. When Emma read it, she thought her fever had made her delirious.

It began with Elsie announcing that she was "worried sick" about her darling grandson, who she felt was abnormally quiet and "apathetic" and "withdrawn" for a boy his age, and then, nothing loath, went on to say that she felt he was reacting to the atmosphere of "disorder and confusion" in his home:

"In violent and chaotic times such as these, our only chance for survival lies in creating our own little islands of sanity and order, in making little havens of our homes. Going further, I think that where children are concerned, an atmosphere of reason and order and well-being in the home does more than anything else to stave off all the ills young flesh is heir to nowadays: the rebellion against authority, the rebellion against sexual mores, the taking of drugs.

"Now I certainly hope you won't think I'm criticizing you, my dear Emma, but in trying to run your *ménage* in your absence, I naturally had to delve into some of your previous household expenses and arrangements, and I was terribly shocked. What with your laundry bills averaging *eighteen* dollars a week, and a cleaning person costing you *fifty* dollars a week (and with The Situation being what it is now, I doubt you could ever even replace her), plus your "baby-sitting" fees, which Harold told me sometimes run as high as *thirty* or *forty* dollars a week during your Busy Social Season, you are not getting your money's worth. In fact, you are just throwing money down the drain. But the worst part of all this is that after such an expenditure, you still have many gaps, certain things never get attended to and are neglected —particularly *my darling grandson,* who is continually left alone and left to fend for himself. This breaks my heart. The terrible wastefulness and disorganization of your arrangements of course distresses me, but darling Benjamin is my primary concern.

"The presence of such a person as Maria Nonez in your home could solve all your problems. I feel it would make the greatest difference in little Benjamin's life to find a warm, cheerful person like Maria Nonez in his home when he returns from school. I speak now for that future time when, God Willing, you are fully recovered, back at work and out so much of the time, as well as for the present, when illness deprives Benjamin of your company. Maria Nonez has told me that she loves children, and I can well believe it. In just the short time it has taken me to break her in, I have found her to be an unusual young woman. She is modest, pleasant, intelligent, honest, sober, clean about her person and about the house, industrious, experienced and takes a great deal of pride in the quality of her work. To find all these virtues embodied in the person of someone in Domestic Service is nothing short of miraculous nowadays, when people of that calling are a vanishing breed. You have a golden opportunity in Maria Nonez, who is a paragon. Though she has a permanent visa, her aunt has informed me she is eager to become a citizen of this wonderful country of ours. I think it would be wise to keep Maria on beyond the allotted seven weeks if only for Benjamin's sake. If the money is an issue, I would be only too happy to share part of the expense of her salary. With the welfare of my darling grandson at stake, no expense should be spared.

"Well, the time for my flight is drawing nigh, but in closing I would like to offer a few words of advice. While Maria Nonez has worked for two American families, she is not acquainted with the customs and pace of life in such a large metropolis as New York City. I therefore urge you to be kind and patient, and help instruct her in New York ways. Do not patronize her, but on the other hand do not spoil her. You must strike a delicate balance between the two. Like her aunt, she is a very proud person and must be treated as your equal, as a human being in short. I say all this because I know your experience in handling Domestic Help is rather limited, dear Emma. And I am sure I need not remind you that her aunt, Constanza Vallejo, is *indispensable* to me.

"With all affectionate wishes for your speedy recovery,
Elsie"

When Emma finished with this letter, she wordlessly handed it to Harold, who'd been standing over her cranked-up hospital bed all the while. Harold read it, frowning, then shoved it in his pocket: "I think she makes a lot of good points, Em. *I* certainly never dreamed our household operations were so half-assed or expensive, and I think she's onto something important about Benjy. He *is* alone a helluva lot, and he *has* gotten awfully quiet. Maybe Elsie goes a bit overboard—I don't think he's apathetic or withdrawn—but he seems kind of down. And maybe having somebody capable in the house, and having a more efficient operation at home *would* give him a sense of stability and help cheer him up."

Emma said nothing, and Harold soon left—but she was sure her fever went up two degrees and stayed there all afternoon.

Now, weeks later, fever free and out of the hospital, but still far too weak to handle her household alone, Emma had to face it: at the moment, Maria Nonez was (to carry through on Elsie's equine metaphor of "breaking-in") a gift horse she could hardly afford to look in the mouth, like it or not.

And it was hands down not. Though she was the first to admit Elsie's digs were well-founded—she was a spectacularly rotten housekeeper and manager—she was, at heart, a thoroughly domesticated creature who had always treasured the time she spent at home with her family. Alone. *In privacy.* And when the chips were down, her finicky scruples and guilt about having a full-time servant didn't matter half as much as this new lack of privacy. She had never realized until just now, now when they were gone, how much she had loved and needed her rare moments of solitude, times when she had come back early from work and had sat drinking tea and reading the paper she'd only skimmed at breakfast, or had just sat daydreaming, savoring, without knowing it, things like the patterns of sunlight on the floor, the clock-ticking stillness. She had also never realized how absolutely essential it was to be able to speak freely, unguardedly, in one's home, or to be able to move freely through the rooms of that home without its constituting an event or precipitating a crisis—go into the kitchen, say, for a snack, without somebody popping out of the woodwork to offer assistance she didn't need, or worse, without having somebody guiltily jump up the minute she appeared and begin putting on a great surly show of busyness . . . as though suspecting she'd come out there just to spy or check up.

This latter had been going on constantly the last few days. And Surly was the ticket. Because as she might have known, Elsie's character report on Maria Nonez had been wildly misleading. "Pleasant" and "modest" and "warm" and "cheerful" and "unusual"—good old Elsie. But then Maria Nonez was certainly "unusual." She, for one, had never met anybody so testy and temperamental and given to such wide swings of mood—anybody who, in split seconds (and without provocation), could go from a dull, broody kind of passivity to a barely-concealed full-blown state of rage.

Thus the "companion" who was to cheer her son's lonely hours. And her own companion for two or three more house-bound weeks. But there was nothing she could do about it. She had to put up with it as best she could until she was stronger, and meanwhile try to get out of the house for little relief periods as often as possible. Her doctor had recommended short walks around the neighborhood, and though she had a few problems on that score, now was as good a time as any to have another go at it. Particularly now that the dizziness and shortness of breath were gone.

Resolved, she got up off the bed, and was in the bathroom washing up, when she finally heard the tapping on the door above the rushing water. Holding a towel to her face, she opened the door on Maria. Who angrily announced she was wanted on the telephone, and took off before she could ask her to tell whoever-it-was she was busy. Bracing herself, Emma went to the phone; she knew who whoever-it-was, was.

"Hi, Em. It's me."

"Minda dear, I'm sorry, but I really can't talk now because I . . ."

"I can't talk now either," snapped Minda. "I'm only calling to see if you'll meet me in the park this afternoon. It's just *gorg*eous out and the fresh air would do you good. I'll be in the playground from two-thirty on and would adore some company."

Wavering, Emma stood clutching the towel. She had just finished telling herself she had to get out more. She had also just finished telling herself the night before that she would avoid Minda from now on. But . . . the playground. She hadn't been in a playground for years. It had never been one of her favorite places, but the very thought of being out of that apartment, away from Maria, out among people, just sitting on a bench and soaking up sun and looking at the golden turning trees and listening to the sounds of playing children (instead of listening to Minda)—was powerfully appealing. "What playground?" she finally said.

"The one near Benjy's school."

"I'm not sure I know where you mean."

"Well, you know where Benjy's school is—right?"

"Quite right."

"Well, you go into the park entrance a block above his school and keep going. You can't miss it."

"I remember now. But that's a lot of walking."

"It isn't. Not if you take a cab over to the entrance. Besides . . . didn't your doctor tell you to take walks?"

Indeed he had. But Minda already had her boiling, and this was only over the telephone. And yet . . . the afternoon, the whole long day stretched emptily ahead. She wouldn't even have Benjy to break the monotony and loneliness: at breakfast, when she'd tried to arrange to pick him up at school and take him for the fall clothes they'd never gotten to buy on Friday, he'd told her he couldn't do it today because he had soccer practice until five. "What time did you say you'd get to the park?"

"Two-thirty, after the twins get up from their nap." Minda laughed happily, pleased with her victory. "See you then. Don't you *dare* let me down."

Nobody Cares

"What do you call that, Benscherman? That is not my bowl of fruit."

Three livid pink plastic peaches, a bunch of magenta plastic grapes, three real oranges, one real lemon, one real green banana, all piled into an old-fashioned tan pottery mixing bowl—Miss Sugrue's bowl of fruit.

Benscherman-Benjy turned and looked at the woman who stood behind his chair, glaring down at the wetted paper where splotches of brilliant primary colors were fuzzily blending and soaking in. "It's the way I see it, Miss Sugrue," he said, ever polite.

"I do not teach art in this way, Benscherman," said Miss Sugrue. "You are not at liberty to paint what you 'see,' particularly since you 'see' things in such an unnatural way. In art you must first learn the *rhu*-daments. You must master the basic rules and forms. Once you have become master you are then permitted to hexperiment, to hexpress yourself. But this . . . this you have painted does not mean *any*thing, Benscherman."

"Excuse me, but why does it have to mean something, Miss Sugrue? Art doesn't have to *mean* things, Miss Sugrue."

"You are not hexcused, Benscherman. And if I report you to Mr. Porter that will make time number four since the beginning of the fall term." A knobby-knuckled hand reached down and snatched the limp paper away, putting a dry blank sheet in its place. "There are twenty minutes of class time remaining. You will please to start again, Benscherman, and paint my bowl of fruit as it is and as the rest of your classmates are doing so beautifully."

From all around came the coughs and throat-clearings of these classmates, trying to make him look up. Without success. Instead, he kept his eyes lowered and carefully cleaned his brush with the piece of paper towel he'd been given at the start of the class, along with five little fluted paper cupfuls of paint and a piece of tin foil to use as a palette. The art class, the last period of the day, was conducted in a large sun-filled room on the top floor of the huge old mansion that housed the progressive school he had attended since second grade. Though every art teacher since nursery school had found him to be an "unusually gifted child," he had not been found to be so by the Winthrop School's new Swiss art teacher, Miss Melanie Sugrue.

Now, dipping his brush first in one cup, then another, using the foil palette to blend the glaring primary colors into subtler shades, he swiftly began to paint Miss Sugrue's bowl of fruit, the brush moving expertly—and satirically—over the paper.

"We never did get you any new fall clothes," she said as he was going out the door at eight o'clock Friday morning. "I'm feeling much better today—I'll pick you up at school. What time do you get out on Fridays—two?"

"Two-thirty. I don't need any new clothes, ma."

"Of course you do. You're a growing boy."

"I haven't grown an inch since last December."

Her big, troubled eyes, flickering doubtfully over him, had reluctantly perceived this was true. "Well. Maybe so. But you still could use some new clothes. I'll be out in front of school at two-thirty."

And so she was. When he came out through the massive oak front doors, she was standing by the curb, wearily leaning against the fender of an old car, sun beating down on her shiny pale hair, looking so worn and thin and weak he couldn't stand it and quickly turned away. Thinking he didn't see her, she loudly called his name and came swooping down, kissing him on the cheek, slipping her arm through his and leading him away—completely unaware of the gestures Gorvey and Ulrich were making behind her back. "Let's take buses instead of cabs," she said, giving his arm a squeeze. "It's such a beautiful day, and I can get a little exercise that way. Dr. Tepp told me it was very important to get a little exercise every day. . . ."

She was off. On and on she went. She talked all the way to the bus stop, all during the ride across town, and all the time they stood waiting for the second bus that would take them down Lexington Avenue. Tense, nerved-up, sometimes slyly squinting upward at the sky or at tall buildings they passed, as if she maybe expected something to come dropping down on them, yet all the time going on about how wonderful it was to be out on such a wonderful day, how wonderful it was to be feeling well again. Wonderful. Wonderful. When they were on the bus heading downtown she finally stopped, and for a while just sat there peering sideways at him. "Is . . . something wrong, darling?" she suddenly asked after they'd gone several blocks.

"No. Nothing's wrong."

"You're so quiet. You seem . . . angry."

"I'm not angry. I'm just hot."

"You wouldn't be hot if you took that blazer off. Why don't you take it off?" The bus lurched along another block while he kept his blazer on. "I noticed that Robert and Oliver and all the other boys were wearing jeans. Wouldn't you be more comfortable in clothes like that?"

"I like the kind of clothes I wear, ma."

"Yes. Well. They're very *nice*. But they're the same kind of clothes you've always worn. Wouldn't you like something newer, a little more . . . swinging? Some jeans instead of those chinos, some nifty far-out patterned shirts instead of those same old button-downs for a change."

"No. Thank you. I really don't want any . . . swinging clothes, ma." Or Nifty Far-Out Patterned Shirts.

She laughed. Or rather, forced out a terrible sound that made two people turn and stare at her. "It's really funny. I mean most mothers would do anything to get their boys to cut their hair and wear nice simple shirts and jackets and ties . . . and here I am, trying to talk you out of all that."

Seeing nothing "really funny," he neither laughed nor spoke for several blocks.

"Listen, Benjy dear. There's a drugstore with a soda fountain in the block beyond the next stop. Let's get off at the next stop and get a nice big soda and then walk the rest of the way to Bloomingdale's."

He didn't want a soda, he didn't want to go to Bloomingdale's, but he said nothing, and after she'd stood up and pulled the cord, reluctantly followed her down the aisle.

"The drugstore's on the other side of Lex," she said once they were off the bus, taking his arm and steering him across the street. "I don't know what's making me so thirsty. It must be those awful iron pills. Instead of a soda, I think I'll have a tall lemonade or iced tea, that is, if they're still making iced tea in October. . . . Oh. God. Benjy—*look*."

He looked to where she pointed, and saw a huge German shepherd with concave flanks and matted fur bounding across Lexington Avenue. Zigzagging through the heavy one-way traffic, the solid phalanx of down-bearing cars which wildly swerved, honked horns, applied brakes, the dog miraculously reached the opposite side of the street unharmed. Climbing onto the curb, the dog then just stood there, scraggled tail pressed between its legs, panting, bony flanks heaving, dazedly looking at the people rushing unheedingly by on the sidewalk.

"Come on," she said, as the light turned red, and before he knew what was happening, she'd grabbed him by the wrist and dragged him across the street to the place where the dog stood. There, letting go his arm, she held out her hand and softly crooned, "Here, boy, here nice old boy," to the dog—who, close up, tongue lolling from between jagged teeth, looked like some half-crazed timber wolf.

"Jesus, ma—don't *do* that. He looks pretty wild and sick."

"He's just a lost dog. A poor lost dog half-starved to death. Look . . . he's still got a collar on."

He looked, and yes, there was a collar under matted fur. But there was also the wary tension of the head, the terror in the dazed yellow eyes.

"Here, nice old doggie," she crooned, edging nearer now, hand still held out. Much to his surprise, the dog suddenly stopped panting and, cocking its head, considered her with a changing, almost hopeful look. Its right ear, he saw now that they were closer, was torn and clotted with blood, its nose dry and gray with caked dirt, its coat scruffy and filthy. It looked as if it had been living in some excavation for a new building, or as if it had been lying, burrowed, under some condemned old building—which it probably had.

"Don't touch him, ma," he cried out as she continued to advance inch by inch. "He's probably diseased. He's probably been eating rats and garbage to stay alive. . . . What're you trying to *do*."

Hand still outstretched to the dog, she turned and glared at him. "Benjy. I'm surprised at you. What I'm trying to *do* is get its trust, get close enough to get hold of its collar, and see if there are tags. If there's no license, we can take him home, or take him to some animal shelter where . . ." She broke off, as the dog, perhaps finally aware of her nearness, suddenly backed away, ears flattening on the narrow skull. "Oh, God. Look how *frightened* he is. People have been abusing him."

Perspiring heavily under his blazer, he stared bleakly at other "people," passing them without so much as a glance. "Come on, ma. Please leave that dog alone. Dad will have a fit if you bring it home. And if you really want to give it a chance, the last place you should take it is one of those 'animal shelters,' since they'll stuff it in a gas chamber the

size of a washing machine. Besides, if you try to get hold of its collar,
it'll bite you—can't you see the way it's looking at you?—and then you'll
have to get something like a rabies shot."

Luckily she heard none of this. "Listen, Benjy darling, I've got an
absolutely terrific idea," she said, no longer edging forward, just standing very still with her hand outstretched, a pose that seemed to
hypnotize the dog. "Take the wallet out of my purse—please try not to
make any sudden movements—and go into that hamburger place up
the block. Offer them five dollars for two raw hamburger patties and a
piece of any kind of rope or string—yes, *five dollars*, they won't even
listen to you if you offer them less—and meanwhile I'll stay here and
keep the dog calmed down. I'm sure he'll stay with me—he seems to
trust me now—and when you get back you can feed him bits of the
raw meat, while I take the rope or string and slip it under his . . ."

A car screeching to a stop at the red light drowned her out. Alarmed,
the dog skittishly reared, then took off, loping to the corner of the side
street and careening around it out of sight.

"Oh *no*," she moaned and took off after the dog.

He watched people turning to gape at the pale, skinny woman, blond
hair flying, shoulder bag flapping, tearing after the wild-looking dog—
then grimly set out after her. As he rounded the corner, he saw that
the dog, terrified, convinced she intended him harm, had picked up
speed and was now half a block ahead of her. Then she suddenly
skidded to a stop by the stoop of an old brownstone, her face twisted,
clutching at her side.

In the same moment he reached her, the dog disappeared around the
distant corner onto Park Avenue. She stood holding her side and panting like the dog, her face so pale it almost looked green. "Listen, ma,
you're not in any kind of shape for this. You'll have a relapse or something. Let's forget about the clothes and the dog and go home. Come
on, ma—it was just some old lost dog."

"*Just* a lost dog? It was a dog that loved and trusted somebody
and . . ."

An explicit series of sounds came from Park Avenue: a rubbery
screech of tires, an impacted thumping bump, a volley of yelps that
climbed some terrible ear-splitting scale, then stopped.

She stared at him round-eyed. Then, making a dreadful whimper-
ing sound, she clapped her hands over her face.

Near tears himself, he stood helplessly watching her weep, convinced that people were standing at the windows of houses all around

them, furtively peeping out, laughing at them. "It probably wasn't really hurt, ma. It probably just got . . . grazed."

She made a feeble protesting noise from behind her hands, shaking her head, the pale hair twirling and glinting in the sun.

"Okay, since you don't believe me, I'll go up to the corner and make sure. Only you stay here. You better sit down on that stoop—you look like you're going to faint or something—and don't move until I get back."

She nodded without lowering her hands, but didn't sit down.

A taxi was pulled up at the curb just around the corner on Park Avenue. The front door nearest the sidewalk hung open, the driver stood on the pavement next to it, hands-on-hips, peering in an uptown direction.

"You see a dog, mister?"

The man slowly turned and took him in, then pointed many blocks uptown to a distant galloping blur of fur. "He yours?"

"No. You hit him bad?"

The cab driver shrugged morosely. "I sure as hell *thought* I did—he came tearing out of nowhere—but he couldn't run that way if he was badly hurt. I couldn't help it," he added angrily, grievingly, and climbed back into his cab and slammed the door.

"It was nowhere in sight," he said coming up to the stoop where she stood anxiously waiting. She'd stopped crying. "It must've taken off when it was sideswiped."

She stared at him with swollen red eyes, clearly wanting to believe him, clearly suspecting she shouldn't. "Maybe we should get a cab and go cruising around looking for him, Benjy. He's probably hurt—*you* heard him—and if we found him we could take him to a vet."

"For God's sake, ma. Please cut it *out*. Let's just go home."

She gave him a long sober look, really seeing him for the first time since she'd spotted the dog. "All right, we'll go home," she finally said softly, and led the way back to Lexington Avenue where they immediately got a cab. She gave the driver their address, then slumped back in the corner, and said in a weak, small voice, "I'm sorry, darling. I can see you think that was pretty peculiar. My getting so worked up about that poor dog. But you see, Benjy dear . . . it's more than the dog. It's because nobody cares."

Not wanting to look at her—he was full of churning, violent feelings—he looked out the window instead, staring bleakly out at the sunny sanity of the busy avenue where the sidewalks were swarming with people, not a lost dog in sight. "I'm sorry but I don't get it, ma," he finally said in a choked grudging voice. "How does one ratty old lost dog prove that nobody cares?"

"Oh, it does. Believe me it does. You know how many lost dogs I see around this city in the course of a week? Or at least saw before I got sick?" Still refusing to look at her, he shook his head. "I'd say on the average of two or three a week. I really began to notice, to pay close attention to it last spring, and started keeping count. In the course of one week, as I traveled around the city—either on my way to visit Grandma Pittman at the hospital or on my way to work—I'd see at least two or three lost dogs. Do you know how they got lost? *Why* they got lost?"

"No. Why," he said, not wanting to know why, uneasily keeping his eyes on the profile of their driver, who had pulled up at a red light, and was busily talking through his rolled-down window to the driver of the cab next to theirs.

"They got lost because somebody didn't care. Because some stupid, selfish person—the kind of person who should never be permitted to *own* a dog—broke the law and walked their dog without a leash. Of course, some of the lost dogs you see around the city were just turned loose by their owners, heartless monsters who either just got tired of the responsibility of having a dog, or had to move, say, to some faraway place and couldn't take the trouble to find the poor dog another home. Though, actually, that turning-loose thing happens more out in the country than here in town, I'm happy to say."

Happy to say. Just as she'd come out with "heartless monsters," the light had changed, but before making the left turn heading them east, their driver had given her a long appraising look in his mirror—then caught his eye and winked.

"But most of the lost dogs you see around the city," she continued, "were owned by people who broke the law and walked the dogs on the street without leashes, or let them off the leashes the second they hit the park, long before they were anywhere near the dog runs. I've gotten so mad when I've seen that happen, I've even stopped a few of them, but they've all said the same thing: It's the only chance their 'poor doggy' gets to exercise. And the 'poor doggy' is always some enormous dog like a setter or wolfhound or Dane. Which they shouldn't keep in a New York apartment in the first place. But then, so many people who don't even really *like* dogs get them because they like the idea of themselves as dog owners, like some image they think they're creating. The ones who walk their dogs on the street without leashes are perfect examples of that. All you have to do is watch the way they walk along, swinging and jingling the leashes—so pleased and involved with themselves, they either don't even look back to see if the dog's following, or else try to impress everybody by screaming fancy dog-training-school commands like 'heel' or 'stay' at the poor dogs—and you just *know* it's not the dogs they care about, but just some figure of Dog Owner they think they cut. And all kinds of types go in for it. Hippy brats walking beautiful shepherds like the one we just saw—without leashes to show how natural and free they are. Fat old men all gotten up in tweeds walking boxers and pugs without leashes, playing at being country squires. Fa . . . fancy young men with leashless Afghans and standard poodles, airing themselves, not the dogs. They all have one thing in common, though: most of them have never owned a dog before, and *none* of them really deserves to own a dog at all. They're the same people who walk the dogs while doing all their neighborhood errands, too lazy to make a separate trip. They'll use a leash then, damn them—they'll use it to tie the poor dog to a hydrant or traffic sign in front of the supermarket or laundromat, and sometimes leave them out there for hours. I've seen dogs tied up out in the pouring rain. I've seen dogs chained to a pole in a blizzard, sitting and shivering on icy snowdrifts, howling as if their hearts would break. I've seen dogs so tangled up in the leashes they were tied with, it was a wonder they didn't break their legs. Once, I was waiting for a bus, and a man came along and tied his dog to a No Parking sign and went into the bank. After a while—it was a York Avenue bus and they take forever to come—this raggedy little kid came up and began to untie the dog. Everybody else at that bus stop just *stood* there, watching the boy steal the dog, and finally I couldn't stand it, and went over to the boy, and he dropped the leash and ran. I was tying the dog back up again, when the owner came out of the bank and got very excited and asked what the *hell* was I doing with his dog. While everybody at the bus stop stared at me as if I were stark raving mad. I wasn't mad. I cared. But they didn't. And nobody does any more. They just break the law and let the dogs off their leashes, and the dogs get lost. They get frightened by a loud noise in the street and start running, they chase a squirrel or a rat into some part of the park they don't know—and before you know it they're lost. And the poor things run wild in the park and die of hunger or exposure, or come out and get picked up by somebody who sells them to some laboratory for experiments, or run out into traffic like the one we just saw, and it's . . . good-by dog."

Good-by dog. All during the last part of this speech, he had felt the driver urgently trying to catch his eye in the rear-view mirror, while he'd sat, face burning, staring at the floor, hoping, praying, she would stop. Now, still two blocks from home, he thought maybe she finally had. But no. No. She couldn't stop. Couldn't stop.

"I had a dog when I was your age," she went on, softer. "My father gave her to me for my tenth birthday. I called her Loopy. She was a springer spaniel with a silky white coat and liver-colored spots and a pale pink nose. She was only six weeks old when I got her. She was completely *my* dog, my responsibility. I walked her three times a day—we lived too near the highway for me to risk letting her run loose. I bathed her, cooked her special food, picked the ticks off her with a tweezer every night, and when she was sick, which was only once, I took her to the vet. I *loved* her. And she loved me. She slept in my bed, sat in any chair I sat in—I was always covered with long, silky white hairs—and followed me all around the house just like Mary's lamb. When I was in school or out somewhere, she would lie upstairs on my bed, waiting for me. One day when she was almost three—it was the year after Da . . . my father died—I had to play in a hockey tournament at some school near Danbury and didn't get home until long after six. When I got home, Loopy was gone. My mother didn't even know she'd gotten out. Later, we found out that she'd slipped out while my mother was talking on the phone, and the washing-machine repair man had propped the back door open to carry in a big piece of equipment from his truck. I guess poor Loopy had just gotten desperate. She was such a *good* dog and never broke training, and I usually walked her by four. Anyway. She was hit by a car. My mother and I were just getting into our car, to go out looking for her, when the man who killed her brought her body home. He hadn't been able to help it. She . . . she'd just run out onto the highway before he could stop. He was so upset he was crying, poor man."

Well, *there* was somebody who cared, he thought, staring out the window with relief: only half a block more to go.

"I never got another dog. Never wanted one. Your father's never wanted a dog either, but I see now that it might have been very selfish of us. You've never mentioned it, but if you'd like a dog you could have one, Benjy dear. It could be your very own, like Loopy was mine, and you could . . ."

"No thanks. Ma. I don't want a dog," he cut in as the driver pulled up with a jerk in front of their house. While she rummaged distractedly in her purse for her wallet, he opened the door and hopped out. But not before the driver had swiveled all the way around in the front seat and, leaning forward to the pushed-back plastic partition, had given him a look he'd never forget.

"Benjy dear, I'd really rather you didn't mention this to Daddy," she suddenly said in the elevator, where she was holding onto the chrome side rail for support.

"Mention what."

"This . . . business about the lost dog we just saw."

"Why would I do that?" he said just as the door slid open, and, always the little gentleman, he stood aside to let her out.

She didn't seem to think this a question she need answer, and they walked in silence down the long, gloomy corridor of peepholed doors. Their own peepholed door was opened by Maria, who didn't seem to notice how sick she looked, and who told her in this crazy angry way that the *Señora* Wolfe had called three time and said it was of great importance that the *Señora* Soller call her back the second she arrive. So the *Señora* Soller, looking even sicker, had gone into her room to call the *Señora* Wolfe, and he'd gone into his own room and shut the door and standing on his desk chair had spent the next half hour rearranging the electrical parts on his shelves, until calmer, he'd finally climbed down and tackled his math homework.

Now the bell just outside the sunny art studio jangled, and he stared blankly down at the picture that had automatically come out under his hand: a duplicate of one of the gaudy illustrations from those twenty-five-cent Little Golden Books, that endless stream of storybooks his mother had bought him at a neighborhood Whelan's when he was a child.

"Well now. That is what I call a painting, Benscherman. *That* is art. Now I see you are the talented little boy I haf so often been told. This I am going to hang on the bulletin board for to display."

As the art teacher triumphantly bore the flapping wet paper away, he cleaned up his desk in record time and was the first to leave. "Hey, Rembrandt—wait up," called Gorvey as he rushed from the room, but he didn't wait up and, grabbing his things from one of the steel lockers out in the hall, headed for the stairs. "*Hold* it, Sohier," called Ulrich from the studio door, but he didn't hold it, and down he went, plunging down six flights of the white marble steps the school discreetly gave out had once been brushed by ballgowns of ladies named

Twombly and Van Pelt and Van Renssalaer—and finally pushed out through the heavy main doors into the blinding October afternoon.

It was freakishly hot, hot as mid-July, and upper Fifth Avenue was swarming with people, most of them heading for the park. Heading there himself, secretly glad of the company, he crossed Fifth Avenue and turned into a path glutted with nursemaids and mothers pushing carriages or shepherding along herds of small children just out of school. Like his, their destination was the playground, and he fell in behind them, contentedly trudging along until the playground loomed in sight. Then, suddenly veering off the path, he cut across a broad stretch of grass, making for a dense clump of bushes encircling the base of a giant old oak. Reaching the shrubs, he set his book bag on the grass and, carefully parting the springy branches, waded in to the precise spot where he had watched a piece of metal trailing a spray of wires sink out of sight five hours earlier. "You still playing with Tinker Toys, Sohier?" Mr. Avery had said, unluckily catching sight of the piece of metal he'd found while waiting his turn at stickball, and had been about to sneak back to school now that recess was over. "I'm surprised at you, Sohier. Throw that dumb thing away," Avery had said, sneering. So he'd thrown it, but not away, taking careful aim, using the powered curve that had made him famous at camp, observing the precise formation of the leafy branches that closed over it as it sank down.

Now he was in that very spot and the piece of metal was gone. Angrily pushing deeper into the bushes, he parted the branches even wider than before and, crouching down, began to grope in the dirt among the roots. "Did you see that disgusting little boy, Mildred?" said one of the nursemaids he'd seen passing on the grass as he ducked down, her affected English voice filtering down to him through tangles of branches and leaves: "And with a water closet right there in the playground—beastly little pig!" Muttering a response to this, he kept on groping and searching in the pebbled dirt between the roots, until finally, hot and discouraged, he stood up to get some air, surfacing among the meshes of branches like some strange creature from the deep. He stood there a moment, breathing heavily, frowning, wiping his earth-stained hands disgustedly on his chino pants, then decided to go back for a final look. As he sank back down into the greeny underworld, he heard what seemed like someone calling his name, but angry, desolate, distracted, he resumed his fruitless search, poking and fumbling among the branches and roots, blindly patting the loamy earth.

Hearts of Romaine

". . . bobby pins, hair-rollers, light bulbs, stationery, dish towels, hangers—only the expensive kind for hanging up skirts and slacks—pantyhose, gloves, silk scarves, tiny utensils like fine French paring knives or garlic presses or poultry pins, tiny cans of things like anchovies or imported smoked mussels and imported pâté. Soap in every known shape or form—if it's liquid they put it in some old empty jelly jar, if it's powdered they put it in those sandwich-size Baggies—the invention of Baggies was a godsend to them. And so was the invention of the tote, because the whole haul gets stuck in their purse, which is always some huge carryall or tote. Which is exactly the word for the whole damned procedure: obligatory tote."

"Tote? What on earth is tote?" said Emma, opening her eyes. All during this recitation of things Minda claimed that cleaning women and maids had stolen over the years (and over the years Minda had employed an astonishing number of cleaning women and maids), she had been sitting, eyes closed, leaning back against the playground's netted wire fence, soaking up hot October sun.

"I thought you took American History with Pennington."

"I did. But I don't remember anything about tote in the course."

"Well, maybe it wasn't actually in the course, but in some reference book Pennington had us read," said Minda, digging in her own huge tote bag for a cigarette. She had smoked incessantly ever since Emma had sat down half an hour ago. They were sitting on a bench at the far end of the playground, right up against the fence; across the teeming stretches of cement, Minda's four-year-old twins, Chrissy and Missy (Christina and Melissa), were playing on the slides. Tireless, joyous, they would climb to the top of the ladder, tinnily bang their heels and shout, "Mommeemommee lookit*me!*" and when Minda looked and waved, would let go and go zooping down the slide. Minda had stopped looking and waving ever since the subject of maids had come up. It had come up because Minda's latest maid had just quit. Which explained the mystery of her bringing her daughters to the playground—something she never did.

"*Anyway*, tote is a ritual that goes back to the days of slavery," continued Minda, savoringly blowing out smoke, happily settling down. "It started for valid enough reasons, God knows. The poor mistreated, overworked slaves who worked in the main house—'house niggers' was their charming name, I believe—would often sneak little things back to their cabins at night: candles, salt, lard, sugar, bread. Staples. Things they needed and never got enough of, poor old things. Occasionally, on some plantations, when the situation got out of hand, the plantation owner, the dear old massah, would frisk them before they left for the slave quarters at night . . . a brilliant idea, now that I think of it." Minda laughed, tossing her long slippery, reddish-black hair around. "Now, of course, it's just vestigial, it's evolved into a purely symbolic act. An obligatory ritual, you might say. Acts of petty thievery done more for what they express than the loot. Did you notice that none of the things I mentioned were particularly valuable?"

"Yes," lied Emma, who had only noticed from a glance at her watch, that it was too soon to get up and leave, and had wearily shut her eyes again.

"Well, that's particularly important. In fact, that's the whole point. The *act* of thieving, which is always petty, is far more important than the take itself. It expresses all the pent-up hostility and contempt for the employer, and is really an act of revenge, a way of getting even with the boss for all the humiliations of being a servant, a slave. A maid. But, mind you—and this is *really* important—this doesn't just apply to blacks any more. *Every*body in any kind of domestic service practices obligatory tote now. And that includes your high-type fancy caterers with bartenders and waitresses who'll take anything from Cuban cigars to bottles of booze and all the leftover food—and not just the leftover caviar and filet of beef—anything that's not chained down. In all the years I've been running a house, and that includes the years in Rome and L.A., I've had cretins of every nationality working for me. Italian, Swiss, German, English, French, Chinese, blacks from this country and the Caribbean islands . . . you name it, and they've worked for me. And every goddamn single one of them, whether mother's helpers or maids or laundresses or cooks, practiced obligatory tote. I swear to God. Of course it's just the last gasp of the class struggle. But soon there won't be a struggle any more—soon nobody will do that kind of work, and nobody will be in a 'servile' position they think they have to get even for."

And what will you do then? thought Emma. Aloud, she said, "Even if they do really take any of the stuff you claim they do, couldn't it just be because of poverty instead of some twisted motive like hostility or revenge?"

As the silence prolonged itself, Emma opened her eyes. Minda's face was half hidden by enormous, opaque sungoggles, but the finely plucked brows above them met in fury, the full-lipped mouth below them was pulled into a thin and ugly line. "I just *love* that. Stuff I 'claim' they take. They damned well took all that stuff, and I ought to know, because once I started getting wise I began keeping track. With each new charmer. Some of the things that went on, some of the things they took, were enough to make your hair stand on end. And it wasn't because they were poor. I mean for God's sake how much does a lipstick or bar of soap or a light bulb *cost?*"

"Enough to make a big difference to somebody who earns less than two thousand dollars a year."

"God. I might have known. My friend, the social worker. God. When you go into that pious routine you make me absolutely sick."

"Yes. So I see," Emma said dryly; though her voice was quiet, she was angrier than Minda. "But I'm not being pious, I'm merely sticking to facts. Reality. And you're not. You're completely distorting things just to accommodate this . . . batty obsession of yours."

"It's not batty or an obsession and the shoe is on the other foot. *You're* the one who's not sticking to facts or reality . . . the grubby facts and realities of everyday life, of doing something as dreary as running a home. The responsibilities involved in being a woman and a housewife that the rest of us have to face. And don't start giving me any of that Women's Lib crap: you've been running from all that for years, long before Women's Lib ever showed up to make it seem respectable. Oh, I know what you're going to say—I can see it on your face. You're going to tell me you're *not* running, but, on the contrary, are facing realities of a more important sort, facing the Real Thing—what poverty and hunger and neglect and abuse do to those slum kids you work with, and how in helping to see to it that some poor kid gets placed in a foster home where he won't get beaten up and will get enough to eat, you're doing something damned important. And okay, I won't knock that—it *is* important—I'm just questioning your motives, that's all. And questioning the way your being so hung up with other people's problems and other people's kids has made you blind to what was going on in your own house, to your own kid. I'm also sure you'd tell me that sitter, Mrs. Burbage, you've had ever since Benjy was born, or that paragon of a cleaning woman you had for eight years—Chloe or Coretta—I'm sure you'd tell me that neither of them had a hostile bone in their bodies or ever took so much as a bobby pin. But the fact is, how would you know? The fact is, they could have been burning up with hostility and walking away with half your house, and you wouldn't have known it either because you weren't home, or, if you were home . . . because your mind was on more important things."

Emma sat silent, feeling sick. You asked for this, she reminded herself. You know exactly what she is, yet you came to the park. But knowing didn't make it any better, and she felt so dizzy—from anger, not anemia this time—she couldn't even get up and go as she wanted, really couldn't even speak. Except to say at last, "Maybe you're right, Minda," hoping that would placate her and make Minda switch to some other subject until she felt well enough to get up and start for home.

But hardly. "You bet your sweet life I'm right," said Minda, somewhat pleased and softened by what she thought was a victory, but using it as ammunition. "I'm sorry, Em, but I've wanted to say all that ever since we ran into each other again last spring. God knows the changes in both of us are enormous—in fact, we seem to represent the two extremes of the way women can go. And I know you can't understand the way I've gone, and I'll admit sometimes I can't either, but most of the time, thanks to Weiglitz, I know that going this way has made me sane, has saved my life. Okay, I have my bad spells, as you know, but most of the time I know I've made a commitment and have to stick by it, even though it means putting up with a lot of shit. Housework is shit. And since there are limits to how far I'm willing to go in this role, and since I can afford it, I hire people to do the housework for me . . . but they constitute another kind of shit. Sometimes I think it's a tossup as to which is worse. Lucky for you you've been spared up to now, and maybe now that you've got that Mexican creep you'll find out for yourself—but I'm telling you that the hostility of these people is unbe*liev*able. And the different ways they express it are even more unbelievable. The obligatory tote thing is only a small part of it. For instance, another way they let off steam is to break things, always the things you're sure to love or treasure most—the Steuben ashtray, the Baccarat decanter, the Creil plate, the crystal lusters on the eighteenth-century chandelier.

To say nothing of every expensive electrical appliance in the house. *Dish*washers, clothes washers, blenders, the Electrolux, the electric knife sharpener, the Water Pik, the . . ."

She was off again.

As this new list expanded, Emma heard what sounded like one of the twins, and glancing up saw that yes, it was Missy, on top of the slide, shouting for her mother to look at her, but Minda was too deep into broken rotisseries and electric carving knives to hear her. Emma waved, and somewhat appeased, Missy shot down the slide with a squeal, but Minda, groping in her tote bag for still another cigarette, noticed none of this. Lighting up and luxuriously inhaling, Minda now branched out from breakage to still other forms the hostility could take —the burning of food, the "accidental" throwing-out of important letters and documents, the deliberate failure to answer ringing phones, the deliberate failure to write down messages on the occasions the phone *was* answered, the deliberate garbling of names and return numbers on the occasions the phone was answered and the messages *were* written down.

As she went on to describe, with particular relish, an Irish Catholic "au pair" girl she said she knew for a *fact* had used her douche bag, and who she suspected had stuck pins into her diaphragm in a fit of muddled religious zeal, since the diaphragm had suddenly been full of mysterious holes—Emma sat back and closed her eyes and ears. That is, using a trick she'd learned as a novice diver at camp, she tensed the inner muscles of her ears, producing a watery roaring that drowned Minda out. But only for the moment. Because whether it was on that park bench (where she and she alone had put herself) or on the phone at home, she'd soon have to listen to Minda again. Minda, who had turned up in her life again (like a bad penny, claimed Harold, who'd never even met her) after fourteen years late last May and had been relentlessly pursuing her ever since, determined to renew a friendship that had never really existed.

Fourteen years ago she and Minda, then Melisandre Harris, had gone to Radcliffe together, or, more exactly, she had gone to Radcliffe and Minda had transferred there from Berkeley in their senior year. Though Emma saw Melisandre Harris around the first part of that term—you couldn't miss her with her big bra-less breasts bobbling in T-shirts, and her streaming hair and sandals and jeans (still a freaky getup in those days)—she and her friends had avoided her, like everybody else. Poor Melisandre was a sort of instant campus joke, a slobby sexpot with a famous movie-mogul father, who wandered around campus looking distracted and ignoring the packs of panting Harvard boys forever trailing her across the Yard, and took off for New York every chance she got. Then in November, Melisandre submitted some poems to the magazine Emma coedited with Casey Rowland, an English transfer student from Cambridge—extraordinary poems—which they immediately published and which immediately got Melisandre a lot of attention . . . but not one single friend. Feeling sorry for her, Emma invited her to drop by her room once or twice, and before she knew what had happened, Melisandre had latched onto her. And for the next three and a half months she was virtually a prisoner in her own room, a captive audience for Melisandre, by then Minda, who would sit by the hour giving herself free therapy in Emma's favorite red chair—talking nonstop about her father, the succession of shrinks she'd been going to since seven (because of her father), and a lover named Nando, a sculptor who lived in New York. Then suddenly in late February, Minda proudly announced she was pregnant and was going to have the baby even though Nando wanted her to have an abortion; in early March, Nando panicked and took off for Rome and two weeks later Minda took off after him. And aside from one postcard late the next summer, announcing that Minda was now *Signora* Servio Nando and had given birth to a nine-pound boy named Sebastian, it was the last time Emma heard from her for the next fourteen years. Years in which her own life took shape.

During those years—busy, happy years, extraordinary years she realized now—the only time she ever thought of Minda was when she bumped into someone from Radcliffe and heard some wild new rumor about her (which, like most rumors, she eventually learned, contained some germ of truth). One, a terrible story about Minda's having committed suicide, got her so upset she did some checking through the Radcliffe Alumnae Bureau (of all places), but as soon as she found out it wasn't true, she forgot it like all the others, and returned to her own busy, happy life.

Then just last May, shortly after her mother died, Benjy came down with a terrible cold that went to his sinuses, and she took him to an ear-nose-throat specialist named Dr. Fenster. They were sitting in the surprisingly overcrowded waiting room (there seemed to be a remarkable number of respiratory infections for late May), where people sat miserably snuffling and hacking, when someone cried, "Emma! Emma

Pittman!"—and not wanting to believe it, Emma raised her eyes from the tattered copy of *Time*. But yes. There she was. Minda. Minda Harris for-all-she-knew-still-Nando. Standing in the doorway, looking absolutely unchanged, holding a homely little girl by the hand.

And there, in the packed waiting room, where there weren't enough chairs to go around and Minda and her red-eyed daughter had to stand, and where in the suddenly deafening silence the only other sound was the faint rustle of magazines, Minda filled her in on the last fourteen years. While her rheumy little daughter (one of twins, it was hastily explained) stood blinking up at her, and while Benjy hid his agonized embarrassment behind an upside-down copy of *Vogue*, Minda talked in a loud, strident voice. About a suicide attempt in Rome. A divorce from Nando, made possible by a whopping settlement from her father. A long stay in a Los Angeles sanitorium. (While her father and a new stepmother took care of Sebastian.) A romance and marriage to a designer of California sports clothes named Peter Wolfe. A move to New York, the birth of the twins—and the crackup of nine-year-old Sebastian, who after two years of therapy with a "genius therapist," was sent back to Rome to live with Nando, his adored and adoring father. Where he'd always belonged, according to the "genius therapist."

All this in the stuffy waiting room, where people sat glassily glaring with their mouths open (from outrage, not blocked respiratory tracts), and Benjy and Missy sat balefully glowering at each other with instant, murderous loathing. By the time Benjy was called in to see Dr. Fenster, Emma was limp. As she followed Benjy out of the waiting room, Minda handed her a slip of paper with her phone number, and begged her to call—but while Dr. Fenster put a clamp up poor, terrified Benjy's nose, she crumpled the paper and dropped it into a plastic sanitary receptacle, along with soggy wads of Kleenex and mucky cotton swobs. Fitting.

But Minda got her married name from the Radcliffe Club and called *her*. And Emma was wild. The ferocity with which Minda tried to latch back onto her frightened her. It was history repeating itself, but what did Minda want from her *now*? Fourteen years ago Minda had been alone and friendless, and though she apparently was still friendless, she now had a husband and children, a life—so why this compulsion to latch onto somebody who obviously didn't want anything to do with her?

For a while the circumstances of her Rough Year helped her avoid seeing Minda more than two or three times before the summer, when

Minda went off to Fire Island, and she herself was finally hospitalized
with her FUO. But she was never able to avoid Minda's calls, and
Minda called all the time, *all the time,* sometimes twice a day now that
she was housebound in convalescence. Minda called to tell her one of
the twins had impetigo. Minda called to tell her that the washing machine had broken down. Minda called to tell her that she'd had a fight
with Peter. (They fought all the time.) Minda called to tell her that
she was having a "whopping anxiety attack." (She had them all the
time.) She called to tell Emma that she had fired the latest maid
or "cretin," as she called them. (She fired them all the time.) She called
to tell Emma what they were having for dinner—she prided herself on
being what she called a *"numero uno* gourmet cook"—or to tell her what
she'd bought at Bendel's or Bergdorf's or Bonwit's that afternoon. She
called to tell Emma the details of a visit to her dermatologist or hair-
dresser or exercise class, she called and tried to tell Emma the details of
some "super, kinky sex" she'd had with Peter the night before. Tried—
Emma always cut her off when she started *that.*

Actually, Emma tried to cut her off all the time, but Minda always
came bouncing back for more. The big difference between now and
the days at college was that now Minda wanted to know all about
Emma's life, and when she finally realized Emma wasn't going to tell
her *any*thing, was furious, but not furious enough to give up and go
away. She still kept on calling, but childishly tried to get back at Emma
for being reserved by sniping at her, making dumb, snide remarks
about her social work (as she had just now), one day even going so far
as to accuse Emma of having sold out, of having traded the uncertainty
of a literary career for the smug rewards and safety of social work. Fed
up, Emma rose to the bait in spite of herself, and dryly pointed out that
Minda could hardly afford to be critical, since she had given up the
"uncertainty" of her own literary career—had completely given up her
wonderful poetry—for the "smug safety" of what she kept calling The
Feminine Role. Which, after a seething silence on the line, produced
one of Minda's most memorable speeches. "God*damn*it, Emma, sometimes I think you don't listen to a word I say!" (True, thought Emma,
wishing she had the courage to hang up.) "I told you that one time we
had lunch in June that I've never regretted that, *explained* that my
whole drive to write poetry came out of unresolved incestuous fantasies
about my father. Since it didn't make a dent, I'll run through it again.
Weiglitz, my last analyst, the only good shrink I ever had, a genius really—Weiglitz made me see how I'd always subconsciously thought that

the only way I could ever be a real woman was to have my old man screw me . . . which of course was only the dirty old bastard's secret wish projected onto me. Now interestingly enough—and *listen* this time, Em, this is just beautiful—I stopped writing poetry in Rome just after Sebastian was born and never wrote another line from that time on. Never wanted to. I attributed it to a lot of things, a lot of fancy crap like my new responsibilities as a mother and my troubles with Nando and so on and so forth, but years and years later Weiglitz made me see what it really was, made me understand the *dynamics* of the whole thing: giving birth to Sebastian made me realize that I *could* be a real woman without my old man screwing me—and the minute I realized that, even though it was just subconsciously, my whole need and drive to write poetry went up in smoke. Which I gather strikes you as sad, but let me tell you, it was one of the most important break-throughs in my life!"

Sad? It was obscene. My last analyst. My last duchess. What that string of shrinks had done to Minda made Emma's blood run cold, and if she'd been any kind of friend, she would have pointed out to Minda that she'd been had, been brainwashed, transformed by that endless parade of shrinks into a poor, quivering ambulatory wreck continually racked by anxiety attacks, who, like some wind-up toy, acted out some ludicrous travesty of The Feminine Role. But she didn't point any of this out to Minda. Even if she *had* been a friend, she saw that any meddling could be dangerous.

But she wasn't a friend, and trying to help Minda would only get her in deeper. All she wanted was out, was to get Minda out of her life, but she seemed to be getting in deeper all the time. Part of this was because her convalescence made her a captive audience for Minda's calls, but another part of it was the way tricky Minda knew how to play, unerringly, on her sense of guilt: though she could be cruel and even bitchy if it was called for, she liked to think of herself as an essentially kind and gentle person—and Minda knew how to make her feel just the opposite. Ever since May, for instance, Minda had been trying to promote an evening where "just the four of us—you, Harold, me and Peter—can go out to dinner and get acquainted," a prospect so appalling, that Emma had repeatedly put it down. Then, during a phone call late last week, Minda had suddenly said, "I was thinking of asking you and Harold to come here for a quiet dinner as soon as you felt up to it—but I've decided, screw that. I've finally gotten the message, and you're probably right. Harold and Peter probably *would*n't

get along, the literary world and Seventh Avenue just don't mix."
Which had immediately made Emma so guilty, she'd angrily protested,
saying that could hardly be true since she'd been planning to invite
Minda and her husband to a little dinner party they were giving in
two weeks. And had promptly invited her. And Minda had promptly
accepted. Which was hardly the way to go about getting anyone out of
your life.

". . . particularly the ones who drank the liquid off some marvelous
ragoût or *pot au feu* I'd slaved over for hours," said Minda, still very
much in her life, still on the subject of "hostile" maids.

"Did what?"

"Drank all the beautiful, concentrated liquid or sauce off something
I'd cooked that had reached the point of perfection. Drank it like it was
some kind of beef tea or nourishing soup," said Minda, and went on to
describe how the "cretins" who did this would either fill the stew pot
back up with water, or leave the meat stranded in the pot without
sauce.

As she talked, Emma stared out into the middle of the playground,
where the twins, off the slides, now forlornly stood considering a conclave of little girls on tricycles: Though the dizziness (and anger) had
subsided enough for her to get up and go, she was beginning to have
other sensations that were even more disturbing and unpleasant than
the dizziness. Sensations she was determined to ignore: she would go
anyway and just take a cab instead of the bus.

"I'll admit that only a few of them did that. But every goddamn maid
who's ever worked for me has eaten the lettuce hearts."

". . . Lettuce hearts?"

"Yes, lettuce hearts. I know you're no cook and proud of it, but even
you must know what they are—those teeny little perfect greeny-yellow
leaves in the middle of a head of romaine or boston or escarole? The
best part of the lettuce, which is exactly the point. I'm a salad addict
and we have one every night. Though I certainly don't do the cooking
every night, I always do the salad. I'm a genius on salads. Nando taught
me the art back in Rome—the only good thing, outside of Sebastian,
that bastard ever did for me. I'm really fa*nat*ic about the way the
greens are prepared, and always go through this big routine—endless
sinkfuls of icy water, the arm-breaker with the lettuce basket, the
wrapping in layers of paper towels, the crisping in the icebox for hours
ahead of time. Before I finally caught on to what was going on—and it

took me years—I'd always try to save myself some time by teaching the current treasure how to wash the greens. And the first few times each one washed them things would be okay. Then gradually, maybe say about the fourth time, I'd go into the kitchen about ten minutes before dinner, as always, to make the dressing and toss the salad so it would have time to get properly 'fatigued' . . . and when I'd unroll the paper towels the hearts would be missing. All that would be left were the lousy bruised outer leaves I'd always teach them to discard, and maybe some of the medium leaves surrounding the heart. But the heart itself—that pretty little bouquet—was always gone. Gobbled up. Every goddamn time. I couldn't believe it, even though it happened with each new cretin I got. Each time I would think that maybe they'd misunderstood me and had discarded the hearts instead of the bruised outer leaves, and after checking the garbage can, would ask them where the hearts were. With great tact. But each one would get huffy and sore as hell, and tell me the lettuce I saw in the towels was exactly what the grocer had delivered. One, a German girl we had in Beverly Hills, took the prize. 'Hots?' she said, giving me a look that would've made Ilse Koch seem like June Allyson: 'Wass is hots? In my country the only salad we eat iss made from the cabbage. I haff never before seen such a thing as this lettuce you buy. Iss most peculiar that lettuce.' Peculiar. You bet your ass it was peculiar—two enormous heads of romaine at seventy-nine cents a head and nary a heart or tender inner leaf in sight. I told her it was the most goddamn peculiar thing I'd ever heard of—and told her to pack her things and clear out."

Emma laughed in spite of herself. "Maybe they all think the hearts have special powers or are good for their health. Like being good for constipation or night vision or the teeth."

"Special powers. They could think the hearts had the power to ward off *cancer*, and it still wouldn't give them the right to eat them. And every single creep who's worked for me has eaten them, no matter what their nationality. It's the same thing as obligatory tote, it's their feeling about property. Share the wealth, baby. They all think they have a right to everything you have—and then some. This last one was unbelievable. What's that expression, 'She beats as she sweeps as she cleans'? She took everything, from my lace stretch pants to bottles of Dessaux Fils vinegar—none of your A&P vinegar for *her*. I would have given anything if I could have pulled the old massah routine and frisked her before she left for her weekends off. I tried to ignore it, I know what the maid situation is now, but she finally got me so wild that last week I began putting little signs around the apartment in all her favorite spots for filching. Which I'm sure is why she quit."

"What kind of signs?"

"Well . . . notes. Little messages written with bright green Magic Marker on pieces of note pad. Things like HANDS OFF and KEEP OUT and THIEF. I put one of the THIEF ones in my underwear drawer last Thursday, and by Friday I noticed she was acting rather . . . Em. Isn't that Benjy?"

"Benjy? Where? It couldn't be. He's at soccer practice until five. It's only twenty to four—I just looked at my watch."

"Well, it certainly looks like Benjy. Over there, rooting around in that clump of bushes under the big tree."

With a sinking feeling, Emma looked through the steel netting to where Minda pointed and saw that it was, indeed, Benjy. Rooting around in a clump of bushes.

"Of course that's Benjy!—What's he *doing*, Em?"

"I . . . don't know. Probably looking for something he dropped at recess. I think his school sometimes uses this part of the park for nature walks and games."

"That's a damned strange place for a nature walk or game. Aren't you going to let him know you're here."

Though Emma's impulse was quite to the contrary—in fact, the last thing she wanted to do was let him know she was there—she weakly called his name.

Lifting his head, Benjy quizzically squinted into blinding sunlight, then bent down to beat the bushes again.

"Ben—jee." A trifle louder, but only a trifle.

Straightening up with a startled jerk, he now stared in Emma's direction, the sun making opaque yellow discs of his glasses.

"Over here. In the playground. It's me. Ma."

"Ma," said Minda. "Is that what he calls you? Ma. How sweet."

Letting this pass, Emma watched her son stand motionless for a long, eloquent moment, then push out of the springy bushes, pick up the book bag lying on the grass, and resignedly start trudging across the turf toward the playground.

"He certainly doesn't seem overjoyed to bump into you," said Minda, tittering.

Emma let that pass too and unhappily watched her son approach, wondering how he would gloss over the lie about soccer practice, wondering why he had lied. Small, solemn, poker-faced, a miniature

Harold with his horn rims and short pointy nose and tan crinkly hair, he walked to the playground's distant side entrance, then headed toward them across the teeming concrete, picking his way between the tiny staggering children and careening tricycles with obvious distaste.

"Hi, ma. Hi, Mrs. Wolfe." No kisses. Laconic.

Emma decided he had the right approach and stood up. "How nice to run into you, Benjy dear. I was just getting ready to go home, and now we can go together." More laconic than he.

"What on earth were you looking for, Benjy?" asked Minda, who had been carefully taking him in—the navy blazer and striped rep tie and dirt-smeared chinos, the wizened little face. "Something you lost?"

"Ya."

"What did you lose, Benjy?" persisted Minda, arch.

Bitch, thought Emma, as Benjy shot her a quick quizzical look, then turned to Minda: "Actually, it wasn't something I lost. Mrs. Wolfe. It was something I found at recess that Mr. Avery wouldn't let me take back to school."

"That wasn't nice of Mr. Avery," said Emma, knowing exactly what sort of "something" it would have been—some beat-up old toggle or sproggle or greasy coil of wire.

"What sort of thing *was* it that he wouldn't let you bring it back to school, Benjy?" persisted Minda, in a tone Emma did not care for. At all.

Furious, Emma was about to announce that they were leaving, and grab Benjy's arm and march him off, when she saw a curious thing. Saw the boy of eleven stare at the woman of thirty-four with the jaded, insolently assessing gaze of a man of fifty—and saw the woman blush.

"It was a low voltage multicontrol relay frame, with an RT-5 transformer wired to a RA-9 rectifier. Mrs. Wolfe."

"Oh, *I* see," said Minda, nervously simpering.

See what? said the small, pale face, which turned to Emma with another message: Let's *go*. And without another word he started off.

"Complicated little chap, isn't he," Minda said dryly.

"Not really. Just shy, Minda." And murmuring good-by, Emma set out after her son, almost colliding with Minda's little daughters on borrowed tricycles, gleefully pedaling toward their mother on the bench.

Hot Spaeces/Old Times

As they walked in silence toward the entrance to the park, she knew she ought to say something, call him down for being so fresh to Minda, but she didn't speak until they came out onto upper Fifth Avenue, and then it was only to say, "Let's walk home, Benjy,"—having decided that this, not taking a cab, was the only way to face down the ominous sensations she'd been having for the last twenty minutes.

"Aren't you overdoing the walking, ma?" he said as they paused at the curb, waiting for the light to change.

"What?"

He shot her a nervous look. "I mean, I know your doctor told you to exercise, but the last time we did some walking you did yourself in. Remember Friday? When we saw that lost dog?"

Oh she remembered all right, suddenly realizing that "that lost dog" probably had a great deal to do with today's lie about soccer practice. Which got her so upset she went striding across the street ahead of him when the light changed, and made her say coldly, when he caught up with her on the other side, "I'm feeling just splendid today, Benjamin, and would like to walk home. But of course if you're tired, we can take the cross-town bus."

"*I'm* not tired."

"Fine. Then let's go."

And go they did. As they walked down Fifth Avenue and turned east into the broad cross-town boulevard, the unpleasant silence between them deepened, just as the space between them on the sidewalk widened—Benjy walking nearer and nearer the curb, Emma walking nearer and nearer the towering wall of buildings on their left. As he trudged along, Benjy viciously slammed his book bag into any stationary object he passed—a hydrant or lamppost or traffic-sign stanchion—an activity that bore no resemblance to that pleasant old-fashioned childish pastime of rhythmically tapping fence slats with a stick. Is that me or Minda he's slamming? wondered Emma, trying to draw her attention away from the noxious crawling going on under her scalp, a sensation which had prefaced the two frightening attacks she'd had since leaving the hospital. She called them attacks, a word used by Minda to describe a variety of states ranging from mild anxiety to full-blown hysteria, because it seemed as good a word as any to describe the state she'd fallen into two times—a state which fell in the middle of Minda's range, being a strong sort of anxious dread, which was always accompanied by the nasty tingling. Though she knew exactly what she dreaded and what caused the tingling—and it actually wasn't as irrational as it seemed—knowing hadn't made the attacks go away, as she'd thought it would: after the last one, when she'd faced what she dreaded, she thought she'd routed them for good. But far from it, since just that morning she'd begun having one in the house (both others had occurred on the street). Now, with what felt like a third full-blown attack getting underway on the street again, she crept along, hugging the buildings, so distracted she didn't realize Benjy had fallen behind. Finally missing him, she turned and saw him several paces in back of her, standing by a wire trash can brimming with greasy garbage and papers, holding a long piece of rubber tubing glistening with iridescent slime.

"Benjamin. Put that disgusting thing back. Right away."

"I need it, ma. It's just the kind of piece I've been looking for."

"Put it back, Benjamin. It's filthy. I'll buy you one just like it at the hardware store." She paused and glared forbiddingly at the doorman who stood listening to this exchange with sheer delight—the same doorman who'd just been watching, with fascination, her creeping progress along the wall of his building.

"You can't buy one like it. It's the drainage tube from inside a washing machine. I'll clean it with formaldehyde the minute we get home, then wash my hands with Phisohex. I promise."

"We don't have any Phisohex," she said, unthinkingly falling in with this idiotic line of argument. Hearing herself, she turned and set off, disdainfully trying to ignore the grinning doorman as she passed.

"Dad has some Phisohex in his medicine cabinet," said Benjy, catching up with her, carefully holding the slimy tube straight out in front of him. "I ran out of Band-Aids while you were in the hospital and went to get some from Dad's medicine cabinet—I don't want you to think I was snooping or anything. I saw the Phisohex, and later, when

I asked what it was for, he said he used it to wash up with after he visited you in the hospital. He said that hospitals were just loaded with all kinds of crazy germs."

Emma stopped in the middle of the sidewalk. "He . . . did?"

"Ya. He did."

"Well, he's right," she said after a moment. "Hospitals *are* full of germs." And she set off again, Benjy trotting to keep up at her side.

They walked another block in silence, Emma watching the way people coming toward them gave the boy with the slimy tube a wide berth —when she suddenly realized the terrible tingling and feelings of dread had stopped. Completely.

"I asked him wasn't Phisohex the stuff full of hexachlorophene, and wasn't that dangerous," he said after they had gone another half block.

"You did?" Coming to a stop again.

"Ya. I did. And he said it was only dangerous for newborn babies." A whoop of a laugh. And they moved on.

"Don't tell him I told you any of that . . . will you, ma?"

"No, Benjy. I won't."

Another block. Then: "He's pretty worked up about things like germs. Did you know that, ma?" Sly. Very sly.

"Yes. I know that, Benjamin."

A sidelong weighing glance. "But just about everybody's got some kind of hangup now. And when you think about it, a hangup about germs isn't as bad as some."

Though that more or less summarized her own feelings about this peculiarity of Harold's, she finally said, "I don't think your father really has a hangup, Benjamin," and they walked in silence the rest of the short distance home—Emma striding fearlessly down the middle of the sidewalk all the way, the symptoms of the attack mysteriously, and totally, gone.

Upstairs, after ringing the doorbell several times, she let them in with her own key. As she opened the door, a terrible smell came rushing at them—a powerful aroma of onions and olive oil and garlic, mixed with something unidentifiable, something foul, something pungently sour like vinegar, only nastier. "Jesus. What's she cooking this time? Can't she cook any normal food?" said her son, and preceded by the oily tube, headed down the hall to his room.

More curious about the smell than why Maria hadn't answered the doorbell, she went out to the kitchen to investigate. A large meaty brick was sitting in a pan on top of the stove, the meat loaf, she now remembered, Maria had said she was going to make for dinner. Which accounted for the pleasanter parts of the smell. The offensive part, stronger and more distinct now, a disgusting brininess tinged with an herby-charry underbase, seemed to be seeping out through the crack under Maria's door. Suddenly nervous—it certainly smelled like something was burning in there—Emma went and timidly tapped on the door: as far as she knew, Maria didn't smoke, but maybe she did after all, and had fallen asleep, leaving a lit cigarette burning somewhere dangerous like the edge of the bureau or night-table. Something woodsy was burning.

Beyond the closed door, she could hear the faint babble of the radio. After knocking three times and getting no answer, her nervousness changed to alarm. And overcoming her reluctance, she cracked open the door. And stared:

She had made a great point of neither looking nor going into Maria's room since coming home from the hospital, not even during the two weekends Maria had gone off to the Bronx—partly out of respect for Maria's privacy, but more out of the resolve not to give in to a particular failing of her own. Now she stood blinking around the little room where the air was thick with the sickening smell, and where the shade was pulled, but, in spite of the gloom, she could see enough. The first thing she saw was a large gilt crucifix nailed to the wall above the bed, which seemed to glint softly with some inner light of its own; the bed beneath it was unmade and wildly mussed. What looked like a votive candle stood in a saucer on the bureau, but the wick was uncharred, and in any case she didn't think either a candle *or* a cigarette could have produced the awful smell, which was overpowering now. Then suddenly, above the steady chatter of the bedside radio, came the rush of water and squeak of tub taps from the little bathroom beyond the foot of the bed: Maria taking a bath.

Quickly closing the door, she went up front to her own room, where the sound of rushing water came from behind her own bathroom door: Benjamin Sohier washing up with his father's Phisohex?

Going limp, she sank into the armchair near the windows, craving a cigarette: she hadn't smoked in five years, but the way she felt at that moment, she could easily have picked up where she'd left off, and gone right back to two packs a day.

Benjy finally came out of the bathroom. Though he seemed somewhat startled to find her sitting slumped in the armchair, he kept on going to the door, where he suddenly turned: "Listen, ma, I'm sorry about this afternoon. They . . . called off soccer practice at the last minute. If you want, we can go for clothes tomorrow or any other day this week. You name it."

"We'll see, darling," she said, deeply touched by this lie, even though it made the second one that day—something of a record for a child who never lied. "Would you like me to get you something—some of those cheese things with a cold drink?"

"I'll get it, ma. You stay where you are. You look . . . bushed."

Bushed. She was more than bushed. A torporous heaviness had descended, and each of her limbs seemed to weigh five hundred pounds. Though it resembled the terrible stuporous lethargy that had accompanied the depression she'd sunk into her third week in the hospital, she wasn't depressed now. Just . . . down. And physically exhausted. She was still much weaker than she wanted to admit, and probably Overdoing, in spite of Tepp's warning. What an idiotic thing to do—making herself walk home just to face down the attack: it had gone away, true, but she had no idea why—just as she had no idea why it had started up again in the first place. All in all, it had been a very trying day. To put it mildly. As she sat there, slowly reviewing some of the things that had "tried" her, tears, idle tears, came into her eyes, and she angrily hauled all two tons of herself out of the armchair: none of *that*.

Maria had the right idea. She would follow her example: she would take a long soak in a hot tub and maybe take a nap after that—it was only four-thirty, so there was plenty of time. Brightening, she went to collect some comfortable clothes from her closet, hearing what sounded like angry voices coming from the kitchen, but she told herself her trying day was making her hear things, and carried the clothes into the bathroom and turned on the water. Coming back out for a pair of sandals, she found Maria in the bedroom doorway, her face an ominous, blotchy red.

"Señora. The Benjamin think I eat his Cheese Drundles. You must tell the Benjamin I never eat other people's food, *Señora* Soller."

From far out in the kitchen came the sound of The Benjamin banging and slamming cabinet doors.

"I'm sure he wasn't implying that you ate them, Maria. You probably misunderstood. He probably was just trying to find out if you knew where they were."

"He no implying anything. He *mean* he think I eat them. I no misunderstood. My English is getting very good and I understanding everything. *Everything.* Because is not just the Drundles I come see you, *señora.* I hear you come in my room when I taking the bath, and I come here to tell you I no think this be right. My room is my *castillo,* my *dominio,* and no one on any other job ever come there. Not Mrs. Lewis T. Spratt or any other boss."

Emma stared down the hall, where Benjy had come up behind Maria and now stood outside his room; clutching a bag of Cheese Doodles with one hand, making the pinwheel crazy-sign with the other, he flashed her a brilliant grin, then slipped inside, soundlessly shutting the door behind him.

"Maria. Maria, I didn't go *in*to your room. For your information, I have not gone in that room since you've come to work here, nor has anyone else. The only thing I did was crack open the door and peep in —and that was only because I got worried when you didn't hear the doorbell or my knock on your door. I wanted to make sure you were all right." She decided not to mention the nasty smell.

"All right? Of course I all right. What you think could happen to me, *Señora* Soller? I never open the door the stranger, and I never be sick. I just here working hard, cooking, cleaning the house, and then I take the bath to clean myself. Is no crime. I very clean person and take the bath every day. *All* my people very clean, in spite what the Americanos think."

And now an international crisis. "I know you work hard and are a very clean person, Maria," she finally said in what she hoped was a bland, soothing tone. "I'm also certain you never heard anyone in *this* house say anything about people from your country not being clean. You can take as many baths as you want—five a day, if you feel like it." Immediately regretting this sarcasm, she forced a vapid smile: "I often like a hot bath during the afternoon myself, in fact I'm running myself a tub this very minute, as it happens. And now if you'll excuse me, Maria, I'd better go turn off the water."

So saying, she firmly shut the door on the unconvinced-looking Maria, and went into her bathroom, announcing, "I can't stand it, I can't *stand* it!" to the white tiling, which bounced her voice hollowly back at her. Delivered of this, she turned off the water and quickly threw off her clothes, and was climbing into the tub when she suddenly stopped, holding one foot poised above the steaming water like the wood nymph in *September Morn.* Withdrawing the foot, she set it down on the pink bath mat, and marched to Harold's medicine cabinet, throwing open the louvered door. She and Harold each had their own medicine cabinet. His and Hers. Hers was the one above the sink. Harold's, a deluxe model from Hammacher Schlemmer, hung above the laundry hamper on the opposite wall. She never looked in Harold's medicine cabinet. Or Harold's closet or bureau drawers or any of his other private places. Or rather, she tried never to look: all her life she'd had to battle the one trait she'd inherited from her mother, ironically (or maybe fittingly) one of her mother's worst traits—a powerful predilection for snooping, for prying into other people's personal effects and affairs. Though she had pretty well managed to keep this humiliating weakness under control over the years, she had occasional lapses. And had one now.

Now she stared long and hard at the tiny bottles and phials cramming the shelves of Harold's medicine cabinet, duplicates, she saw from the labels, of the ones she had seen in Harold's desk drawer last May—the occasion of another lapse. The bottom shelf held the tallest bottles and containers: shaving cream, after-shave cologne (the awful new one?), mouthwash—and a huge can of Lysol disinfectant spray, and, yes, an enormous bottle of Phisohex.

Shivering, her long thin body going prickly with gooseflesh, she shut the medicine cabinet door and, not even wincing at the hotness of the water, stepped into the tub and lay back, resting her head on the porcelain rim and shutting her eyes.

One afternoon at the end of last May, three weeks after her mother had died, a station-wagon mover had come down from Connecticut with the few things she'd salvaged from the auction of her mother's treasured antiques—a Hepplewhite settee, a curly maple dining table, some gesso candlesticks, and a little Federal mirror Harold had always admired, that she was going to give him as a surprise present. Though she still hadn't seen the place herself, Harold hated the furniture in the new office he'd been given as vice president, and she thought the mirror might be the very thing to cheer him up and brighten up the decor. Now that it had come, she couldn't wait to give it to him and decided to take it right down.

When she arrived, unannounced, Miss Mayross said that Harold was "upstairs," but would be down soon, and ushered her into his office, telling her to make herself at home. Taking the secretary at her word, she prowled around the office (which was just as bad as poor Harold had said, was for a fact very "Grand Rapids Executive Suite" with all its massive oiled woods and leather)—first inspecting the tiny private bathroom, then the view from the three windows, then the titles of books in the huge bookcase, then finally sitting down in the elephantine leather chair near the desk, which was Executive-bare, except for a small fat book lying open on its slick surface. As she sat there, bored, waiting for Harold to appear, her curiosity finally got the better of her, and she got up to see what the book was.

What it was, she discovered, was the *Merck Manual*, opened to a section titled "Liver and Biliary." On the right-hand page was a heavily underlined paragraph headed "Indications for Liver Function Tests." Frowning, she read the underscored passages several times, her uneasiness growing with each reading: she didn't think Harold was doing any research or personally checking out some Phaedre Press book— he had a staff of bright English majors fresh out of Vassar and Bennington and Yale, hired for just that purpose. Suddenly feeling very weary, more than weary, she sat down in Harold's leather desk chair . . . and immediately spotted Harold's John Kennedy key ring, dangling from the lock of the bottom right-hand desk drawer.

For Emma, afflicted as she was, a key in a lock was irresistible. She didn't resist. She bent down and pulled out the drawer as far as it would go. Every inch of the 17 x 26 space was meticulously organized, utilized. In the front of the drawer were two tightly packed rows of little bottles and phials, which she drew out and examined one by one, carefully setting each one back in place. Going from left to right, then back again, they held (according to their labels): Probanthine, Lomotil 2.5 mg, Compazine 10 mg, Mysteclin F 250 mg, Chlortrimeton 4 mg, Ornade capsules #12, Phenobarbital ¼ gr, Librium 10 mg, Darvon 65 mg, Bonine 25 mg, Alka Seltzer and Amphojel in tablet form, "Natural" vitamin-B complex capsules made from wheat germ and brewer's yeast, "Natural" vitamin-C capsules made from rose hips, "Natural" iron tablets made from a mixture of organic sea salts and ground bone meal and pulverized kelp. So much for the small containers. A row of larger ones stood behind them. Repeating the same process, she found herself examining a green plastic bottle of Phisohex, a jar of vitamin-E wafers, a box of Wheyfers (crackers, stated the label, made of bone meal, yoghurt, whey and carob), a stack of what looked like candy bars where large print on the wrappers announced they were TIGER'S MILK BARS, and small print claimed they were made of peanut butter, "assorted vitamins," cocoa . . . and yes, tiger's milk.

Behind the rows of bottles and containers lay two manila folders, the top one marked *Rx* with a red felt-tip pen. Really into the swing of things by now, still wondering how one milked a tiger, she was about to lift it out, when she heard Harold talking to Miss Mayross out in the hall. Sliding the drawer shut—or at least thinking she had—she just had time to scramble across the room to the bookcase, where she appeared to be thoughtfully browsing when Harold strode in, beaming, genuinely delighted to see her and genuinely delighted by the mirror, which he said would "tone the whole place up." "I think I'll hang it over here," he said, carrying it around in back of his desk and holding it up between the two windows: "How's this, Em?" "Perfect," murmured Em, and, smiling with satisfaction, he set the mirror on the desk —and saw the *Merck* he'd left lying open. His smile fading, he hastily flipped the book shut and nervously glanced down at the drawer, which he had *not* left open—but apparently was open now. Paling, he gave her a long quizzical look. Then, forcing a smile, he brightly proposed a tour of all five floors of the newly decorated office . . . while he furtively shoved the drawer clickingly shut with his foot. "Some other time, darling," Emma demurred; "I'd like to be home when Benjy gets in from school." And, distractedly kissing him on the cheek, fled.

It had given her quite a turn, that drawer. That and the *Merck*. She'd always known Harold was a secret hypochondriac, but like most of his secrets, with two notable exceptions, it had always struck her as being harmless and trivial, a little funny and foolish . . . and a little sad. Though few people besides herself knew it—and she'd never dreamed how far it went until just recently—Harold was an extremely secretive man. Harold, of course, had no idea that she knew just how secretive he was, or that she knew what any of his secrets were, but over the years, just through the proximity of marriage, she had accidentally discovered what many of his secrets were without any active prying on her part. She knew, for instance, that he had a separate savings account with $3,070.51 put by—but for what, she couldn't imagine, since they had a joint savings account with $19,302.06 put by for Benjy's education and the remote dream of a country house. She knew that he had an almost erotic passion for fresh caviar, which he sometimes bought in quarter-pound jars, and secretly (or so he thought, poor dear) gobbled behind the locked bathroom door. She knew that he had a more straightforward passion for Elizabeth Taylor, was immoderately fond of the novels of Émile Zola and the poetry of Edna St. Vincent Millay and the paintings of Thomas Hart Benton and the recordings of Peggy Lee—and that he would sooner die than admit any of this to anyone in the New York literary subculture. She knew that he was afraid of lions and elevators and interstate freeways, that he loathed his own podgy looks, that he was inordinately proud of his sexual prowess, and that (the one following upon the other) he'd had two fly-by-night affairs with two girls who worked at Phaedre Press—something he never dreamed she had discovered, something she had almost left him for the second time. Most important, she knew that starting several years back he had begun having some sort of an identity crisis —that current overworked phrase for a time when someone faced what he really was, in contrast to what he'd once dreamed of being. In Harold's case it was the slowly dawning realization he was never going to be any of the things he'd planned on back in Princeton or up in Cambridge—a brilliant "creative" editor (though he'd actually been a fine, much respected editor for years), one of the intellectual leaders of The Establishment—and that he was merely what his promotion in March confirmed: a tiny cog in the business machine that Phaedre Press had become, a cipher in the vast, conglomerate empire of a giant corporation that owned, along with Phaedre Press (and himself), whole city blocks, TV stations, oil wells, airlines, chains of motels. What this confrontation, this final moment of truth had cost him, she would never know. Harold didn't confide in her about certain things, particularly things where his pride was involved (which had worked for their marriage), but she'd been able to guess how he felt.

Of all his secrets, she had thought his identity crisis the most important, his hypochondria the least. After the shock of her surprise visit to his office had worn off, it occurred to her they were interrelated. Though she usually took great care never to play shrink (she hated when anyone did it to her), she decided after the visit to his office that his suddenly stepped-up hypochondria was what they called a displacement—was his way of channeling and working off all the bad feelings and disappointment and anxieties about himself he still hadn't come to grips with, still hadn't been able to consciously face. A bit pat, but true, she'd felt. And compared to some other supposedly secret compulsions and obsessions she knew of, Harold's hypochondria was a rose. A rose.

So she'd told herself back in May, and so she now told herself in the tub, where she saw her skin had puckered from being in the water so long, and quickly washed up and got out. Once dressed, she realized she felt thoroughly rested and refreshed, and decided to fix herself a drink instead of taking a nap. She had completely stopped drinking during her illness and had only recently started again because Tepp had recommended it, saying it would stimulate her badly damaged appetite. Appetites, she now guiltily amended as she started down the all, thinking of how a lot more than the desire for food had gone by he boards.

Benjy had opened his door while she was bathing, and as she passed she saw him sitting at his desk, doing his homework like any other normal child. Cheered by this, not letting herself consider the slimy tube or what he might have done with it, she went to the bar built into the bookcase covering the far wall of the living room. All the living-room walls were covered with bookshelves. In fact, every room in the apartment, which resembled a library, was covered with shelves of books. Even the dining room, which wasn't a real "room" at all, but had been carved out of too much badly designed free-floating space by a ceiling-to-floor bookcase-divider wall, which created a dining area on one side and a tiny book-lined entrance hall on the side nearest the door.

The ice bucket on the bar was empty. She hated giving orders, and the only thing remotely resembling an order she'd ever given Maria was a request to have the pail on the bar filled with ice by five every day, since the first thing Harold did when he came home was make a beeline for the bar. In the ten days since she had made the "request," the bucket had been filled twice.

Wondering if Maria belonged to some Colombian temperance league, she picked up the bucket and came to an abrupt stop in the kitchen doorway:

Home early, still wearing his topcoat and carrying his dispatch case, Harold was standing by the stove with Maria alongside him. They stood with their backs to the door, giving the meaty brick in the pan on top of the stove their full attention.

"What else besides green pepper and onion, Maria?"

"The temerra, *señor*. And garlic. And egg. And oh yes the bread crumb."

"And what about the meat. What kind of ground meat is that?"

"I no know, *señor*. Is what they send from the super store."

"Is there any ground pork in it?"

"I no know. The package say Chock."

"Ah, chuck. That's okay. What about any other seasonings. Are there any hot spices mixed in?"

"Hot spaeces?"

"Chilis. Peppers. Cayenne. Tabasco. Any of those strong Spanish-type seasonings."

"What are you doing home so early, Harold dear?" said Emma, sail-

ing into the room, and they both turned, Harold looking sheepish
Maria ominously pale.

"The sales conference broke up early," Harold said with embarrass
ment. "I didn't get any lunch, so I came out here to get a snack and to
find out what's for dinner."

"I tell him dinner is the meat loaf," said Maria, turning to Emma in
some appeal, her black eyes like Hot Spaeces—fiery peppercorns. "The
señor think I put bad things in his food, but is exack meat loaf
his *madre* show me how to make."

"My . . . mother?"

"Yas. Your *mamá*. When I first come here and the *Señora* Soller is
still in hospital, your morther show me how to make all your favor thing
She tell me you absolute crazy for the meat loaf the way she make, and
she make it one night to teach me. You eat it then and I even hear you
say is wunnerful. You no remember?"

"Ah yes, I remember now. I just never saw an uncooked meat loaf
before. Speaking of which—shouldn't it be in the oven if it's to
be thoroughly cooked by dinnertime?"

"I put in the oven at five, *señor*. Is not even yet five."

"Maria's a marvelous cook, Harold darling," Emma said emphatically,
taking ice trays from the refrigerator. "Why don't you leave the meat
loaf to Maria and go on up front and get comfortable. I'll bring you a
nice relaxing drink and some kind of snack to tide you over till
dinner."

Visibly brightening, Harold got as far as the door. "Just don't make
the drink *too* relaxing, sweetie. I didn't get any lunch, as I said, and I
don't want to end up on my ear—I've got a lot of work to do tonight."

As he went out, Maria opened the oven door and shoved in the meat
loaf, with what seemed to Emma like a lot of unnecessary banging and
slamming. She quickly filled the ice bucket and was looking in the icebox for a jar of olives, when Maria suddenly said in a strangled voice:

"You very funny eaters in this family. I never see people eat so
funny before. Every day the Benjamin come in from school and eat the
what you call snax, and then have no happetite for what I cook. His
padre also always eating the snix, and beside that always ack like he
think I maybe poison him. You are the only one in this house who eat
normale, *señora*, but you still eat pic-a-pac like the *pajaro*, the bird. I
know is just because you getting over being sick, but I very good cook
and is important to me I see people enjoy my food. Mrs. Lewis T. Spratt

always tell me I better than most fancy cook, and she and Mr. Lewis
T. always eat up every single thing I make."

Emma set the bucket and olives on a tray. "I think you're a fine cook
too, Maria. Didn't you just hear me say to Mr. Sohier, 'Maria's a
marvelous cook'? But we are *not* funny eaters, Maria, and Mr. Sohier
doesn't think you're trying to poison him. He just likes simple, wholesome food."

"Holsome?"

"Plain. Without much seasoning or spices," said Emma, and returned
to the bar where voices came drifting down the hall as she fixed the
drinks.

". . . thought it might be a computer."

"If I wanted to make something resembling a computer, I'd make
something that *looked* like one. Dad. It's just what it looks like. A lot
of old electrical junk."

"You thinking of maybe becoming an electrician, old boy?"

No response.

"Well. I'll leave you to your math. You seem to have a lot of it."

She took a deep swallow from her glass, replenished the drink from
the bottle, then carried the tray up to their room, where Harold's coat
and dispatch case lay on the bed. The sound of running water came
from behind the closed bathroom door: washing up with Phisohex?
She set the tray on the bureau and carried her drink to the armchair.
"Beautiful," said Harold, finally coming out of the bathroom and immediately spotting the tray. "Thanks, sweetie—it's just what I needed,"
he said after a few sips of scotch, popping olives in his mouth.

For several minutes she sat watching him busily drink scotch and
eat olives and tear open the mail he'd carried in from the hall table.
"Why didn't you get any lunch today, Harold dear?"

"Told you . . . had a sales conference," he explained wetly through
a mouthful of pimento and olive, frowning at the stiff card he'd just
pulled from an envelope.

"I thought they always had lunch sent in."

"They do. But it's always sandwiches, which they have sent in from
some filthy pesthole of a delicatessen that just opened last. . . . Listen,
Em. Just what is this invitation to a ball on November tenth? And who's
this person who wrote that coy little note on the bottom—who the hell
is Sally Emerson?"

"A tall, attractive brunette, who also happens to be Jack Desprez'
cousin. We met her at that party Jack gave when he opened his agency

last year. Or rather, you did. I'm surprised you don't remember—she
took quite a fancy to you."

Harold shot her a quick, shrewd look. "Amh, yes. I remember now.
Some fancy, sending an invitation to a ball at fifty bucks a head. —Were
you by any chance wanting to go."

"I wasn't, but I thought you might." By way of answering, Harold
tore the invitation card in half, then returned to the rest of the mail
and his drink and olives. Emma sat deep in thought for several seconds.
Then: "Harold dear, can you think of some way—some tactful way—
we could get rid of that girl? She's driving me right out of my mind."

"Girl. What girl?" Startled, Harold came up out of a bank statement
he'd been reading with obvious displeasure.

"Maria. She gives me the creeps. I honestly just don't see how I can
take three more weeks of having her around."

Harold grinned disarmingly. Charmingly. "She gives me a lot more
than the creeps, but I don't see how we could send her away without
its turning into some kind of federal case."

"I'll tell you how. We could pay her for the remaining time. Since
Elsie's already paid her, she'd be getting double pay for work she'd
never have to do. I should think *that* would take care of any hurt
feelings."

"I wouldn't be so sure, Em. She's touchy as hell—*you* saw that little
crisis about the meat loaf just now. As you know, her aunt—Constanza?
—is my mother's right arm, and I certainly wouldn't want to do anything to jeopardize that. Besides, if you'll pardon me for saying so—paying her double for work she'll never be doing seems pretty damned
extravagant to me. How much time was it you said she had left?"

Before Emma could answer, the telephone rang and Harold picked
it up, and, finishing some leftover argument from the sales conference,
stayed on for the next three quarters of an hour.

"How much time does she have left?" he repeated four hours later,
picking up where they'd left off. Dinner, a surprisingly good meat loaf,
had long since been eaten, and they'd all scattered the minute it was
over—Harold to do some work in the living-room corner they used as
a makeshift "study," Benjy to watch a Jacques Cousteau Special in his
room, Emma to watch *The Thirty-nine Steps* in their bedroom, and
Maria, once the dinner dishes were done, to watch God only knew what
on *her* TV: much as it pained Harold, they seemed to own three little
portable television sets.

Now Benjy was in bed, and Harold, finished with his work, had just come into the bedroom where Emma lay stretched out on the bed in pajamas, reading.

"Three weeks," said Emma.

"And how much does Elsie pay her? I always forget."

"One thirty a week."

Harold paused, one foot out of his trousers, and finally whistled. "Jesus Christ. I don't forget—I *repress* it. Listen, Em, no matter how bad she is, she isn't that bad. That would be taking three hundred and ninety dollars and just pissing it away. To say nothing of plane fare. Or did Elsie pay for that too . . . I never got that straight."

"Elsie paid her plane fare. Round trip."

Finally struck by a certain dryness in her voice, Harold glanced at her, then stepped free of his pants. "Well, I definitely think we should stick it out. That meat loaf was pretty damned good. But the important thing is that you really need her, Em. You look just lousy, yet you told me all you did today was go sit in the park with Hinda, that buddy of yours. You'd get a relapse if you tried to handle this place by yourself. And you're certainly going to need her for that dinner party next week."

"Minda. For Melisandre. And I have Cora coming to do the dinner as you suggested. Or have you forgotten that too."

Harold busied himself with putting his clothes on the armchair, letting that pass. "Well, I still think you should keep her," he said mildly, trying to placate her. "I really don't like the way you look."

"Well maybe you don't, Harold—maybe I look 'lousy,' as you say— but I'm actually feeling much better. In fact, I'm beginning to feel like my old self."

Naked by now, Harold turned and stared at her. Behind the horn rims his yellow eyes suddenly kindled and glowed. "Well, that's good news," he said softly. "Do you feel well enough for a terrific fuck?"

"Yes. I do."

"*Now* you're talking. Will it take long to get things . . . arranged?"

"No."

It didn't. And by the time she came out of the bathroom, he'd shut the door, pulled the blinds, and had the bed stripped for action—covers drawn down to the foot of the bed, pillows ready to hand.

"How do you want it?" he asked.

"Neat. Straight."

Laughing—it was an old joke—they climbed onto the bed with a businesslike air.

For a while there was silence. Busy silence. Intense silence.

Then: ". . . Ah, Em. Ah, Em. It's just like old times."

Then: "You're right . . . you *are* your old self."

Falling Bodies

And this seemed to be true for the next three days. For the next three days, while it wasn't exactly like Old Times—and she didn't think it was ever going to be like that again—she did feel like her old self, in fact felt so well she called Knickerbocker House to say she would probably be able to start the storefront tutoring project in early November, in about three weeks. Though she knew she would have to get the official go ahead from Tepp on that, she was convinced he would give it to her when she saw him on Friday, felt certain he would tell her she was all right at last, and discharge her.

For three days life seemed back on the right track: Benjy seemed more cheerful and talkative and didn't bring any new electrical equipment into the house, Harold seemed less depressed and preoccupied and didn't do anything peculiar about his food—which could just have been the return of good, active sex, but she somehow felt it was more than that. For three days even Maria seemed less touchy and sullen (and as a result she was less aware of her), but best of all, for three days she didn't hear a word from Minda, who was undoubtedly too busy facing life without a maid to call.

On the fourth day, the minute she opened her eyes she knew she was in for it. Fear and danger and the aura of one of her full-scaled attacks (something like a migraine's aura) hung in the sunny October air like woodsmoke. Determined to face it down, she got out of bed to make breakfast, a chore she'd always liked and had reclaimed from Maria for the last three days. Her slipshod housekeeping notwithstanding, she had always made a great point of getting up to fix breakfast for fourteen years, her feeling being that it was tremendously important for a family to start the day with a proper, nourishing meal—together. Which she knew was like trying to live out some near parody of magazine Togetherness straight out of the early fifties, but which she also knew was precisely the point—the early fifties, when her father was alive, having been the only time there was anything remotely like family-Togetherness in her life.

But that morning, unlike the previous three, there was hardly any atmosphere of what one might call Togetherness at their breakfast table. Aside from her own badly nerved-up state (which she thought she was successfully hiding, but soon found out she wasn't), Harold was jumpy and irritable, Benjy, pale and silent. "You're looking pretty washed out and shaky this morning, Em—you sure you're all right?" Harold suddenly asked toward the end of this depressing meal, where the table was glutted with barely-touched plates of eggs and toast. Because she felt so far from all right, Emma tartly came back that she felt just fine, *wonderful* in fact—so wonderful she was sure Tepp would give her a clean bill of health when she saw him at noon. "I hope you're right," Harold muttered doubtfully, then said good-by to Benjy who was getting up to leave for school. "Have a nice day, Benjy darling," said Emma, trying not to mind his leaving without kissing her good-by (there hadn't been any good-by kisses since she'd come home from the hospital), wondering, as she took in his marked pallor, if she shouldn't take a cue from Harold and ask if *he* felt all right, but deciding against it: she really couldn't wait to get the two of them out of the house.

Though it seemed to take forever, Harold finally left too. But the minute the front door closed behind him, Maria came whisking into the dining room where she was scraping and stacking the plates. Bracing herself for a long speech about William O'Dwyer or the Lewis T. Spratts, she was pleasantly surprised when Maria merely softly wished her a *"buenos días,"* and suggested she leave her the "matter of the dishes." Which she promptly did . . . Maria's hissing comments about the untouched food following her all the way to her room.

Closing the door, she went to the windows Harold had pushed wide to the golden October day and slammed them down, lowering the venetian blinds and pulling the slats tightly shut. She then flipped on the FM radio standing on a table behind her, dialing to the station she'd discovered her first day home from the hospital—a wonderful station that played the complete scores of old musicals for three solid hours every morning, with no commercials, just breaks for the time and random bits of zany information and news. When she reached the station, Ella Logan was singing "Look to the Rainbow" in her rich, gravelly brogue—which normally would have delighted her, *Finian's*

Rainbow being one of her all-time favorites, particularly when sung by the original cast. But there was nothing normal about the present situation, and for reasons that had nothing to do with loving the score, she turned the sound up full blast, and then went to sit on Harold's side of the bed, her place of reckoning. Where she hadn't sat since Monday morning.

With a shaking hand, she snatched up the pad and ballpoint pen by the phone, and began to make a list of things she had to do. Or, more precisely, to have something to do, she began making a list:

"Call Cora and fiinnnalize nxt friday menu," she wrote in a wildly lunging hand. "Make copy of mnu for H. so he can decide what wine," she scribbled, not at all distracted by Ella Logan's roaring—on the contrary, needing it to write. "Get Tepppp to give exact date when U can go back to work," she wrote veeringly, as Ella Logan burrily sang *"follows the dream,"* and after a blasting instrumental reprise, silence fell. Which lasted several seconds, too long for Emma, who sat apprehensive, pen poised above what looked like a cardiogram for paroxysmal tachycardia, until an unknown voice boomed, "Good morning. This is Thomas Brevitt, replacing Eliot Fletcher, who is on vacation. The time is eight thirty-two. Today is Friday, October fifteenth, National Poetry Day," and she immediately felt better: this was her favorite part of the program—the nutty part.

The morning star on October fifteenth was Saturn, continued Mr. Brevitt, his top-volume voice crashing around the bedroom, the evening stars Mercury, Venus, Jupiter and Mars, the Zodiac sign Libra, the Balance—and he wished to extend his personal Happy Birthday congratulations to all those born on October fifteenth, "a natal date" they shared with such "distinguished personages" as Friedrich Wilhelm Nietzsche, Ina Claire, William Menninger, Frederick William IV of Prussia, John Kenneth Galbraith, Mikhail Yurievich Lermontov, Sir Charles Percy Show, Arthur Schlesinger. And Mervyn Le Roy.

Beginning to relax, she put the pad and pen aside and swung her legs up on the bed, leaning back against the headboard, as Mr. Brevitt began to give a random sampling of some of the "memorable events" that had "transpired" on October fifteenth within the last hundred years:

On October fifteenth in 1928, he offered chattily, the dirigible Graf Zeppelin landed at Lakehurst, New Jersey, after a four-day flight from Friedrichshafen, Germany, with twenty passengers and thirty-eight crew members.

Brief pause.

On October fifteenth in 1946, he went on, his voice darkening a shade, number-two Nazi, Hermann Goering, committed suicide by poison in Nuremberg Prison two hours before he was scheduled to be hanged.

Long pause.

On October fifteenth in 1902, he said rapidly, as though someone in the control room had signaled him to cut the histrionics and hurry it up, the steamer *General Halliday* burned off Hell Gate, New York, and one thousand, two hundred and forty-seven passengers died.

Then running it all together: On October fifteenth in 1942, a hurricane in Bengal India "claimed" eleven thousand lives, on October fifteenth in 1964, Soviet Premier Krushchev was ousted as premier and Soviet Communist Party chief and on October fifteenth in 1858, the Lincoln-Douglas debates came to an end in Illinois.

Short pause for much-needed breath. Then: "And now our thought for the day. In honor of National Poetry Day, I would like to quote one of our greatest but most sadly neglected poets—Ralph Waldo Emerson—who in his immortal 'Merlin's Song' wrote, 'A day for toil, an hour for sport,/But for a friend is life too short.'" A long, vibrantly electronic pause to allow time for the pithy import of these immortal lines to sink in. Then: "The time is now eight forty-seven. And *now* the music from *Carousel!*"

She smiled. *Carousel* was another great favorite, but not at top volume. Realizing she felt fine now, she decided she didn't need the deafening roar of the radio any more, and was just about to get up off the bed and go turn it down, when over the opening bars of the overture she heard exactly the sort of noise she'd dreaded hearing and had hoped to drown out with the turned-up sound. A long, high-pitched screeching, whether human or metallic it was impossible to tell, finally ending in a sickening impacted scrunching thump.

Refusing to believe she had heard what she had—it was her worst dream come true—she sat paralyzed, the calliope pumping of the *Carousel* overture thunderously crashing against her deaf ears. Then, deciding to get it over with, she rushed to one of the windows and tilted a slat in the closed blind, but all she could see were the sunstruck upper floors of the building across the street. Gripping the sill with one hand, she used the other to yank up the blind and, forehead pressed to sooty glass, peered downward. The impeding glass and steepness of the angle made it impossible to see very much of the street, but even so she saw enough. Saw the front of the taxi that had obviously been making an illegal U-turn and had rammed into the middle of a delivery truck, and now stood broadside, blocking traffic. Saw what was clearly the two drivers standing and angrily gesticulating by the curb, while horns began blaring and a few curious passersby paused on the sidewalk to watch.

Even if she hadn't seen the jammed cars or their drivers, the faces of those bystanders would have been enough. If it had been what she dreaded, there would have been a huge, gaping, rubbernecking crowd, faces stiff and blank with horror, some of them even streaming with tears.

Near tears herself, she let down the blind with a crash and, oblivious to the roaring radio, went and sat back down on the bed. As her blurring eyes slowly cleared, she found herself staring at the block of lucite and the face of Elsie-Erasmus, who seemed to be smirking, sneering, "If that's not sick, then I don't know what is."

Knowing just how sick it was, she shouted, "Oh shut *up*, you old bitch!"—and then, frightened and demoralized by the sound of her own voice, burst into tears.

A little over a year ago, in late November, shortly after they had moved into their present apartment, some poor young woman had pitched herself and her two miniature poodles off the penthouse terrace of the building diagonally across the street. Emma herself hadn't seen it—it had happened two hours before she arrived home, and she couldn't have seen it in any case, since they had all landed in a rear courtyard out of sight, thank God—but Fitzclarence, the doorman, a born ghoul, had pounced on her as she stood in front of their building, confusedly blinking at the crowds and police cars across the street, and had told her the whole story in grisly detail. It seemed that the poor girl, "a rich divorcey" as Fitzclarence happily put it, had suddenly come out of her penthouse terrace, stark naked (on a day of 28 degrees), a tiny poodle under each arm, and had clambered up and sat down on the low stone parapet enclosing the terrace. For several minutes she'd just sat there, dangling her legs and wriggling her toes in outer space like someone testing the water in a swimming pool, while horrified workmen, retarring a lower neighboring roof, pleaded with her not to jump. Ignoring their shouts, her mind finally made up, the girl had first tossed one furry bundle, then the other, high into the air like some queenly vaudeville juggler—and as they came down past her (yowling?), had stood up on the low wall, spread her arms wide, and in a perfect Esther Williams swan dive, had taken off into space herself.

A sad and terrible and really horrifying story. And Emma had been properly horrified at first. But she felt it was basically like so many other New York horror stories one was always hearing or reading about, and wouldn't let herself dwell on it. Though certain images lingered—more, actually, of the poor poodles than the girl—they quickly faded, and she soon forgot the whole thing, never once thinking of the girl or poodles until her last night in the hospital, when another New York horror story brought it all back.

The hospital. The hospital. For someone who had always been afraid of hospitals—like many people, she secretly believed that once you got in, the chances were good, through iatrogenics or whatever, you might never get out—she'd had her powers of endurance pushed to their limits during her Rough Year. Having to spend a month first in one hospital watching her mother die, then spending another month in another hospital herself, burning with a mysterious fever no one could diagnose, had been a terrible ordeal, but she had come through it all with flying colors. Yet, ironically enough, in spite of the fear and grief involved in both experiences, and, in her own case, in spite of the physical misery caused by the fever and the grinding desolation of having to spend a whole month in a hospital—the worst part of the whole ordeal had been the depression she sank into at the beginning of her third week, even outdoing the nightmare of the first week.

The first week, terrified—she knew they suspected some "malignancy" might be causing her fever, and she had just watched her mother die from a malignancy—she was subjected to every conceivable kind of test and X ray, every kind of mortification of the flesh; when she wasn't being jabbed with needles that either drew out blood or injected some alien (and dangerous, she later discovered) dye or substance *into* her blood, she was being violently reamed out, only to be filled right back up again with barium, and carted off and laid out under some huge, futuristic machine (resembling no X ray she had ever seen) that took pictures of her insides. Small wonder that in any time left between all these goings on, she was much too knocked out to do much besides sleep.

With the bulk of the tests behind her, the second week was a dramatic improvement. Particularly since the reports on the first and most important of the studies began coming in, and her primary fear was allayed: her fever wasn't caused by any malignancy. Though as results on other analyses began coming in, it gradually became clear they couldn't discover what *was* causing the fever, she was too relieved and grateful to let it get her down. And feeling better, or more accurately, seeming to feel better as her body became accustomed, in its fashion, to a steady fever of 101.8 degrees—she began to read and watch television, at first sporadically and listlessly, but soon steadily and voraciously. It was really terribly strange, but once she started, she couldn't get enough, couldn't stop. She read three daily papers from front page to last, not missing one tiny news item or squib or classified ad, and when she was through with the papers she would read any news magazines the hospital bookshop had just gotten in, and when she'd finally finished the magazines, she would lie back, depleted but not sated, her bed adrift on a papery sea, watching any news program—on-the-hour spot bulletins, ponderous summaries by stellar newscasters, weighty roundtable discussions by experts—that she could find on the TV set.

At the time it never occurred to her she was doing anything peculiar, or occurred to her to stop and ask herself what she was doing, but if she had, she would have answered without hesitation that (a) she was trying to keep her mind off the fact that she was in a hospital, burning up with a mysterious fever no one could diagnose, and (b) she was simply getting caught up at last. Of course she had always read the papers and kept up with what was happening in the world, but she had never felt it was enough—and with good reason: her quick, abortive sessions with the *Times* at breakfast (and mostly the second section, at that, since Harold invariably commandeered the first, and then often took the whole damned paper to the office), and her after-dinner sessions with the *Post*, that is, when she wasn't too tired from her long day at work and from cooking and doing the dishes, which she often was—all that had left her feeling cheated, unsatisfied. She had always wanted a more complete picture, had always wanted to know the whole story, had wanted to be in possession of more of the facts.

And soon enough she was.

By the end of that week she was a veritable repository of facts, was a supine News of the Week in Review. On any given day of that week she could have supplied you with an endless variety of vital statistics and fascinating facts. On any given day of that week, for instance, she could have given you the pollen count or the body count. She could have told you whether or not that day's air had been Acceptable (and it had not been Acceptable in anybody's sight, O Lord, that whole week long), what passenger and mail ships were "Incoming" and "Outgoing," what had been served at a White House Breakfast Conference, and what the President had said at the Conference—which, considering what he'd said, was a pretty remarkable feat in itself. She could also have repeated, almost verbatim, a speech made by the Secretary-General in the UN that morning, a tirade delivered by the spokesman for a group of angry citizens (protesting a low-income housing project in Riverdale) on the porch of Gracie Mansion at noon, or what Bronx neighbors had said to reporters about the "nice, quiet" boy who lived in their building—who had taken two little girls to the basement and doused them with gasoline and set them afire. A sudden expert on numbers and statistics, she could have given you the day's scores at Shea Stadium or Forest Hills, the Dow-Jones averages, or told you the exact number of people who had "perished" in an earthquake in Peru, in a tenement fire in Brooklyn, in a small town in Maine where a madman had run amok down the main street with a Sten gun . . . and the exact number of years a Nobel Prize-winning biologist, speaking at an international conference on Human Environment, had given the world before total pollution of its resources was effected: seven.

Thus her second week in the hospital.

At the beginning of the third week, a black depression, like one of the oil-slicked breakers fouling the beaches of the world, came rolling in and washing over her, leaving her like one of those sea birds she'd seen photographed for years—bedraggled, immobilized, beached. She would lie for hours on end, unable to move, unable to speak, big, dumb, gelid tears streaming down her cheeks. It was—and she knew it right away—her little crash course in Contemporary Civilization paying off. Lying there, bedridden, a captive audience for the doomy generalizations of the seers and pundits of the press and TV, force-feeding herself on a diet of bad news, she had given herself a whopping case of spiritual indigestion, of accidie. Muzzy-brained from the fever, her powers of judgment and objectivity at their lowest ebb (leaving her unable to distinguish the bad from the worst), she had come, without realizing it, to that stupidly facile, romantic conclusion: the world was on its way out. Yes. She, Emma Sohier, apparently thought that. She, Emma Sohier, realist and pragmatist, had become the sort of doom-mongering creep she'd always laughed at. Facts. All the time she'd thought she was supplying herself with facts, cold facts, with her required reading and compulsive viewing, what she'd *really* been doing was supplying her poor fevered brain with portents, which it torpidly took to mean only one thing—the end was in sight. For sure. Doomsday. The Apocalypse.

Judgment Day. All that. It was like having some crackpot suddenly loose and wandering around in her head, one of those bearded nuts who wandered around New York in loincloths and sandals, wearing sandwich boards splashed with red paint: PREPARE! REPENT! THE END IS NEAR!

At the end of the second day of her depression, after asking her a lot of puzzling questions about Harold and her relationship with Harold, Martin Tepp put her on a powerful antidepressant drug. With a candor she found rather refreshing, if not downright disarming, Tepp said her depression was normal under the circumstances, since it was "damned depressing" to have an ailment doctors couldn't find a cause for—and added to that was just the condition of being hospitalized and bedridden, of being reduced to a weak and helpless and dependent state . . . all of which was bound to be "damned depressing" for someone as strong and active as herself. And, of course, added to *that*, concluded Tepp, were all the possible side effects a steady fever of 101.8 degrees might be having on her body: Though they still hadn't come up with an accurate way of gauging any of the effects a FUO might have on the nervous system, there were bound to be some, "indubitably."

Ah yes, Indubitably, Emma concurred. She saw no point in either correcting his grammar or in contradicting him, in telling him she knew what the real cause of her depression was. And thinking it could do no harm, she docilely took the antidepressant pills he prescribed, which immediately got her so jazzed up she had to be taken off them within two days, but it didn't really matter, since she had her own little antidepression program well underway by then.

It was really very simple, her program. Though she'd never believed in running, and happened to believe that banal slogan THERE'S NO PLACE TO HIDE, she saw that until she was well and up and about, it was stupid to snow herself with all that bad news. So while she didn't stop reading the papers, she only skimmed the news sections and editorials, and concentrated on the pages devoted to theater and movies and books and fashions and sports. She completely stopped reading all the weekly news magazines (she found their editors the worst self-appointed prophets of doom and gloom) and read all the murder mysteries and adventure stories the hospital lending library had on tap. On TV she watched old movies and soaps and programs where they ran quizzes, and gave away prizes ranging from pet goats to camper-trailers and wigs, and talk shows which all seemed to be run by ego-

maniacal idiots. When she was too tired to do anything but just
lie back, she would program her thoughts with the same fanatic insistence on no-think displayed by those unsung geniuses who programmed
daytime TV. She made herself think only Happy Thoughts, made herself think about only Happy Things, things as bland and comfortable
and wholesome as the breakfast paps and "home-style" soups they
dished up on TV commercials all day long:

Her childhood in Connecticut, or at least the part when her father
had been alive and Joseph McCarthy was still somewhere in Wiscon-
sin, plotting his evil career. The look and feel of the Connecticut coun-
tryside in those days—the big open fields, the tall old trees, the
comfortable old houses—the days just before the developers moved in.
The only dog she'd ever had, her beloved dog, Loopy. A boy named
Burt Tovey who had been her first real love, a big love, even though
she'd been too frightened to face up to it at the time. Her years at Radcliffe, where all the unhappiness of her adolescence slipped away, and
doors swung open in her mind, worlds unfolded. Those first novels read
for an English Lit course, and the words she'd kept jotting down as
she read—gumboots, plimsolls, lobelias, ayah, pelmet, loofah—words as
exotic as any in some foreign tongue, and which, sixteen years later,
still had some magical soothing and evocative power as she said them
aloud in her hospital room. Harold. First falling in love with Harold in
Cambridge. Harold and all the good years they had had. All those years
in that miraculous apartment—the first two floors in an old town house
in the East Fifties—with its garden and wood-burning fireplaces and
ceiling-to-floor windows and resinous smells, its aura of leafshade and
creaky boards and ticking clocks. Benjy. Benjy as a baby and little boy
in that leafy garden, that house. Benjy, the happiest of babies, the
happiest of little boys—sturdy, self-sufficient, endlessly busy, completely content. Benjy, who hadn't been permitted to visit her in the
hospital, and who she missed with a . . .

Well, it worked. Sentimental, self-indulgent, escapist, but the point
was her little program worked. All by herself, without the help of jazz-
you-up-let-you-down-with-a-bang drugs, she fought her black depression with its sludge of Doomsday thoughts, and made it go away. It
went, and so too, miraculously, did her fever—though there was no
connection between the two—and she was finally told she could go
home.

Her last night in the hospital, she was sitting in a chair by the window, an untouched supper tray in her lap; she was too excited about

going home to eat. The window was open to the mild late-September dusk, and a warm wind smelling of the river blew in, rattling the untouched evening paper on her bed. She had the TV turned on, but the sound was tuned down very low, and she just sat vacuously blinking at the screen, where pictures of birds and animals flickeringly came and went. The program was a documentary film sponsored by some wildlife-conservation outfit, which had just kept several thousand acres of Florida swampland from being filled in and turned into a monster jetport. Heartened that such a group should exist and succeed, childishly soothed and cheered by the pictures of the wild swamp creatures, she was staring absently at some shots of strange, huge, pelicanlike nesting birds, when the noise outside her window began. A high-pitched, eery kind of wailing or keening, an unnervingly fierce and frightening sound, like a solo of one of the women's voices in *The Battle of Algiers* —which reached a crescendo as she turned her head, and out of the corner of her eye saw something like one of the huge swamp birds flap past her window—and which suddenly ended in a hideously sickening clunk. The kind of noise a sack of rotten apples might make when dropped from a great height.

For one second she sat staring out at the dusky sky, where some unknown evening star twinkled and blinked (she'd had no FM radio in the hospital, no Thomas Brevitt to tell her its name). Then, determined to convince herself that she hadn't seen or heard what she already knew in her heart she had, she set the tray carefully on her bed and went to the window opened to the balmy twilight. Tightly gripping the sill (the open window space felt like a sucking vortex), she first looked straight out, in the wild hope that she might see some huge bird winging across the darkening ruddy sky, but all she saw was another unknown evening star, prettily twinkling above one of the bridge's steel lace towers. Abandoning all caution and leaning far out, dangerously far out, she finally looked down—and there it was, on the jutting terrace of the solarium seven flights down. No bag of rotten apples, that. The body of an old man, or what had been an old man, lying face-down on sooty red-brown brick, the hospital gown hiked above pathetically withered nates, limbs splayed at impossible angles, like a puppet with cut strings. Thank God there's no blood, she found herself stupidly thinking, while tightly clutching the sill and staring, mesmerized, at the bare soles of the old man's feet: delicately high-arched, coated with dirt (as though he had padded about his room barefoot, in endless agitated indecision before he jumped)—they brought the horror home more powerfully than anything else.

"Mrs. Sohier, Mrs. Sohier! Whatever are you doing, child? You want to have a terrible accident?" Low enough not to startle her and make her fall, as strong hands closed on her upper arms.

Mewling, she tightened her grip on the sill.

"Come away, come away, come away, dear," softly said the voice, which she now recognized as belonging to Miss Grundel, the night charge nurse, who kept forcefully tugging at her arms. "Come now, Mrs. Sohier dear . . . you're not yourself. I could see that right away from the look of your back, when I was passing by in the hall."

The sturdy hands finally succeeded in prying her loose and in getting her turned around with her back to the window. Unable to speak, desperately trying to swallow all the saliva flooding her mouth, she goggled at the square-faced nurse. "Och. God. Oook down," she finally managed.

"Look down at what, dear?" Suspicious, gray eyes narrowed, as though she thought that if she so much as shifted her grip, Emma might break free and turn around and jump herself.

"You'll *see!*" shouted Emma, and breaking free of those hands, bolted for the bathroom, locked the door, and barely made it to the toilet bowl in time. Through her misery, over the sounds of her own retching, she heard sounds outside the bathroom door that told her Miss Grundel had finally looked down—pounding footsteps, excited voices, phones ringing in her own room and outside in the hall.

After several minutes the doorknob rattled, someone sharply rapped on the bathroom door. "Mistress Sohier. Are you all right?" asked Miss Steele, the pleasant Haitian student-nurse who sometimes gave her back rubs and got her ready for bed every night.

"Yes, thank you, Miss Steele. I'm all right."

"Then please to unlock this door, Mistress Sohier. Nurse Grundel wishes that I assist you to your bed."

Ready, at that point, to be "assisted" in any way, she unlocked the door and passively let the student-nurse lead her to the bed. The window was shut, the shade drawn all the way down, the air conditioner going full blast—puffing the shade, flapping the corded shade pull.

Shivering, but not from the air conditioner, she wondered if they had locked her window.

"Who was it?" she asked Miss Steele as she gently smoothed out the covers on her bed.

". . . Mistress?"

"The man who jumped. Do they know who it is? Or why he jumped?"

Looking frightened and distressed, Miss Steele deliberately avoided her eyes and began edging away. "Nurse Grundel will be in to see you presently, Mistress Sohier . . ." she began, just as Nurse Grundel came through the door. Smiling. Carrying a doilied tray which held a paper cup filled with water and two yellow pills.

Miss Steele fled.

"Well now, Mrs. Sohier—how are you feeling? Better now?" Cheerful as hell.

"I'm feeling all right, I guess. All considered. Why did he do it? Do they know?"

"Please take these, dear."

Emma glared down at the tray being thrust at her. "What are they?" She knew what they were. Good old yellowbirds. They'd put her mother on them in the beginning, long before they'd brought in the big guns of Demerol and morphine.

"Something that will help calm you down and let you get a good night's sleep."

"I'm perfectly calm. I just want to know what happened. You can't pretend it didn't happen, though that's obviously what you're trying to do. As the only witness, I certainly think I have a right to . . ."

"There were three other witnesses, Mrs. Sohier," sharply cut in Miss Grundel, dropping the phony cheerfulness. "Three other people —all of whom were closer than yourself, in terms of distance—witnessed the . . . event. And saw a great deal more than you did. You're lucky you didn't see more than you did. Now. Please take these. My dear. You won't sleep a wink otherwise."

Knowing this was true—she could feel the nightmare hours of insomnia looming and banking like thunderheads—she swallowed both pills while Miss Grundel watched with gray pebble eyes. Then she decided to try a different tack. "Miss Grundel, I just saw a man take his own life," she said in a much softer voice, assuming what she hoped was a woebegone expression, as she set the empty paper cup on the tray. "I may not have been close enough to see what the others saw, but I saw enough to shake me up. Terribly. Knowing what was behind it might help. I'm not being morbid . . . I just can't help wondering what could be bad enough to make someone *do* such a thing. Didn't he leave some sort of note, or anything like that?"

While she had talked, the charge nurse's expression had shifted from weary disapproval to deep distaste. "If it will help set your mind at rest, Mrs. Sohier," she said in a thin, testy voice, "he was a very old man. A very old and very sick man who was going to die soon anyway."

"You mean he had some terminal illness. Like . . . cancer?" Careful, Emma, warned something in her head: Easy does it. Leave that alone.

Miss Grundel stared.

"Isn't an attitude like that against your code?"

"Code?"

"I guess I mean oath. The Aesculapian oath that declares the sanctity of human life. Or do only doctors take it. Are nurses required to take the Aesculapian oath?"

That particular nurse, no matter what oath she might have taken, now looked at Emma in a way that violated all the rules of her profession—with undisguised loathing. Then she quickly buckled the professional armor back on and forced a bland, ingratiating smile. "I think we've carried this discussion far enough, Mrs. Sohier," she said softly, suavely. "You tell me you're perfectly calm, but the fact is, you're terribly agitated. It's only natural for you to be upset—you witnessed a dreadful thing—but you're far more than upset, and I'm not going to contribute to your agitation by prolonging this conversation. I'm going to turn off your phone and leave instructions that you're not to be disturbed. You've a big day coming up tomorrow. A happy day, Mrs. Sohier. Try to concentrate on that and give those pills a chance to do their work. The horror will be gone by morning. A good night's sleep will bear it all away."

A good night's sleep did not bear it all away: the old man was the first thing she thought of as she came out of that bombed sleep—against the screen of her closed eyelids, she saw his body spread-eagled on the rusty tiles again—but by the time she was up and dressed and waiting for Harold, the excitement of going home did bear it away.

Harold took the morning off to help get her through the exhausting complications of a hospital discharge—the paying of bills, the distribution of little gifts and tips—something she never could have managed by herself: much to her dismay, she was terribly weak, far weaker than her shuffling walks up and down the hospital corridors had led her to believe. Once home, there was so much excitement and confusion—her reunion with Benjy (who was distressingly cold), her introduction to Maria Nonez, the barrage of phone calls from Minda and other well-wishers—that the old man completely slipped out of her mind. And during those first days home, it never occurred to her to tell Harold about the old man. (As it turned out, she never did.) Though later, after the first happy flush and commotion of being home had faded, having been replaced by more sober concerns, she did think of the old man once or twice, she didn't dwell on him very long. By then she had too many real and disturbing problems of her own to contend with: her demoralizing weakness, Benjy's continued coldness, the endless bombardment of phone calls from Minda, the disquieting, ever-obtrusive presence of Maria Nonez.

And so she completely forgot the old man. Or so she thought.

Her fourth day home, while following Tepp's instructions and taking her first short sortie out into the neighborhood, she suddenly found herself pressing up against the plate-glass window of a laundromat, a nasty tingling going on under her scalp. Frightened, she told herself it was just some awful new offshoot of the damned anemia, and went into the laundromat and sat down on a bench, not sure whether the whirring noises she heard were produced by twenty sloshing washing machines or her own head, and desperately tried not to cry: at the rate she was going, it would take *months* for her to get back to herself.

After a while the tingling and noises stopped, and she felt well enough to get up and go home, where she promptly forgot the whole thing. Then two days later she was returning from another short jaunt to the corner drugstore, when she felt the same noxious crawling under her scalp. With two more steps it had spread through her whole body— a vibrant sort of tickling, tinged with some terrible kind of expectancy or dread—which suddenly had her hugging the limestone bricks of the building next to theirs. Luckily, she was only a few yards from the entrance to their building. Luckily, Fitzclarence was off duty, and there weren't many people on the street. Somehow she managed to edge crab-wise to the glass doors, tears streaming down her face, and once inside the lobby the tingling and fright abated enough for her to get upstairs, and let herself into the apartment with her own key.

Luckily, Maria was on the phone, and rushing, unobserved, into her bedroom, she shut the door and sat down, violently shaking, on Harold's side of the bed—the first time she was to use it as a place of reckoning. And there, with icy sweat pouring off her and the tinny taste of terror still in her mouth, she had her moment of reckoning, she made herself face exactly what it was that had sent her up against the bricks of the building next door: the fear that a human body was about to come hurtling down out of the sky. Not, mind you, just *any* body. No. No accidental body. Not, say, the body of some poor window washer whose belt had snapped, or some poor old lady who'd leaned too far out the window to look for the mail truck with her pension check— but a body shoved off into space by its own impetus. A body going *whooooish* through the air, cutting a shrieking trajectory as the ground rushed nearer, and regrets, too late, came rushing in . . . finally landing with that sickening sound on the street or sidewalk or on top of a car. Or on top of *her*.

A pretty impressive phobia, that. And she'd been properly impressed. But also tremendously relieved, once she'd tracked it down: it was just the old man, of course. Or really the old man and girl and poodles combined. Less than two weeks before, she had witnessed—in spite of bitch Grundel's quibbling—she had *witnessed* the horror of an old man taking his life. And it had rocked her, had had a devastating, traumatizing effect on her. Which was only natural. The *un*natural thing was the way she'd managed to repress it for two weeks. And though, admittedly, another strange if not unnatural thing was the way she had somehow hooked up the old man and girl and poodles— almost as though she'd secretly thought of them as constituting a . . . trend—she was sure as more time passed, and the freshness of the horror receded, the weird phobia would recede along with it.

Now, a week later, when more time had passed, it was clear that the phobia or attacks or whatever she wanted to call them weren't receding at all, but were in fact getting so out of hand they happened in the house. Now, sitting there with the radio blasting away and tears drying on her cheeks and her shouts at her mother-in-law's photograph still ringing in her ears, she had to face it: there was nothing "natural" going on, and she had some more reckoning to do. There was something here that went far beyond any morbid or traumatized preoccupation with the old man and girl and poodles and she'd damned well better sit there until she'd figured out what it was.

It didn't take long. It was all there, of course, just waiting for her to carry it one step further than she had last week. And it was really pretty funny . . . in a macabre sort of way. Some message. The same old message. She turned out to have a pretty comical subconscious, had some bossy, joky kind of monitor in there—a cross between one of the Marx brothers and one of the pioneer animators at Disney's studio, with an added touch of fiendishness—determined not to let her get away with a thing. Particularly the smug idea that she'd managed to get rid of her depression and Doomsday thoughts singlehanded, with her own little do-it-yourself kit. Because the fact was she hadn't. A lot of that was still kicking around. And probably just at those times she was feeling most self-congratulatory and optimistic—such as during the last three days, when she'd felt that not only the world, but *her* world was going to be all right—the monitor in her head would growl like Groucho, "Think so, girlie? Then get a load of this!" and would send her one of the attacks. Which were really, now that she saw it, like some early Mickey Mouse cartoon expressing the idea of a mass, collective despair, the kind of despair she'd felt her third week in the hospital . . . and now sometimes highhandedly projected onto everybody else. It was as though the monitor in her head had taken the old man and girl and poodles and all the bits of hearsay she'd ever collected about 1929—a time of real enough despair, when people had pitched themselves from windows and rooftops and real bodies *had* come whooshing and tumbling down—and made it into this souped-up Donald Duck version of what she thought everybody was feeling now.

Only they weren't. And she knew they weren't. It was just that some tenacious and destructive part of her mind wouldn't let go the Doomsday thoughts. Maybe she was more of a masochist than she'd ever dreamed, and some part of her (the mean monitor) didn't want her old dynamic, optimistic self to come back and take charge. Maybe it just was a build-up of guilt from lying around, useless and trapped, for almost a month and a half. Maybe. Maybe. The point was the whole damned thing had to *stop*. Another manifestation of the same thing was the way, ever since she'd gotten out of the hospital, her eye kept seeking out and fastening on the cruel, the ugly, the sordid—trying to turn every nasty little incident or detail into some sort of concrete proof of just how rotten the world had become. Like the time, exactly a week ago to that very day, she'd gotten poor Benjy upset (she'd belatedly realized) by carrying on about that lost dog.

All that had to stop. For the rest of her convalescence she had to be on guard against these wild swings of mood and lapses into pessimism, had to try and find something constructive to do. In less than three hours she'd be seeing Tepp and would know exactly when she could go back to work. Though she had a feeling she had probably jumped the gun by calling Knickerbocker House, maybe Tepp would let her take some small part-time job, something that would get her out of the house for a few hours every day, until she was well enough to go back to work full time. Knickerbocker House ran a thrift shop called

Knickerbocker Knick Knacks just a few blocks from where they lived. If she had enough time, she could drop in on her way to Tepp, and see if there was any small volunteer job they'd let her do—typing inventory lists or sticking price tags on old clothes and cracked Meissen plates. Anything. She wasn't proud.

Cheered by even this rather pathetic plan, she got up off the bed. The attack was completely over. She wasn't at all shaky or frightened—just deafened by the radio which had been roaring away all the time. She was just about to turn it off, when the phone next to her on the chest began ringing, making her jump. It was Minda, she was sure of it; her three days of peace had come to an end in every way. She decided to let it ring, and when Maria picked up the kitchen extension, would tell her to tell Minda she wasn't home. But Maria didn't pick up, and the phone kept ringing, almost jouncing and jiggling on the walnut surface of the chest. When it rang a sixth time—where *was* Maria?—she couldn't stand it and picked up.

"Oh, thank God you're there!" said Minda, and she could hear the suppressed hysteria in the voice, even with Ezio Pinza singing "Some Enchanted Evening" at top volume. "Can you *hear* me, Em? What's all that racket at your end?"

"It's the radio. Hold a sec while I turn it down." As she crossed the room, she desperately tried to think of something that would get her off the phone, fast. "Minda dear, I really can't talk now," she said, coming back. "I have an appointment with Dr. Tepp, and before I go I have to . . ."

"Why'd you have the radio turned on loud like that?" Minda cut in suspiciously, momentarily diverted from herself.

"They were playing the score from *South Pacific,* and I wanted to make sure I could hear it while I was washing up in the bathroom." The day's ration of lies had begun; each time she talked to Minda, she found herself lying more and more, with greater and greater ease. "As I started to say, I have an eleven o'clock appointment with Tepp" (another lie, the appointment was at noon) "and I have a lot of errands to do first. I have to go to the bank, and then to . . ."

"It's only twenty past nine, for God's sake. You've got an hour and a half. Just give me ten minutes, Em. That's all I ask. I need your help. Badly."

Something about the pressured, breathless voice made her say, reluctantly, "What's the matter, Minda. Something wrong?"

"Huih. J-j-just about everything you can think of is wrong. That's all.

I'm so frightened, Em. I have this horrible, godawful feeling of dread, of being on the verge of losing control. You know what I mean? It's hard to describe, except to say that it feels like . . . if I made one wrong move, said one wrong thing . . . I might . . . fly apart."

Emma heavily sat back down on the bed, tempted to lie back and close her eyes: therapy-position in the reverse. "What triggered it off?" she asked, remaining upright, playing therapist as always. "Did something specific happen, or is it just sort of . . . free floating." At least she hadn't used the word anxiety.

"Oh, it's specific, all right. Peter's got a woman. I know it for sure."

"How can you be sure. Did you hire a private detective, or did someone write you an anonymous letter—something like that?"

"No, nothing like that. But it doesn't have to be. There are hundreds of little giveaways."

"Such as."

"Such as his buying an enormous bottle of mouthwash, and some horrible new sandalwoody after shave at the drugstore last week."

"I see," Emma said quietly, and, taking hold of the extra-long phone cord, distractedly began winding it around one of the brass drawer-pulls of the bachelor chest.

"I can tell from your voice you don't see at all. I also can tell you think that's pretty crazy, but that's because you don't really know Peter. You only met him that one time you were here with Benjy, and he came home early. You only saw the facade—that sun-lamp tan, the fancy haircut, the expensive clothes—what looks like a handsome, well-groomed man who's meticulous about himself. But let me tell you, under all that lies an absolute slob. He has a lot of disgusting personal habits you'd never *believe*. For instance, he'll go for months without cutting his toenails, and then suddenly starts cutting them while lying on our *bed*, watching TV. Charming? Or he'll often go two or three days without changing his underwear or brushing his teeth, and if I didn't put his pajamas in the hamper every Friday, he'd wear the same pair for a month. All right, I know a lot of men have some pretty disgusting personal habits, and compared to Nando, Peter's actu-ally . . ."

"Minda. I'm sorry, but I really have to go."

"Wait. *I'm* sorry for rambling on. I'll get to the point. Tell you what triggered me off. You see, when I've got someone working here, I never get up to make breakfast, but all this week I've been up at seven to get the twins off to play group. What I do is get up, wash, rush in the kitchen to put the coffee on, rush in to wake the twins, then rush back to our room to change from pajamas to slacks. Well. Every single morning this week, when I've come back to change, I've heard Peter Wolfe using the Water Pik in the bathroom: zroom zroom gurgle gurgle. Now get this, Em: we've had that frigging Water Pik for two whole years—each of us with our dear little private nozzle, mine pink, his blue—and he's never touched it. And he hasn't been to any dentist lately who might have told him his gums are in terrible shape; I know because I asked . . . very subtly, of course. Anyway. The first time I heard him in there googling away, then finishing off by gargling with his new high-powered mouthwash, I almost broke up. Caruso of Central Park West. When it happened every day, I stopped thinking it was so funny, and from the second day on began paying attention to the other things. The waves of after shave he gave off when he came in the kitchen for breakfast—it was so disgusting it's a wonder the twins didn't throw up in their bowls of Kellogg's K. The new clothes—all of a sudden he broke out with all these new shirts and ties and even *underwear* from some Italian boutique. But the clincher was his never being in his office in the morning. He leaves this apartment at ten to eight every morning: he told me long ago, even when we were living in L.A., he likes to be the first one in the office, likes to open up the place. Okay. If he leaves here at ten to eight, he ought to be in his office by eight-thirty, quarter to nine the latest, right? I mean we live on the West Side, and even though it's forty blocks down, the subway ought to get him there in twenty minutes, tops. Right? Well, let me tell you, I've called his office at ten three mornings in a row, and he's never been there. This morning I called at a quarter past nine, just before I called you, and the switchboard operator said nobody was in the office yet. And he left here at twenty to eight *this* morning. Yesterday, when I called around ten, his bitch secretary—I could tell she knew exactly why I was calling—said he was 'out in the market' and couldn't be reached. 'Out in the market.' He was out in some hotel or motel, or the pad of one of his showroom models or one of those rich-bitchy young fashion editors, who are so hot for his new spring line, and are doing a big promotional thing. Well, it's not just his spring line they're hot for, let me tell you."

All during this speech, Emma had sat winding fourteen feet of phone cord around the brass drawer-pull. Now she stared at the shiny knob strangled by rubbery coils: guess who.

"Say something, Em."

"I really don't know what to say. You're right, I don't know Peter at all, but even so, I think the things you've . . . Listen, Minda. The back doorbell's ringing, I'd better get it."

"Why doesn't that Mexican creep get it?"

"I don't know. Maybe she's in the can. And she's Colombian, not Mexican."

"Well, whatever she is, go get it. I'll hang on. It's still only twenty-five to ten. I'll only keep you a few more seconds, I promise."

Putting down the phone, Emma walked soundlessly across the thick-piled carpet, and for a count of forty, stared at herself in the full-length mirror on the bathroom door. Finally, twisting her pale face into an Imogene Coca expression, she stuck out her tongue at her reflection and went back to the phone: "I've *got* to get off this phone, Minda."

"Who was at the back door?" Suspicious again.

"The cleaner. Maria was taking a bath." How many lies had she told—eight? nine?

"A bath at nine-thirty in the morning? She sounds like some treasure."

"Please listen to me, Minda. I know you're upset, but I've *got* to go. Let me say, fast, that I really don't think you can hang Peter on such slender evidence, but if you like, I'll call you back after my doctor's appointment, and we can go into it a . . ."

"I have to talk to you now. *Now.* D'you understand. Just give me two more minutes. I beg you, Em. In all the time we've known each other, have I ever begged you for *anything* . . . ?"

As she listened to the sounds from the other end, Emma shut her eyes. "Don't, Minda. Nothing's ever that bad. Nothing. If you feel it's a help, I'll stay on a while longer, but what I really think you ought to do is call your old analyst . . . Weiglitz? I realize he's living like an invalid up there in Connecticut, but a telephone conversation certainly isn't going to put any strain on his heart." She paused, knowing this might not be true if Minda was the caller. "I mean you keep telling me Weiglitz is the only one who ever really helped you, and, after all, he *does* have a certain responsibility to you."

"Responsibility. That's the right word," said Minda, weeping stormily. "He and all those other shrinks are responsible for the shape I'm in. For my ending up in this blind alley. I hate my life. *Hate* it. Maids. Nursery schools. Play groups. Groceries. Meals. Keeping this fucking place running. Living with a sadistic prick like that. Having to take care of his lousy dirty laundry and then having to wonder who he's sticking his cock into. Why should *I* care. Why should I even have to *consider* filth like that. Sink that low. Oh God, Em. What happens. What *happened*. To you. To me. Yes, to you too. My *God*, but you were an exciting person in the old days. I'd never met women like you or Casey Rowland before—so damned smart, all fired up about everything, that room of yours with piles of books toppling and spilling, Tate, Ransom . . . and now the fire's gone out. D'you remember those days, Em? D'you remember the feeling in the air?"

Emma sat holding a shading hand over her still-closed eyes. "Yes. I remember."

"A sort of feeling that anything—*any*thing was possible. Endless vistas opening up. 'Flights of arches.' Like Sitwell said somewhere in 'The Gothick North,' I think. He also said—and I've never forgotten it—and it catches what I mean here—'It was an early morning of the senses with a cold and energetic freshness, clear and brilliant light . . .' Oh. God. D'you remember *Songs from Palma*, Em?"

"Of course I remember."

"D'you remember how you and Casey and *every*body was so damned excited, and I got all those letters, one from Garrigue, and one even from Louise Bogan, and a feeler about reading with a few other young poets at the Y?"

"Yes," said Emma, only remembering Weiglitz's explanation for Minda's "drive" to write poetry—and suddenly hearing what sounded like a click and the acoustical opening-up meaning someone had picked up on the line. But before she could say anything, Minda went barreling on.

"I had style. Class. Individuality. Integrity—at least intellectual integrity. And O God, look at me now. Listen to me now. Carrying on like somebody out of Chekov. The Feminine Role. Okay, Weiglitz was better than the others, he *did* help me, but he conned me into believing all that shit, and I don't want to talk to him, I want to talk to *you*. You may not be who or what you wanted or started out to be back in those days, but who am I to say that's wrong—and *you* made the choice. You have control over your life, you make things work. You're the only stable, effective woman I know. I might pick away at you about your social work and the way you live, but it's just jealousy. You've got it all licked, got it made. I mean you're married and have a kid and run a home, yet you haven't been sucked in or sucked under, you're still your own woman. How do you do it? Do you know how *lucky* you are, Em. For instance, do you have any idea how unusual it is to have a smart, successful husband who really loves and respects you, and doesn't go around screwing every little . . ."

"Minda. I think there's someone on the line. In fact, I'm sure I heard somebody pick up."

"Well it couldn't be here. I'm all alone, needless to say. The twins left for play group over an hour ago.—It must be at your place."

With that there was a loud click, an acoustical sealing-off.

Minda laughed. "It *was* your place—your Colombian treasure has obviously finished her morning soak. You poor baby. I warned you they were all alike, but you didn't believe me. You never do. But, to get back to what I was saying, you better believe me when I tell you how lucky you are. I know you've got problems—with Benjy and probably Harold too—but somehow you manage to handle them, manage to keep on going no matter what. Strong. You're strong as hell. Look at what you've just been through. I didn't see you while your mother was dying, but I saw you right after she'd died, and the way you handled her death was just typical. Then, right on top of that you get sick yourself, but instead of just crumpling under all . . ."

"Cut it out, Minda, knock it off. You're embarrassing me." Making me sick was more like it. Making my blood boil. What did she *mean* by "problems with Benjy"? And all this carrying on about the past and "vistas" and "feelings in the air" was getting her nervous and upset, like all the talk of luck: though few people knew it, she was tremendously superstitious, and like all superstitious people believed one should never talk of one's luck. "I'm flattered that you think I'm all those things, but you're really going overboard when . . ." A loud click on the line stopped her cold. "Maria. Is that you?"

This time the phone loudly clattered down, no furtive clicks.

Minda was gasping with laughter at the other end.

"Minda. Minda, *listen* to me. I'm going to hang up now. You certainly don't need me any more. You're in good shape. If you can laugh like that, you're in terrific shape. And I'm late. As it is, I'll be lucky if I get to the bank before I'm due at Tepp."

"Oh, God. Sorry. Selfish as always, that's me. But you're right, I'm fine now—thanks to you. You ought to hang out your shingle. I have a lot more to say about dear Peter Wolfe, but I'll save it for Monday. We're going away for the weekend, to someplace near New Milford. *With* the twins, but our hostess, this high-powered sportswear buyer named Selma Shrick—I swear to God, that's her name—has *three* in help, and one of them's a nursemaid type. We won't be leaving until five, but I won't bug you again today. You've done enough, and I don't know how to thank you, Em. Well. I hope Tepp finds you in *assolutamente* splendid shape. And have a good weekend. And . . . bless you, bless you, pussycat."

Emma waited until she heard the dial tone, then shoved the receiver under Harold's pillow so she wouldn't have to listen to the operator signaling that the phone was off the hook. She wasn't going to replace the receiver until she was on her way out the door: in the time it took her to wash and dress, Minda might suddenly remember some fresh piece of incriminating evidence, some further proof of Peter's infidelity —a new pair of shoelaces, a jar of a new brand of deodorant, a pack of suspicious-looking matches she'd found while searching his pockets.

She was in her closet, trying to decide what to wear, when there was a volley of loud staccato raps on her door.

It was Maria. Rather excited. "Please, *señora*—is something with the telephone. Is important I call my friend who share the apartment in the Bronx. I must know if a letter come for me there *now*—I cannot wait until I leave the weekend tonight. I trying and trying to call, but first you be on the phone, and now is broken. It just making the funny sound. *Por favor* . . . perhaps you know how to fix?"

Could she see the receiver under the pillow from the doorway? "Wait just a second, Maria—*uno segundo*—let me check." Rudely shutting the door, she raced back and hung up the phone. "Sorry," she said, reopening the door on a flaming-faced Maria. "The phone isn't broken, it was just off the hook."

" . . . *señora?*"

"Is okay. I mean the phone's all right now. *Multo bueno?* You can call your friend now. And in case you're on the phone when I leave —I'm going out and probably won't be back till one or two o'clock. Also, I know you like to do heavy cleaning on Fridays, but the place doesn't really need it, Maria, just straighten up. I'll send something for dinner from the A&P."

The sallow face, which had remained uncomprehendingly blank throughout this whole speech, lit up at the mention of dinner. "Please, *señora*—for the dinner you send the pork roast. You send, and I will make like I do for the Spratt. You remember I tell you about Mrs. Lewis T. Spratt, the cousin of the onetime wife of Mayor Bill?"

"Ah, yes. Indeed I remember Mrs. Spratt. Of course, I'll send the pork roast. And now, Maria . . . *adíos*." She shut the door and was dressed in ten minutes: she really did have to get to the bank before her appointment with Tepp, she hadn't lied to Minda on that score—but she also had to get to the A&P and Knickerbocker Knick Knacks shop, and all before noon.

As she slipped out the front door, she heard Maria excitedly talking in Spanish on the phone. Though it was hard to tell, she sounded upset: maybe her friend in the Bronx was reading the important letter to her over the phone—and it had some sort of urgent message about the necessity of her returning to Colombia. At once.

Though she felt a twinge of guilt at wishing any kind of trouble on poor Maria, the very idea of her leaving their household ahead of time made Emma walk with a light, buoyant step down the hall, for once not minding the dimness and fusty smells and depressing lineup of peepholed doors—not even minding the familiar amber puddle on the floor of the elevator, left by the pathetic old incontinent Dandie Dinmont that lived on the fourteenth floor.

Her high spirits suffered a minor setback when she reached the lobby, where she looked across expanses of orange carpet and saw a frail old black woman, in demeaningly authentic nursemaid rig, trying to maneuver a huge limousine of an English pram up the steps to the street—while Fitzclarence watched from outside the glass doors, a bemused expression on his ravaged old alcoholic's face. The minute she appeared at the woman's side to help her jockey the carriage up the steps, Fitzclarence sprang into action; swinging the glass doors wide, beaming obsequiously at Emma, he playfully poked a nicotine-stained finger into the carriage as it passed: "And how is darlin' Rosaleen Shuster on this gadgious October day?"

Rosaleen Shuster, aged five months, swoddled in layers of monogrammed pink batiste and wool, did not respond. Nor did Emma or Rosaleen's nurse, all of them filing out past Fitzclarence in dignified silence, the nurse and Rosaleen heading west for Central Park, Emma heading east for the bank—hearing as she went, an explicitly juicy splat as Fitzclarence expressed himself by spitting on the sidewalk. *Do something.* Turn around and tell the old bastard where to get off, she told herself, her steps lagging, but kept on going, promising herself she would do something later on—report him to the super or the management, see if she could get him fired. She would. This time she would.

Ahead on her left soared the new building they had finally finished last March, an ugly white-tiled tower with jutting slabs of cantilevered terraces. In the months before she'd gotten sick, particularly during the time she was visiting her mother twice a day in the hospital, she had amused herself, diverted herself, by closely following what each tenant did to make his terrace truly his own—within the restrictions imposed by the management, that is. She had really made a little game out of it, watching the endless variations of potted shrubs and outdoor furniture and fences and divider-panels and dangling things like plants and mobiles and lamps slowly pile up—with her former optimism, seeing all these accumulations of stuff, of junk often, as signs of spirit, as brave assertions of individuality and the resolve not to knuckle under to the grinding regimentation of life in New York.

Not so this morning. This morning she indulged in no such florid flights of fancy. This morning she wasn't interested in the terraces. At least not in their furnishings (with the exception of all those dangling things). Today she was primarily interested in their occupants, who, without looking directly upward, she could still see moving around— watering plants, wielding mops and brooms, or just sitting or lying in the sun, taking advantage of still another Indian-summer day. Her interest in them was rather limited, however: *Just stay where you are,* she found herself thinking as she passed under their terraces, in some sort of final spasm of her earlier attack. But grimly determined not to let it go any further than that, she slowly kept on going up the block toward the bank, hewing to the middle of the sidewalk, looking to neither side. Though the sun was in her eyes, she could see all the things going on around her in the street, but she doggedly narrowed her eyes, diffusing the focus, not letting herself fasten on ugliness as she recently had. The man whipping his collie with its steel leash. The black boy, younger than Benjy, pedaling the heavy, overloaded grocery cart, his arms and legs like burnt matchsticks, his toes bursting from the sneakers pumping the pedals around. The old woman whose grocery bag had burst, and who was gropingly trying to retrieve rolling canned goods and oranges, while people (like herself) walked briskly by. The young nursemaid with the face of Himmler, bending over the weeping little girl in the stroller, softly whispering threats in German. The boy unscrewing hub caps from the car at the curb, the emaciated cat cowering under the car . . .

None of it. She saw, yet permitted herself to "see," none of it. She wasn't going to let old Lady Doomsday get started, get any ammunition or proof of how ugly and heartless the world had become. No. *No.* And keeping her eye slitted against the sunglare, pleasurably scuffing her heels on the pavement dividers like a child, she finally reached the corner bank, where, hand on door, she paused, triumphant, and tremulously smiled: On such a gadgious day in October—why would any bodies come tumbling down?

Sheets

FRIDAY 11:10 A.M.

"Horrors, Benjamin. What *can* your mother have been thinking of
. . . letting you come to school with a throat like that."

Lost dogs. Broken families and starving children in the slums. Thus
he would have answered if he hadn't had a tongue depressor jammed
down his throat. Now, the pressure of the wooden stick and the greeny-
cheese smell of Miss Tibbs's breath made him gag, and the depressor
was removed. "She didn't know I had it, Miss Tibbs," he mumbled, as
that lady took herself and her foul breath a sparing five feet away, sitting back down at her desk with a flutter of paisley and tick of amber
beads.

"What's that you said, Benjamin?" said the student-counselor-cum-
school-nurse, as she began to scribble on several pads at once like some
spindly octopus.

"I said she didn't know I had the sore throat, Miss Tibbs. It wasn't
this bad when I left the house."

"That's hard to believe, seeing that you've got what looks exactly like
a strep throat." She ferociously ripped sheets of paper off the pads and
stood up. "You have a responsibility to other students in this school,
Benjamin. If you are feeling even the teensiest bit poorly, you have an
obligation to let your dear parents know." She stalked to the door.
"Please wait here for me, Benjamin. I have to give these discharge slips
to Miss Gancy and Mr. Bolt, and phone your mother and ask her to
come and fetch you home."

Remembering he'd heard his mother say something at breakfast about
a noon appointment with somebody named Tepp, he called out after
Miss Tibbs, but she was already down the stairs.

After watching fifteen minutes tick away on the wall clock, the
frosted door rattled open, and Miss Tibbs came in carrying his jacket
and book bag, a wild look in her eyes. "O goodness gracious," she said
breathlessly. "*Something* is wrong with the phone at your house,

Benjamin. I got a busy signal for ten minutes straight. I happen to know your dear mother, and she is not the sort of woman to hang on the phone. The operator tried to put me through to Verification, to see if the phone was off the hook at your house, but Verification wouldn't pick up, though we rang and rang." Putting a bony hand to her bony breast, Miss Tibbs took a deep and steadying breath: "The New York telephone system will be the death of us all. Do you know if your mother is at home, Benjamin?"

"Yes. She's just come out of the hospital. She's home all the time." He had decided not to mention the noon appointment with Tepp.

"Ah yes, ah yes. Now I remember. Poor lady. Well." Obviously still shaken by her bout with the New York telephone system, Miss Tibbs handed him his jacket and book bag and a pink slip, and sank down at her desk. "This is highly irregular, Benjamin—the school always insists that sick children be picked up by someone from home that we know—but if we wait to get through to your mother on that telephone, you might be here for the rest of the day. Mr. Anson, the new assistant Latin instructor, has a free period coming up. He'll meet you at Miss Gancy's desk in ten minutes, and take you home in a taxicab. Meanwhile, we'll try to get through to your mother, to let her know you're on your way." She forced a wan smile. "I hope you feel better soon, Benjamin. You have a whole weekend to get well in. But you mustn't rush things. If you're not well by Monday, you mustn't *think* of coming to school."

Politely thanking her—he was famous for his beautiful manners at the school—he went down three flights of marble steps, to the receptionist's desk at the back of the main hall. The receptionist, Miss Gancy, a moon-faced young woman with heavy black-rimmed glasses, was talking on the phone. As he sat down on a bench near her desk, she absently nodded and smiled at him, and when she finally hung up said, "Hallo there, Benjamin. Sorry to hear you're under the weather. Don't fret—Mr. Anson will be here soon."

For twenty minutes, while clanging bells announced the change of classes, and the sounds of scuffling feet and voices and banging doors came floating down from the upper floors, he sat patiently on the bench. In between tapping on the typewriter and answering the phone, Miss Gancy kept giving him encouraging smiles. At the end of the twenty minutes, her phone rang again, and after a short conversation, she hung up and, wringing her hands, came to the bench where he sat. "I'm *most* sorry, Benjamin, but there's been some dreadful mixup. It seems Mr.

Anson has a Cicero class over in the Upper School. Miss Tibbs just called me from upstairs. She said she *still* can't get through to your house and asked me to take you in a cab myself, as soon as Mrs. Frumpke relieves me for lunch."

"Thank you, Miss Gancy. And when will that be?"

"In fifteen minutes. At noon. I'm *so* sorry, Benjamin, but it's the best we can manage. Are you feeling very poorly? Very tired? Would you like to lie down? You could stretch out on the chaise in the teachers' lounge until Mrs. Frumpke comes."

"No thanks, Miss Gancy. I'm just fine here." And to demonstrate this, opened his book bag, took out a math book and started to read.

For five minutes he sat turning pages; Miss Gancy's phone rang twice. "Oh *dear*," she said to the second caller. "He's in the science lab on the third floor. There's no phone up there, so I'll have to run up and fetch him myself. I'm sorry—yes, I *know* it's urgent—but I'll go fast as I can."

And did. Depositing the receiver on the green desk blotter, Miss Gancy flew up the broad marble stairs on her chunky legs, her sturdy oxfords making a loud echoing report in the hollow hall. The moment she rounded the bend in the landing, he shoved the math book back in the leather bag, picked up his jacket, and walked out through the main doors of the school.

Outside in the sunny brilliance of upper Fifth Avenue, he shivered and put on his jacket: a chill, cutting wind was blowing, coming over the treetops of the park across the street. Not liking the wind or the deserted look of the broad avenue, he walked one block down, then turned into the next side street—so blinded by the refraction of sunlight off yellow leaves, he didn't see the two figures slipping over the low stone wall enclosing the park. Walking briskly, he had almost reached Madison Avenue, when he saw the old electric shaver sitting on the top of an uncovered garbage can. He came to an abrupt stop and glanced at the house behind the can—a strangely deserted-looking place, with grimy windows where shades were pulled all the way down. Picking up the shaver, he checkingly glanced to either side. Looking to the left, he saw them—grinning, lurching with a rolling sailor's gait, making straight for him. Slowly, as if he hadn't seen them, he turned, and using all his will power—he knew better than to run—walked the short distance to the corner, which he rounded onto Madison Avenue with short-lived relief: it was just as deserted as Fifth Avenue had been, with only a few cars and cabs cruising up the street.

They were just a few feet behind him now—he could feel them with a crawling of his back—and he yanked open the first shop door he came to and ducked inside, a bell wildly jangling over his head. It was, he saw in a glance, the kind of "delicatessen" he hated, not a real delicatessen at all, the kind that sold things like stale old bologna and cheese and cellophane-wrapped packages of cupcakes and sliced pound cake coated with dust.

"Yes?" said a fat mustached man, surfacing like a walrus from behind a glass case filled with bins of gluey-looking salads and slabs of angry red wursts and hams. The face above the white storekeeper's coat was the color of the wursts.

He slipped his right hand into his pocket, where his fingers closed on gritty emptiness. Not so much as a dime or quarter for one of those rolls that looked like rocks. In the other pocket was his wallet, which held his bus pass and Junior Life-saving card—and nothing else.

"What do you *want?*"

"T-t-to stay here a minute, sir, if I may." He'd decided to slip into the Roddy McDowall-Oliver Twist routine he'd picked up from old movies on TV. A sure-fire approach with certain adults.

"What? *What?* Speak up."

"I said, sir, please sir, I'd like to stay here a few moments if I may. Sir. Two . . . goons are after me." The strain of the role was too much.

The man glared past him, out through the plate-glass window, and, turning, he saw what the man's pale, bulging eyes were focused on— totally empty, sunny stretches of sidewalk.

"Get out. Get *ouda* my store!"

He backed to the door, fingers closing on the doorknob, weighing where the greater danger lay—in or out.

"You deef or something? Get your fancy private school ass ouda my store, or I'll give you what to be frightened, you yellow-bellied little cunt."

In lay the greater danger, he saw—and went wildly crashing out.

For a second, while the shop bell still faintly jangled and the white hulk loomed menacingly behind the glass door, he looked carefully around. The two were nowhere in sight. A policeman was writing tickets at the curb—the reason they were nowhere in sight. During his brief stay in the delicatessen, Madison Avenue had come to life, other human beings had appeared on the street—a woman walking a dog, a man staring in a shop window, a storekeeper sweeping the pavement in front of his door. Relaxing, smiling, he turned and exhibited his rigid middle finger to the man still glowering at him through the delicatessen door, then marched to the corner and looked down the side street. They weren't there either. But other people were: far up the block, near Fifth Avenue, a man was unloading steel pipes from a truck, and down the end of the street nearest him, a woman was slowly bumping a marketing cart down the basement steps to a brownstone house.

The shaver was still sitting on top of the open trash can. The shades were still pulled in the house. He quickly grabbed the shaver, only to find its trailing wire snagged on something buried deeper in the can. Reluctantly setting down his book bag, he began burrowing in the papery trash with both hands.

"Stop messing with that shit, Jasper, and give us your wallet, fast."

He put down the shaver and glanced sideway. Teeth and switchblades flashing in the sun. Shorter and smaller and younger than he was. Scrawny and greasy pale. Exactly the same size as last time, only last time they'd been black. Not looking directly at them, he silently handed his wallet to the taller of the two, who pocketed it without glancing inside.

"And that watch, Clarence."

He unstrapped the watch, and handed it to the smaller one, the one who'd snarled the request. As he did, he slyly glanced up the street: the woman with the cart had disappeared, the man had climbed into the back of his truck where he was busily rolling pipes around with a thunderous clanking.

"What about the ring, hey, Charlie. That's one cool ring this jerk-off mother's got on."

"That ring is five-and-ten crap, you idjut. I ripped off one just like it last week—don't you remember, shit-for-brains? . . . Hey. You. What's a rich little asshole like you doing wearing crap from the five-and-ten?" The switchblade was pushed up close to his throat.

"C'mon. Cut the social hour, Charlie. We cleaned this faygola for sure. And something tells me that pig is going to show any second and start writing tickets for *us*." Turning, he started jogging up the block.

For one second the switchblade remained perilously close to his throat. Then, as it was withdrawn, the other hand snatched the glasses from his face and threw them into the air. "Goodnight, Irene! See ya in the men's at the BMT." Joyously whooping, he took off after his friend.

By some miracle the glasses had landed next to the shaver on the mound of soft, papery trash. Though he couldn't see much without his glasses, he could see that much. Sighing, he went to retrieve them, carefully wiping them with the end of his tie before putting them back on. Then he picked up the shaver, and finding the wire mysteriously released from what had snagged it, tightly wound it around the shaver's body and stuck it in his book bag—which they hadn't seen on the far side of the can. Squaring his shoulders, he set out for Madison Avenue, but hadn't gone two steps when there was the snap of a rolling shade and the shuddering rattle of a window opening in the house beyond the trash can.

"Little boy. Little *boy!*"

Coming to a stop, he wearily turned and looked up at the bony old woman in a lacy nightgown, leaning far out of a third-floor window in the house.

"Little boy. Were those other little boys mo*les*ting you?"

For one long second he took in this old woman, the double of the other old woman who had spent one week in his house and made his life miserable while his mother was in the hospital. Then he turned and trudged toward the corner, her voice following him up the quiet block: "Little boy, little *boy!* You mustn't be afraid, darling. If you tell me, I can report it to the police. Things must be reported . . . only way . . . stopped. Little boiyeeeee . . . ?"

Not having any money or a bus pass, he walked the seven blocks home.

"Well. If it isn't Barnabas the Junkman. Watcha doing home from school this tima day? Catch you in a little misdeemeener in the terlet, hey?"

Displaying the same rigid finger to Fitzclarence that he had exhibited to the owner of the delicatessen, hissing a word that sent the doorman's grizzled eyebrows soaring toward his cap, he trotted down the steps to the lobby and punched the elevator bell.

Upstairs, as he walked down the long, dim corridor, unfamiliar late-morning noises and smells came from behind the domino-lineup of peepholed doors. From behind his own door came the distant whirring-grinding of the washing machine, and the high, excited gabble of Maria's telephone voice. Setting down the book bag, he inserted a finger in his collar and drew out the chain which held his door key—an arrangement he'd initiated early in the fall—and lifted it over his head. After letting himself soundlessly into the apartment, he stood in the front hall, listening, making sure Maria was on the phone. Then he went up the hall to his sunfilled room, where his bed was just as he'd left it three and a half hours ago—unmade, the covers turned down to the foot to air. Completely disinterested in the bed, he took off his blazer and hung it away in the closet, then pulled the shaver from the book bag and set the bag on the closet floor under the jacket: he wouldn't be needing anything in it for at least two days. He then carried the shaver into the bathroom, and set it on the sink while he took a tin of Sucrets from the medicine cabinet and popped two tablets in his mouth; a look of immediate relief flooded his face—his throat had been hurting powerfully. Quickly cleaning the shaver with wads of toilet paper drenched in formaldehyde (from the bottle under the sink), patting it dry with still more toilet paper, he brought it out to his desk, where he lifted a small tool kit from the bottom drawer, and finally sat down with a happy sigh.

For ten minutes he sat snipping and screwing and tapping, using several tools from the little kit. When the shaver finally lay in neatly dismantled piles on the green blotter, he put away the tool kit, scooped up the separate pieces, and, standing on his desk chair, carefully deposited them in a small empty space on the fifth shelf above his desk. While sunlight poured in, splattering his rug and desk, he stood shifting small pieces of equipment and wires, so absorbed he didn't hear the sounds from the other end of the apartment—the ringing of the back doorbell, the slamming down of the phone, a man's rumbling voice, a woman's high, excited laughter. When the laughter grew louder and more excited, he stood frozen on the chair, clutching a fistful of screws; finally realizing from the pounding of feet that they were heading his way, he leaped off the chair and shot into the closet across the room.

Just in time. The minute he was in there, crouched between his bathrobe and rubber camp poncho, the sounds erupted into his room. Dropping the handful of screws into the pocket of his chinos, he grabbed the inner latch of the doorknob, trying to pull the door tightly shut, but several things were in the way—his book bag and three of the boxed games he'd recently moved from the shelves above his desk. Though only a crack of about two inches was left, and he was sure he couldn't be seen in the stuffy darkness of the closet, he could still see out. It was at an oblique angle, and he couldn't see much, but he saw enough, and found himself staring with burning eyes at the back of a starched white skirt covered by a large, hairy hand, and at the stained tan leg of a workman's coverall thrusting its way between the legs beneath the skirt.

"Ha. Gotcha!" the man's voice growlingly gurgled.

"Aiyeeee."

"You betcha I-ee. Ooh. You hot-blooded little Latin devil! What you *do* to old Joe!"

Old Joe. But even without this information he had already recognized Joseph, the back elevator man.

The hand now had the white skirt hiked way up and was frantically clawing at the pink iridescent pants that covered a rear end like a luminous full moon. Suddenly then, the pants were down, and the hand had flown between the white cheeks, and was busily reaching and working there, the legs beneath it eagerly opening wide and stretching the pants to a taut pink band about the knees.

He shut his eyes, but his ears took the place of his eyes. Growls. Moans. Grunts. Floorboards creaking. Gasping sighs. Then, "*Aprisa! . . . Aprisa!*" and stumbling steps, and a thrumming twang from the innersprings as they fell on the bed. His bed.

In the same second they hit the bed, the telephone began ringing. He opened his eyes. That would stop it. The phone went on ringing. His bed was out of his line of vision, but he didn't need his eyes to realize that they weren't going to answer the phone. For several seconds he stood, roundeyed, in the rubbery-tweedy smelling dark. Then he clapped his hands tightly over his ears, but nothing would keep out the sounds. Even through his sweaty palms he could hear those sounds. And the thwack of his maple headboard against the wall. And the ringing of the phone.

Then suddenly the phone stopped ringing. And seconds later the other sounds and the thwacking of the headboard also stopped. Through his drenched palms, he heard the woman, Maria, say something high and shrill. "Next time, sweetheart," said Joseph, as he took his hands off his ears. "I done yeoman work just now . . . and I'm no superman. Besides, it's too damned *dang*erous here. C'mon now, doll . . . s'only because you're such a hot little tamale I lose my control like that. S'a *comp*lamint."

A creak of bedsprings. A rustle of clothes and bedclothes were smoothed into place. Then Joseph backed into his line of vision, zipping his pants, restrapping his belt. "*Come* on, sugar—don't be mad. And leave that damn bed alone and come see me out. I'd better vamoose before the missus comes in."

He waited until he heard them start down the hall, Joseph keeping up a wheedling mumble as they went, then pushed the door wide, but stayed in the shelter of the closet until he heard the distant slam of the back door. The minute he came all the way out of the closet the telephone began ringing. When it stopped after two rings, he crept to the open door of his room, and stood listening to Maria talking to someone in Spanish again.

Finally turning back into his room, he stood over his bed and stared down at the sheets and pillowcase with slitted eyes. Except for a few wrinkles, the pale blue percale looked exactly as it had before—clean, free of any stains. But suddenly gagging convulsively, wincing at the pain this inflicted on his raw throat, he viciously ripped the sheets and pillowcase off his bed, and balling them into a loose, floppy bundle, carried them down the hall. As he paused to slip the latch on the front door lock, he heard Maria weeping, pleading in Spanish with someone named Constanza on the kitchen phone. Pronouncing the same word that had sent Fitzclarence's eyebrows soaring, he let himself out without a sound, heading for the incinerator cubicle at the far end of the hall with the flapping bundle of his sheets.

Tepp had found her still anemic. "In spite of my warning, you've been overdoing, Emma," he said after the quick physical examination and after studying the slide his technician had made from her blood sample. But when she angrily protested that she *hadn't* been overdoing —all she'd been doing was hanging around the house, taking short walks, and her morale was so low she'd been hoping he would let her take a part-time job—he said no, that was absolutely out of the question. "You're pushing, Emma, and you're going to get yourself into a totally debilitated state if you're not careful. I know it's hard, but you've simply got to try and relax about this, and take it very easy for another two or three weeks. Pamper yourself. For instance, go straight home from here, stretch out in front of the TV with a nice, nourishing lunch on a tray, and don't think a single thought." Too discouraged to tell him that she'd just spent a month stretched out in front of the TV, and it had almost scrambled her brains, she meekly left his office—with an appointment card for another checkup in exactly two weeks, on a Friday again. And riding home in the cab, she realized it was lucky she hadn't had time to stop at the Knickerbocker Knick Knacks shop, where she would have made a fool of herself; as it was, she'd have to call Knickerbocker House and tell them she'd miscalculated, tell them she wouldn't be coming back to work for quite some time.

Now, going up in the elevator in her building, she tried to think of what to do—not only with the long afternoon stretching in front of her, but the whole seemingly endless weekend lying beyond that. If only she could get away. Escape. A change of scene, a two-day pass out of that apartment, would do wonders for her morale. Then she had an inspiration: maybe she could persuade Harold to rent a car, and tomorrow they could all drive up to the Berkshires and stay overnight at some peaceful, picturesque country inn. Yes. *Yes.* It would be good for all of them. Harold could put in some time with Benjy (the time they'd spent together when she was in the hospital was not what she meant), something he hadn't done in a long time, something she was convinced Benjy needed; the last time Harold had deliberately done something pleasant with Benjy had been back in June, when he'd taken him to a double-header at Shea Stadium. While they went on nice rambling hikes together, she could just lie around as Tepp ordered. But on a lovely soft tester bed, with a roaring fire going across the room. If she had to spend time lying around, it might just as well be in a pleasant place for a change—a place where she could look out the window and know that only pretty autumn leaves, not falling bodies, would come drifting down.

Growing more and more excited by the whole idea, she stepped off the elevator at her floor and turned right, so absorbed in making plans that she walked three steps before she registered what she'd seen—or thought she'd seen—out of the corner of her left eye. Whipping around, she squinted through the dimness at the small, sturdy figure trundling down the far end of the hall, an unmistakable figure in a pink shirt and chinos, carrying a bundle of something with trailing, flapping ends toward the incinerator cubicle. But could it be? Her son? Carrying his sheets to the incinerator chute? Ah yes, she saw in another second. Her son. Carrying his sheets to the incinerator chute.

Some strange and powerful instinct—a combination of caution and stealth—kept her from calling out his name. This same instinct also made her duck through the open door next to the elevator before she knew what she'd done—the door to the fireproof stairs. Confused, ashamed, she stood in the grim, gray stairwell, listening to the incinerator-cubicle door bang shut: Wouldn't he be home from school at that hour only because he was sick? And if he was sick, what was she *doing* sneaking around and spying on him instead of going to find out what in God's name was wrong? Then, as she heard the distant, repeated tinny slamming of the trapdoor to the incinerator chute, she asked herself the most important question of all: And what was he doing burning his sheets?

Suddenly feeling every bit as "debilitated" as Tepp had warned her she might get to be, she backed deeper into the stairwell, and sat down heavily on the bottommost step of the flight of iron stairs leading up to the next floor. From where she sat, she'd be able to see him when he passed the open doorway—but he wouldn't be able to see her. Shivering, she sat waiting, and the tinny slamming finally stopped. Then a moment later he went sailing past the open doorway with quick, purposeful strides, his half-averted profile pale and grim-looking, and after another moment she heard the distant click of their apartment door closing.

The same, powerful new instinct for caution and stealth—for cunning, really—told her to stay where she was for another five minutes, to give him time to . . . to do what? She didn't know. *She* didn't know. God only knew.

She was sitting there not letting herself think, counting down the minutes on her wristwatch, when she heard someone enter the stairwell on the floor above her, and start down—a woman, from the great clacketing of heels. Not caring who it was, too exhausted to stand up, she merely moved closer to the wall, and as the steps grew louder, wearily turned her head and stared up at the woman rounding the bend of the stairs—tall, gaunt, beautifully and expensively dressed, decorously picking her way downward. Momentarily disconcerted to see Emma sitting on the steps a flight below her, the woman then proceeded to ignore her, carefully making her way down past her, the gleaming burnished pumps narrowly missing Emma's arm. But when she finally reached the landing, and Emma had assumed the whole little interlude was going to take place in silence—which completely suited her mood, peculiar as it was—the woman paused at the bend in the stairway, and turned to give her an icy little social smile: "I have a thing about self-service elevators."

Emma blinked at her. Now what. Now was she supposed to say *she* had a "thing" for sitting in fireproof stairwells? "Do you walk all the way back up too?" was the way she finally resolved it.

The woman tittered. "Sometimes. It depends. Sometimes I just wait in the lobby until somebody I know comes along, and then ride up with them. I always use the elevator when I'm with my husband."

Saying nothing—what was there to say?—Emma glanced at her watch.

"I was mugged by a delivery boy in a self-service elevator, in another building, five years ago. They had elevator men in *this* building when we first moved in, it was one of the reasons we moved here . . . but like everything else, this building's gone down." And down she went herself, katicket, katucket, kerslap.

Shaken—all she *needed* was a run-in with a nut like that, on top of everything else—Emma got up and stiffly walked down the hall and let herself in the apartment with her own key. Not making a sound. Emma, the sneak.

As soon as she stepped into the little front hallway, she heard Maria excitedly talking on the phone—just as she'd left her two and a half hours ago. Maybe she'd never gotten off and had just been sitting out there, talking nonstop for two and a half hours straight. Maybe—but so what? Worse things were going on.

She started down the hall toward Benjy's room, neither making a lot of unnecessary noise, nor deliberately muffling the sound of her footsteps. She was almost at his open door, when she heard the squeak of casters as his bed was moved, and used it as her entrance cue: with the air of someone taken by surprise, she walked into the room where her son, back to the door, was putting the finishing touches to a neat hospital corner on his bed. ". . . Benjy?" she said, with just the right mix of confusion and incredulity. Emma, the master sneak.

He jumped a mile, as well he might have, poor boy, and wheeled around, ashen. "Jesus, ma—you scared the shit out of me!"

And so she had. She blushed, too guilty to care about the way he had put it. "I'm sorry, darling," she said, glancing at the sheets on the bed, which were linen-closet fresh, with knife-sharp creases, "but I heard Maria on the kitchen phone when I came in . . . and couldn't *imagine* who was in your room. Why are you home? Are you sick?"

"No. I just have this nothing scratchy throat. All I wanted was a Sucret, but Tibbs took one look down my throat and made me come home."

"How did you *get* home?"

"I walked," he said, backing away as she started toward him, right hand outstretched.

"You *walked?* Have they gone mad at that school?" Having backed him up against the night-table, she clapped her hand over his forehead. "You must have fever. You're burning up."

He ducked out from under her hand. "I don't have fever. It's you. Your hand's all cold and wet," he said with disgust. "And it's not the school's fault. They tried calling here, to get someone to bring me home, but they couldn't get through. . . . The line was out of order or something." As he paused, they could hear the "or something" still talking on the kitchen phone. "Then one of the teachers was going to bring me home in a cab, but they got their signals all screwed up, he had a class—and I got tired of hanging around."

"And then what. You just left? Did you just go ahead and leave without telling them?"

A mumble.

"Benjamin. *Answer* me."

"Ya. But so what."

"So *what*. They're probably frantic, that's what. What on earth's come *over* you, Benjamin. Why do you do these things? And why, may I ask, were you making your bed?" For the moment, she'd decided to skip the matter of the sheets being shoved down the incinerator chute.

Clearly wrestling with something, he gave her a long, chillingly assessing look. Then: "It wasn't made when I got in. Maria was on the phone, and I decided to go ahead and make it myself so I wouldn't have to have her in here messing around."

They stood there for a minute, warily blinking at each other, the air thick with both their lies. "Let me have a look at your throat," Emma finally said.

Resigning himself to this, he stood where he was and opened his mouth in a cavernous gape, like Tweedledee. Telling herself to stay calm, she went and peered down his throat, which was fiery red.

"Well, Miss Tibbs was right. That's an awful-looking throat. I'm going to take your temperature. Meanwhile, you get into your pajamas and get right into bed."

"But I don't want to get into pajamas and go to bed. I'm all *right*, ma. It's just a lousy sore throat."

She stopped by the door. "Benjamin. You are behaving very strangely and very badly. And you are getting me very upset. *Very* upset."

A long glimmering look through the glasses: That's obvious.

"You will do what I've asked," she said breathlessly. "If you don't you'll be sorry." With that she stepped into the hall—while he sped across the room and shut the door behind her, turning the key in the lock with a loud click.

She rushed through her room (where the bed was still unmade) into the bathroom, making straight for Harold's medicine cabinet. Where there were three oral thermometers. She took one out of its case and began savagely shaking it down, when she was suddenly hit by a surge of dizziness and, closing the lid on the toilet, sat down and shut her eyes. Benjy, she thought, fighting off waves of fear and nausea. *What* was happening to Benjy?

Pushing aside all the other upsetting things he'd recently been doing, she focused on this latest freaky act, this burning of his sheets, and for several minutes just sat reviewing all the possible explanations for his doing such a thing—each more pathetic and ludicrous than the next. But the thing that really hit her the hardest wasn't the variety of ways he could have stained or soiled his sheets (all of which were perfectly *normal* for an eleven-year-old boy, she flappingly assured herself like Billie Burke—even a regressive bed-wetting), but the fact that he would be so ashamed and afraid of her seeing them, he would throw them down the incinerator chute. Oh God. It was so *sad*. So terrible. And that pathetic little act, it suddenly occurred to her, summarized the de- terioration of their whole relationship. That extraordinary relationship, she thought rushing on, her eyes flooding with walrus tears—once so open and easy and trusting and spontaneous, so totally unlike any mother-son relationship she knew of. Now gone. All gone.

About to plunge into a sea of bathos, she paused, as several jarring inconsistencies presented themselves: how, for instance, could shame and fear of herself figure so largely, when Maria was the one who always made his bed? And if he'd been so afraid of anyone seeing them, why hadn't he changed his sheets before leaving for school? But she dismissed them with a ready answer—he probably hadn't even seen the sheets were stained until he'd come home sick just now, and then, panicking, decided to burn them—and made herself face the *real* issue: something horrible was happening to her dear little boy. Her darling. Her baby. And it was suddenly all too much for her. The sheets, the electric junk, his coldness, his freshness, all the lies . . . it was all too much. It made her sick. Literally. And maybe Harold had been right—maybe he *was* turning into a "disturbed child," joining that army of "disturbed" children quaking and cowering in high-rent apartments all over New York. Maybe. But the point was she suddenly knew she couldn't handle it all by herself. She needed help. Professional help.

She got up and headed back toward Benjy's room, shaking down the thermometer as she went. The door was still locked. She gave it a sharp kick. "Benjamin. Unlock this door and let me *in*. Right aw*ay*. You hear?"

He unlocked and opened the door with one hand, buttoning up his pajama top with the other. "What're you so excited about, ma?"

She never hit him and wasn't going to start now. "Why did you lock your door?"

Not answering, he sat down on the edge of his bed and sullenly glared at her.

"Answer me, Benjamin."

"Because I was changing into my pajamas."

"Are you ashamed to have me see you naked, Benjamin?" She realized she'd blundered even before she saw his face.

"For God's *sake*. I'm eleven years old. I have a right to privacy like anybody else. This goddamn place has gotten like a *zoo*. And you're treating me like a Mongolian idiot, like some kind of freaked-out mental case."

The knowledge that he was right, dead right on all counts, kept her from breaking the rules of eleven years—and smacking him, hard. "Put this under your tongue," she finally said in a dry deadly voice, handing him the thermometer. "And keep your mouth closed until I come back. I'm going to fix a gargle for your throat."

Not waiting to see if he was going to follow her orders, she rushed back to the kitchen where Maria stood with her back to the door, stuffing Windex and furniture polish into the shopping bag she carried from room to room when she cleaned.

"*Haie, señora* . . . how you fright me!" she cried, whirling around at the sound of Emma's footsteps on the linoleum floor.

It seemed to be her day for startling and frightening people—guilty people—by walking in on them unexpectedly, she reflected cynically, noting that Maria's eyes were swollen and red, but only found herself callously thinking that considering the morning she'd put in on the phone, it was a wonder Maria had found time to cry. "I'm sorry, Maria," she said, hardly sorry, taking out a container of salt and a glass and turning on the hot water. "I didn't mean to frighten you."

"When you come in, *señora?* I no hear you come in," Maria said uneasily, shoving a can of Lemon Pledge and some dust-rags into the shopping bag.

"A little while ago," said Emma, wincing as the water scalded her testing finger, thrusting the glass under the tap.

"You drink that, *señora?*" asked Maria, annoyingly hovering, watching as she poured salt into the hot water, then stirred the cloudy mix with a spoon.

"No. It's a gargle for Benjy's sore throat."

"*Ben*jamin? Is the Benjamin here?"

"Yes, he's here. He came home sick from school."

"When he come in? I no hear him come in either. How long *he* be here?"

"Not very long," Emma said dryly, fed up with this barrage of guilty questions, and took the glass of hot salt water up to Benjy's room.

He was sitting and morosely staring off into space, the thermometer jutting jauntily out of the corner of his mouth like a glass cigarette. As she put down the gargle and took the thermometer out of his mouth, he slumped back on the pillows, wearily shutting his eyes.

It hadn't been her cold hand. He did have fever. Not much, true—the mercury only stood at 100.6 degrees—but it was an oral thermometer, making it 102.6 degrees, and for Emma, somewhat of an authority on fevers, four degrees were enough. Leaving the suddenly (and ominously) docile Benjy gargling with the hot salt water in his bathroom, she went to her room to call Dr. Leonard Ingleman, one of the last pediatricians in New York who still made house calls.

Or so she'd thought. Ingleman seemed to be hopping on the band-wagon. The earliest he could get by to see Benjy was seven that night, possibly much later, he explained: he was due in half an hour at the hospital clinic where he did volunteer work every Friday afternoon, and still had three patients in the waiting room; however, if she felt it was urgent (he added dourly), she could throw a coat over Benjy's pajamas and rush him right over, and he would take a quick look at the throat before he left the office.

Quickly weighing the alternatives—trying to get Benjamin Sohier to "throw a coat over his pajamas" and get him to rush anywhere, or having Harold the Hypochondriac, arrive home to find his son sick and still unseen by a doctor, she said, "We'll be right over, Doctor Ingleman," and slammed down the phone, which immediately began ringing.

"Hel*lo?*" she shouted forbiddingly into the receiver, convinced it was going to be Minda—but it was Miss Tibbs, the student-counselor-nurse from Benjy's school, in a state bordering on hysteria. Though it almost put her in the same state to do it, she heard the poor woman out, and when she'd finished, apologized for Benjy, assuring Miss Tibbs that he'd arrived home safely, adding they were just on their way out to see a doctor about the throat.

"Well, in that case I won't hold you up, Mrs. Sohier," Miss Tibbs said tremulously, proceeding to hold her up, "but I simply must tell you that we are all terribly concerned about Benjamin here at the school." (*You're* concerned, thought Emma with a frantic glance at the clock.) "Benjamin hasn't been himself since the beginning of the fall term, Mrs. Sohier, he's not the happy, considerate child we've always known and loved. Benjamin has always been one of the most polite children at school, and his leaving without permission this morning is just one more example of the new thoughtlessness and rebelliousness he's dis-played all fall. Not a week goes by without one of Benjamin's teachers having to report him to Mr. Porter for insubordination. We are all *most* concerned, Mrs. Sohier, and Mr. Porter feels that a conference be-tween himself and you and Mr. Sohier should be arranged at the earli-est possible date. . . . Would that be at all possible, Mrs. Sohier? Would that be agreeable to you and your husband?"

No, it most certainly would *not*, thought Emma. And suddenly de-ciding that this, in its way, was almost more important than getting Benjy to Ingleman, she took a deep breath. "I certainly appreciate the school's concern, and I'm certainly sorry that Benjamin has been troublesome, Miss Tibbs," she said in a cool, self-confident voice, "but I don't think it's serious enough to warrant any sort of conference. As my husband informed the school in early September—but perhaps it's been overlooked—I've just spent a month in the hospital. During the time I was away, things got a bit . . . disorganized here. Now, I'm sure you'll agree, Miss Tibbs, that any disruption in the normal routine of a home, any sudden upheaval or disorder is bound to have some impact on a child—bound to create feelings of confusion and disorder *in* the child, which would naturally be reflected in his behavior. And that's all that's been happening in Benjamin's case, Miss Tibbs. But things here are finally getting back to normal now, and I'm sure *Ben*jamin will be getting back to his old self too. Of course, if his troublesome behavior continues, I'll be glad to arrange a conference, but for the moment, I'd like to ask everybody at school to be patient. And now, I'm sorry, but I *must* get Benjamin to the doctor or he'll miss his appointment. *Good*-by, Miss Tibbs."

Hanging up, she stood there, hand on the phone: Now where on earth had all *that* come from?

Then she dashed off to Benjy's room.

Since Benjy insisted on getting fully redressed, they almost did miss Ingleman, who was walking out the door of his ground-floor office when they pulled up in a cab. With something less than graciousness, he went back inside and with one quick look at Benjy's throat, made the diagnosis: an allergic reaction to some powerful new pollutant in the air; Benjy's was the fifth case he'd seen in two days. Though it had all the characteristics of a strep throat, it was relatively "benign" and responded beautifully to treatment with antihistamines, he said; rapidly scribbling prescriptions for antihistaminic pills and gargles, he added that while Benjy didn't have to stay in bed, he had to take it *very* easy over the weekend, and could go back to school Monday. And with that, bolted for the clinic—leaving Emma sick with disappointment: she'd been pinning all her hopes on getting Ingleman alone for a minute . . . to ask him the name of an experienced child therapist.

In the cab going home, she and Benjy (having had a terrible row about his getting fully redressed) didn't exchange one word. In the cab going home, she decided to make an extremely painful but essential phone call once they reached the apartment.

Once they reached the apartment, Benjy refused her offer of lunch, saying that he wasn't hungry, and went into his room, shutting the door. Bracing herself she went to her room to make the call. Maria, finished with her cleaning, was just on her way out.

Clutching her shopping bag full of cleaning equipment, Maria paused in the doorway: "I am sorry the house be so late in getting clean today, *señora,* but I have a bad morning, many bad thing happen."

Her eyes, Emma noticed, looked even more puffy and red than before: had she been crying all the time they were at Ingleman's? "Don't worry about the apartment, Maria. I've noticed you were upset. Is there anything I can do to help? I mean, if you've had bad news from home or are having some kind of trouble, I'd be glad to help if I could."

"*Gracias, señora.* Yes, is trouble. But nothing you can help." For one more second she remained there, something ugly flickering then dying away in her face, then turned and went down the hall.

With a little involuntary shudder, Emma went to close the door, first glancing down the hall at Benjy's closed door and shuddering again: it was fast turning into a house of closed doors and lies and secrets— and just a while ago she'd told Miss Tibbs it was turning back into a normal household again. Hand on doorknob, she considered the other things she'd told Miss Tibbs, but decided it had been a lot of slick, glib rubbish, a lot of hot air, and made herself face the job at hand.

For the second time that day, she snapped on the radio and turned up the sound—not to drown out any possible sounds from outside, but to drown out the sound of her own voice: even with the thickness of two closed doors, she wasn't taking any chances of Benjy's overhearing what she had to say. As she went to the phone, she found it hard to believe that the morning's attack and her visit to Tepp had ever happened. Not only did all that seem as if it had taken place in another century, but Tepp's depressing announcement about the state of her health now seemed completely irrelevant: strangely enough, in spite of her blood count, she felt *fine,* not at all weak or tired out from all the running around and tension she'd been through in the last few hours. Which was really more than strange, but it wasn't the time to sit and try and figure it out.

She picked up the phone and dialed.

"Oh, Em, I'm *so* glad you called! It must be some kind of ESP," said Minda. "I've been feeling so damned rotten and guilty ever since we talked, so damned ashamed . . . dumping my problems in your lap like that. I've been here for the last half hour, trying to pack for the weekend, and went to the phone twice, and started to dial your number, but then hung up. I felt I'd bothered you enough for one day. But all I really wanted to do this time was tell you that you were absolutely right. As usual. You see, I took your advice and called Weiglitz up in Connecticut. He was an absolute *angel* . . . he stayed on the phone for about half an hour. He told me he's actually fine now, but he's not going to come out of retirement; when we'd finished talking, he gave me the name of some other shrink to call, and said I should go see him, and maybe go back into treatment for a while . . . but I don't think I'll ever call him. I mean it would mean shrink number *six*. And Weiglitz was such a help I don't *need* to see anyone else for the time being. He's an absolute genius. I forgot what a genius he was. He spotted the trouble right away, the same old trouble. He said it was perfectly *normal* to have lapses. I guess when it's happening, I just don't want to see that it's happening. I mean it isn't exactly pleasant to realize that you have a tendency to confuse all the men in your life with your father. And, actually, with Peter the confusion's not completely unjustified. I mean Peter's aggressive and driving and ruthless in business like my father, and somewhere along the line I get confused, and assume that, just like my father, he must be tricky and unfaithful and . . ."

Shutting her eyes, Emma sat out this sickening explanation of Minda's paranoid suspicions about her husband, this *reducto ad nauseam* of all poor Minda's problems to the same disgusting thing—and, belatedly, had second thoughts: and she was going to let her son in for some of *this*?

"Don't thank me, please, Minda," she finally said, cutting in on the profusion of apologies and thanks. "I didn't really do anything at all. But if you think I helped you, I'm glad." She took a deep, fortifying breath. "And now the tables are turned. I've called to ask you for your help."

". . . *My* help?"

"Yes. I'd like the name of that doctor Sebastian saw. The child therapist who found out that all Sebastian needed was to go back and live with Nando in Rome? The one you said saved his life."

In the silence, vibrations of surprise—and pure pleasure—came humming over the wires. "Why? What happened, Em? Is Benjy in some kind of . . . trouble?"

"No. Nothing as dramatic as that. He's just been rather . . . withdrawn lately, and I think it might be a good idea if he went and talked to someone for a while. He might open up to a stranger, air whatever it is that's bothering him."

"This isn't *talk*, Em. As usual, you weren't really listening. This is a whole, new, dynamic concept of therapy—it's not the old Freudian one-two."

Well, *that's* something, thought Emma, immediately heartened.

"And she'll want to see you too, you know. You'll have to go for an initial conference before she starts with Benjy—*if* she takes him on, that is—and then probably more sessions with you later. Harold too."

No, she hadn't known that. And that ended it right there. She would pretend to take the doctor's name and forget it. "Yes, I know that."

"Well, it's important you understand that. I mean, naturally Benjy's problems didn't originate in a vacuum." A deprecating little laugh.

Naturally. She looked down at the drawer-pull, which she was throttling with the phone cord again, then let the rubbery wire drop: as always, she had only herself to blame—as always, she'd asked for this.

"When you say 'withdrawn,' what exactly do you mean?" asked Minda. "If it's sluggishness, I mean *leth*argy, it could be drugs, you know. Have you looked for any other signs, like dilated pupils or sharp swings of mood?"

"It isn't drugs," she snapped. "They don't have any drug problem at his school, and he just isn't that kind of child. If he does have any kind of problem, it's being too strait-laced, too conservative. No. He's just been a little uncommunicative and moody." Too late, she saw she was giving out far too much information. "Can I have the doctor's name please, Minda?"

"Just a sec, the address book is up front in the bedroom. When I'm without help, I seem to spend the whole goddamn day in the kitchen. Hold on."

As the phone clattered down on some hard surface, Emma thought: God, how she's enjoying this. Reviewing her stupidity, she realized she would never get Minda out of her life now.

"Got a pencil?" asked Minda, picking up another extension, breathless from her sprint through the huge apartment.

"Yes," she said, ignoring the pad and pen on the chest.

"It's A. Hobbema—A. for Alison, Hobbema just like the painter, but no relation, at least not as far as I know. I always meant to ask, but always had too many other things on my mind once I was there," said Minda, forcing a laugh, then reading off a phone number and address on West End Avenue. "Got that, Em?"

"Yes. Thanks a lot."

"Em. Listen. Now that you're going to do something about Benjy, I guess I can tell you. I mean I'm really terribly relieved you're going to take him to see someone."

"Tell me *what*."

"Well, actually, maybe I shouldn't tell you. It's just a silly thing, and I'm sure there's a simple explanation, but it will only upset you."

"What are you talking about, Minda?"

"You . . . won't like it."

"You simply can't do that, Minda. Now that you've started, finish."

"Well. Okay." Anticipatory relish. "You remember that day last June when I bumped into you and Benjy a block from here—you'd just taken Benjy to the dentist for a pre-camp cleaning—and I made you come back up here for a drink? It was sort of sticky, because Benjy didn't want to come?"

Oh, she remembered all right. She could hardly forget, since the whole thing had centered around the one issue she and Benjy invariably fought about—her refusal to have him stay alone in the apartment for any length of time. She'd stood absolutely firm that particular day and had made him come up to Minda's with her—touching off a rift which had lasted over a week. "Yes, I remember that afternoon. What about it."

"Well, maybe you don't remember this, but I was without help then too. It was a beastly hot day, and after I'd put the twins inside for a nap, and given you a quick tour of the place, we sat in the living room with some cold drinks—while Benjy watched TV in the bedroom—we figured the combo of air conditioning and color TV would ha ha cool him off? Well, to get to the point, I got up once because one of the twins was whining—and when I passed my bedroom door, there was your son, wearing the new Dynel wig I'd had sitting on a wig stand, this campy thing I'd gotten to wear after swimming on Fire Island, a blond pageboy like Garbo in *Ninotchka* . . . there he was, doing pirouettes in front of the mirror like Melissa Hayden, I mean oh Jesus he looked like Little Eloise or something."

Emma sat remembering the look Benjy had given Minda in the park playground.

"Did you hear me, Em?"

"Yes, I hear you. Did he see you out in the hall?"

"You bet your sweet life he saw me out in the hall! He turned . . . green. The poor lamb. But I just rushed on up the hall as if I hadn't seen him."

Emma began laughing—harshly, raucously.

"Well, I'm glad you can laugh . . . but, frankly, I don't see what's so damned funny."

"It really isn't funny. It's actually terribly . . . sad. What's funny is your interpretation of the whole damned thing. But you were right when you said there was probably a simple explanation. I mean the poor darling has Harold's hair, he'd give anything to have that long Prince Valiant hair all his friends have . . . and I guess he was just seeing how he'd look if he'd been luckier. The thing I don't understand is why, if you thought it was so *sin*ister, you didn't say something before now."

"I didn't say something before now because I didn't want to upset you," exploded Minda. "You had enough troubles at the time. You were still settling your mother's estate when it happened, and though you were being very good about all that, it was obvious that way deep down you were really pretty rocked by her death. I certainly wasn't going to call or write you about it from Fire Island, and by the time I got back you were in the hospital. So this is really the first chance I've had to bring it up, and I would never have done it if you hadn't called about Hobbema. I happen to think your whole explanation of it is rather *over*simplified, wishful thinking, really—I happen to think it's some kinky kind of transvestite offshoot of the homosexual thing they all go through at that age . . . but whatever it is, Hobbema will get to the bottom of it. *If* she can take Benjy on, that is. Being one of the best in the business, she's madly busy and may not have any free time. You'll just have to see what she says when you call. Mention my name, of course, say that I'm the one who sent you, and . . . what did you say?"

"I said Benjy's calling. He's home from school, sick in bed . . . and probably needs something."

"Oh, God. You poor baby. You've got it in *spades*. Well, go see what he wants and then call Hobbema. I'd love to hear what she says, but Peter called a while ago to say we'd be leaving at three instead of five to beat the traffic. It's going to be heaven to get out of this dump for a few days. I think I told you that Selma, our hostess, has three in help? Anyway, if we get in early enough I'll call you Sunday night, otherwise I'll call first thing Monday. Meanwhile—*courage*, sweetie." The French pronunciation.

"*Courage* yourself, sweetie," Emma said to the dial tone, converting the noun to a transitive verb, and hung up.

For several seconds she sat thinking intently, then bent down and took the phone book out of the bottom drawer of the bachelor chest.

To her surprise—and dismay—Dr. Hobbema answered the phone
herself: she had expected, really counted on (she realized) an answering service or secretary to pick up. The doctor had a warm, pleasant,
Midwestern voice, and after responding to the mention of Minda's
name with a spectacular lack of enthusiasm ("Oh? Ah, yes."), asked
Emma a few basic questions—Benjy's name, his age, whether or not he
had "siblings," the name of his school. To Emma's steadily mounting
surprise, Dr. Hobbema didn't ask her the one question she had really
expected . . . and dreaded: Why was she calling? Just what seemed to
be the matter with Benjamin Sohier, aged eleven, only child, attending
the Winthrop School? None of that. Just a mild and rather offhand
inquiry as to whether Emma wanted to come and "see" her "sometime
soon," and when Emma promptly answered in the affirmative, she set
up an appointment for Wednesday at three in the coming week, and
after politely wishing Emma a pleasant weekend, hung up.

Limp, but somehow feeling better, Emma hung up too. Though
she knew it was completely ridiculous, just that brief exchange with
Dr. Hobbema had comforted and reassured her in some way. She had
sounded so, well . . . *nice*. So warm and open and friendly, so un-
shrinklike, in short, or at least unlike what she had come to expect a
shrink to sound like. And she felt she had made a wise move in calling.
Even if Benjy never got to Hobbema himself, just the prospect of her
own visit, the idea of unburdening herself to someone who sounded
so pleasant and reasonable, was tremendously soothing. She would
definitely keep the appointment and not tell Harold a thing until after
she'd gone. Not a *thing* about the sheets, the lies, the freshness, the call
from Miss Tibbs . . . or about Hobbema herself. Particularly Hobbema, since Harold had developed a powerful aversion to all psychia-
trists and psychoanalysts during the last few years. She saw no point in
needlessly setting Harold off. Though he was a fairly casual father, he
was given to sudden fits of alarm about Benjy if anything serious
seemed to be involved, and sometimes the slightest thing was enough
to make him push the panic button. This was far from the slightest
thing—and if there was one thing she didn't need at the moment, it
was having to cope with a panicky Harold on top of everything else.

Harold pushed the panic button anyway, as it turned out. Not because she told him about Hobbema or any of the things that had made
her call Hobbema, but because Benjy was sick. And not because he

was concerned about Benjy—but because he didn't want to catch whatever it was Benjy had.

He arrived home at quarter to six, rather late for him, and within ten minutes destroyed the peaceful atmosphere that had existed in the house since midafternoon: after a late lunch, an unusual calm had settled over the apartment, and for several hours she and Benjy and Maria had all contentedly kept themselves busy—Benjy, sitting in his room (with the door open), doing some painting and drawing, or just puttering (but *not* with the electrical junk); Maria comfortably clattering in the kitchen, preparing the famous Spratt pork roast for dinner; she herself doing small chores like straightening her bureau drawers and closet, then finally stretching out on the living-room couch with a trashy new Phaedre Press best seller Harold had recently brought home.

Then Harold arrived.

Without even taking off his coat, he came into the living room where she was happily stretched out, reading, and after listening to her story about the visit to Ingleman, he exploded: Ingleman had made her bring Benjy over to his office with a fever of four degrees? The *bast*ard. Ingleman had said it was an allergic reaction to some irritant in the air? The *moron*. With that, he marched up the hall to see Benjy, or, more precisely, he marched up to Benjy's room, where, remaining in the doorway, a safe fifteen feet away, he fired some questions at Benjy while she listened from the living room, incredulous. Finally, looking extremely agitated, he came back and stood over the couch: "Let me tell you something, Em. I happen to know a great deal, a *great* deal, about air pollution, and I've yet to hear about any new 'irritant' that can cause a fever of four degrees and a bad sore throat. He just finished telling me that his throat still hurts a lot, and he looks perfectly *lousy* to me—and in spite of what that idiot said, I think he ought to be in bed. At any rate, I certainly think he ought to have his supper on a tray in his room, if that's all right with you."

It was far from all right with her, but she quietly said she supposed that could be arranged, and with an astonishment that was growing as fast as her anger, watched him, still wearing his coat, go to the bar, where he looked in the ice bucket, then let loose a stream of invectives that finished up with ". . . and *she* has the nerve to complain!" He then poured some warm scotch into a glass, tossed it off and said: "Would you please come up to our room, Em? There's something I'd like to discuss in private."

Sitting upright by now, she just glommered at him.

With an impatient jerk of his head, he indicated the closed kitchen door and poured more scotch: "It's about *her*."

She quickly scrambled off the couch and led the way down the hall to their bedroom.

Coming in behind her, Harold closed the door. "My mother called me at the office late this afternoon. Christ—I've never *heard* her so worked up. It seems that that . . . that Maria called her aunt Constanza out there this morning and said she wanted to leave. Said she was unhappy as hell here, and wanted to pull out now."

"She did? But that's *marvelous*," said Emma, and thinking of the morning-long tie-up of their phone, laughed. "It probably cost us a few hundred dollars in tolls to Albuquerque, but it's well worth it."

"I don't happen to think it's very funny, and I don't give a damn if she calls Albuquerque twenty times a day. We're not tight. *I'm* not tight. One of the things she told her aunt Constanza was that we were tight. 'Mean' as she put it. Mean and cruel and peculiar."

Emma laughed again. "*We're* peculiar."

"Okay, *she's* peculiar, I'm with you on that . . . but where did she get all those lousy ideas about us? *Are* we tight with her in any way? Or cruel?"

"You must be kidding, Harold."

"Hardly. I'm upset as hell, as you damned well can see—and so was Elsie. With good reason. That Constanza's indispensable to her. She kept asking what in God's name we were doing to make Maria so miserable, and said she was ashamed to have outsiders get such a terrible impression of us. I am too. I mean that girl must have *some* basis for her rotten opinion of us."

Emma watched him, still in his coat, polish off the scotch he'd carried in, and had to forcibly restrain herself from picking up something— the plastic cube enclosing his mother's picture, notably—and slamming him over the head.

Misinterpreting her silence for some kind of troubled acquiescence, he sighed and finally started climbing out of his coat. "Well, the upshot of the whole thing is that she's staying—her aunt Constanza persuaded her to stick it out. In a way, I'd be just as glad as you to have her leave, Em, but not under these circumstances. I certainly don't want anybody going around with such distorted ideas about us, and I don't want to do anything that would hurt Elsie. She put herself way out on a limb with Constanza, got Maria to give up a perfectly good job, brought her here, broke her in, *paid* for her—we have a terrific obligation to Elsie, and if only for her sake, we'd better watch our step with Maria from now on."

While he'd been talking, she had carefully lowered herself into the armchair. Now, as he tossed his coat on the bed, Harold gave her a long, careful look.

"One thing for sure—you need her, Em. You look terrible. You did at breakfast this morning too, and I spent most of the day worrying about you, to tell the truth. Didn't you go to Tepp today? What did he say, how did he find you?"

"He found me still anemic. He said I was probably overdoing things and had to take it easier." Her voice was hollow, as though it came from the bottom of a deep, dry well. Which was precisely where she felt herself to be.

"*Have* you been overdoing?" Furrowed concern.

"Hardly. Since my main activity consists of short walks around the block."

"You poor baby. You've really had it in spades. We'd probably better call off that dinner party—if Tepp thinks you're overdoing, the last thing you need is a dinner party to worry about."

Poor baby. In spades. Strange, that. Odd that her husband and Minda, who had never met, should have the same limited vocabulary in common. "I do need a dinner party," she finally said wearily, "and we had this whole conversation Monday, including just how rotten I look. But I'll run through it again: Cora is coming to do the party, so there's nothing for me to worry about, and in spite of how I look *or* what Tepp said, I've felt pretty damned fine all afternoon." Until now. She stood up and went to the door. "Are you serious about not wanting Benjy to eat with us? I'll have to fix him a tray."

"Yes. I *am* serious," he said, suddenly less overbearing, eying her nervously. "It's best for him—and us. I just don't buy Ingleman's diagnosis, Em. It's probably some virus, and I can't risk catching it. I have a big week coming up—Scrim's coming down from Maine, for one thing—and I just can't take any chance of getting sick."

"And what about Benjy. What if he minds?"

"What?"

"Nothing, Harold. Nothing." And she went out down the hall.

As it turned out, Benjy, who disliked pork roast, was only too happy to have his favorite meal—a whopping can of spaghetti and meatballs

—on a tray in front of TV in his room. As they passed his door when Maria called them in to dinner, they saw him wolfing down mountains of the stuff, raptly watching Charles Laughton in *Mutiny on the Bounty*. Less fortunate, they silently filed into the dining room, where Maria had painstakingly set the table, as usual, and had put a little Indian brass bell at Emma's place. As usual. Emma particularly hated the bell, which Maria had dug out of some drawer while she'd been in the hospital, and which seemed to her a symbol of the whole depressing new situation in her household, functional as the bell was: having firmly rejected the formal service Maria had been taught by the *aristicrático* Mrs. Spratt, and having worked out with the scandalized Maria a slapdash kind of "service" where she brought in the food and left it, and then only appeared to clear the plates and bring dessert—something other than a boarding-house shout was needed to summon Maria from the kitchen. Hence the bell. But Emma hated and resented it, just as she hated and resented all the other changes in the way she lived.

Now she and Harold took their places at opposite ends of the long table—the beautiful curly maple table that had belonged to her mother —and the minute they drew up their chairs, Maria came through the swinging door with the famous pork roast, proudly beaming.

"That looks just beautiful, Maria," said Harold as she set the platter in front of him. *"Muy bello."*

"I hope you like," Maria said demurely, flushing with pleasure, and ducked back through the swinging door for the vegetables.

Muy bello. The campaign to placate Maria was apparently on, she thought, watching Harold laboriously trying to carve the roast down into chops, but having his troubles, since the A&P butcher had not sawed the chine bone through far enough. As he struggled with the carving knife, Maria came back with bowls of potatoes and stringbeans, and after hopefully dawdling a minute, reluctantly returned to the kitchen. The minute the swinging door closed behind her, Harold laid the carving knife and fork down on the platter, suddenly pale.

"What's the matter?"

"It's pink. Ruddy bloody pink," he whispered, looking sick. "We can't possibly eat the damned thing."

"We have to. There's nothing else. And if we don't, she'll call Constanza."

Some of his color came rushing back. "Okay. Touché. Fuck Constanza. She'll just have to cook it some more. Ring the bell."

"*You* ring it. You tell her." She slid the bell across the expanse of gleaming wood.

Disconcerted, he gave her a long, wide-eyed look, and finally picked up the bell and swung it to and fro.

Looking happily expectant—clearly anticipating loud bravos and *olés* for the famous Spratt pork roast—Maria came in and stood, blank-faced, while Harold tried to explain what was wrong with the meat.

"Pank?"

"Pink. *Rosado?* . . . *Rojo?*" tried Harold, pointing to one of the dissected chops, which was oozing reddish juice onto the platter, un-nerving Emma with this display of Spanish. Another one of his secrets coming out?

"Is not nice, *señor?*" The hands at her sides were clenched into fists.

An answering mumble from Harold was drowned out by the ringing phone.

"I'll get it!" cried Emma, leaping up, grateful for the chance to escape, and raced to the hall extension, which sat on a little console table on the other side of the bookcase-divider wall. As her hand closed over the phone, she heard Harold behind the shelves of Modern Library Giants, trying to explain the dangers of eating undercooked pork to Maria.

"May I please speak to Mrs. Sohier?" said a Midwestern voice that made her heart sink.

"Oh. This is me. I mean she." Dr. Hobbema.

"This is Alison Hobbema, Mrs. Sohier.—I hope I'm not disturbing you."

"Oh. *Hello.* No. Not at all." Dr. Hobbema.

Silence. Puzzled silence from the other end of the phone, where Dr. Hobbema was undoubtedly registering this strange, to say nothing of impolite, refusal to address her by name. Listening silence from the dining room, where Harold suddenly seemed to be alone—and from Benjy's room, where the sound suddenly seemed to be turned down on Captain Bligh.

"I'm sorry to be calling at this hour," Dr. Hobbema finally continued, "but I wanted to be sure to reach you before the weekend closed down. Something unexpected has just come up, and I'm afraid I'll have to shift our appointment for next Wednesday to some other time."

"Oh."

"Would next Tuesday at two-thirty be convenient?" offered the doctor, after the finest of pauses.

Emma quickly considered two things—the endlessly empty hours of next Tuesday . . . and the possibility of not making another appointment with Dr. Hobbema. Ever. "I think that would be all right. In fact, I know that would be just fine. Dr. Hobbema." There'd been no way out, she'd had to say her name.

"Good. I'll put you down then for Tuesday the nineteenth at two-thirty. I apologize—I have a feeling that I *am* disturbing you by calling now. I hope you have a pleasant weekend, Mrs. Sohier."

"Thank you. I wish you the same, Dr. Hobbema."

More than "disturbed," Emma hung up. Charles Laughton—probably just momentarily silenced for a station break—was booming away again down in Benjy's room, but the silence from the dining room continued. Steeling herself, she went back inside, where Harold, his face carefully deadpan, blinked impassively at her as she sat down. Maria and the pork roast were gone, sounds of pots and pans being slammed and a hissing-sizzling came through the closed kitchen door. And then, just as she'd known he would, Harold playfully smiled and "twinkled" at her through his horn rims: "And just who is Dr. Hobbema? A descendant of the painter, I presume."

Not returning his smile, she said coldly, "A dermatologist. What happened to the pork, Harold?" Thanks to Minda, she now could produce a lie in two seconds flat.

"Dear Maria is frying the chops I managed to hack off. Scorching them from the sound of things. She wasn't too happy about it, needless to say.—Why a dermatologist?"

Momentarily stumped, Emma stared at the brown smoke threading under the kitchen door: her skin, flawless, creamy pale, was the one true claim to beauty she possessed. "I have a few problems," she finally said.

"You? With *your* skin? What kind of problems. You mean you have some kind of rash or something?"

Seeing the turn his mind had taken, seeing his alarm, she laughed. "No. Nothing like that. No skin diseases. The problems brought on by the passage of time, the ravages wrought by time you might say. Dr. Hobbema is a genius about problems like that."

"And who told you about this genius. Your pal, Minda Wolfe?"

"Yes." Which was the absolute truth; Minda had even called her a genius. "Why are you asking me all these questions, Harold."

"Because it just doesn't sound like you. Dermatologists. It's just what object to. It's exactly the sort of idiotic thing that flea-brained broad would think is important, and . . ."

He broke off as the scowling Maria came in with a platter of blackened chops and thumped them down in front of him. "Ah, that's *much* better, Maria. Many thanks. *Muchas gracias.* They're just splendid now."

"Is no splendid to me, I tell you, *Señor* Soller. I never before see anyone eat the pork like that. Is ruin. When I make this same roast for the Spratt, they always eat pank. Is no *peligroso.* No danger. Pank is the only way the Spratt care to eat the pork," she sullenly recapitulated, stomping toward the door.

"Ah yes. The dear Spratt. Long may they flourish, the dear dear Spratt, wherever they are—riddled with trichinoderms, I'm sure."

At the door by now, Maria swung back around. ". . . Señor??"

"What I *said,* Maria, was that I'm quite sure that the Spratts had excellent taste in all matters. But as they say the world over, 'Each to his own taste.' *Chacun à son goût.* I don't know the Spanish version, but the point is—we happen to like pork this way, Maria. Black. Quite black. We think it's lovely like that."

"Well, I certain hope is lovely for you. Is not Maria's fault if is not."

"We just love it, Maria. It's just dandy. And many *multas gracias* once again!" Concluding on this hopefully dismissing note, he forked up two blackened chops and deposited them with a flourish on a plate. As the door finally swung shut on Maria, he clapped a hand to either side of his head, and made a face of such comical despair, Emma laughed. He raised a finger to his lips. "What say we sneak them up to our can and flush them away."

"We'd only stop up the plumbing," she whispered back.

"How's about my slipping down the hall and pitching them down the incinerator chute?"

She had a flashing vision of Harold trundling down the hall like his son, carrying a platterful of blackened chops instead of an armload of sheets to the incinerator. "*No,*" she said with a ferocity that made Harold blink. "That's absolutely out. We've just got to try and choke them down as best we can."

"In that case, you'd better ring for the ketchup or Worcestershire, my dear."

"On the contrary, you'd better. My dear. You're the one who has the bell now." Giving her another one of those startled looks—was this the

Emma he knew?—Harold braced himself and timidly tinny-winkle
the bell.

"Let's see those ravages wrought by time," he said three hours later
in the privacy of their own room. The blackened chops, drowning in
commercial sauces, had long since been choked down, the still
seething Maria had departed for her weekend in the Bronx, and
Benjy, suddenly overcome by the narcotizing side effects of the anti
histamines, had been in bed, soundly asleep for over an hour.

Rising from the armchair where he'd been sitting and taking off his
shoes and socks, Harold padded to the side of the bed where she lay
reading the novel she'd started that afternoon. Tilting the shade of her
bedside lamp so that it threw a strong, naked light on her face, he
said, "Let's just see this time-ravaged skin of yours," and bent low to
run light, caressing fingers down her face. "Hn-m-m. I see," he said
and, finished with the inspection of the flawless skin on her face and
neck, deftly unbuttoned the top of her pajamas and bent still lower to
examine the dazzling skin he'd uncovered. As he slowly took first one
breast, then the other in his mouth, Emma moaned and dug her fingers
in his rumply hair. "Harold. Darling," she finally gasped. "The door's
open . . . and Benjy . . ."

"*His* door is closed, and he's out cold with those pills," said Harold,
kicking free of his shorts and tugging her pajama pants down.

"*Please* shut the door, darling. And turn off the lights or close the
blinds, and move the head of the bed away from the wall."

"What do you want—a furniture mover—or a fuck?"

"A fuck," she replied in a very small voice.

"Okay. You've got a deal," he said, and grabbing her legs, roughly
pulled her to the edge of the bed, where, after wrapping her legs around
his waist, he came to a tantalizing stop. "Listen. Let's just fuck and
forget everything else—even the diaphragm. You won't get pregnant. I
know you won't." And with that, went ahead.

You're damned right I won't, thought Emma, incapable of speech by
then: sensing this might happen, in fact having wanted it to happen
ever since dinner, when she'd been charmed by the sudden return of
their old rapport—she had taken care of matters well ahead of time.

"Come on, Em baby. Let's just fuck and fuck and fuck."

And so they did. With the door wide open. The lights still on. The
blinds still unpulled. And the head of their bed tapping its Morse code
on the wall.

Burt Tovey: "In Dreams Begin Responsibilities"

The next morning, just before waking, Emma dreamt that she and Burt Tovey were making love. They were lying on what seemed to be some part of the Eaton Club golf course, a putting green—she could feel the turfy tickling grass, springy as a deep-piled carpet, beneath her bare legs. She could also smell the brackish water of Long Island Sound, hear its faint lip-a-lap against the edge of a nearby dock. She and Burt were moving together in the rhythm of the water, gentle, persistent, slow, pleasure mounting steadily, steadily, unbearably, finally exploding into a cataclysmic climax—in reality as well as the dream: she woke up churning and writhing and moaning on flowered percale, to blink confusedly at bright October sunlight seeping through the blinds. First embarrassed—it had been a real, honest-to-God orgasm—then alarmed, she rolled over and looked at Harold sleeping soundly, thank heavens, mere inches away, noisily breathing through his nose. Then, still shaken, as guilty as if she and Burt had been making love with Harold right alongside them in the big bed, she flipped onto her back and stared at the sun-striped ceiling: Burt. Burt again. But why Burt after last night?

Burt Tovey was a boy she had loved when she was nineteen. She hadn't thought she loved him at the time, and it wasn't until years later, just recently in fact, that she realized she'd been protecting herself. Against what she still didn't know. That summer she was nineteen, Burt Tovey was the tennis instructor at the Eaton Country Club, where Jane Robbins, her best friend since childhood, had often taken her as a guest. Emma and her mother had never been asked to join the Eaton Club, which was only five years old that summer. But even if they had been asked and could have afforded it, her mother never would have joined the club, which, as her mother ever-so-fumigatedly put it, was filled with "all those people" who weren't "our sort." By which her mother meant Jewish—just like they were—only richer. Nouveau-richer.

But Emma didn't really react to remarks like that any more, and in this case only resented the inclusiveness of that "our." She had done all her violent reacting at thirteen when, still grieving and trying to get over the shock of her father's death, she'd had to stand by and watch her mother try to make up for lost time, try to be accepted by what passed for society in that small Connecticut town—and with great, grim satisfaction had seen her fail. Though, at nineteen, it still made her faintly sick to think of all those useless ploys and come-ons for the people her mother wishfully considered her "sort"—those genteel (perfect word for what her mother was up to) hobbies of painting and collecting Colonial antiques (suddenly turned into a means of supporting them), her mother's volunteering for all those equally genteel charity drives and causes (Red Cross, Community Chest, Gray Lady at the local hospital)—it didn't really touch her, she found it more depressing and pathetic than anything else. Certainly, by the time that summer she was nineteen rolled around, and she met Burt Tovey, the fact that he wasn't Jewish meant nothing to her, just as her being Jewish meant nothing to him. But the fact that it mattered to her mother, and was the only reason her mother accepted him at first (and only at first), almost put Emma off him. Almost. Actually . . . nothing could.

Though she didn't know it at the time, it was the last summer she would ever spend in Eaton. It was a summer of record-breaking heat. In late June and early July, when she was first home from Radcliffe, she did part-time volunteer work at the local library, but when the terrible heat wave struck, she cut down on her hours at the library and spent most of the days at the public beach. Jane, on vacation from Smith, had been sent to stay with hated relatives in Buffalo while her parents traveled in France, but returned at the end of July. On her third day home, she invited Emma to the Eaton Club for the day, the rough plan being that they would play some tennis in the morning and spend the rest of the day at the club's private beach.

When Jane came to pick her up at ten, it was already in the low nineties, with locusts parchily rasping in the fields. Hardly a day for tennis, but Jane was determined to make up for all the time she'd missed on the beautiful club courts, all the miserable weeks in Buffalo. The club courts were usually all taken by nine in the morning, but when they pulled into the empty parking lot behind the pavilion, the courts were

as deserted as the rolling greens they'd just driven through in the car:
everybody, of course, was at the beach—the only sensible place to be.
But Jane was unbudgeable, so they played. They were both fairly good
—good enough to have made the high school tennis team several years
before—but as the sun beat mercilessly down on the clay courts, they
both began playing badly, sloppily, lobbing wild balls everywhere.

Emma was winning, but hardly cared. Occasionally smashing back
some of Jane's crazily soaring balls with stunning precision, she kept
waiting for Jane to say they'd had enough, say they could quit and go
to the beach, but Jane wouldn't. During the last game of the first set
(Emma was taking it 6–1), someone came and sat down on the
awninged pavilion at the side of the courts; from the glare of the base
line, Emma could only make out someone very brown dressed in white.
When Emma took the last game and set, they took a break and went to
splash their faces and rinse their mouths at the faucet near the foot of
the pavilion stairs. Jane, given to erratic bursts of politeness, let her
guest use the faucet first. Jane's face was an alarming red and streaming with sweat, but when Emma had finished with the faucet and
timidly asked if they couldn't stop and go to the beach, Jane snapped,
"Let's play three more games," and bent to hold her face under the faucet's gushing stream.

Leaving her spluttering like a porpoise, Emma went up onto the
pavilion to use the towel she'd left on the back bench with her canvas
purse. Sitting on a middle bench was the figure in white—a deeply sun-
tanned boy with hay-colored hair and a thick coating of zinc ointment
on his nose. Too angry at Jane to pay any attention to him, Emma
snatched up her towel and began drying her face, while he swiveled
all the way around the bench and said softly, in a thick southern accent, "Not bad, girl. Not bad at all, considerin'." Considerin' *what*,
wondered Emma, still fuming at Jane, but as she lowered the towel to
give him a long chilling look, she stopped wondering anything and just
stared. She had always hated—and avoided—overly handsome boys.
Their conceit bored her, she wasn't afraid of getting hurt. But this . . .
this person was something else. And as he returned her stare with eyes
like cornflowers suspended in ice and softly said, "Hey there," something thwocked in her chest like one of the balls Jane had slammed
into the net. And she hated it. Resented it and feared it. Finally giving
him the withering look she'd originally planned, she quickly turned her
back on him as Jane came up onto the pavilion. Ignoring the boy after
one quick, flickering look, Jane dried her face and, taking an elastic

sweatband from her purse, skinned back her thick auburn hair. Ignoring Jane, the boy went on staring at Emma—she could feel the scorching trail of his eyes on the backs of her legs. Why me and not Jane? she wondered. They were good legs, and many boys liked her pale blondness, but never when Jane—sleek and dark and voluptuous—was around. Yet he sat there, his eyes fixed on her, eyes she could feel trying to force her to turn around (she didn't), ignoring Jane, who finally announced bossily, "Okay, just *two* more games and then we'll go get a swim."

As Emma followed Jane back down the pavilion steps, she heard him softly laugh.

They played four more games, not two. He moved down from the middle bench to the front row. In spite of the heat, which was now sickening, she and Jane buckled down and began to play in earnest, each—for some inexplicable reason—now grimly determined to win. When Emma took the first two games, Jane insisted they play two more. Across the net, Jane's face shone pale and wet, her mouth bitterly clenched, the strokes of her racquet jerky and choppy with ferocious intent. During the first two games, each time Emma took a point or made a good shot—and there were many, her form had suddenly opened up, was all loose grace and deadly accuracy—there was a faint drawled comment from the pavilion: "Hey, that was mighty purty, gal!" or "*Now* you're lookin' good, things are lookin' up," or "Not bad. Not bad at all." All of which, for sheer vapid dumbness, should have put her off. But it didn't. Nothing would, she began to see. Affected by this and the heat, she let Jane take the next two games—anything to get *out* of there. As they collected their things from the pavilion, he sat silent, and she could feel him again, waiting for her to look at him, trying to force her to look at him, but she wouldn't. Halfway to the beach, Jane broke the acrid fumy silence in the car: "He's bad news, Em. If you ever hear from him you'd better steer clear. Even though he's only been here a month, the word's gotten around. I gather he was pretty busy while I was away. He's a real tennis bum. A cracker from someplace in Florida. Some tennis coach took him under his wing when he was a kid, and early on it looked like he might make the grade—I hear he even got to Forest Hills—but he never did make it and now just bums around the country working at private clubs. Working at more than just tennis. He's got a terrific chip on his shoulder, and tries to work it off in obvious ways. I hear he's out to make what he calls any 'rich bitch' at he club—young *or* old—who's stupid enough to fall for all that Jon Whitcomb gorgeousness."

Well, I'm certainly not rich, Emma thought bleakly, stepping out of he car onto the crunching gravel of the beach-club parking lot. I oathe Jon Whitcomb, yet I'm certainly stupid enough to fall for whatever it is, but how can I ever hear from him when I don't belong to the club, and he has no way of finding out who I am?

She had underestimated him—as she was always to do.

He had called twice while she and Jane were at the beach, her mother informed her when she arrived home at six. (He later told her that as soon as she and Jane had left the pavilion, he'd gone to the front office and gotten her name off the guest-chit Jane had had to sign.) He called again while she and her mother were having dinner. Dispensing with formalities, he quickly identified himself—"This is Burt Tovey. I watched you playin' tennis this mornin' at the club?"—and asked if he could take her to the movies that night. Dispensing with any fake coquetry, she immediately accepted and told him how to get to her house. "Who *is* that boy?" asked her mother, when Emma came back to the table and announced she was going out. "Someone Jane introduced me to at the club," she glibly lied. Somewhat appeased, her mother didn't ask any more questions; few local boys, from Jane's club or otherwise, ever asked her out. Later, when he came to pick her up, her mother saw at once what he was. But liking what she saw in spite of herself—all that blond "Jon Whitcomb gorgeousness"—her mother gave her one brightly glancing ironic look and let it go at that.

He had an old four-door sedan, which he told her he had bought thirdhand for his two-month stay at the club. He was boarding for the summer with the club steward and his wife, who lived in Stubbs, the town next to theirs. They went to a drive-in theater that sat off the highway between Eaton and Stubbs. On the drive to the theater they made small talk with painful awkwardness. "Your mother's beautiful. Looks like the Duchess of Windsor. Anyone ever tell you that?" *All* the time, since she works so hard to point the damned likeness up. "Yes, a lot of people have." "So are you—beautiful. But in a different way." Incapable of speech, she let him do the talking for a while. He told her he was going to spend the fall and winter in Fort Lauderdale, where he had a job lined up at some other club, and perhaps go to Australia in the spring; he'd never been out of the country, and wanted to travel and had a "contact" in Sydney who could help him get a job. When he asked her what she would be doing that winter, she said she would

be going back to Radcliffe in September for her junior year. Which
had the effect she had known it would—imposed a silence that lasted
until they were in the drive-in theater's vast parking lot, a speaker
hooked up to the car window. For a minute they sat stiffly in darkness,
staring out at the towering blank screen, waiting for the movie to begin. Then he suddenly announced he was going to get them some soda,
and got out of the car and went to the refreshment stand. She put her
hand on the warm place on the seat where he'd been sitting, and
deeply breathed in his smell—a compound of sunburned skin and Old
Spice after shave, and something else she couldn't place.

For twenty minutes they sat and watched the movie. Or rather they
sat staring straight ahead through the windshield at the giant screen.
He kept his arm stretched out along the back of the seat, letting it graze
her shoulders from time to time, only moving it away when he lit their
cigarettes. Emma sat achingly expectant, feeling the arm drawing like
a magnet at the back of her shoulders, hoping he couldn't hear her
labored breathing, listening to his. Then he suddenly threw his half-
smoked cigarette out through the rolled-down window, and gently, almost shyly, bent his head and placed his open lips on the base of her
throat. She shuddered: here it was. And so it was. Slowly moving his
mouth up her neck, lightly grazing her skin with the tip of his tongue,
he at last lifted his mouth and brought it down on hers. Greedily, claim-
ingly. Groaning, they flew together, the old-fashioned gear shift jab-
bing them, impeding their tangling legs. "Let's get the hell *out* of here,"
he finally said, mouth still against hers. "Yes . . . but where?" "You live
here—don't you know of some place?" "No." The smallness and sadness
of her voice made him laugh, made him fold her against him tighter
still: "Then we'll wait until I find out where to go."

He found out by the next night. Her mother, greeting him with less
graciousness, wearing a smug, knowing expression that Emma found
unbearable, saw them off again. He drove without talking, heading for
the back part of Eaton, a heavily wooded section filled with huge old
estates. She didn't ask him whom he'd asked—the steward? the golf
pro? one of the caddies? She didn't want to know. She didn't want to
think about the hours he spent at the club, his daytime life. (His life.
Period.) She just wanted him to get to the place someone had told him
about—the overgrown driveway of an unused caretaker's cottage on a
large estate. The place where they parked, and after several ravenous
kisses, scrambled, laughing, over the back of the front seat (the sound
of the car doors opening and shutting, he explained, might alert the

residents of the big house), onto the broad rear seat, and with legs at impossibly crazy angles, finally made love. Violently. Happily. Found.

They made love every night they could manage to see each other for the rest of the summer—which amounted to about three and a half weeks after that night. Her summer became a vigil of waiting through the long hot days until covering darkness fell. Jane Robbins never asked her to the club again. Two days after Emma and Burt Tovey became lovers, Jane had called and in a rasping voice bluntly asked if she was seeing him. When Emma quietly said that she was, Jane cried, "You moron!" and slammed down the receiver. A week later she called again. Her voice even more grating and metallic than the last time, she said that as Emma's friend, she felt she had to tell her that Burt Tovey was going around the club, bragging to all the help—waiters and caddies and locker-room attendants—about his "hot piece of Jewish ass." Of course Emma didn't believe it. But she hung up on Jane and wept—for the murderous meanness of Jane's jealousy, not for any betrayal by Burt. Sweet gentle Burt. She spent the long dragging days in the library, forsaking the public beach for the fusty coolness of the large old private house that had been converted to a library, doing odd jobs for the librarian, a kind, shy woman she'd known since childhood. Her mother spent her days painting in her air-conditioned studio above the garage (she had temporarily closed her antique shop), never asking Emma how she spent *her* days. She knew without asking how Emma spent her nights. And after the first few times, she made a point of being upstairs when Burt came to pick Emma up. She didn't have to tell Emma how she felt. Emma could feel the searing blasts of disgust and contempt as her mother passed through the living room on her way upstairs—could feel the exact quality of the look her mother gave her as Emma sat on the couch, freshly bathed, wearing light clothes that came off quickly and easily, waiting impatiently for the sound of Burt's old car. Waiting for the covering darkness that preceded, by minutes, the hum and cutoff of his motor.

They never thought of going to a motel, of seeking out a bed. It wasn't just the money: the car, the night, the leafy lanes were their home—were an integral part of their happiness. They parked on the banks of every pond or inlet, on the outer edges of every overgrown field, in every remote lane and every wooded grove in Eaton and neighboring towns. Patrolling policemen, traveling by car in pairs, shoving flashlights through Burt's car windows and muttering crude warnings or orders to clear out, kept them on the move, kept them constantly searching for new places ever more remote. Emma wasn't a virgin—she had slept with two boys from Harvard and one from M.I.T., and had been fitted for a diaphragm by a Boston gynecologist her sophomore year—but the sex she had with Burt Tovey bore no resemblance to the sex she'd had in those Cambridge dorms or Boston hotels. And she was willing to put up with any amount of humiliation or discomfort to go on having it. She told herself it was The Real Thing. It was all she'd ever thought sex might be, and more. Drunk on sex, going around on a perpetual erotic high, she even took to telling herself that she was like a character out of Colette, a woman discovering and fulfilling her deep and true sensual nature. Knowing just how outrageous it was, she kept on telling herself that anyway. Burt told her that he loved her, she told him that she loved him. She thought she didn't mean it. She thought she was being very advanced, very pre-liberated, shattering the damned double standard and lying while she did it, if that's what was required. She even began believing she *was* a Colette heroine, a woman who knew how to enjoy things without guilt, and Burt Tovey, gentle, tender, yet incredibly virile, was her Cheri—a ripe thing to enjoy, to pluck, like summer fruit. On and on. There was no end to the garbage she told herself. She and Burt never talked about the future, the immediate future, that is. About the fact that in weeks, then before they knew it, days, she would be going back to Cambridge, and he, almost the length of a continent away, to Fort Lauderdale. And all this time her mother knew exactly what was going on. She got the scent of all that spermy grass-stained sex, but said nothing to Emma, just continued to be in her studio or upstairs when Burt came to pick her up. She also did a little active prying, and Emma finally realized her mother had discovered her diaphragm: when it wasn't in use, she kept it in her sweater drawer, under the scant stack of treasured cashmeres she had gotten for birthdays and Christmas over the years. One afternoon shortly after she and Burt had become lovers, and hadn't been able to see each other for a record three days, Emma found the diaphragm under a stack of her old shetland sweaters, instead of under the precious Braemers and Ballantines. She was beside herself. Enraged, outraged, but frightened too. Now. Now her mother was going to let out some of that bottled-up venom. Now (she told herself like a child) she was *in* for it. But no. Her mother said nothing. And Emma finally told herself that in spite of all her mother's monumental faults—her coldness, her obnoxious snobbishness and bigotry, her disregard for privacy—she was damned lucky to have a mother who was so liberated about sex, a mother who tolerated her daughter's private little sexual revolution years before anyone knew what a sexual revolution was.

Then, one night at the end of August, the first clear night after three days of heavy rains, Burt's car got stuck in the mud. For three nights, because Burt's ancient car had a leaky roof, they'd sat in the last row of movie theater balconies in Eaton and Stubbs, doing urgent things to each other right under the brilliant shaft of the projector's beam. Several days before the rain, there had been a lurid Lover's Lane murder in the town beyond Stubbs, and the Connecticut police were rigorously patrolling all isolated spots for miles around. All their spots. But Burt, undaunted, ever resourceful, found them a new place near the entrance to the freeway that the local police had overlooked—a once-marshy tract recently filled in by bulldozers, where a middle-income housing development was being built. A bleak, depressing place, filled with the looming silhouettes of huge cranes and derricks that looked like prehistoric beasts, and the flimsy toothpick frames of the future ranch-style houses, but Burt pulled in behind a gigantic cement mixer, and safely hidden, wildly greedy after three days of relative abstinence, they stayed until a quarter past two. When, at her insistence, Burt finally tried to start the car, the wheels flew around, splattering mud. After twenty minutes, they gave up and walked the five miles back into town, not a single car passing them on the way. Not even a police car. Worried about his poor, ancient car, Burt left her on the porch of her house and set out to find an all-night garage with a tow car. As quietly as she could, Emma let herself in: it was three-thirty by then.

Carrying her mud-caked sandals, she started tiptoeing up the front stairs. Eighteenth-century stairs that were her mother's pride and joy, and that her mother had left uncarpeted, in all their warped and ancient glory. Creaking, groaning stairs. Halfway up, Emma finally glanced upward and saw her mother standing at the top of the stairway —a tall, wraithlike figure with blazing eyes, wearing a white nightgown . . . an apparition as frightening and forbidding as one of Blake's wrathful vestal maidens.

"What is the *matter* with you. Have you lost all sense of decency?" her mother hissed as she slowly climbed upward. "Can't you ever think of anyone but yourself? I thought you'd had an accident . . . or been murdered in some lonely lane like those two other disgusting brats. I called the police. They *laughed* at me."

"I'm sorry, Mother," she gasped, breathless from unreasoning terror, not her climb up the stairs. Reaching the top step, she gave her mother a wide berth: though her mother stood with arms placidly crossed, a terrible angry violence emanated from the diaphanous whiteness of her. "Burt's car got stuck in the mud. We had to walk all the way home."

After a long scalding silence, her mother stirred as if she were about to start for her room, but apparently changed her mind, and stayed where she was. "Has it ever occurred to you that you might catch some filthy disease from that person? Knowing you, I'm sure you've taken precautions to keep from getting pregnant—but what about some venereal disease?"

There was a space of about four feet between them. With one step, one shove, she could have sent her mother crashing down the stairs— those precious uncarpeted stairs with sharp-edged risers. Shaken, Emma backed away into the blackness of the upstairs hall. "You've no right to talk about Burt that way." Her voice was thick, slurred. "He's a good and decent person. Gentle and sweet, a fine human being. He loves me. He isn't . . . You've no *right* to make such rotten insinuations. He can't help it if he's poor, if he hasn't had the advantages other boys his age have had. Just because he hasn't had a formal education, it doesn't necessarily follow that he's a bad person, some kind of shiftless . . . bum."

Bum. Without repeating the outmoded word herself, her mother let it hang on in the air, openly and shamelessly savoring the heavy-handed double meaning. Then, rounding things off with an eloquent sniff, she walked across the hall to the door of her room, where, pure ham-actress that she was, she stagily paused, then swung back around: "If you're so concerned about his welfare, then why are you using him? That's all you're doing, you know—*using* him." And with that, went into her room and shut the door.

Emma lay awake until her room was filled with blinding sunlight, and she heard the peaceful whirring of their next-door neighbor's lawnmower. Grainy-eyed, rigid, she lay there raging at her mother and her mother's contempt and cruelty, hating her mother, hating herself more. When Emma finally got up in the early afternoon, her mother acted as if nothing—none of that ugly, demoralizing scene—had happened. Bewildered, irreparably hurt, still raging, she decided to follow her treacherous mother's example and play it as if nothing had happened. But later in the afternoon she phoned Burt on his job at the club—something she'd made a great point of never doing—and told him to pick her up on a corner a block from her house. She didn't have to explain. He understood.

There wasn't much time left to them, just five days, including Labor Day. Burt picked her up on the same corner for all of those last five nights. Nights which seemed to Emma suffused with a special aura of drenching sweetness, undercut by pain and shame. Nights when they either talked evasively of the winter ahead, or gallantly told each other elaborate lies, making plans for meetings they knew would never take place, reunions in some big city midway between Florida and Massachusetts, where, as he put it, they would "hole up in some fancy hotel and just screw our brains out for a couple of days." Which neatly put things in their proper place, she thought, desperately trying to harden her heart, unhappily wondering if she wasn't exactly the bitch her mother made her out to be. They promised to write each other often and phone from time to time. Burt gave her a St. Christopher medal and a green-dyed rabbit's foot on a key chain. She gave him a gold tiepin (she'd never seen him wear a tie) and a gold money clip which she had engraved: "To have and to hold. For always. Emma." Yes. Yes. Her mother was right after all: bitch.

She went back to Radcliffe and the grinding schedule of her junior year. She became co-editor of the magazine along with Casey Rowland, did volunteer work on Senator John F. Kennedy's campaign against Lodge, started the groundwork for a senior thesis on Joyce, and began to think seriously about a literary career as a critic or editor. Though she missed their sex, she didn't miss Burt. Or so she endlessly told herself. Halfway through the autumn, Burt's job at the Fort Lauderdale club folded (fired because of some "rich bitch"?), and he immediately landed another job at some country club in Fort Worth. Which fell through within a matter of weeks. Slowly he began moving across the Southwest, now taking jobs as a tennis instructor at luxurious hotels instead of private clubs. He wrote her postcards, never a letter. Only postcards—tinted photographs of what almost looked like the same hotel facade, where an inky X across some lower window always indicated his room, and where there were always one or two nearly illegible lines scrawled on the back . . . which she would read with cynical detachment, her mind nastily inserting *sic* after each misspelled word: "Wish you were here sweatheart (*sic*)" or "Miss you baby and you're (*sic*) You Know What" or "The living here is easy but the women are dogs. I shure (*sic*) do miss you lover. WOOF WOOF!" Whenever she pulled these cards from her mailbox, she would always find herself wondering if the student volunteers who sorted the mail had read them, and if so, what they'd thought. She hated herself for it, but kept on wondering that all the same. Just as, hating herself, she still kept on writing him the same kind of condescending letters on her Royal portable—always a single page filled with the sort of short declarative sentences one might write to a backward child, sentences that described in monosyllabic words the weather, a visiting lecturer, a new foreign movie she had seen. In spite of their promises, they never spoke on the phone. None of their cards or letters ever brought up the subject of a possible meeting sometime, somewhere. It was rapidly becoming clear that a meeting was impossible. Anytime. Anywhere.

She began going out with other boys all the time, slept with some, finally settled into a spiritless affair with an English instructor at Harvard—and feverishly concentrated on her work and the magazine. With many misgivings, she went home for Christmas. As insulation against her mother (who never mentioned Burt Tovey or referred to him in any way), she brought along Casey Rowland, whose father was an honest-to-God duke and whose family was listed in Burke's Peerage—which meant absolutely nothing to Emma. But like most petty snobs, her mother was an avid Anglophile, and was so bowled over by Casey's rich fruity accent and lineage, she turned into someone Emma barely recognized—someone warm and gracious and almost sweet. Casey, however, was not at all bowled over by her mother or the least bit taken in, and their second night in Eaton as they were getting ready for bed suddenly burst out: "My gawd, but your mother's a frightful snob, Emmy! Howdjevah turn out so *nice?*"

Though it wasn't a question that required an answer, Emma couldn't have answered in any case: at that time in her life the last thing she would have dreamed of calling herself was "nice." The last real message, the last postcard from Burt had come in early December, sent from a Palm Springs hotel. She'd never answered it. Then just before going home for vacation, she'd gotten a Christmas card—a cutout of a fat, lewdly winking Santa sprinkled with sparkly sand and bits of cotton wool glued to his beard and robe's fur border, with HOWZE ABOUT I FILL YOUR CHRISTMAS STOCKING, SWEETIE PIE? printed in red across his bulging sack . . . and a lurching row of inky X's and "Your Burt" scribbled beneath. Her heart beating strangely, she had stopped in the middle of the Yard and re-examined the envelope, which had a Los Angeles postmark and no return address. Suddenly shivering, she had finally moved on, throwing the card and envelope into the first trash can she passed, then rushing off to her next class.

She didn't hear from him again for six months. In May she pulled an envelope from her mailbox addressed in the familiar meandering hand. The postmark was Sydney, Australia. Something terrible began lurching and knocking around in her chest. With clammy hands she ripped open the envelope. A piece of stationery folded around a news-clipping fell out. The clip, from some Australian newspaper, announced the marriage of Miss Sara Brewster of Sydney to Mr. Burtwin Tovey of Sarasota, Florida, the United States. Miss Brewster, briefly stated the article, was the daughter of Alwyn Brewster, the "distin-guished barrister"; Mr. Tovey, a professional tennis player, was "well known in tennis circles" all over the United States. On the piece of stationery wrapped around the clipping, were two dipping, smudgy lines: "Sorry baby girl but thats (*sic*) the way it gos (*sic*). I still love you if you can belive (*sic*) it. Always and forever. Your Burt."

She could believe it. She did believe it. *Sic. Sic* be damned! She wept for days. Amazed at herself. She finally pulled herself together, and, reverting to the role of coldhearted bitch, told herself she was being a sentimental idiot, it couldn't have turned out any other way. She told herself that love her or not, he was exactly what Jane Robbins had called him on that scorching summer's day: a tennis bum out to get himself a rich bitch. Well, he'd gotten just what he wanted. And good for him. She could hardly sit in judgment, seeing how she herself had behaved. How she had treated him. *Used* him. Just as her mother had said.

When the term ended, she went to Denmark for the summer with a social study group. Her exclusive interest in a literary career was falter-ing, she was thinking of branching out. Her mother paid the study group's modest fee and Emma's passage on a student ship, and went off to spend the summer in Chatham with the homosexual decorator who sold most of her paintings to his rich clients, the closest of her mother's pitifully small group of friends. When Emma thought of Burt Tovey—and she thought of him often, in spite of all the things she'd resolutely told herself—it was always only to recall the summer nights of a year ago. (Which now seemed like ten years ago.) She never let herself think of Burtwin (*Burtwin*) Tovey, well known in tennis circles, married to the daughter of a distinguished barrister.

The next fall she met Harold, fresh out of Princeton, just settling into Cambridge and starting *The Cantabrigian Review*. She fell in love with him right away, but managed to hide this from him for many months. Serious, almost scholarly, dedicated to literature in a way she was beginning to face she never would be, witty and charming withal —he was everything Burt, poor Burt, hadn't been. Even—and this was a real shocker—in sex. Trying to summarize things (and therefore be able to let go of them all), she had recently taken to telling herself sadly that whatever else he hadn't been, Burt, sweet Burt, so handsome and physically perfect and virile, was undoubtedly the best lover she was ever going to have. But as soon as she settled down into a steady sex life with Harold, she began to look back and examine her sex with Burt, began asking herself if the gentle sensuousness of Burt's lovemaking hadn't really amounted to a certain kind of . . . passivity. Harold, as unlikely looking a lover as anyone could imagine, with his chunky, stocky body and legs like posts, made love with a crude, well yes, *animal* gusto and abandon that almost shocked and disgusted her at first. Almost. And only at first. Harold, not Burt, she soon realized, was the most exciting lover she would ever have. And once she and Harold were going to bed all the time, all the time, she ended the comparison once and for all with this final thought: Her sex with Burt hadn't been The Real Thing, as she'd once told herself, but had been just one long pretty midsummer night's dream; her sex with Harold— earthy, raw—was The Real Thing, the gutsy stuff of reality, of every-day life.

Those were the exact words she used.

Luckily, her relationship with Harold survived that unfortunate be-ginning. Luckily, they were right for each other in many ways besides sex. It was, everyone said, a perfect match. When they were married, everyone—even her mother—was pleased. For fourteen years their mar-riage had flourished and was the only marriage Emma knew of that could remotely be described as solid or happy in their New York world. In fourteen years she had never been unfaithful to Harold, even though she knew of the two times he had been unfaithful to her, even though she'd had opportunities, and the temptation to pay him back had been almost overwhelming when she found out about the second affair. Though all the other women she knew would have gotten even with a vengeance, she didn't. She decided she would only be hurting herself. In the tough, wised-up world they moved in, she knew she was almost a freak, but the thing was, she loved him. Yes, loved him. There it was. She loved him. She . . . treasured him. She would sometimes watch him while he was sleeping, and as she stared at his face, so naked-looking without the horn rims, she would be overcome by a terrible tenderness. He looked so defenseless. So . . . vulnerable. Things hadn't turned out as he had once hoped or planned. He was just a glorified businessman (in the business of publishing), not the distinguished critic or editor he had once planned to be. But he had somehow learned to live with it. In spite of terrible disappointment, thwarted ambition, he had remained good and kind and thoughtful—a reasonable man. Nowadays, when most other men struck her as unbelievably vain and hostile and aggressive, so ruthless in their drives for power and success and self-gratification that they almost seemed to leave a trail of human debris in their wake, Harold seemed unique, a precious exception, the embodiment of all that was rational and good. A rarity. A good man. A rational man. And oh she was lucky. She told herself just how lucky all the time. Which she supposed made her whatever the feminine equivalent of uxorious was—a word used with contempt by everybody she knew. But she didn't give a damn.

Though during the fourteen years she had been married, she had often thought and dreamed of Burt Tovey, she had noticed a distinct pattern, observed that something unpleasant or unhappy invariably preceded—or actually triggered—the thoughts and dreams. A fight with Harold. The discoveries of Harold's infidelities. (When she'd found out about the first girl, she'd dreamed of Burt Tovey four times in one week, and had even had a few wild thoughts about flying to Sydney.) Doubts about the motives for her work at Knickerbocker House. Doubts about its merit. A siege of minor illnesses in the household that kept her housebound and brought on mild depression and claustrophobia. The terrors and traumas engendered by serious illness and death: during the weeks her mother lay dying in the hospital, she had thought of Burt often, and later, when she herself was hospitalized with the FUO, she had deliberately dredged up and used thoughts of Burt to help hoist her out of her black depression. Used. Her mother had been right about that: used. As always the appropriate verb, the precise word for what she had done to Burt as a girl, and had gone on doing over the years. Used him as a springboard. Used him the way a hypnotist uses a bright light or shiny object to induce a trance—used his memory-brightened persona to induce a trance of reminiscence, of escape from whatever unpleasantness was happening in the present, back to what she seemed to think was a better, simpler time.

And now she had just done it again.

Now, trying not to wake Harold as she finally got out of bed, she went into the bathroom to wash, thinking of the "unpleasantness" of the present she had needed to escape from—thinking of the day before. A day that had ended in fantastic sex with Harold, true, but that had been jampacked with a variety of events, each more ludicrous and dislocating than the next: the attack (which, having no idea of the day ahead, she had promised herself would be the last), the long unsettling call from Minda, the disheartening visit to Tepp, the discovery of Benjy burning his sheets, Miss Tibbs, Ingleman, Hobbema. Why go on? What more did she need? Quite a little day, that. A red-letter day, one might say. A day which in retrospect seemed like some nutsy Marx Brothers or Laurel and Hardy comedy . . . only it wasn't funny.

Giving an ironic little laugh all the same, she cupped her hands under the faucet and dashed cold water in her face, gasping from the shock of it—just what was needed to rip away the last shreds of sticky Dreamland cobwebs away:

That dream of tender sex on the putting green hadn't been a yearning for sweet Burt or their lovely sex, but a yearning for that summer they had coupled on grass and sand and car seats—a summer she had idealized out of sight. A summer which, except for that one ineradicable black moment when she'd stood facing that terrifying specter at the top of the stairs, she persisted in remembering as a summer adazzle with light. A nimbus-enclosed summer which had come to mean far more than itself, had come to stand in her mind for some sort of last golden time for the world, the last time the world was peaceful, unpolluted, undefiled. A summer whose mornings alive with the sounds of locusts and lawnmowers and sprinklers, whose stretches of soaking lawns and baking sands and sunsparked sea and high blue domic skies she had fatuously come to think of as still unpoisoned, pure.

Very pretty, very soothing . . . and a lot of *horse*shit, she thought, reaching for a towel and furiously rubbing her face dry: though it seemed like another century, the hard fact was that that summer had been just sixteen years ago, and all the things she liked to think of as having just recently come to poison and destroy the world had already been at work in that landscape, those skies. Including the clouds of war.

Disgustedly throwing down the towel, she tiptoed through the bedroom and went to the kitchen, angrily clattering things as she put the coffee on: her insistence on seeing that summer as a last golden time for the world was just the same old story—fears of falling bodies, thoughts of Doomsday, flights into dreams—they all came from the

same damned thing: a refusal to accept things as they were. A refusal
to face facts. Just yesterday she had smugly told herself she was through
with all that, yet she had let one bad day push her right back. A day
when Minda's phone call certainly hadn't helped matters, in fact, all
that talk about the past, about "vistas" and "flights of arches" and "feelings in the air" and how she herself had been such an "exciting" person in those days, was undoubtedly part of what pushed her back—but
the crux of the matter was that she had *let* herself be pushed. She
seemed to forget that when Minda had finally finished moaning about
her husband and the past, she had moved up to the present, bringing
things up to date, and had, in effect, told her that if she wasn't a very
"exciting" person any more, she was still one of the strongest individ-
uals Minda knew: "stable" and "strong" and "in control" of her life.
What about that? If any of that was true, she ought to be "strong"
enough to "control" this need to escape.

Well, it was true, and she *was* strong. And she *would* control it and
stop it. Stop all the dumb, frightened vacillating and hedging and
ducking, and be a big brave girl and face things the way they
were now, accept them and find a way to live with them. Face the Age
of Aquarius.

She plugged in the juicer and, taking oranges from the icebox, began to slice them with fierce thwocks of the knife on the cutting
board:

Meanwhile, for less ambitious starters on that bright Saturday morning, she had something nice and limited to face: two days of being shut
in with a man who suddenly wasn't so rational after all . . . and
a child who was suddenly so strange he needed to see a therapist.

I'm Making Happy Memories

"Hobbema? Take the right elevator in the rear."

Footsteps echoing on marble, she started across a vast lobby, an enclosed inner courtyard where stained-glass windows filtered sunlight to mausoleum gloom, and spiraled porphyry pillars formed a colonnade around an empty stone basin, a fish pond without water or fish. Growing more depressed by the minute, she stepped into the rear elevator, where even the ancient elevator man looked embalmed and fit into the general funereal tone of the place. "Dr. Hobbema, please," she said flatly, and he took her up to the seventh floor, crashing open the gates and wordlessly pointing to the left-hand door of the two on that floor.

With a sinking heart she got out and stared at the little metal plaque above the bell, which said RING ME like some fey command straight out of *Alice in Wonderland*. Feeling just as disoriented and out-of-control as poor Alice, in her phase of shooting up-and-down in size, she rang the bell, then waited. Then rang again. And again. At last she heard the opening of some inner door, heard footsteps come to the door where she stood, then stop, and in the long pause that followed she realized she was being inspected through the peephole. Eyes lowered, nervous and self-conscious, she waited. Finally, after a series of metallic clicks and slidings of bolts, the door was opened by a tall, sturdy woman with a broad-planed pleasant face framed by a blond, old-fashioned Dutch bob, wearing a starched doctor's coat over worn shetland and tweed. "Mrs. Sohier?"

"Yes. . . . Dr. Hobbema?"

"Yes. Won't you come in, please?" The voice and manner were warm, but—and this made her even more nervous—the doctor didn't smile.

She hesitantly entered what seemed to be a very small waiting room, while behind her Dr. Hobbema relocked the door with the same rattles and clicks of bolts.

"Make yourself to home," Dr. Hobbema said folksily, finally faintly smiling and glancing at the incongruously dainty jeweled watch on her largeboned wrist. "You're a mite early—fifteen minutes, in fact," she said amiably, still smiling, and with a starchy rustle disappeared through a door on the opposite side of the tiny room. Another lock clicked.

Suddenly wildly nervous—she had been, she suddenly realized, stupidly calm until now—she sank into the nearest of two pale blue plastic chairs. Making no move to unbutton the trenchcoat she'd thrown on as protection against the sudden rawness in the air, she sat there trying to compose herself and catch her breath, a thousand questions jibbering in her head. Why the doctor's coat? Why all the locks? Did the coat impose a kind of professional authority, and the locks a soothing feeling of safety on the children who came? How did that peculiar apartment work? The small, *very* small—about 12 x 14—room she sat in, was strangely placed; several of their friends lived in old West Side buildings just like this, and the apartments invariably had long dark "foyers" leading from front door to living room, with many dim corridors branching off. Had the whole front hall been remodeled to create a tiny waiting room (which was beginning to give her acute claustrophobia), with an adjacent office or treatment room? Did Dr. Hobbema live in the rooms beyond these front two? What was that accent—Kansas? Iowa? The place was as still as a tomb—was it soundproofed? With a doorman and elevator man, why all the locks? To keep out cranks and nuts and hysterical mothers?

Hysterical mothers like herself. She was, she finally realized, in a state bordering on hysteria. What in God's name was she so frightened about? Or of? That nice pleasant woman? And why did her mind seem only capable of producing thoughts in the shape of questions?

Oh. Dear God.

To distract herself, she began minutely examining the room where she sat. Pale blue-sky walls that matched the plastic armchairs, a grass-green carpet (nature's soothing color scheme), an old-fashioned bentwood coat rack with a child's poplin jacket (could be either a girl's or boy's) hanging off one of the arms, two large armchairs with a lamp table next to each. Besides the lamps, the tables held stacks of magazines and groups of clay or ceramic objects made by childish hands (she could tell from the crude overlaps and thumbprints left in the hardened clay), all painted in bright colors and baked to a glaze in a kiln—bowls, pitchers, ashtrays, human figures, animals, agglutinated lumps. Hanging on the walls was still more work by childish hands: large brilliant pictures done in finger-paints, crayon, colored pencil, pastel.

Still not taking off her coat (and she was getting very warm), she reached out and picked up some of the artifacts on the table next to her —a bear, a bowl, a gorillalike hand making the peace sign, a lopsided ashtray—examining them, then setting them back down. Each had a name scratched into the clay while it had still been soft, with some sharp tool like an orange-stick. Getting more jittery by the second, she put down an ashtray which Carol Muntz had painstakingly signed on the rim, and got up to inspect all the other objects made by Childish Hands I Love in the room. Like the clay sculptures, every picture bore a name. Tracy Devlin. Margo Heddle. Peter Salkin. Emily Shoan. Lewis Tufts. Timothy Edelberg.

And Benjamin Sohier printed on what?

She immediately sat back down in the chair and snatched up a magazine. It turned out to be some children's magazine called *Happy Hours*, but she began reading it anyway. As she turned pages with a shaking hand, her stomach gave a faint troubled squerk, which was immediately followed by a volley of loud borborygmus yowls. She froze. What was that? Not hunger—she'd eaten lunch. A simple lunch, plain food, nothing to produce such ferocious complaints. As her stomach went on making the terrible noises, she tensed her stomach muscles and finally succeeded in silencing it. Which was very unpleasant, if not downright painful. But the moment she relaxed it began rumbling again. Was her crazy stomach going to make these awful sounds during her conference with Dr. Hobbema? As she considered the embarrassment, really humiliation, of that, she heard another small sound, one that wasn't produced by her hysterically protesting insides, thank heavens.

A funny tiny sound she couldn't make out at first. A faint vibrato. A tiddely pom. A tiddely pom. A thumpety pum from behind the far door. As if in response to it, her stomach gave a faint answering squawk. Painfully knotting her stomach muscles, trying to control and use them like someone in childbirth, she stared with disgust at her fingers, all smeared with colored inks from an illustration in *Happy Hours*. She threw down the magazine. As she dried and wiped her repulsively wet hands with some Kleenex from her purse—Dr. Hobbema struck her as the type to start an interview with handshake—another tum-piddy came from behind the closed door. Silence. Silence. Then tiddely pom. Tiddely pom. Thumpiddy *pum*. Picking up momentum and volume until there was no mistaking what it was: someone energetically bouncing a rubber ball.

A bit strange, she reflected, but probably part of the therapy, like all the clay sculptures and paintings. Minda had said it was a "dynamic" new concept of therapy—and this was "dynamic." Indeed.

The bouncing was steadily growing louder and more spirited. The far wall, clearly coincidental with some wall in the room beyond, was being used as a backboard of sorts. Was the inner room stripped of furniture, stripped for action and fitted out like a combination artist's studio-handball court?

She sat contemplating this rather unnerving possibility, realizing with relief that her stomach had quieted down, when the ball gave a rubbery, ricocheting double bounce, which was followed by a shriek of childish pleasure and a woman's chuckle, low and warm.

How . . . *sweet*. How touching. How dear. They're interrelating or whatever you call it—in this new and "dynamic" way.

No sooner had she told herself all this with a certain ferocity, than the bouncing, which had momentarily stopped, resumed. Starting with a first tentative tiddely pom, then quickly attaining a whamming rhythmic speed, the childish laughter and womanly chuckling making a background duet.

Clutching the arms of the chair as if it might fly out from under her, Emma shut her eyes and tried to make herself remember exactly why she was there. She tried to make herself think of the wall of shelves crammed with wires and electrical debris. Of Benjy fishing filthy electric gadgets from garbage cans. Of Benjy throwing his sheets down the incinerator chute. Of Benjy telling lies and being fractious at school and suddenly being friendless and suddenly being cold and hostile to herself. But it was no go. She couldn't seem to do it. Swamped by sentimental tenderness, all she could think of was Benjy, not the peculiar boy who had brought her to that room, but Benjy as a small child, a little boy—a totally happy little boy. Benjy standing in the doorway to pre-nursery school play group on his first day, confidently waving her off to graduate school, while all around him frightened children wept and had terror tantrums as their mothers tried to leave. Benjy, climbing into endless conveyances—buses, mini-buses, station wagons, cars which whisked him off to play groups, schools, day camps—so busy returning the joyous shouts that greeted him, he usually forgot to turn around and say good-by to her. Benjy, coming out of his room to see her the minute she got in from graduate school or the Child Guidance

Center or one of her Knickerbocker House projects—rushing up to kiss her while she dug in her purse for Milly Brundage's sitter fees, happy to see her and have her back in a pure and straightforward way, not harboring one ounce of hidden resentment about her having been gone for hours.

She had been, and had always been proud of it, the most casual of mothers, too casual according to many people, her mother-in-law included. But it had always seemed to work for them, he'd thrived on the setup they'd had until . . . until this summer. Even earlier, really. Until late spring. Early spring. Though she kept forgetting it, he'd acted very strangely when her mother died. *Very* strangely.

In her head something clicked like one of Dr. Hobbema's locks.

What was it she'd said off the top of her head to poor, overwrought Miss Tibbs way back on Friday? ". . . any disruption in the normal routine of a home, any sudden upheaval or disorder is bound to have some impact on a child—bound to create feelings of confusion and disorder *in* the child, which would naturally be reflected in his behavior." Quite a little mouthful, that. But right on the button, the way things said on the spur of the moment so often were. Excited, so pleased with herself she managed to overlook, again, exactly who was really the author of these "spontaneous" blinding insights, she went rushing on: the only thing wrong with what she'd said to Miss Tibbs was understatement. Chaos, not disorder. Chaotic was what the state of things at home had been, not disordered. For a long time now. And it was all very well to sit there, salving her conscience as always and telling herself that Benjy had done beautifully without her hovering over him like some anxious mother hen, telling herself he'd thrived on their casual routine, but the fact was things had gone way beyond that in the last year: "neglect," not "casual," was the right word to describe the treatment he'd gotten in the last year—a year when she had been almost totally absent, a year that had been Rough for her, but had undoubtedly been even Rougher for Benjy. A year which had begun for both of them when she'd plunged into the confusion of finding them a new apartment and getting them moved, had continued through the long ordeal of her mother's dying and the settling of her mother's affairs, and had probably climaxed in Roughness for Benjy when he'd come home from camp and found her gone, *really* gone this time, not to return for a month. A month when his only companions at home had been a grandmother he loathed, a father whose behavior was clearly beginning to make him edgy, and a complete stranger, Maria, whose behavior clearly made him a lot more than edgy.

From the inner room the sounds of the merry therapy grew louder, but Emma sat there, deaf to the sounds of ball-bouncing and laughter, flush with her sudden insights, something opening and bursting into bloom in her chest—like one of those bouquets of paper roses magicians create from cones of newspapers with the flick of a wrist. Yes. Oh, yes. Blind, selfish idiot that she'd been. Minda had been right that day in the playground—she *was* blind to what was going on right under her nose. Not because she'd been too preoccupied with her social work, as Minda had said, but because she'd been so busy worrying about the state of the world—worrying about whether or not the world was coming apart—she hadn't seen that her own little world was coming apart at the seams, hadn't seen something as obvious as what was happening to Benjy. The poor darling. The poor lamb. The poor baby. He didn't need a therapist. He needed a Mother. He needed . . . *her*.

She flew out of the chair, across the room, soundlessly turning locks and bolts, shutting the door on laughter and rubbery bouncing—and it was only when she stood in the blinding sunlight of West End Avenue, hailing a cab, that guilt hit her: shouldn't she at least have stayed to explain to Dr. Hobbema that she'd had a last-minute change of heart about the whole thing? No. *No.* She would call the minute she got home. If she was as nice and understanding as she seemed, Dr. Hobbema would certainly understand a change of heart . . . particularly when she made clear she had every intention of paying for the skipped hour.

Delighted with herself, she climbed into a cab. A block from home she got out at a sidewalk fruit-and-vegetable stand, paid the driver, bought a pumpkin as big as a volleyball and carried it, staggering, the block to her house.

"Going to make a Jack-o-lantern for the little marster?" said Fitzclarence as she tottered past him down the steps. Ignoring him (she had seen him spot her struggling down the street with the pumpkin, then seen him duck inside the glass doors), she wriggled one finger free and jabbed the elevator bell, and once upstairs, repeated the same procedure. After several minutes of ringing, she set the pumpkin on the dusty flowered carpet and let herself in with her own key.

It was only five to three, still too early for Benjy to be home, but where was Maria? Taking a bath again? She carried the pumpkin into the kitchen and set it on the formica table. The kitchen was clean and sunny and still, but a terrible smell—the same nasty, faintly-burny pungence of a week ago—hung in the air and seemed to be seeping through the crack under Maria's door, just like the last time.

Feeling she was reliving the whole idiotic episode—and hating it— she knocked on the door, calling, getting no answer. Though she remembered all too well what had happened last time, when she'd merely peeped into the room, fear of fire won out again: something was *definitely* burning in there this time. Turning the knob, she found the door unlocked, but something on the floor was caught under it, making it impossible to open it more than a crack. Crouching down, she inserted a groping hand and pushed what turned out to be a pomponned satin slipper to one side, while the smell rushed at her, sickening, overpowering, then stood up and opened the door.

Everything was the same as last week—the pulled shade, the crucifix gleaming on the wall—even the wildly disheveled unmade bed, she saw, snapping on the overhead light. The only new addition was the huge pottery ashtray on the floor next to the bed, a gaudily painted monstrosity Elsie had brought on one of her visits, gilt-lettered THE HAPPY HACIENDA MOTEL, ALBUQUERQUE, NEW MEXICO. Emma had banished it long ago to the top shelf of some cabinet, but here it was, resurrected by Maria, filled with what looked like charred twigs or scorched stubs of punk—the source of the foul smell. Gagging—it was re*volt*ing, burnt woodsy matter undercut by something vinegary and fetid—she was about to make sure that none of the charry stumps were still on fire, when she heard the distant scrabble of a key in the front-door lock.

She quickly snapped off the light and pulled the door shut, or as far shut as she could get it—the damned pomponned slipper got in the way —and managed to scuttle over to the table just as Maria came into the kitchen, wearing a hideous old black coat over her uniform and carrying one of the striped corner-drugstore bags.

"*Cielos*—how you fright me, *señora!*"

Fright herself—it had been a close shave—Emma forced a smile. "Sorry, Maria. I just got in myself. Were there any calls while I was out?"

"No. No call, *Señora* Soller. I have the terrible headache and go to the drugstore for the haspirin. Is only reason I go out."

"Goodness, you don't have to exp*lain*, Maria, you can go out any time you like. Only next time you need something like an aspirin, just go up front and help yourself to what you need from our medicine cabinets."

"I never goes in other peoples private places, *señora*," she said with a certain emphasis, and proceeded to her door, where after a long pause, she gave the wedged slipper a kick and went in, slamming the door behind her.

Feeling that she could do with an aspirin herself—terrible forky flickers were shooting through her head—Emma left the pumpkin where it was and went up front, where, after gulping down two aspirins, she phoned Dr. Hobbema.

"But I quite understand, Mrs. Sohier," the doctor said mildly, after listening to her excessively long and detailed explanation for leaving, and suddenly laughed: "In fact, that's happened many times. People seem to achieve sudden insights into their problems while sitting in my waiting room . . . but I never charge for that. I wouldn't think of accepting payment for the hour, Mrs. Sohier. And now . . ."

"But your time is valuable," Emma cut in protestingly, growing more confused and upset by the second. "I mean I tied up time you would have filled, and it's only right that I pay for it."

A sigh. "There are certain types of therapists who would insist on payment, Mrs. Sohier, but I'm not that type of therapist. Please don't give it another thought. And now, I'm sorry, but I really must go. Goodby. Good luck."

Good-by. Good luck. Feeling strangely shaken, almost bereft, Emma stood by the phone after hanging up. With each brief new contact, Dr. Hobbema seemed more wonderful. Maybe she'd made a terrible mistake. Maybe she should have stayed, if only to tell Dr. Hobbema the full story of her Rough Year and the effect she thought it had had on Benjy—if only to be reassured that she was right. Because that's what she'd *really* wanted, she saw now: she had wanted the doctor, after hearing just an abridged version of the story, to assure her she was right. Over the telephone.

Good-by. Good luck. Tough luck, Emma. She took off her coat and threw it on the bed: she'd made her decision and had to stand by it. As for Hobbema—she'd burned that bridge behind her—it was too late now for second thoughts, for doubts.

She saw by her bedside clock that it was a quarter past three. Benjy wouldn't be home for a good half hour. They hadn't carved a pumpkin since he was seven, but she still remembered how he hated the job of digging out the pulp, and decided to get it done ahead of time, leaving him the job he loved and was so good at—the drawing and carving of the Jack-o-lantern face.

She threw off what she'd decided was the very thing to wear for a visit to a child therapist—a drab knitted dress, the sort of thing she imagined suburban mothers wore to PTA meetings, the sort of thing she never wore any more—and climbed into some comfortable old jeans and a shirt. The kitchen was still deserted when she went back; Maria was still in her room, *gracias a Dios*. She set out a cutting board, carving knife, small paring knife, big ladling spoon, plastic garbage bag, then took a sponge and tried to scrub off the price—$4.87—that someone had stupidly scrawled across the pumpkin's only unflawed side with a greasy black crayon. As she futilely rubbed and scrubbed, Maria came out of her room, took a bag of peas from the icebox, a colander and bowl from a cabinet, and carried everything to the sink where she began shelling the peas.

Giving up on the smeary numbers, Emma decided to rush through the messy de-pulping fast, then move everything to some other room for the carving: Maria was giving off waves of hostility, as powerful and fumy as the smell of the charred stubs in her room. Though she was sure she knew why—yesterday, when Maria had come back from her weekend, she'd finally gotten up enough nerve to tell her about the party on Friday and tell her that Cora was coming to do the cooking—it was still unbearable. And she took up the carving knife and angrily sliced into the pumpkin about a fifth of the way down from the top, the force of the thrust briefly embedding the knife in the cutting board.

Meanwhile Maria stood at the sink, working off *her* anger by tearing at the pods, savagely shooting peas against the side of the stainless-steel bowl.

A charming situation, thought Emma, as she set the top of the pumpkin aside, and plunged the big spoon into the mulchy pulp. Digging as fast as she could, she planned a move to the dining room: she would cover the curly maple table with that big piece of oilcloth, left over from the days when Benjy did finger-painting in . . .

"I must say this, Mrs. Soller," Maria suddenly announced in a choky voice. "I tell you once before but I see it make no difference. Is no right you go into my room. As I say the other time, my room is my *dominio*, and no one else should come there. Is mine. Is *privado*. Is only right."

Leaving the spoon standing upright in the turgid muck, Emma brushed a strand of hair back from her suddenly flaming face and stared. "I'm sorry but that's not accurate, Maria," she finally said. "As *I* told *you* that other time, I didn't really go *into* your room, I merely opened the door and peeped in. Which is exactly what I did again today. And I only did it today because I smelled something burning in there, and was afraid a fire might be starting. The smell was definitely coming from your room. You didn't answer when I called, and I wanted to make sure you were all right. You could have taken sick or fallen asleep and left a cigarette burning, or lit a religious candle that toppled over.—I assure you that I have no interest in your room, Maria. I respect your right to privacy and never go into your room. Not even on weekends when you're not here."

Madness, she thought, hearing herself. *Madness.* What am I *doing* running on like this.

"I do no smoke and I never sleeps on the job," said Maria, viciously shooting peas at the side of the bowl in a rapid fusillade of pinging. "The only candle I ever light is in the *iglesia*, and I never get sick except every once the while the headache like today . . . but the headache is no what I call sick."

You notice how she hasn't offered one word of explanation about the smell of burning? thought Emma, grimly digging at the pumpkin again. She may only burn candles in *iglesia*—but what about those charred stubs in the ashtray? Then: To hell with the stubs—she's got to *go*.

Eerily, the moment she thought this, Maria did one of her unnerving schiz-y switches. After watching her dig at the pulp, she said sweetly, "Wot is that? We eat for dinner?"

"No, it's not for dinner. It's a pumpkin. Benjy likes to carve them. For Halloween," said Emma, barely able to speak, scooping out great gobbets of the stringy pulp and depositing them in the plastic bag.

"Harroween?"

"It's a holiday we have in this country. For children."

"Ah, *si*. Is when the witches fly and all the evil spirit coming out and running around. Is tomorrow this Harroween?"

"No. It's not until over a week from now," she said, noisily rattling the plastic bag, hoping a show of busyness would intimidate Maria and keep her from speaking any more—but no.

"It last until next week, that pumper? It no spoil before Harroween?"

"No, it probably won't last."

"Tcha. I see is very expensive that pumper. You no eat at all?"

"No, Maria."

With a rush of water, Maria rinsed the peas, then turned off the faucet with a loud squeak. "In my country I see children eating from the garbage can. Sometimes mens and women too."

Emma said nothing. There was nothing to say. She was always guiltily aware of the poverty in Colombia, of Maria's own poverty. Things like that ugly black coat she'd just had on (some castoff of the Generous and Aristocratic Mrs. Spratt?) were constantly reminding her of Maria's situation and had helped keep her tolerant. Until now. Now she said, "Excuse me, Maria, there's something I have to get up front," and rushed out.

Though this was true—she'd forgotten to put out a crayon to draw the face on the pumpkin—it could have waited until Benjy was home; she'd just had to get away from Maria for a few minutes. Where *was* Benjy? she wondered as she went into his room, which only got sun in the mornings and was depressingly dark now. Though the continuing heat-wave made it seem like some endless midsummer, the light had been failing earlier each afternoon; the days were getting shorter, winter would be coming on fast. The faster the better, she thought, and went into Benjy's bathroom to wash the pulp slime from her hands, pausing to stare for one long sobering moment at the huge bottle of formaldehyde under his sink.

Without turning on a light, she went back out and started searching through his desk for crayons, opening and shutting drawers where the contents were arranged with an almost fanatic neatness . . . in contrast to the bulging clutter of the shelves above her head. As she went through the desk, she was unpleasantly aware of the shelves hanging over her like some brooding presence, and at one point even shivered involuntarily: how she *hated* that damned thing. (She'd come to think of it in the collective singular, sometimes even calling it The Machine.) She finally found the crayons in a bottom drawer filled with beautifully ordered stacks of art supplies, and after selecting what looked like a dark brown one, stood up and glared at the packed shelves—at The Machine. What was it, and how did it fit into the revelation she'd had in Hobbema's waiting room? Why would missing her and needing her have made him start collecting all that awful junk?

Why indeed. Momentarily at an impasse, she finally sighed: she hadn't meant to assume that everything referred back to herself. It probably had nothing to do with her at all. It probably was some last assertion of childhood, of some childish belief in magic, she thought, not exactly sure of what she meant; she didn't think he expected all that junk to *do* something, perform in some way, but she was sure it must have some secret sort of significance for him, must stand for something. She hadn't the least idea of what the something could be—but maybe when she'd recovered lost ground, and they were back where they once had been, warm and close, he would tell her.

She went back to the kitchen, hoping to find Maria finished with the peas and gone, but, finished with the peas, Maria had created another job for herself, and stood at the sink vigorously polishing the copper bottoms of the Revere Ware pots—a thing Emma had specifically asked her not to do many times.

"Please, Mrs. Soller," said Maria, rubbing on swirls of Noxon as Emma defeatedly went back to finish de-pulping the pumpkin, "tomorrow you will put out all the silver and china and glass for the party and I will clean. At Mrs. Spratt *every*thing be done before the party—the tablecloth, the napkin, the window, the floor, the china, the silver. Everything shine like the diamant when the guest come."

"Thank you, Maria . . . it's very sweet of you to offer, but the only thing that needs polishing is the silver. We're a lot more casual about our entertaining than the Spratts . . . and we don't have their staff."

"Staff? You mean many *sirvientes*? Ha. Is me. I be the staff for the Spratt. I and this old man, Jorge, who drive the car and drink the Spratt whiskey and sleep the rest of the time. I do everything, even the shopping for the food."

"How did you manage all that by yourself, Maria. How wonderful you were able to do all that." Done. Triumphantly spooning the last of the pulp into the plastic bag, she quickly started cleaning up: *Now* she could move out of there.

"I manage because I never mind the work. I no like the other *criadas* in this country who afraid the work. And you say is wunnerful, but I never have the chance to show you just how wunnerful I be. You eat the plain food, the very strange food. You no run a fancy house. You no let me do things like the shopping—and now you have this party and you ask someone else to come and do the cook."

So she'd been right. It was the party. And Cora. Clutching a wad of old newspapers she'd just taken from the broom closet, she said: "Maria. Maria. I'm terribly sorry if I've hurt your feelings, but as I tried to explain yesterday, I've known Cora for years—*years*—and I have an obligation to her. I promised to let her do all our parties when she went into the catering business, and this is the first chance I've had for a long time. And as I also told you yesterday, I thought a dinner for ten people was just too much for you to handle alone."

"I sometime cook for sixteen at the Spratt. Twenty even. I cook *and* do the serve. Everybody say, Maria you just a marvel, a genius . . . and that be the true."

The true, thought Emma as she started to leave the kitchen with the newspapers, was that Mrs. Lewis T. Spratt had been a ruthless slave driver who had shamelessly taken advantage of this poor, misguided girl.

"Wot she cook this Cora?"

With a great reluctance, she paused in the doorway, but the sound of the front door slamming provided an escape from Friday's menu. "Benjy?" she called eagerly.

"Yah?"

"Come back here to the kitchen for a second, darling. I want to show you something."

". . . later, ma." A distant rattle of paper, the sound of a door closing.

Not looking at Maria (who she could feel looking at her with a burning interest), Emma went up front and knocked on Benjy's door, and when there was no answer, let herself in. The sound of running water came from the bathroom, on the bed lay a bag marked Hungermeyer's Hardware with two long wires spraying coppery filaments sticking out the bag's open end. Presently Benjy came out of the bathroom, patting some small piece of machinery dry with Kleenex; though he seemed less than overjoyed to see her, he gave her a jaunty grin and marched to his desk. She stared at the piece of junk he set on his blotter —it looked like some inner part of a radio—and said: "I guess you didn't hear me, Benjy. I wanted you to come see the pumpkin I bought. It's a beauty. I've got it all de-pulped. I've been waiting for you to come home and do the face. Where were you?"

"I dropped in at Hungermeyer's. Needed something, ma."

She watched him carefully move the radio innards to one side and heave his book bag onto the desk. "Well. I'm going to move everything into the living room. As soon as I'm set you can come carve it."

He turned and gave her one of those long gleaming looks through his glasses. "I'm sorry, ma, but I really don't have time. That ba . . . Mr. Fowler gave us a mountain of math homework."

"If you had so much homework, why did you go to Hungermeyer's?"

Another look, then he wearily pulled open the accordion top of the book bag and began unloading books and notebooks onto his desk.

"Benjamin. Do you mean to tell me you're not even going to come see the pumpkin? That you're not going to carve it?"

"I'm sorry, ma, but I guess that's just about the size of it."

"But . . . I bought it just for you."

"Why."

"Why what, Benjamin?"

"Why'd you buy it just for me?"

She stood blinking at this stranger, this owlish dwarf.

"What're you doing, ma?" Soft, very soft. In a grieving tone.

"Doing with *what?*"

"With . . . the pumpkin. The dogs. What's bugging you, ma?"

A good question, better than he could possibly dream but she stood there, stricken, longing to give him a clout that would have sent his glasses flying off his nose. "I will expect an apology, Benjamin," she finally said in a low, shaking voice, and went out, quietly shutting the door behind her.

She automatically started back toward the kitchen, then realized she was still clutching the old newspapers, and carried them into the living room, dumping them down on the corner coffee table. Shutting her eyes, she stood for several seconds with her fists pressed to either side of her head, which suddenly felt like one of those huge balls made out of layers of twisted rubber bands. Anger, a terrible despairing anger at herself and her son, made it impossible to think. Then as she felt a rushing return of some of the anemic symptoms that had been gone for days, she opened her eyes and grimly marched to the kitchen where Maria, through with the pots, now stood scrubbing potatoes at the sink. She could feel Maria watching her gather up the pumpkin and the small tools, but Maria made no comment . . . luckily for her. Carrying everything into the living-room corner, and setting it all on the floor, she spread the Sunday *Times* real estate section over the glass coffee table. Then, setting the pumpkin smack in the middle of an article titled "The Frightened Flight to the Suburbs and Back Again," she sat down cross-legged on the floor and began drawing a face on the pumpkin with stiff, clumsy fingers. From a great distance she heard the telephone ring, but she doggedly kept drawing, then drew back to view her handiwork: a hideous, snaggle-toothed gargoyle face.

"Señora . . . is telephone."

Looking up, she blinked at Maria, who stood in the doorway blinking at her on the floor. "Who is it? D'you know, Maria?"

"Is same *señora* who always call. You want I should tell her you busy?"

"No, thanks, Maria. I'll take it out in the hall."

"I couldn't call yesterday," said Minda as Maria clattered down the kitchen extension, "but I've just been *dying* to talk to you. How was your weekend?"

"All right." Which was true: though it seemed a thousand light years away, the weekend had been surprisingly all right. "How was yours?"

"Fabulous. With the best part being I think I got a maid. Selma has this Finnish marvel named Inga who takes care of her kids and took the twins off my hands all weekend—and Inga has a cousin she thinks might be interested in working for me. The cousin's coming here at five today for an interview, and I've got every finger crossed. Just think, if it works out I can start *living* again.—But another marvelous thing that happened was that we rented a house up there."

"Rented a house for the winter?" Dully.

"Winter weekends. A two-day escape hatch from this town. A place to go on holidays like Thanksgiving and Christmas and New Year's Eve. It's only a two-hour ride and it's absolutely gorgeous up there, another world. Autumn leaves and log fires, all that. You'll see—as soon as we get settled you'll be our first weekend guests. You can even bring Benjy, and if this cousin of Inga's . . . oh God. Benjy. I completely forgot. I've been so excited, so *up* for a change, I completely forgot all the awful things happening to you. How's Benjy's throat. And what did Hobbema say?"

"Benjy's fine. He went back to school."

"And Hobbema? What about her?"

"I didn't call."

"You didn't? Why *not?*"

"I decided I didn't want to start all that." Pause. "I decided I could handle what was wrong."

Pause. "Oh, Em. I think you're making a terrible mistake."

"It all depends on your point of view. In any case, I can't go into it now."

"Oh. You mean Benjy's around. I *thought* you sounded peculiar."

"Yes."

"Well, I won't try to find out any more now. —Is anything else wrong aside from Benjy's being there? I mean you sound pretty strange."

"No. Nothing's wrong. Everything's fine. Just great."

"Ha. Some great. Well, I'd love to call back later and hear more, but after the interview with Inga's cousin, I'm rushing off to meet Peter—I've got a sitter coming—at a promotion party for some Italian fag designer. Oh God, Em. The creeps we have to see. I can't *tell* you how much I'm looking forward to your party Friday, to seeing some civilized human beings for a change. I want to talk about what to wear, but I'll have to get back to you, though maybe not for days. If the cousin takes the job, I'll hang around long enough to break her in, then take off—I've a ton of back errands to catch up on. But before I go . . . are you *sure* you're all right? I don't like the way you sound at all."

"Yes, I'm all right. Never better. Splendid. Good luck with the maid."

Hanging up, she stared at herself in the little mirror fastened to one of the bookshelf dividers above the console: the twin sister of the pumpkin-goblin sitting inside on the coffee table.

Returning to this piece of art work, she picked up the paring knife and began to carve it with short, savage thrusts of the blade. Just who was she carving up? she wondered, aware of a pleasant sense of release. The possibilities were endless, ranging from herself and Minda to her dear mother-in-law, the true author, she now belatedly realized, of all those blinding Insights and Revelations she'd had about Benjy in Hobbema's waiting room. That brilliant bit of Instant Child Psychology she'd snowed poor Miss Tibbs with—lifted, gratis, from Elsie's memorable letter to her in the hospital, merely inverted. Chalk up another one for Elsie. Bitterly smiling, she continued to cut up the thick orange rind, only glancingly considering her son, focusing on herself: wrong again, Emma. Wrong and fatuous beyond belief. God only knew what was the matter with Benjy or what he needed—but *she* certainly wasn't what he needed. On the other hand, maybe she was what was the matter with him. In which case *she* needed a therapist—not him.

As she carved out the precise triangle of a nose, she considered this with surprising calm. Did Dr. Hobbema ever take adult patients? If not, maybe she could still just go there and talk for a few sessions. Maybe Dr. Hobbema could be persuaded to let her come by a few times, between the hours when children kneaded clay and splashed paint and bounced balls, and after letting her talk, could maybe help her sort it all out—help her to understand something as basic as why she kept shifting the focus of her attention from her own little troubled world to the big troubled World at large.

Strange. Either just through thinking about Hobbema (who, given their brief exchanges, she knew she was idealizing into some totally unreal tower of Wisdom and Kindness and Strength), or by unconsciously practicing some version of Hobbema's "dynamic" new therapy —those ferocious thrusts of the knife—she had somehow managed to quiet herself. The raging anger had died away, the rubber-band tension was gone from her head. She considered the pumpkin: she had finished the eyes and nose, and just started on the tricky job of the teeth. "Dynamic" therapy or whatever, she was, she realized with surprise, enjoying herself. Which, in view of everything that had been going on, was no mean feat. And deciding to keep on until she'd finished, she began cutting into the rind, slowly, taking more care— when the front door suddenly slammed and there was a muted jangle of pocketed keys.

Damn. Harold. Home early again. But really early, since it was only about twenty to five. What was it this time? Another call from Elsie, reporting Maria had called her aunt Constanza to beef about Friday's party? Something alarming he'd read in *Merck*? It hardly mattered. What mattered was that he was *there*, long before she'd expected him, about to find her doing what she was doing. And guessing what his reaction to this might be, she decided not to call out and let him know where she was: hidden as she was by the corner wall, he couldn't see her. Knife poised, she listened as he went up to their room with a heavy step, heard him call her name, then heard him come out and tap on Benjy's door, going in at some muffled response, shutting the door behind him. As she absently stuck the knife back into the yellow rind, and carved out a little wedge between the snaggle teeth and laid it on the *Times*, she heard muffled voices, the sound of Benjy's door opening and shutting, heavy footsteps advancing down the hall. Silent, impassive, she watched him whisk past the open end of the room and start through the dining room toward the kitchen, obviously looking for her—and, bracing herself, finally called out, "Harold? I'm in here."

He turned and came into the living room where she sat on the floor, paring knife in hand. Yes. Just what she'd expected. Pale, bewildered, he stopped and stared at the pumpkin, sitting in its litter of neat little geometric rind cutouts, then came over and bent down to kiss her cheek. He smelled just like he looked—weary, stale.

"Why are you home so early?" she asked brightly, deciding to take the initiative and try and forestall things she could feel rushing her way like a roaring express train—things, she suddenly sensed, that were going to be a lot worse than having to explain what she was doing sitting on the floor carving a pumpkin.

"I didn't feel well, so I left the office early. I've had a perfectly lousy day—one of the more charming high spots being my lunch with Scrim."

Scrim—Harley Scrim—was the prize possession of Phaedre Press, the only author Harold still worked with himself. "What happened with Scrim?" she asked, thinking she might be spared after all. "Is he leaving Phaedre Press?"

"No. Nothing like that, thank God. Scrim wasn't really even actively involved. It wasn't anything he said or did. It was the husband of that pal of yours."

"I'm afraid you've lost me, Harold."

"Hinda whatever's husband."

"Peter Wolfe? How could he spoil your lunch when you've never even met him?"

"A mere bagatelle to that pushy prick. Scrim and I were having this very important private conversation about his new book—Bruno had purposely given me an isolated table so nobody could eavesdrop—when I suddenly looked up and saw this creep standing over our table, wearing this shit-eating grin. 'Ex*cuse* me, but I heard Bruno mention your name, and I thought it was high time we met, seeing that our wives spend half the day on the phone together,' he said, and proceeded to introduce himself. But after I'd pulled myself together and made the proper noises, he didn't go away but just stood there, waiting for me to introduce him to Scrim. What he'd really come over for and which I wasn't about to do. But that didn't faze him. He just turned to Scrim and started oozing all this crapola about being one of Scrim's biggest fans, and his waiting 'breathlessly'—I swear to God, 'breathlessly'—for the next masterpiece. It was unbel*ie*vable. Finally, he must've seen the looks on our faces, because he started laughing. Nice recovery. I'll give him that. 'Well, it's been terrific talking to you boys. Guess I'll see you Friday, Hal—hear you're giving quite a little shindig,' and with that took off and joined some other creep who'd been waiting for him up by the door. Who he'd obviously been trying to impress by knowing Scrim."

She sat blinking at him, not sure which was more "unbel*ie*vable"— the way poor Peter Wolfe had been treated, or this newest revelation about her husband's Rational nature. "I'm afraid I don't understand what's got you so upset," she finally said. "D'you mean to tell me that dumb little episode is what spoiled your lunch—and ruined the rest of your day?"

His face was swollen, livid. "What's got me so upset is that he's a vulgar, pushy slob, and I don't understand why I have to have a pig like that shoving his way into my life—particularly at *this* time of my life. What's got me so upset is your getting so chummy with that idiot wife of his, who I gather's even more disgusting than he is. What's got me so *upset* is not being able to understand a goddamn thing that's going on around here any more. Like, for example, what you're doing sitting on the floor, sitting and carving some stupid pumpkin for Chrissake— and what my son's doing, sitting alone in his room and crying *while* you're in here on the floor. Why shouldn't I be upset? What the hell's going *on* around here?"

"Stop shouting, Harold.—Crying, did you say?"

"Yes, crying. Not bawling. But his cheeks were wet. He kept his face turned away, but I could still see . . . sit *down*, Emma. Don't you dare go in there. Leave that kid alone, let him hang onto *some* shred of dignity. You stay where you are and tell me what the hell this is all about. Why's he crying? You two have a fight?"

She tightened her grip on the paring knife. "No. We didn't have a fight. We just had a little misunderstanding about carving the pumpkin."

"Ah, yes. Carving the pumpkin. I see." Caricaturing fascination, he studied the pumpkin sitting on the littered newspapers, then lifted slitted eyes to her face: "What are you doing, Em?" Pitying, soft. It was like hearing a replay of a recording.

She felt a terrible chill. "Just what it looks like. Carving a pumpkin."

"Yes. But why?"

"Because," she said slowly through her teeth, "I've always *loved* Halloween, that's why. Because I loved building bonfires and roasting mickies and carving pumpkins when I was a little girl. Because Benjy always loved it too, and I thought it would be fun to make a Jack-o-lantern together again."

"Ah. I see."

She stood up, dropping the knife on the coffee table with a loud clatter. "I don't know what it is you think you 'see,' but we'd better finish this conversation up in our room. Behind a closed door."

Too late. As she strode from the room and turned up the hall, she was sure she heard another door hastily closing. Benjy's. Dangerously close to tears herself, she wondered if he'd stopped crying, wondered how much of that exchange he'd heard and if she shouldn't go in and see him, but made herself keep on going to their room, with Harold close behind her. As he shut the door, she sat down on the end of the bed: she hadn't felt this weak since leaving the hospital. Looking as drained and exhausted as she felt, Harold collapsed in the armchair. "Now," she said, shivering. "Now it's my turn. What the hell is going on? Just what the hell are *you* doing, Harold? What are all those snide questions and innuendos?"

"They're not snide and they're not innuendos. All I'm trying to do is find a way of saying something without hurting you, but I'll stop beating around the bush and come right out with it: I think this family is falling apart—*has* fallen apart. And I can't stand it. We used to be so happy . . . and it's like a nightmare now."

"And I'm responsible. Is that what you're trying to say?"

"Getting angry will get us exactly nowhere, Em. I love you and I love our life—at least I loved our life the way it was, but it's changed. No, I don't think you're solely responsible for its changing—but I do think you've been behaving in a way that has *some*thing to do with all the changes around here."

"I can't imagine what you're driving at, but may I remind you that I've recently been sick. That I've just been through what you keep calling a 'rough year'—and that anything different or odd about my behavior is a direct result of that fucking, lousy year."

"You don't have to remind me. And you don't have to use foul language. I know better than anyone that you've been through absolute hell, Em, and my heart goes out to you. And what you just said is absolutely right. Only the one thing that really affected you most during that year, the thing that had the most damaging effect on you—is something you can't even bring yourself to face."

"Stop talking in ellipses, Harold. Spit it out."

"You . . . won't like it."

Amazing the way everyone was cribbing everyone else's lines. With just the same relishing air of anticipation, Minda had said exactly the same thing to her on Friday before bringing down the ax—or what Minda had thought would be the ax, but had turned out to be something totally ludicrous. And the chances were this would be just as ludicrous, if not more so. "I don't like it already, so you might as well just get it *out*, dammit."

"Flying off the handle isn't going to help matters, as I said . . . but then, your anger is really just a sign of how deep the problem goes."

"Problem. *What* problem? Jesus Christ."

"Please keep your voice down. And please try to get ahold of yourself. I'm only terribly concerned about you and trying to help you . . . not attacking you, as you seem to think. Okay then: the problem. The problem is unresolved guilt about your mother's death. Ever since she died you've been struggling with a colossal load of guilt—guilt you don't actually even know you feel, on a conscious level. But it's there, all right all righty, and I happen to think that it's not only what's made you so strange and made you do strange things—but it's also the thing that undermined your health by eating away at you, lowering your resistance and leaving you wide open to whatever bug it was that caused your FUO. They haven't gotten too far in the field of psychogenic disorders, but every doctor's files are packed with case histories where the mind has affected the body, indirectly causing . . . what's that you said?"

Since what she'd said didn't bear repeating, she mumbled, low, "I said I couldn't decide who you were trying to be—Freud or Osler."

"What? I still can't hear a word you're saying. Speak up."

"One minute you tell me to keep my voice down, the next to speak up. Make up your mind. I *said,*" she went on, lying again, worn down, "you'd better tell me what this great guilt is supposed to be about."

"Oh I'll tell you. I'm only too *happy* to tell you. Guilt about your real feelings for your mother. Guilt about the way she died. About some of the circumstances surrounding her death. If you remember—or maybe you've repressed it—on the day she died you carried on like a *mad*woman about her drug dose and practically accused some of the nurses of swiping her drugs."

Emma leaned forward, gripping the edge of the bed.

"D'you remember all that?—Just what do you think that was?"

"I loved my mother." Hoarse. Slurred.

A glinty ironic stare.

"I loved my mother. And she died a horrible death. In unspeakable agony."

"She was *not* in agony when she died. I happened to be there when she died, and you weren't. Or have you repressed that little detail just like you've managed to repress practically everything else?"

She sat shivering, trying to swallow.

"And you didn't love her. You wanted to love her and tried to love her, though God only knows why—but you *hated* her. With damned good reason. She was a castrating bitch, who cut your poor father's nuts off and finally drove him to drink himself to death."

"You. You don't know what you're talking about. My father drank all his life. But when he lost his job at the university it broke his heart. My mother didn't do that to him. Joseph McCarthy did."

"That's a lot of melodramatic *crap!* Lots of men got blacklisted and still had enough guts to go on and survive. But she'd battered him down to a pulp long before that—and losing his job was just the *coup de grâce*. God. It makes my blood run cold just imagining what that poor guy must've gone through, and what you must've gone through as a child. I've always felt it was proof of your terrific strength that you'd managed to come out of that relatively unscathed. But now she's finally gotten at you anyway. Finally did it by dying, the bitch—and screw that business about not speaking ill of the dead: she was a *bitch*. And I just can't take it any more—can't stand around watching you punish yourself, keeping my mouth shut." He moved his head ponderously from side to side: "You didn't kill her, Em. Cancer did."

Was he really saying all this?

"Don't look like that, Em. I'm only telling you these things because I love you, *love* you, don't you understand . . . and can't stand seeing you flagellate yourself. I love you and love the life we've had together all these years. We've got the only happy marriage I know of, and . . . what did you say?"

"I said what took you so long to speak up? You've obviously had all this figured out for months, so why didn't you come out with it before now?"

"I was afraid of upsetting the delicate balance, triggering off something maybe even worse. You've built up such elaborate defenses, I thought it might be dangerous to try to get through them, might blow up the whole shooting match. I'd even begun to think that maybe you ought to go and see a shrink, but I'm still not sure that would be the answer. You're the strongest woman I know—and maybe all you've needed was someone to level with you, make you see what you've been doing and help get you back on the right track."

"Why would I need a shrink when I've got one right here in my own house?"

"Don't stoop, Em—it isn't like you. I guess you'd do anything rather than face the truth, but I've got news for you: you've damned well *got* to face it. You're not living in a vacuum, you know—you have a responsibility to the other members of this family. You're not the only one who's been having a bad time, we've all been affected by what you've been going through. These things rub off. And I'll tell you something else: I think all those not-so-secret conflicts of yours have a lot to do with how peculiar that poor kid of ours has gotten."

She stood up. "He's not a 'poor kid,' and he's not so peculiar. And I'll tell *you* something: if he *is* at all peculiar, maybe it just comes from having a father who's so afraid of germs he takes a bath in Phisohex every other second . . . who's some kind of a hypochondriacal nut."

They glared at each other, and for one second Harold's face hung naked, pale. Then he said, almost whispering, "Listen to us, my God, *listen* to us—snarling and tearing at each other just like everybody else." Then, as she started for the door, louder, on a rising note: "You won't face it, will you—there you go, running away again. Come *back* here, Emma, I haven't finished, I have more to say. You can't keep on running, you've got to face things *now*."

Hand on the doorknob, she turned. "I faced what I had to six months ago. And I'm not running away—I'm just going to get a drink. I *need* a drink. And I don't want to hear anything else you've got to say. You've already said enough. And you don't know what you're talking about." She opened the door and stepped into the hall, softly adding, "You've just got things reversed."

No ice in the bucket as usual. Pouring some whiskey into a glass, she began nursingly sipping it like brandy, when she suddenly realized the pumpkin was gone from the coffee table. In the same instant, Benjy came in carrying it in his arms. His face pale and sternly forbidding, he marched to the coffee table and set it down with the carved side turned toward her: with just a few expert thrusts of the knife, he'd managed to transform the evil-looking goblin into a normal Jack-o-lantern—wearing a wide and soppy grin. Wordlessly turning, he got halfway to the door, then stopped and swung back around. His face suddenly alight, he gave her a grin matching the pumpkin's, gave her the peace sign—then went up the hall to his room.

"Spring is like a perhaps hand"

A MAY MONDAY 2:20 P.M.

Holding the bunch of violets she'd bought off a street vendor's cart, Emma walked down the hall toward her mother's room, brightening at the sight of the open door: maybe her mother was having a good day —for a change. As she passed the desk, she smiled at Miss Bruce, the pleasant charge nurse, then turned into her mother's room, stopping just over the threshold and staring through a gap in the door's inner curtains, pulled for privacy:

Propped up by pillows, steadied by the nurse's hand, her mother was having her hair—or what had been her hair—brushed by Miss Moody, her private-duty nurse. Miss Moody, an Australian, was a plump blond woman who wore too much makeup, and wore, even though it was no longer required, the frilly cap of her nursing school atop her old-fashioned pageboy with the air of a duchess sporting a coronet. Miss Moody normally worked the day shift, from eight to four, but for the last two days, when they hadn't been able to find a nurse for the four-to-midnight shift, she had heroically worked both shifts, making a total of sixteen hours. Which was her style. Skilled, selfless, dedicated—a paragon of a nurse, in short—Miss Moody was revered by the whole hospital staff. Withal, Emma detested her.

"There you are, dear girl," the nurse now crooned, vigorously wielding a stiff-bristled brush, merely displacing lank gray wisps on the pink scalp. "You're certainly looking fine today. And high time, Iris says." With that, Iris took away her supporting hand, and while the head lolled to one side, put down the hairbrush on the bedside table and plucked a Q-Tip from a tiny phial of oil. "This'll make you feel better too," she said, plunging the oil-soaked cotton swab into a pinched nostril; "this'll soften those nahsty crusts and let you breathe."

As the tip went into the other nostril, the mouth beneath it fell slackly open, a faint sound came out.

"Trying to thank me, are ye? Well, you're welcome, I'm sure. Iris does the best she can."

With a loud clacket of curtain rings, Emma pushed into the room, and the heavily powdered face swung her way.

"Well naow, just look who's here on this lovely spring day! It's your charmin' little girl, looking like the breath o' herself in a sweater the color of daffodils."

"Hullo, Miss Moody," Emma said coldly, and went to the bed, where because of the raised sidebars, she had to stand on tiptoe to get at her mother's cheek. "Hello, Mommy darling," she said, kissing the sunken cheek, sickened by the reek of baby oil and some other strange yeasty smell. "How are you feeling today?"

Her answer: a blink from milky unfocused eyes.

"For shame!" scolded Miss Moody from the far side of the bed. "Aren't you going to say hello to your little girl? Why, look. She's even brought some vilets—surest sign of spring."

The gray eyes widened with some tremendous effort, then snapped shut.

"She's a mite temperamental just now," the nurse confided across a body that outlined itself under the sheets in the wrong way—swelling in the middle, sinking in concavely on top. "They oftimes do that. Take on. Get angry at the teensiest things."

"What's she angry at?" asked Emma, so angry herself she could barely speak.

"Being put on the throne. I had her on it for twenty minutes before you came. But to no avail. Still, I had to try. S'crucial to try to keep things moving along by themselves. All that morphine tends to bind up things."

"She can hear every word we're saying, Miss Moody," Emma finally burst out, unable to control herself. Her face burning, she quickly pulled a chair alongside the bed and sat down, taking care not to look at the nurse. As she shifted the violets from hand to hand, slipping her arms out of her trenchcoat and letting it fall over the back of the chair, a whiff of terrible animosity and terrible lavender cologne drifted across the bed.

"Are you planning to stay long, Mrs. Sawyer?"

"An hour or so. It depends."

Miss Moody pointedly did not ask what depended on what. "Well then, long's you're here," she said, busily gathering up a pink cardigan and large white plastic purse from the chair in the far corner, "I think

I'll run downstairs for a cup of tea—I had an early lunch—and give you a chance for a little visit with your ma. Though it won't be much of a visit, I'm afraid—she's just had her medication, and seems to be going off."

Emma watched her throw the pink cardigan jauntily about her shoulders, and found she couldn't keep still. "I'm sorry, Miss Moody, but I don't understand. If she just had her medication . . . why were you brushing her hair?"

Miss Moody stopped in front of the bureau: behind black-framed harlequin glasses, lids tinted a delicate blue descended, making slits of eyes which shone yellow-ly, like a cat's. "Yes. I would say that's rait, Mrs. Sawyer. You don't understand." The voice was calm, measured. "Your mother was a bit restive after her shot—they sometimes have a reaction like that until the medication takes hold, and need some smoothing down. She likes to have her hair brushed, your mother does. It cheers her up to primp a bit. You see, in spite of how it mait seem to you, Mrs. Sawyer, she's still very particular about the way she looks."

With an angry squeak of gumsoles and a whoosh of cretonne curtains, she sailed past Emma, out of the room.

You deserved that, Emma told herself, trying to make herself feel guilty, but not succeeding. The nurse, she knew, was only doing her job, and what's more was doing it brilliantly—Eliot Barney, her mother's doctor, continually told her that Miss Moody was one of the best private-duty nurses in the city, and with the nurse shortage being as acute as it was, they were incredibly lucky to have her on the case. But in spite of knowing all this, and constantly reminding herself of it, she still couldn't control a deep, visceral aversion to the woman, which had sprung up the minute she'd met her and grown steadily worse in the eight days she had been on the case. It had gotten so bad in the last few days, she could hardly stand being in the room when the nurse was there. And she was always there, always remained in the room during her visits, sitting and reading or knitting in the far corner like some fat white toad, while Emma sat silently raging and grieving on a chair next to her mother's bed.

Which made today a lucky break. And finally realizing that she was still clutching the violets, she got up and went around to the bedside table where a pitcher of water and two tumblers stood. She put down the violets and was reaching for one of the tumblers to use it as a bud vase, when she saw that her mother had rolled around to face her on the pillow, and was staring at her with wide eyes. For one long second the eyes—bright and lucid with recognition, shining with fierce intelligence—fixed her compellingly, then suddenly clouded, the eyelids drooping sleepily.

Unnerved—her mother had seemed to be asking something—she moved close to the bed and reached over the bars to pat one of the bony hands on the coverlet. "Yes, it's me. Go to sleep, Mommy darling. Emma's here to stay with you."

In response to this nursery incantation, the eyelids fluttered, then closed all the way; docile as a child, her mother went off to sleep.

Afraid to take away her hand or make any other sudden movement that might disturb that sleep, she stayed where she was, her hand covering what felt like a bundle of twigs. As she stood there, she slowly, unwillingly, looked down at the face where blue-veined yellow skin, as transparent and vulnerable as a baby bird's, stuck too tightly to temple and cheekbone and jaw—and finally shuddered convulsively. Not because she was remembering how that face had been just a few weeks before, or was marking the newest ravages of the disease—but because, while staring at it, she really wasn't seeing that face at all, was seeing something even worse, something more horrible. Something she "saw" for split seconds every time she was confronted with her mother—a set of morbid and hideously graphic images produced by her own mind. Her own *sick* mind. But no matter what she called herself, no matter how savagely she attacked herself, no matter how hard she tried—she couldn't stop the awful flow of images from coming. Couldn't stop this terrible thing that happened for brief moments each time she visited her mother and had begun happening the first time she had seen her mother right after being told she was going to die.

She had been told the news by Dr. Eliot Barney, a total stranger. Old Dr. Wolsey, the Connecticut doctor who had taken care of her mother for thirty years, had retired in December, and in early March, her mother, who hadn't been feeling well for months, had come down to see Eliot Barney in New York, on the recommendation of a friend. After a complete checkup, Dr. Barney had sent her mother to the hospital for some tests. On the same day her mother returned to Connecticut, Dr. Barney phoned Emma and asked her to come to his office for a talk—that afternoon if possible. Emma went, and without any hedging Dr. Barney told her that her mother had a "widely metastasized" carcinoma of the pancreas and had, at most, a month to live. (As it happened, he was wrong: by that May day she had already lived two.) He also told Emma that the decision about whether or not her mother was to be told the truth was in her hands: because he was a relative stranger, who scarcely knew her mother, he wasn't in any position to advise her, and though her mother struck him as being an unusually strong and probably courageous woman—she, being an only child, was the one who knew her mother best and would know what was best for her. As it happened, Dr. Barney was wrong again—she'd never really known her mother or ever remotely known what was "best" for her. But stunned by the news, almost buckling under the burden of grief and responsibility suddenly thrust on her shoulders, Emma went home, and after two anguished days of indecision (when she asked no one, not even Harold, for advice), decided that her mother shouldn't be told the truth. Because Dr. Barney had been right about one thing: her mother *was* a strong woman, stronger than he dreamed—a woman whose contempt for weakness and helplessness and dependency was so great, Emma was afraid she would kill herself if she was told the truth.

Dr. Barney accepted her decision without question and phoned her mother in Connecticut with a covering story: the tests revealed that she had a "mild pancreatitis," he explained, and prescribed some "medicine" that he said would take care of it—the first and mildest of the long succession of painkillers she would eventually receive. And on a sleety March day, two days after Barney's call to her mother, Emma drove up to Connecticut to see her. Halfway up on the treacherously slippery parkway, she belatedly realized her visit was probably stupid and risky —it might make her mother very suspicious—but she kept on going. She had an overwhelming need to see her mother. It was as simple as that. And as it turned out, she needn't have worried about giving anything away. Exasperated, as always, to have her painting hours interrupted, her mother hadn't hesitated to let her know just how exasperated she was. As always.

"I really can't *imagine* why you dragged yourself up here in this weather," her mother said testily. "The pills have helped me tremendously, I feel much better. I feel fine, in fact." And she in fact looked fine. And as she continued to fume and fuss at Emma, while she poured them some sherry and they moved into the living room, Emma had to remind herself not to be upset by her mother's nastiness, had to remind herself why she was there. But not for long. Once settled into her favorite crewelwork wing chair (her favorite reading place as a child), facing her mother on the couch across the room, she soon stopped having to remind herself why she was there—soon had something far worse than her mother's carping to be upset about. Because as she sat there, sipping sherry, listening to her mother complain about the recession and the terrible market for her antiques and paintings (she painted remarkable reproductions of American Primitive portraits and still lives, which she sold to decorators for a great deal of money), the horrible thing began. Unspeakably horrible. Because sitting there and staring at her mother, who looked the same as always—handsome, well-groomed, even healthy—she gradually stopped seeing that face with its good bones and broad brow under center-parted hair, stopped seeing the trim body her mother had always prided herself on, and instead, as though given X-ray vision, given eyes that could penetrate the smooth envelope of covering flesh, began to "see" the burgeoning horror, the disease at work within. Began to "see" monstrous images of teeming, swarming cell life, cells run amok: cells widely proliferating and expanding, cells piling themselves into microscopic towers and pinnacles like autonomous sand-castles building themselves, cells swelling and looming and bulging and finally bursting into bloom—like those buds in multiexposure nature films that exploded into flowers under one's eyes. . . .

Asking her mother to excuse her for a minute, she went upstairs and was violently sick in her old bathroom, which was luckily well out of earshot under the eaves. "Cancer," she whispered aloud to the sloping walls, still covered with the same daisy-patterned paper that had been there for fifteen years. "Cancer," she whispered again, giving a name to her terror, trying to make the demon audible—in the same way she had just tried to make it visible downstairs. Because that's all the hideous images were, she soothingly told herself: a reaction of pure and primitive terror to the dread disease. And somewhat calmed and fortified by this oversimplified explanation, she washed her face and rinsed her mouth and went back downstairs to stay another half hour—without the frightening images coming back.

They came back again for seconds the next time she saw her mother, and each time she saw her mother after that. Just seconds, but that was enough. She couldn't stop them. Though they never upset her as violently as that first time in Connecticut, they always made her sick and ashamed—ashamed, because she was sure that other people, forced to watch someone they loved die of cancer, behaved more rationally, handled the grief and fear and recoil from ugliness in some superior way. (All her life she'd been convinced that "other people" knew some secret code of Ideal Behavior she'd never learned, would never know.) But love was the important word. The key word. And as the terrible images continued, and her mother slowly continued to die under her eyes, she stopped being so hard on herself. There was something far more important than the demonology of cancer at work here: she cared more deeply for her mother than she had ever dreamed. Loved her, to be exact. Yes. Loved her. Amazingly enough. For most of her life, having only focused on that cold, arrogant woman who had never given her the affection and approval she craved—that mother she thought she hated—it now turned out she'd been shortsighted, been wrong. She loved her. And admired her. And was deeply grateful to her: when her poor, dear, weak father had died, leaving no money, her mother had rallied and supported them both, and if she hadn't given her the warmth and approval and understanding she'd so desperately wanted, her mother had given her everything else—schools, trips, comforts, luxuries. A life. A woman who had been cold and narrow and often terribly cruel, yes—but who had also been resourceful and generous and courageous and strong. And standing helplessly by and watching her suffer and die was more than Emma could bear. It was as simple as that.

By now the gruesome images had receded, as always, and she only saw her mother's face. The face her mother had been so proud of, playing up its resemblance to the Duchess of Windsor's for all it was worth, but which now, stripped to the bony essentials of heredity, was the face of some remote, unknown Jewish-Hungarian ancestor. Her poor, driven, tormented mother. In these last days, did she see that Magyar-muzhik staring back at her when Moody held a hand mirror up to her face?

With a racking sigh, she finally lifted her hand off her mother's: asleep. Not even wanting to risk waking her with just the sound of pouring water, she left the violets lying on the bedside table and turned to the open window behind her for a breath of air: the room was full of sickening, cloying smells—the baby oil used on the Q-Tip, a wilting bunch of three-day-old freesia, the aftermath of Miss Moody's lavender cologne.

Outside, across the river in Long Island City, smoke rose from industrial smokestacks in thin, unbroken threads to the upper sky, where it diffused into a haze—a polluting haze, she thought cryptically. Sun shone brassily on the river, and twenty-two stories down an invisible dog barked, the sound carrying clearly on the newly softened air. Trees along the sidewalks were covered with yellow-green furze, and the cretonne curtains hanging on either side of her puffed and belled in a faint wind. Spring. Spring had sneaked in without her noticing it.

Ever since she'd been a child in Connecticut, she'd loved watching the change of seasons, her favorite being the shift from late winter to early spring: the sudden blurring of sharp lines between sun and shadow on a tree trunk, the sudden change in acoustics—an opening up, like many windows being flung wide on the world; a new greeny-gold richness to the thin washes of sunlight, a change in the density of the air, so that flags and awnings hung slack instead of snapping in the wind, and smoke rose in long unbroken lines instead of choppy puffs. For the first time since childhood she hadn't looked for any of these signs; moving almost blindly between their apartment and the hospital twice a day, she hadn't seen any of the minute changes taking place in the streets around her, hadn't cared. But then just an hour ago, while waiting at the bus stop, she had suddenly heard the voices of children in a play street two blocks away, and suddenly seen the unfurling leaves on the spindly maple sapling growing in a wire-enclosed plot of earth next to the bus stop. And when she climbed off the bus at the other end, a horse-drawn cart was pulled up at the curb, banked with potted tulips and hyacinths and paper cones spilling daffodils and narcissi and violets—bringing the message bloomingly home: spring, so late in coming, spring, which she had forgotten, had arrived.

Now she stared out at the May day, determined not to let herself think of what would have happened by the time that still-cool wind turned warm, that still-wan light turned to full gold, those furzes opened into meshes of thick, shiny leaves. Trying to fight off a sudden sickening, sticking-aching in the middle of her chest, she began to manufacture an elaborate diversion for herself, making herself consider the soft open quality of the day outside, and study it like a lesson: fifteen or sixteen years ago, in some modern poetry course at college, she'd read a poem that caught the essence of a day like the one in front of her—what was the poem? Frowning, she tried to remember. She was absolutely certain Cummings had written it, but except for some lines about an open window, the poem completely eluded her. Which was really very strange, since she had an almost photographic memory for poetry. But what was even stranger was that in spite of not being able to remember the poem itself, and in spite of its having been well over fifteen years back in time, she could remember the exact circumstances of first reading it. Total sensory recall. It had been a snowy day in her junior year, and she could hear the hailstones picking on the window, could smell her wet wool mittens steaming dry on the radiator, could even feel the slippery plastic of her favorite red chair sticking to . . .

Unable to believe what she'd heard, she stood rooted, immobilized by fear. When it came again—a hideous, guttural, choking-gargling— she turned and saw her mother gripping the raised side-rails on the bed, wildly glaring at her with bloodshot eyes.

Almost tripping over the little bench behind her, she stumbled to the side of the bed. "What is it, Mommy? Can you tell me?"

Only the sound, the unspeakable sound, came out of the gaping mouth.

"Mommy. Can you hear me? Listen to me: I'm not leaving you, I'm just going around to the other side of the bed to ring the nurse's bell." Leaving her mother gawping blindly at the window, she rushed around the bed and pushed the button on the wall. As she held it down with her finger, she called out to the back that was curved and bent taut like a bow under the force of the pain: "Hold on, Mommy. I'm still here. Don't be frightened. I'm getting the nurse."

As if in response, her mother weakly rattled the bars.

Furiously blinking back tears—she hadn't wept since that day in Dr. Barney's office, and was proud of it—she kept her finger on the bell, repeating over and over: "Hold on. One more second. Help is on the way."

But it wasn't. No one came. No one answered the bell. And as she stood scrubbing at her filling eyes with her free hand, the rattling of the bars grew louder, the back turned toward her reared up and outward, a graph-curve charting the purest agony. Letting go the button, she flew back around the bed. Teeth bared, her mother goggled with unseeing eyes. "Mommy. I'm going down the hall to get help." She was almost shouting, as if her mother were feeble-minded or deaf. "The bell is broken. I'm going to get Miss Bruce. Don't be frightened. I'll be right back."

She was at the cretonne curtains, when the voice rang out. *"No!! Don't go. Come back. Talk."* Hoarse, but distinct. Utterly lucid. And imperative.

Her mother hadn't spoken so clearly in a week, but she didn't feel any relief or joy. On the contrary, her whole body began to loosen with a terrible kind of dread, which turned to sheer terror when she reached the far side of the bed, and her mother fixed her with a glowering, commanding stare, working her corded throat, trying to force out words.

"Hush. Don't try to talk. I know the pain is awful. Let me go for help."

"*No!*"

". . . No? You're not in pain? . . . Or don't want help."

"No."

"Mommy, darling. Please. Please let me go. I'll be right back."

". . . Emma?"

"Yes."

"Kill me, Emma."

Almost a whisper. But clear. Oh, how clear. As clear as the eyes, no longer clouded, which glared compellingly at her, as she stood frozen, mute.

"Emma. Listen. Get me . . . gun."

"Oh, no. Please don't. I beg you, Mommy."

"A knife. A . . . towel. Stuff down . . . throat. Anything. You hear me, Emma?"

"Yes, I hear you," she said in a sludgy voice that wasn't her own, and, needing support, put a steadying hand on the bars her mother still gripped. "You mustn't talk like that. You're just having a bad day. You'll be much better soon. You'll feel much better in a few minutes, as soon as I get the nurse and she comes and gives you another . . . more medicine."

"No."

"You . . . don't want more medicine?"

"Medicine." Withering scorn. "Injection. No injection. Had *no* injection. Today. None atall."

The voice, suddenly coming with more ease, was full of a blasting authority Emma knew all too well. "Oh, you must be mistaken, Mommy. I think you forgot. Miss Moody told me she gave you a shot just before I came. But never mind that, instead of all this talking, let me go for . . ."

"*Liar.* Moody. Just like. You. . . . Why have you lied to me, Emma?"

"Oh, God. Please stop, Mommy. You're killing me."

"Killing you." An ironic whisper from the bloodless lips, which now stretched into what some part of Emma's overstressed mind ludicrously informed her was a rictus—the literary cliché for the smile of death. Only this was a smile that held other things, things worse than death. Infinite rage. Malice. Contempt. Searing bitterness. Hate. Hate. Naked hate. And then words more annihilating than the smile: "Help me.

For once. In your life. Emma. *Do* something. For me. Once. *Help*. You never . . ."

Making a high, whirring noise of protest, Emma ran from the room, up the hall to the nurse's station, where a blond nurse she had never seen before sat typing at the desk. As she rushed up, wild-eyed, breathless, the nurse calmly went on typing until she had finished the line and the carriage bell pinged. "Yes?" she said coolly, glancing up, touching pale hair pulled back tight as an onion skin.

"My mother. She's in terrible pain. She needs a shot of something right away. I rang and rang, but the bell must be broken."

A delicate lifting of finely plucked eyebrows. "Who is your mother, please?"

"Mrs. Pittman. Mrs. Agnes Pittman. Room 2207."

Spinning around in the swivel chair, the nurse opened a drawer in a yellow file. As she flipped through cards, pulled one out, and frowning, began to read, Emma stared distractedly at a tin of Dutch cookies on the desk: She didn't mean it. Not *any* of it. She wasn't rational. She *sounded* rational, but she was out of her mind with pain.

"I see here," said the nurse, who wore a plastic name badge Emma was too distraught to read, "that your mother received her medication at 2:00 P.M. She's not due for any more until 5:00 P.M."

"I'd like to speak to the head nurse. Miss Bruce."

"Miss Bruce is holding a head nurse's conference just now. Most of the floor staff is there, which is why we're shorthanded. I'm the assistant head nurse, Miss Clarkson, replacing Miss Bruce until she returns." Ice.

"Miss Clarkson. My mother is in uns*peak*able pain. She can't possibly wait three hours for another shot." Though the nurse's face had nastily hardened, and though Emma knew that what she was about to say would have ugly consequences—more for herself than anyone else—she decided to get it out: "In spite of the pain, my mother is quite rational, Miss Clarkson," she began, knowing it was the truth as she spoke, knowing she had cut off any avenue of escape for herself. "She just told me she hasn't received any medication at *all* today. But instead of all this dis*cuss*ion, why don't you just . . ."

One of the three phones on the desk rang, cutting her short. The nurse picked it up, warily watching Emma while she talked—as though Emma were possibly dangerous and violent, and might pick up the tin of cookies and slam her on the head. Registering all this from some icy pinnacle of detachment, Emma knew she shouldn't stay there, but ought to go back and try to comfort her mother until this flinty bitch came to the room. Yet she didn't budge. Comfort? Her mother needed morphine, not comfort, she told herself, and it was senseless to go back unless she brought someone along who could give it to her. What she meant, of course, was that it was senseless to go back and face, alone, any more of those demolishing accusations and pleas.

Miss Clarkson put the phone down and stood up. "I see that Miss Moody is on this case. Why didn't Miss Moody come out to the desk?"

"She's down in the cafeteria having tea. She said it was all right since my mother had just had her shot. But my mother *didn't* have her shot. She told me herself. Clear as day. For God's *sake* . . . come see for yourself!"

The nurse's neat little nostrils flared. "This desk must be covered at all times, Miss Pittman. Please try to stay calm. If you return to your mother's room, I'll join you there immediately."

Her face burning, Emma turned and slowly walked back to her mother's room. Through the opening in the curtains she saw her mother, no longer gripping the bars, her back turned to the door, lying very still. Absolutely still. She's dead, thought Emma. She's dead. And with this terrible dread-hope mushrooming out in her chest, she tiptoed around to the far side of the bed—and immediately saw that her mother wasn't dead. The eyes were closed, but the chest was moving, and a faint puffing snort came out of the yawning mouth. Without really knowing what she was doing, she picked up one of the bony wrists. At the same moment her icy fingers found the faint but steady throb of a pulse, Miss Clarkson, followed by an intern, pushed through the curtains at the door.

Pausing for a split second in front of the curtains, they took in the spectacle of Emma taking her mother's pulse, exchanged eloquent glances, then proceeded toward the bed.

"You can leave everything to us, now, Miss Pittman," the nurse said heartily. "Would you mind stepping out of the room?"

"Sohier," said Emma, gently putting the bony hand down on the coverlet. "My name is Mrs. Harold Sohier. And I *do* mind stepping out of the room. I'm not leaving this room until I find out what's going *on* around here."

Exchanging another look, the intern and nurse advanced to the far side of the bed. "Please move aside, Mrs. Sohier," said Miss Clarkson, her voice soft—but distinctly menacing.

Conceding that much, Emma moved to the foot of the bed, and

watched Miss Clarkson pick up her mother's wrist and take her pulse, while the young intern, his stethoscope dangling like a necklace, moved in next to the nurse.

"Mrs. Pittman?" called the nurse like someone shouting across a valley. And maybe, thought Emma, it was a valley at that. In the last few minutes the Twenty-third Psalm had certainly been in her heart, if not her mind. "Can you hear me, Mrs. Pittman?" continued the nurse.

Her mother's eyelids fluttered open, then closed. She made a tiny sound.

"Does something hurt you, Mrs. Pittman? Where does it hurt you—can you tell me that?"

The figure on the bed didn't move or make a sound.

"Try to tell me, Mrs. Pittman. Try."

"Why don't you stop torturing her and just *give* her something! What kind of a place *is* this anyway?"

Without so much as a glance at Emma, Miss Clarkson whispered something to the young doctor at her side, who nodded and inserted the rubber lobes of the stethoscope in his ears. As he changed places with the nurse and bent over the motionless figure in the bed, she came up to Emma: "Mrs. Sohier, would you please come outside. I'd like a word with you. And would you please bring your coat."

Suddenly crumpling into passivity, Emma took her trenchcoat off the chair, and followed the nurse out into the hall. As they stopped several feet beyond the door, two student nurses chattering at the desk, fell silent and stared.

"Mrs. Sohier, I hope you won't mind, but I'd like to give you a word of advice," said Miss Clarkson in an unctuously solicitous tone Emma found worse than the menacing one. "If I were you, I'd go straight home and rest. You've been coming to see your mother twice a day for almost four weeks, and it's time you took a little break. Relatives of terminal patients often don't know how badly they've been stressed. I suggest you go on home and stay there . . . don't come back to visit your mother for a day or two."

Muddled, fighting back another outburst, Emma stood silent. How did this . . . this *myrmidon* she'd never seen before today know how often she'd come to see her mother? Was it recorded on her mother's chart? At last she said: "Are you going to give her a shot?"

An ugly flicker in the gray eyes. "No one," said the nurse, clearly weighing her words, "is authorized to change the orders for medication that Dr. Barney marked on your mother's chart. If the order were marked PRN, it would be different, but for some reason this medication order is not. Your mother received her medication at two, as I told you, and it seems to have taken hold now. Patients are often restive until the medication takes hold—what you thought was pain was that sort of reaction. Restiveness."

"Restive. *Restiveness.* She was in excruciating pain—not *restive.* She was also more articulate than she's been for a week. She told me—distinctly, there was no mistaking it—that she didn't receive any medication today at all." For one second a trap door yawned open, and Emma considered what else her mother had said distinctly, no mistaking it, then slammed it shut. "What do I have to do to get her another shot? Call Dr. Barney myself? Okay, I will. I'll call him and tell him what's been going on here today. And after I do, I'm going to sit in the solarium until I'm sure she's gotten what she needs." Giving the nurse a wide berth, she started down the hall.

"Just one minute, Mrs. Sohier." The voice rang out in the discreet hush of the corridor.

Reluctantly Emma turned. The student nurses at the desk were gaping. Miss Clarkson, a sheety white, came up.

"There is something you had better understand, Mrs. Sohier," said the nurse in a low, shaking voice. "All medications containing narcotics are kept in a locked cabinet in the medicine room next to the nurse's station. Every dose of medication taken from that cabinet is signed out by the nurse who takes it and recorded on the medication sheet on the front of the patient's chart. Miss Moody has recorded that your mother received her medication at eight and eleven and two today." Miss Clarkson took a deep and steadying breath. "Your hysterical insinuations about Miss Moody—which actually include the nursing staff of this whole floor—are shocking and irremissible. Miss Moody has been with the Wellship Registry for seventeen years. She is a credit to her profession, one of the most outstanding private-duty nurses that has ever worked at this hospital. You've been incredibly lucky to have Miss Moody taking care of your mother, giving so generously of herself and her time—and you should be thinking of ways to thank her, not . . . *vilify* her. I can't, of course, force you to leave this floor, but if you really have your mother's interest at heart—and I'm beginning to suspect you really might not—you will go straight home. And phone your own physician and have him prescribe a sedative."

Turning on her rubber heel, Miss Clarkson marched back into

Emma's mother's room. The nurse's last words—"and I'm beginning to suspect you might not"—echoing in her ears, Emma slowly moved down the hall toward the phones. The student nurses nudged each other as she passed the desk.

The phone booths were around a bend in the hall, opposite the elevators. Both booths, Emma saw with relief, were empty, neither held an Out of Order sign. She settled herself into the booth nearest the wall, and after clumsily bundling her trenchcoat into a ball in her lap, was rummaging in her purse for change and her address book, when one of the elevator doors slid open and Iris Moody stepped out. Unaware of Emma fifteen feet away in the glass booth, the nurse smoothed her Ginger Rogers' pageboy with a loving hand, tugged her starched skirt down over full hips, hiked her white purse higher on her plump arm, and fortified for the fray, briskly turned the corner and headed back to Emma's mother's room.

An answering service told her that Dr. Barney was out of town for the day, and was signed out to Dr. Miles Lambert until eight that night. Dialing the number the answering service gave her, she was informed by a secretary that Dr. Lambert was in the examining room with a patient and couldn't come to the phone. In a flat, deadly voice Emma informed the secretary that Dr. Lambert had better come to the phone since it was a matter of life or death—and several seconds and several clicks later, Dr. Lambert, breathing hard, was on the phone. In a controlled voice, she quickly told her story. When she finished, Dr. Lambert raspingly said he was certain that Emma had things wrong and her mother had received her shots, and he wasn't authorized to change Dr. Barney's orders for medication, in any case.

"Dr. Lambert! Dr. *Lambert*," she called out before he could hang up. "You weren't listening to what I said. My mother told me *distinctly* she had no medication at all today."

Somewhere in that remote office, a phone rang; an exasperated sigh blasted Emma's ear. "Mrs. Sohier. There's something you don't understand. Patients taking narcotics often hallucinate. Their perceptions are often grossly distorted, they can lose all sense of the passage of time and can't distinguish between one hour and five, between one day and the next. Ten minutes after receiving her medication, your mother could think she got it yesterday. As soon as I get a chance, I'll call and check with the floor desk—twenty-two?—but at the moment, I've a waiting room full of patients, and left someone in the examin . . ."

"She wasn't hallucinating. She was perfectly rational. She said some pretty frightening things." She paused: no—*no* one, including Harold, was ever going to know what those things were; she had to live with them herself. "She knew just what she was saying. She was—*is*—in unbearable pain and can't possibly wait until you . . ."

"What looks like pain can be something else. Sometimes, after medication, there's a certain agitation, a restlessness which . . ."

"I hope to God I know the difference between restlessness and agony!" she cried on a cracking note, and slammed down the phone.

The booth was steamy with her anger. Needing air, she folded open the glass door, and then just sat there, trying to calm herself and decide on her next move. As she sat, the sounds of muted voices and clattering carts and ringing phones drifted down the hall. One of the phones could be Lambert, unsettled by her outburst, calling to check up—but she suddenly didn't give a damn what Lambert or any other doctor said or did. All she wanted to do was go back and see how her mother was, see what state she was in, but decided to call Harold at the office first. Dear, rational, unflappable Harold would tell her how to handle this, tell her what to do. Why hadn't she thought of it before?

But she'd run out of change; her change purse held only pennies, no silver coins. The nearest place she could get change was the cashier's office, twenty-two floors away. Unless, that is, she swallowed her pride and asked one of the student nurses at the desk if they could change a dollar or lend her a dime. . . .

Swallowing her pride, she left the booth, carrying the bulky wad of her coat and purse. As soon as she rounded the corner, she saw them outside her mother's room: Miss Moody, Miss Clarkson, Dr. Cooney, the medical resident, and Miss Bruce, the pleasant charge nurse. She took a few more steps, then stopped, the terrible dread-hope filling her chest again. But if . . . something had happened would they all be out there having a conference? If . . . something had happened what would there be to talk about? Miss Moody, the only one who faced her, seemed to be doing all the talking, her bright red lips curling and snapping on words, her white cap bobbing like a sail on a storm-tossed sea. Then Miss Moody caught sight of her standing and clutching her belongings, halfway up the hall, and said something to the others which made them all turn. A second later the conclave dispersed—Miss Moody ducking back inside her mother's door, Miss Clarkson and the resident heading in the opposite direction down the hall, and Miss Bruce, looking pained, coming to where Emma stood.

Looking even more pained, the head nurse informed her that Miss

Moody had just resigned from her mother's case; had she herself been
on the floor at the time, continued Miss Bruce, she was certain the
"unpleasant misunderstanding" about her mother's medication would
never have occurred. But although Miss Moody had been upset by the
"unpleasant misunderstanding," she had really resigned from the case
because of what she described as "the family's general attitude." (The
"family" being Emma, a family of one.) In spite of this, Miss Moody,
with the selflessness she was known for, had agreed to stay until seven,
to give them time to try and find a replacement at one of the registries.

"I don't think we'll get anyone," concluded Miss Bruce, who had
been avoiding Emma's eye all during this speech. "It's close to three-
thirty now, and as you know, we've had an order in at three of the
registries for a night nurse for days, without any luck. But since Dr.
Barney won't be back until eight, and Dr. Lambert—I just finished
talking to him on the phone—is all tied up, I'll call all the registries now
myself." She paused, looking straight at Emma now, and Emma saw
her decide against going into just what the "unpleasant misunderstanding" had been about. "You really mustn't worry, Mrs. Sohier. If we
can't find a night nurse, the floor staff will take good care of your
mother, never fear. You have a steady nurse—Miss Hammond?—for
the midnight shift, and in between seven and midnight the staff will
look in on your mother constantly."

Though Emma had many questions—*many* questions—she decided
to let them all go for the moment, because she liked this nurse. Instead,
she asked something less charged: "If we can't get a night nurse, Miss
Bruce, can . . . some member of the family come and stay with my
mother until Miss Hammond arrives?"

"Well, yes. Of course. But it isn't necessary. And whatever you decide, I don't think that 'member of the family' should be you. I feel
very strongly about that, as a matter of fact, Mrs. Sohier. You've had a
trying day, and I think you should go straight home now and get some
rest."

Admiring the nurse's talent for understatement and restraint, Emma
didn't get angry, as she had when Miss Clarkson had "suggested" that
she go home. "I'll be going soon, Miss Bruce. But I'd like to look in on
my mother before I leave."

For one moment the nurse stared at her, distinctly annoyed. Then,
with a remarkable lack of irony, she said she didn't think that would be
a good idea: her mother was resting comfortable (weighty pause), the
medication had "taken hold" (another pause), and, "all considered,"

she thought it would be best if Emma just went home and left her mother in Miss Moody's capable hands.

Which translated: "all considered," she thought it best there not be another confrontation between herself and Miss Moody. And Emma decided she was right.

So she thanked Miss Bruce for her kindness (and meant it), took an elevator to the main floor, went into the gift shop, bought a magazine she hated—and with a jangling fistful of small change made for the nearby phones.

"Where are you now, Em?" asked Harold, after she'd told him her story with what she felt was extraordinary restraint.

"In a phone booth on the main floor of the hospital."

"Go home, Em. Get a taxi and go straight home. I'll be there soon's I can get away."

"Harold. Dear. There's no earthly reason for you to leave the office. I'm fine. I really am. I'm just not sure I should leave here until . . ."

"Emma. Go home. Right away. You hear?"

Emma heard. She went home.

At home she found Milly Brundage watching TV in the living room, and Benjy doing his homework in his room. During the month her mother had been in the hospital, she had arranged for Milly to be in the apartment every afternoon when Benjy came in from school —an arrangement Benjy bitterly resented: while he was deeply attached to the sweet old widow, he didn't see why, when he was almost eleven (he would be eleven in August), he needed a sitter. Particularly during daytime hours. They'd been squabbling about this for many months. And though Emma knew he was right, and didn't know just what she was afraid of (a fire? some sex-maniac-pervert disguised as a door-to-door salesman? some robber disguised as a United Parcel deliveryman?), she wasn't ready to give way. Especially now, when the thought of him coming home to an empty apartment every day was more than she could bear, on top of everything else. So, in spite of the friction it produced, she had overridden all his objections and continued with the arrangement, which sometimes extended into the evening hours if Milly was needed.

She would be needed tonight, Emma had decided in the cab going home, having also decided she was going back later to stay with her mother until the midnight-shift nurse arrived. And even before taking her coat off, she explained the nurse shortage to Milly, asking if she could stay through supper and Benjy's bedtime: Harold, as Milly knew all too well, wasn't very good at fixing scratch meals, or seeing to it that his son got to bed at a reasonable hour . . . without some huge row erupting, that is. Then something very peculiar happened. In the few seconds that elapsed before Milly answered, Milly stood looking at her with deep concern—while she, looking at Milly, was barely able to keep from flinging herself on that ample breast and bursting into tears like a baby. Unnerved, humiliated—what *now*? what did she want from poor *Milly?*—she effusively thanked her when she said she could stay and went rushing off to see Benjy. Who gave her one of his icier greetings and said, "How's Granma?"

"Much better," she said, not knowing why she lied, adding as she started for the door, "but I may have to go back to the hospital—they're having trouble getting a night nurse."

"If she's much better why does she need all those nurses?"

Having no answer, she returned his grainy, sober stare, then went into her own room and stretched out on the bed.

Where Harold found her bleakly staring at the ceiling a half hour later. With a strange mixture of somberness and tenderness, he came and kissed her on the cheek, then settled himself in the armchair and asked her to repeat the afternoon's sequence of events. Slowly. In detail.

She was halfway through the story (which she found almost unbearable in the retelling, even though she left out the "details" of those moments alone with her mother), when the phone rang. Harold answered and stayed on, talking, for the next few minutes. Or rather, for the next few minutes he held the phone to his ear, occasionally saying, "Absolutely" or "That's quite right" or "I couldn't agree more" into the mouthpiece.

It had been Eliot Barney, who was back earlier than expected from Philadelphia, he explained when he finally hung up. Barney had made the call from the nurse's desk on her mother's floor. He had just seen her mother and said she was resting comfortably. He had also said there definitely weren't any nurses available for the next shift, but— and Barney had made a particular point of this, said Harold, raising his voice—she, Emma, was not to worry, since the floor staff would take excellent care of her mother until the midnight nurse arrived. "He was damned emphatic about something else too, Em. Seems you said something to one of the nurses about going back and staying with your mother until the midnight nurse comes in?—and he said that was absolutely *out*. In fact, he gave me strict orders to keep you home and to see to it that you get to bed early, with two sleeping pills under your belt."

By now she was sitting tensely upright. "Why didn't he ask to talk to *me*? Was he afraid I'd have hysterics or something? I had all sorts of important things I wanted to discuss with him, very im*portant* things. Why am I being treated like this? Everybody, and that even includes you now, is treating me like some sort of . . . mental case."

Sighing, Harold came trudging around the bed and tried to hug her, but she remained stony in the clumsy embrace. "Em. Em, *darling*," he said, defeatedly letting go of her, trying for heartiness but not having any success with that either. "No one's 'treating' you like anything. Everybody's just very concerned about you, that's all. You've been terrific until now—an absolute tower of strength—but things have finally gotten through to you, are beginning to rock you. The amazing thing is that you haven't been rocked long before now."

"I am not 'rocked,' whatever that is. I'm just as I have been all along —calm and steady and completely realistic. And I have no intention of letting my mother stay all alone in that room for five hours. Because that's what she'll be. Alone. The floor staff. I just love that. They don't have enough staff to even *begin* to cover that floor. I ought to know— I've been there twice a day every day for a month. As I just finished telling you, but it didn't seem to make a dent—I rang and rang and nobody came. And my mother can't even *ring* for help. Assuming help was there to come in the first place. She'll be all alone in that damned room, and . . ."

"She won't be alone. I'm going over there in a little while to stay with her until the midnight nurse arrives."

Emma stared at his worn, podgy face, and for the first time made herself consider what a five-hour stretch alone with her mother might hold for her. "I won't let you. It's wonderful of you, and I can't tell you how grateful I am, but you're all worn out. I can see it. You look absolutely exhausted."

"So do you."

"I'm exhausted in a different way. Besides . . . she's *my* mother."

"Now you're just being childish. I want to go, Em. And I'm going. And that's that. I'll just grab a sandwich and go on over and tell that bitch Moody to clear out. And you just stay right there . . . I'll make the sandwich myself."

But she would only follow his orders up to a certain point. She got up, made them both huge drinks, made him a huge Dagwood sandwich, and sat with him in the kitchen while he ate it. But when he finally left at six, equipped for his vigil with the evening paper and a dispatch case full of work, she promised to do the rest of the things he asked—to be in bed at nine, the latest, with two Nembutals "under her belt."

And she was even better than her word: she was in bed by eight. After a dismal supper with Benjy and Milly—she couldn't eat, Benjy wouldn't talk—and after helping Milly with the dishes, she said good night to both of them and went into her room: Milly was going to stay overnight, sleeping in the unused maid's room as she often did. Telling herself not to be so upset about Benjy, telling herself that children were extraordinarily sensitive to the presence of death and reacted to it in the strangest of ways, she took two Nembutals, read for twenty minutes, and fell into the deepest sleep she'd had in a month.

The first thing she saw, on opening her eyes, was the face of her bedside clock: was it eight forty-five the next morning, or had she slept just twenty minutes? Then she saw Harold, sitting in the armchair, bathed in refracted sunlight, still in his pajamas and bathrobe, reading the *Times* with a subdued Sundayish air.

Her mother was dead. She had died during the night, Harold told her in a voice that matched his manner—not Sundayish, just the strained "respectfulness" people assumed when dealing with death. She had died just a few minutes before a quarter to twelve. He had been with her when she died. It had been utterly peaceful and painless—a total release.

Sitting up on the bed and hugging her knees, Emma made Harold repeat the simple sequence of events several times. After the third time, she said: "Why didn't you call me from the hospital? Or wake me when you got home?"

"I didn't see the point of it, Em. There wasn't anything you could have done, except give permission for an autopsy—and I got them to hold off until this morning on that. I felt it was more important for you to have a good night's sleep before tackling all the unpleasant stuff ahead."

After a long silence, Emma said: "Did she say anything during the time you were there?"

His face puckered with concern, Harold studied her, sitting all clenched-up, sickly pale, tensely gripping her knees. "No, Em. She was out from the time I got there until the time she died. She got her medication twice—at eight, and again at eleven—I saw the head nurse shoot the stuff in her arm with my own eyes."

Darkly brooding, Emma let that pass. "Are you sure she didn't suffer?"

"Em. I *told* you. She was unconscious the whole time. Her breathing was very peaceful and regular—I was reading the paper, but I kept listening to her breathing as I read. I heard her take one breath, let it out—and that was it. She didn't take another. I lowered the paper, and she was . . . gone."

"How was her face?"

"What?" Harold was frowning, his face a seeping red.

"The expression on her face. Was it peaceful? Or was it . . . contorted in some way. With pain . . . or anger."

"Please stop, Em. Let it alone. She didn't feel pain or fear or anything. She just . . . slipped away." Shame for the cliché turned his face an even deeper red.

"Where's Benjy? Did you tell him?"

"Yes. Of course. I think it hit him very hard. He went into his room and shut the door. Cried, I'm sure—his eyes were red when he came out. He pleaded with me to let him go to school. I'd told him I wanted him to stay home out of respect, but he seemed so damned strange and so bent on going, I let him. . . . I hope you don't mind, Em."

"No, I don't mind. Anything that makes him feel better is all right with me."

Harold stared at her, the yellow eyes behind the horn rims, troubled, perplexed. "And what about you? What can I do to help you feel better, Em?"

What he really meant, she knew, was, What can I do to help you to cry? He was sitting there, hopefully waiting for her to break down and weep. "You're doing it," she finally said, the cloying words like glue in her mouth. "You're helping me tremendously just by being here. But now I think you ought to get dressed and go to work."

"I'm not going in today. There are too many arrangements, too many nasty things to be taken care of—I'm not going to leave you to handle them all alone."

"Harold, please. I can manage all that by myself. I've had two months to prepare myself for all this. And I'm all right. I really am."

Again, the yellow eyes studied her through the glasses: If you're all right why don't you cry? Then, incredibly, he said it. "I'm not going into the office today, I've already called and it's all settled, so forget it.

But I think you're far from all right. You shouldn't keep everything
bottled up inside you . . . it'll only make it worse later on. Go on.
Give in. Cut loose and bawl. Don't be ashamed."

She couldn't believe it. What was wrong with him? "I'm not ashamed.
Which, I might add, is a pretty peculiar word. I'm just handling it my
own way."

"Yes. So I see." Wry. Dry. Very dry. "But I think this has hit you
much harder than you know."

I know just how hard I've been hit, she grimly thought, and whipped
back the covers and climbed out of bed.

Looking suddenly contrite, he watched her step into her slippers and
put on her bathrobe. "Milly made a big pot of coffee. She's already left,
she had an early appointment somewhere, but she asked me to tell you
how sorry she was and said she'd call you later in the day. . . . Why
don't you get some breakfast, Em. Or at least some coffee to counteract
those Nembies. Meanwhile, I'll get started on some of the calls. I said
you'd let them know about the autopsy first thing this morning, but
I'll make the call for you. What should I tell them, Em?"

"Tell them to go ahead," she said softly, and went into the bathroom
and shut the door.

When she came out, he was still busily talking on the phone. Hurry-
ing from the room (she doubted it was still the call about the autopsy,
but she didn't want to hear *anything*), she started toward the kitchen
and was passing the open end of the living room when she stopped in
her tracks. Someone, probably Milly, had pushed up all three windows
to air the room, and sunlight, bouncing off the buildings across the
street, came pouring in over the sills, along with all the street sounds
of a brilliant spring morning—the voices of schoolchildren, a small dog's
high excited yapping, a doorman's whistle, the jazzy blare of music
from a car radio.

Finally stirring, giving herself a shuddering sort of shake, really,
she strode through the dining room and went to the kitchen corner
where a small stepstool stood against the wall. Carrying it up to the
front entrance hall, she flipped open the steps and, placing it next to
the console against the bookcase-divider wall, quickly clambered up
to the next-to-last step. Ignoring the ladder's wobbling, she leaned from
side to side, scanning the titles of books on the top shelves—books she'd
haphazardly stuck in the shelves seven months earlier, when they'd
first moved in, planning to rearrange them in careful sequence at
some later time—a time that had never come.

Then there it was. Jammed into a far corner, a reddish-brown book with *e. e. cummings* printed in black on the spine. With a swooping reach that set the ladder dangerously swaying, she plucked it out, backed down the steps and, absently wiping the dusty book cover on her bathrobe, went into the living room and sat down on the settee in the middle of the room. The Hepplewhite settee that had belonged to her mother. She quickly flipped from the front of the book to the back, then returned to the front with a rasping sigh: no table of contents, no index. Just the poems. Undeterred, she slowly began going through the book page by page, reading the first line of each new poem, then moving on.

Halfway through the book she found the poem she wanted.

The poem she had desperately tried to remember while standing at her mother's window yesterday afternoon. Yesterday afternoon—when, with death in the air, with hatred and pleas and rage for that death just moments way, she had stood desperately trying to hook up life and art, desperately trying to escape. As always.

Now, pressing the book open with icy hands, she quickly read the poem a first time, then went back to the first line and started again, reading more slowly, inchingly. But as her eyes moved across the words they became meaningless, the print smeared into a blur. And finally taking her dust-streaked hands from the pages, she covered her eyes and quietly began weeping—aware of Harold standing, shocked, on the outer edges of the room. She had felt him materialize there as she finished the first reading of the poem, had felt the full impact of his dismay: Dear God, what's she *doing?* Reading? At a time like this? Now, even through the growing violence of her weeping, she could feel the change, the switch to relief: *Now* she's facing it—now she'll be all right.

Which only made her weep more bitterly.

Which only made her weep as though her heart would break.

A Good Girl Is Hard to Find

Darlin'. She used to call me Darlin'. Laughing. Smacking her thigh. "Hoo, Darlin', that sure beats all!" or "Darlin', you do takes the cake!" or—and this was best—"Darlin', now you just go on about your business, and don't worry your head about a *thing*. You just go on and scoot and leave everything to Old Cora now—you *hear*?" Darlin' would hear and would do as she was told, not worrying her head about a *thing*. Would watch Old Cora pick up the mop or vegetable peeler or laundry soap, and would go on about her business, leaving Old Cora everything. The cleaning, the laundry, the dinner to be reheated later, Benjy waiting for Milly to come take him to the park. Benjy, muckily chewing the banana or bread thick with butter-and-sugar Old Cora had just handed him. Benjy, not caring if Milly ever showed. Benjy, happy as a clam. Like Darlin'. And Old Cora too.

Emma was making a tour of the dining-room table (enlarged by a leaf to accommodate ten), depositing tiny ashtrays at each place, this lament for the Old Cora going through her head. This refrain which for sheer idiot-racism outstripped anything Minda Wolfe had ever said. The New Cora, meanwhile, was sitting in the kitchen less than thirty feet away, making the stuffing for her veal—a frightening stranger Emma didn't know. A tall, forbidding woman with a modified Afro and tinted granny glasses who had walked through the door two hours ago. While the physical change had been unnerving, Emma had quickly gotten over it; she'd seen too many changes like it in the last few years to stay surprised long. What she hadn't gotten over was the steely coldness, the sternness, the absolute refusal to talk. Though, granted, in their phone conversations (mostly apologies on her part, explanations about her Rough Year and why they couldn't do any entertaining) she had gotten a certain . . . frosty reserve, nothing had prepared her for this woman of solid ice.

Now, as she went to the sideboard for matches, a turgid silence drifted through the open door to the kitchen where Maria and the New Cora were hard at work. The Old Cora had never stopped talking, had kept up a running commentary on everything. The New Cora commented on nothing at all. Not even obvious things. The new apartment. ("It's nice, but it don't hold a candle to the old one, Darlin'.") Emma herself. ("I know you've been through a turrible time, but you're still looking mighty good.") Benjy. ("How's my baby? What time he get in from that fancy school?") Harold. ("How's the boss? Still so picky about his food?") None of that. Nothing. Absolutely nothing. Absolutely nothing at all. Silent, unsmiling, acknowledging the introduction to Maria with only the barest of nods, she had stood poker-faced while Emma nervously opened drawers and cabinet doors, explaining where everything was—and while Maria stood glowering at the sink, taking in all the expensive food someone else was going to cook. Then, once this brief orientation course was over, she'd politely thanked Emma, taken the veal from the icebox, slapped it down with a plop on the cutting board, and turned to Maria at the sink:

"You know how to prepare green beans, Mrs. Nonez?"

Mrs. Nonez gave a visible start. "*Señora* Matthews. I very wunnerful cook."

"I'm sure you are. Quite sure you are. Let's leave off all this *señora* and missus jazz. My Christian name's Cora. What's yours."

"Maria. Maria Carlotta Nonez."

"Well, Maria Carlotta, the big question is—do you know how to fix green beans, French style."

"Again I tell you, *Dona* Cora. I absolutely wunnerful cook. And the name is just Maria. The Carlotta never get use."

"Well, I'd say we're in terrific shape seeing that you're such a wonderful cook. S'pose you start in on those green beans, Maria."

Not caring to find out how they resolved this little matter of the beans, Emma had fled up front where she'd kept herself busy with the seating plan for the next half hour. When she'd finally come back to start setting the table, the silence from the kitchen made it clear that no matter how they'd resolved the problem of the beans, they now had a whopping communication-problem on their hands. Which hardly boded well for the long evening ahead, where the two of them would have to work together, cheek by jowl, so to speak.

But then she herself had a little unresolved problem that hardly boded well for the long evening ahead. If she wanted to get through the long, taxing evening ahead, she thought, as she went to the sideboard for napkins, she'd better cut out all this pining for the Old Cora and get on with the New. Better forget that other Cora, whoever she'd been. That black woman in her shabby-genteel rig: the hand-me-down McMullen shirtdress and Woolworth pearls and steel-rimmed glasses and painstakingly straightened hair tortuously recrimped into two dowdy rows of Helen Hokinson-committeewoman curls. That totally unknown (she saw now) woman, her memory had turned into a cruel caricature-composite—Ruby Dandridge/Louise Beavers/Hattie Mc-Daniel, all togged out in imitation WASP-clubwoman drag. That woman she'd clearly been longing to see, counting on her to come and reassure Darlin' that *some* things in the world hadn't changed.

Which made still another bad-news bulletin about herself. Trying to accept it as best she could, she carefully began rolling bright green linen napkins into cones and set one at each place: ironically—in view of her track record as a housekeeper—she was a highly organized, exacting hostess, and whenever she gave a party paid meticulous attention to every detail. Finished with the napkins, she was taking a box of candles from a drawer in the sideboard (they would eat by candlelight) when the telephone rang, breaking the oppressive silence. A moment later Maria appeared in the doorway to announce that the *Señor* Soller was on the phone, wishing to speak with her. With an unpleasant sense of foreboding—what did *he* want?—she told Maria she would take it up front.

What he wanted more than justified the foreboding: he had just invited Harley Scrim to their party, and wanted to make sure it was all right with her. Or, more precisely, Scrim had invited himself. In a curiously flat, depressed voice, Harold explained that Scrim hadn't gone back to Maine as scheduled—he'd had some sort of acute flare-up in a tooth, and as a special favor his dentist was going to open his office on a Saturday and work on him tomorrow; meanwhile, poor Scrim was at loose ends and feeling rather lonely, and suddenly remembering that somebody had dropped by their table at lunch the other day and mentioned something about a party, Scrim had just called him, saying he felt he didn't have to stand on ceremony with his long-time friend and editor, and had asked if he could come to the party too.

Remembering all too well what Harold had said about the "someone" who had dropped by their table, she was tempted to ask if he was sure he wanted to expose his precious Scrim to a "pushy prick" like Peter Wolfe for the length of an evening. But she decided against it: they had enough bad feeling going between them as it was. So she sweetly said that Scrim's coming to the party was just fine with her—then couldn't resist: "But why do you sound so depressed, Harold? You sound awful. Is it something about the party?"

"You betcha it is. I wish we could call the whole damn thing off. It's going to be a real fiasco—I can feel it in my bones."

"It's going to be a *lovely* party. And if it's Scrim you're worried about, you can forget it. He knows everybody who's coming except the Wolfes. . . . And he's already met Peter."

"It's not Scrim I'm worried about!" he snapped, bypassing the dig, but reacting to it all the same. "It's you I'm worried about—I don't think you're in any shape to give a party."

"I think you'd better stop worrying about the shape I'm in once and for all, Harold," she said scathingly, undone by all this concern—this phony overdone concern she'd been getting in huge doses for the last three days. "I'm just fine, so you don't have to worry about me. *Or* the party. It's going to be great." She slammed down the phone: that was more like it.

It was the first honest exchange they'd had in three days, or at least it was the first time she had let her anger show. And her anger was considerable.

For three days the tension between them had been growing almost unbearable, filling the whole house, her anger mounting along with it: realizing he had blundered with that incredible lecture about her mother and guilt, Harold had been trying to make amends ever since, but his way of going about it—putting a show of almost sickening abjectness and solicitude and concern—had only alienated her more. Though she had pretended to accept all this, hiding her anger, pretending everything was all right—she hadn't accepted anything, and everything was far from all right. Everything was changed, perhaps irreparably. Particularly herself. Something had happened to her. Though she knew something more than his stupid lecture was involved, she wasn't sure what it was. Part of it, she knew for a fact, was simple disgust and amazement at such a lapse in judgment and taste from someone who prided himself on being a reasonable, rational man. Another part of it was what she imagined it would be like to have a whopping negative transference to a shrink who had told one the worst news about oneself—garbled news here, actually news with a reversed message, but bad news all the same—and he was paying the penalty for even *trying* to play shrink. But the worst part was seeing the effect all this had had on Benjy, who had picked up all the tension in the air and reacted to it in a way that upset her more than anything else: probably confused, maybe even frightened, Benjy had unconsciously (she was *sure* it was unconscious, it *had* to be unconscious) begun imitating Harold, dropping his coldness, suddenly becoming extremely solicitous of her. Which drove her right up the wall. She didn't want solicitude. She didn't want concern. Not from *him*.

Now she went to the bureau where she had left the stack of place cards with names written in green ink, and her carefully worked-out seating plan. She always made a seating plan: as someone who was constantly getting stuck at other people's dinner tables, she always tried to spare anybody who came to her house a similar fate. When she began going over the plan, she saw with a sinking feeling what she'd been trying to avoid all afternoon: Harold had been right—though she didn't think it was actually going to be a fiasco, it was going to be a dull, dreary party, and she couldn't understand what she'd been thinking when she had planned it to cheer herself up. Even the guest list was depressing and pathetic, proof of how she hadn't made any friends on her own over the years, but had just settled on the most compatible and sympathetic people she'd been able to find in Harold's world—pitifully few as they'd been.

And for tonight she had certainly picked the most "sympathetic," had certainly tried to cheer herself up with love. There was Jack Desprez, who had run the publicity department at Phaedre Press until last year, when he'd left to start his own public relations firm—Jack who, though Harold didn't know it, had been in love with her and trying to get her into bed for years. Without success. There was Desmund Weiss, a brilliant poet, a sweet, bitter, desperately unhappy man, who'd had three disastrous marriages and was just ending a fourth, and who, like Jack, loved her—but in a purely platonic way. There was Gladys Kirsch, a famous illustrator of children's books, a warm, dowdy, middle-aged woman she loved, who did a great deal of free art work for Knickerbocker House—fund-raising pamphlets, posters. There was Sarah Houghton, a tough, handsome, driving woman she greatly admired—the literary agent she'd worked for many years ago, when she and Harold had first come down from Cambridge. There were Simon and Celia Bates, the only exceptions, not friends of hers at all—a boring couple who were tops on their list of long-overdue social obligations: Simon, who was Harold's protegé and had inherited Harold's job of editor in chief, was a pompous little man with a ginger-colored Commander Whitehead beard and an inflated sense of his own importance;

Celia was a homely, fattish, militantly domestic young woman who made her own clothes and curtains and home-baked bread, and had three little children with a fourth due at any minute. Then there were the Wolfes. Oh Jesus, the Wolfes.

And now Harley Scrim, whom she detested. Though she admired his work, and was even willing to concede he was almost the genius he was supposed to be, he was everything she hated in a man—cruel, even sadistic, a self-styled stud, who tried to seduce every woman who crossed his path and took particular delight in humiliating the poor little wife he kept stashed away (along with five children) in Maine. The only man she knew who completely deserved the title of Male Chauvinist Pig.

Now, wondering where to put him, she studied her diagram of the table, where she had Celia Bates sitting next to Jack Desprez. Scrim hated Jack, claiming that Jack had deliberately never run enough ads for his books or gotten him on enough TV-talk shows when he'd been head of publicity at Phaedre Press. Scrim also hated overly-domestic women like his little wife—and Celia Bates. Maliciously smiling, she quickly scribbled Scrim's name between Jack's and Celia's on the diagram, and after carefully writing his name on a place card, carried everything up to the dining room.

As she began distributing the cards around the table, Maria's voice drifted in from the kitchen: "I still no unnerstand. What is baky bits?"

"Bits of dried up bacon rind," answered her son, not Cora.

"I never hear of such a thing in my life. I never hear people eat such a thing and certain never see in this house," said Maria from the sink as Emma rushed into the kitchen. Cora was sitting at the table, carefully spooning softened cheese onto rounds of toast.

Benjy came out of the walk-in grocery closet clutching a box of pretzels, his tense little face lighting up with relief at the sight of her. "Hi, ma," he said, coming to kiss her on the cheek, which hardly surprised her since it had been going on for the last three days. What surprised her was her reaction: she wasn't sure she cared for these kisses. In fact, she didn't.

"The Benjamin think I take his baky snix, *Señora* Soller," complained Maria, as The Benjamin took a can of soda from the icebox and exited, fast—giving Emma a broad wink on his way out of the room.

"I don't think he thinks that, Maria," she said wearily.

"Then why he always asking me where those things I never see?"

"I think it's because he asks me to get something and I forget, as I explained to you the other day, Maria," she said, trying to catch Cora's eye, but Cora was having none of this, and kept her eyes on her cheese puffs. She decided it was as good a time as any to explain about Scrim. "Mr. Sohier just told me he's invited an extra guest, a very important business connection, to the party," she began hesitantly, while Maria furiously scrubbed at a pot in the sink and Cora doggedly went on piling cheese on toast. "All it actually means is that we'll be eleven instead of ten . . . but I hope that's all right. I mean it really won't make any difference, except maybe having to stretch the food a bit."

"Mrs. Sohier. You've got enough food here to feed a platoon." Cora, addressing her canapés, not Emma.

"I glad to hear you say that, *Dona* Cora. So much food go to waste in this house you never believe. I tell the *señora* all the time is too much food but she no listen. What here go in the garbage can is enough to feed a whole family in my country for a month."

Somehow managing to keep her face expressionless and her voice mild, Emma said, "Well, since an extra guest doesn't seem to create any problems, I think I'll go set a place for him," and strode with scissor-stiff legs into the dining room, wishing she had the nerve to kick the door shut behind her. With clumsy, jerky movements, she took some extra silver from the sideboard and began setting a place for Scrim.

"What country is that you're from, Maria. Mexico?"

"No. Colombia."

"Columbia? You mean Columbia, Georgia, from down our South? I thought sure you were from Mexico. Or Puerto Rico."

"No. Colombia. South Americas."

"South America? Hoo, girl—you're a long ways from home!"

Well, *there's* your Old Cora—now you satisfied? Emma asked herself, but hardly satisfied with anything, this interesting reappearance of the Old Cora least of all, she grimly returned to the sideboard to get china and glassware for Scrim.

"Yes. I is. Very long ways from my home."

"You have a fambly, Maria?"

"My husband, Felipe, is *muerto*. Dead. For six years now. But I have the son, Carlos. Eight. He live with my *mamá* in Santa Marta. I send them the moneys. I go to other country only to work and send my *mamá* and Carlos the moneys—is only reason I here, you unnerstand."

"Ho yes, girl. I understand comp*let*ely.—But it must be awfully hard on you."

"Hod?"

"Hard. *Diff*-ee-cult. To be so far from your own folk, your mother and chile. From your own kine. But you sure don't look old enough to have a chile of eight. You look like a baby yousef."

"I thirty-one, *Dona* Cora. In my country is very strange thing--the woman stay looking young for the long time, then pffffift, all sudden they looking like old lady. Is not a nice thing, I tell you.—Yes. As you say is hard. *Diff*-ee-cult. But that is the life."

"*Now* you're talkin', girl! Truer words were never spoke, Maria girl!"

Leaving them to this abundant, if belated, rapport, leaving the candles still undone, she rushed up front, far away from the two philosophers. As she passed Benjy's open door (it was always open now, another one of the new developments the last three days had brought), she saw him sitting at his desk in lamplight, his head bent low over an open book; she hadn't seen him tinkering with the equipment on the shelves for three days—another new development. Two steps past his door, she stopped, powerfully struck by something vulnerable in the arch of the thin neck, some intensity in the angle of the bent head, and found herself overwhelmed by a sudden, sweeping desire: all she wanted to do was retrace her steps, go into his room, take him by the hand—and lead him out of that dim chamber with its sinister wall of shelves, out of that apartment, out of that building, that city, that place, that life . . . to where? to what? Another place. Another life.

Instead, what she finally did was retrace her steps and go into his room—to ask him how his day at school had been ("Okay"), what kind of a greeting he had gotten from Cora ("Okay"), what he wanted for his early supper ("canned spaghetti and meatballs"), and what he planned to do with himself while the party was going on ("I'll come out and say hello to everybody, then come on back in here and hole up with TV").

Somewhat startled and unnerved by the latter—she didn't see any need for him to come out and "say hello to everybody," but she also didn't see any tactful way of discouraging him—she went to her room, shut the door, took a quick bath, and was just stretching out for a short rest, when Minda called to check on what to wear to the party. Actually, Minda (who had only called once during the last two days to tell her that Inga's cousin "Gunnar" had taken the job, and that she, Minda, was about to join "the world of the living" again) had a lot more than clothes she wanted to talk about, but Emma cut her short.

"You sure it's all right if I wear pants, Em?"

"You can wear anything you want, Minda. It really doesn't matter

—as I keep telling you, it's just a group of old friends." She decided not to mention Harley Scrim.

"*Your* old friends. As *I* keep telling *you*, it's been so long since I've been with anything besides fashion freaks, I'm not sure I know the right way to behave any more. I'm really all uptight about doing something that might embarrass you or Harold."

Oh make her shut up make her shut *up*, thought Emma, gripping the phone.

"Well." A nervous titter. "I'll let you get back to whatever it was I got you from. —What was the time again?"

"Seven-thirty," said Emma, and after hanging up, lay back and shut her eyes. Though she wasn't at all tired—in fact, to the contrary, felt very well as she had now for days—something told her it might be a good idea to store up a reserve of strength for the long, and probably taxing, evening ahead.

Just how long and taxing she would soon find out.

"You look just great, Em. Terrific. Prettier than you've looked in years."

Demurely thanking him, she moved away from the mirror where they'd been reflected side-by-side: The Happy Couple—he, knotting his tie, she, combing her hair. Though she hadn't finished with her hair, she decided to wait until she had the mirror to herself; that double reflection and the barrage of compliments were more than she could take.

Patting his tie, he said something about checking the bar and went out, and she moved back to finish her hair at the mirror. The compliments hadn't been pure flattery—she saw she did, by some miracle, look pretty—but she also saw she looked pale, and took a box of powdered blusher out of the top bureau drawer.

As she moved the soft brush loaded with pink powder across her face, voices drifted down the hall. "Was it your ma's idea for you to get all spiffed up like that, old boy? Seems to me you're a bit past the age where you have to come trotting out and make an appearance."

"Actually, it was my idea. Dad."

". . . was, eh?"

"Ya. It was. I thought it would look pretty peculiar if I stayed holed up in my room. Like some sort of psyched-out social misfit. Dad."

"Oh? Well, you've got a point there, old bean. I just didn't think any of you kids cared about the social amenities. Thought you kids were against 'em."

"I can't speak for 'kids.' Dad. But speaking for myself, I think the social amenities are pretty important. They impose a certain kind of discipline and order. And there isn't an awful lot of that around."

"Ah yes. Quite. Right on! . . . Well. I gather you've had your supper. Need anything else? No? Well then, want me to shut your door? You sure? There'll be an awful lot of noise and . . . okay. See you round the quad."

Finally unlocking eyes with her own mirror-image, Emma shoved the blusher in the bureau drawer and started down the hall. Benjy's door was closed. Closed by whom—Dad or Old Bean? "Em?" called Dad from the bar as she hurried toward the kitchen. "This pumpkin's beginning to rot. What d'you think I should do with it?"

Forbearing to tell him exactly what she thought he should do with it, she told him to put it up on one of the bookcase shelves, and went into the kitchen where Cora sat reading the morning *Times* at the formica table, and Maria stood in the corner, softly murmuring Spanish into the wall phone. Cora was wearing (though certainly not at *her* request) the traditional black silk serving uniform with lacy white apron and collar and cuffs. Maria, having gratuitously announced on Tuesday that she wouldn't wear the traditional rig, since black brought bad luck, was wearing starchy white. The air was warm and filled with delicious, subtle smells, shining stacks of china plates and platters stood on the counters, with gleaming silver serving utensils precisely laid out like surgical instruments alongside them.

As she came in, Cora lowered the *Times* and piercingly examined her through lilac-tinted granny glasses. Grim silence.

But then she had hardly expected compliments from the New Cora. "I came to see if everything was all right, Cora, and to find out if we're going to use our old system of signals."

"Everything's under control, Mrs. Sohier. But I don't understand what you mean by signals."

Much to her annoyance, she felt herself blushing. "I mean those signals we always used for clearing plates between courses or refilling the buffet platters. I mean . . . we never used a bell. You just used to crack open the door and catch my eye, and I'd nod if it was time to clear or bring more of anything in. . . ."

"Funny, I don't remember any of that, but I guess that way's all right with me. Anything else about the serving?"

Nervously, glancing at Maria, still on the phone, she said, almost whispering, "Well, only the business about who's going to serve and who's going to clear. But I'd really rather you and Maria worked that out between you."

"We've already worked that out, Mrs. Sohier." Loud and clear. Then, even louder: "Maria knows her business. Like you told me on the phone, she's a fine worker, that Maria. A bit touchy and uppity, but a good girl. If I were you, I'd hang on to her—a good girl is hard to find nowadays." And with that, stood up as the front doorbell began ringing.

"*I'll* get that, Cora," she said quickly, firmly. "In fact, we'll get all the doorbells—you and Maria have enough to do," she added and dashed out, but traveling the shorter distance from the bar, Harold had already beat her to it. She came up behind him in the tiny entrance hall, just as he opened the door—on Minda and Peter Wolfe.

For one long, awkward moment they stood out on the dusty corridor-carpeting, looking embarrassed, blinking at Harold, clearly not knowing how to proceed. "Hello, Harold," Minda began shyly. "I'm Minda Wolfe, and this is my husband, Peter. We . . . ah, *there's* Emma."

But Harold was determined to do the honors. In his own fashion.

"Minda. Peter," he said with gravity, stiffly bowing from the waist. Then throwing the door wide: "Come in. Come *in!*"

"Have you ever read *Songs from Palma*, Harold?"

"No-o. Don't believe I have. What is it—Stevens? Or Graves." Wearily polite.

"Neither. It is I. A book of poems I wrote fifteen years ago. Melisandre Harris I was then. It won that year's Parmenter Prize and Young Poet's Award. Emma has a copy. At least I think she does."

"Copy of what?" cut in Scrim—to Harold's obvious relief.

"Copy of a collection of poems I wrote." Demurely lowering her eyes, Minda "playfully" smiled. "I guess what you might call a slim volume of verse."

"*You* write *poetry?*"

Minda's answer to Scrim was drowned out.

Emma softly laughed. She had caught this tripartite exchange in one of those freaks of acoustics that sometimes occur in crowded rooms —when a sort of telephonic tunnel suddenly opens up and one can hear a conversation from many feet away. In this case, it was just from the far end of the dinner table that she'd overheard this fugue before the voices of the others rose again, closing the tunnel, making it impossible to hear another word. Not that she had to. The rest was neatly played out in pantomime: bending over poet-Minda like a vulture, Scrim reclaimed her attention, while Jack Desprez (whom Scrim had rudely abandoned in mid-sentence) and Harold exchanged wild, comic looks —Jack shaking his head and blowing out his cheeks, Harold rolling his eyes; then Jack turned back to the uphill work of Celia Bates on his right, and Harold, relieved of the burden of Minda, happily turned back to Gladys Kirsch on his left. Which wasn't the seating arrangement Emma had so carefully worked out on her diagram. On her diagram, she had taken great pains to spare Harold, and had put Minda far away between Jack and Desmund Weiss—but thanks to Scrim, all that was changed, and Minda was now sitting on Harold's right. On the other hand, thanks to Scrim, the party now had a focus, had a little entertainment which promised to carry them through the rest of the evening.

Going even further, it was actually, thanks to Scrim, that the party had gotten off the ground at all. It had begun badly, so badly Emma was sure her premonitions (and Harold's) had been right. For the first half hour everyone had stood about in stiff little groups, wearing the set, martyred expressions of people facing the worst: three deadly hours to be struggled through before any escape is possible. In the midst of this polite pall, Benjamin Sohier, all togged out in flannels and blazer and tie, had suddenly made an appearance and made a solemn journey around the room, gravely introducing himself, shaking hands, then finally making his exit, leaving a startled, unnerved silence in his wake: What was *that* all about? As the silence continued, and they heard the distant shutting of Benjy's door, Peter Wolfe suddenly gave Harold a thump on the arm: "Man, are you lucky! How'd you get a kid to look or *act* like that now, when all the other kids his age are such freaks?"

"Well. He's an . . . unusual boy," Harold said into the continuing silence, obviously in great pain.

Then someone coughed, someone else said, "Well, as I was telling you . . ." and the buzz of inane chatter resumed. Detaching himself from Peter Wolfe (who'd had him trapped for the last fifteen minutes), Harold began refurbishing drinks, pouring with a lavish hand. Just what was needed—from that point on things loosened up, began to move. And gradually, in this new lubricity, everyone in the room—with the exception of Peter Wolfe—became aware of the way Harley Scrim was staring at Minda. Looking surprisingly beautiful, Minda was sitting on one of the corner couches talking nonstop at poor Desmund Weiss; Desmund, who ordinarily doted on pretty women, was looking extremely pale and peaked. Scrim, his hawky face brooding under the bowl of yellow plopping hair, sat enthroned on the stiff settee in the middle of the room, flanked by Sarah Houghton and Simon Bates—Phaedre Press royalty attended by ministering courtiers. Obviously not listening to either of them, Scrim sat like some motionless bird of prey, devouring Minda with his eyes: starting at the rhinestone buckles of her shoes, the pale yellowgreen eyes would travel upward along black silk pants legs, up past sproddled knees to the silk-covered crotch, thoughtfully pause, continue up to the breasts loosely bobbling in the laced-up buccaneer-style black silk shirt, consideringly pause, climb on up to the wide, shining mouth babbling about poetry to poor Desmund Weiss—then drop back down to the jeweled buckles, to repeat their slow, carnivorous tour upward again. It was, when observed closely, literally obscene—and with the exception of Peter Wolfe, everybody in the room observed it closely at some point. Over and over, while the chatter of his companions reached fever pitch, Scrim's eyes made their ravenous sortie, but, strangely enough, he made no attempt to get up and cross the room for a more direct contact with Minda—who, even more strangely, didn't seem to feel those eyes eating her up alive.

Then suddenly Scrim hauled all bony six-feet-four of himself off the settee, and strode—not over to Minda—but into the three-sided dining room, where in full view of everyone, he strolled around the table inspecting the place cards. When he'd completed one circuit of the table and was back to where he'd started, he quickly reached down and switched two of the cards, then returned to the settee. Minda and Celia Bates's place cards, Emma discovered almost immediately after, when Cora announced dinner was served—which put Minda on Scrim's left instead of Celia, and Minda on poor Harold's right.

But not really "poor Harold," since he hadn't seemed to mind. Harold, in fact, had found the whole thing very funny. Emma, on the other hand, hadn't found it funny at all: she was furious with Scrim and disgusted with Harold, who was acting like some kind of pandering pimp—Nothing's Too Good for Our Golden Horny Boy. But when everyone was lined up at the buffet, and she took Harold aside and tried to tell him how upset she was, he only maddeningly smiled and patted her on the arm. "Don't take it all so *seriously*, sweetie . . . it's only a party. Relax. Enjoy yourself. I certainly don't mind sitting next to her, since it's clear old Scrim's not going to let anybody else get near her, and your inviting her's actually turned out to be a terrific stroke of luck. She's turning what was going to be a disaster into a night we'll never forget." And with another pat and a laugh, marched off to the buffet.

Leaving her speechless. But she finally went and helped herself to some food and joined the others at the table, and in spite of everything, decided to try and take his advice—try to relax and enjoy herself like everybody else. Because everybody else was thoroughly enjoying himself by then. Particularly Minda, who was finally aware of her conquest, and was lit up with a brilliant, flushed gaiety. And watching her childish pleasure and excitement, Emma found herself more touched than disgusted: this was exactly the kind of thing the poor old wreck kept saying she needed—so who was she to sit in judgment, who was she to begrudge it to her? Especially when it wasn't hurting anyone. Not even Peter Wolfe, who still seemed unaware of the whole thing, and didn't seem to see what was now going on right across the table from him.

While she found that rather odd—he'd have to be blind to miss it—she didn't give it more than a passing thought. That was their business, not hers. Tricky as that business was: though she couldn't connect the pleasant man on her right with the sinister man Minda was always describing, there was something definitely sinister and unwholesome about their relationship; seeing them together, both so dark and flamboyantly sexy and handsome, one got a whiff of narcissism or maybe even incest . . . the sort of things Emma found too boring and perverted to want to consider for long. The important point was that, whatever he was to Minda, Peter Wolfe was a disarmingly intelligent, charming man, and though she'd put him on her right to keep someone else from being stuck, she enjoyed talking to him as much as Desmund Weiss, whom she'd put on her left.

But Peter or Desmund, it didn't matter; by the time Minda had dragged out her book of poetry, Emma was really enjoying herself. The reason for giving the party was paying off: she was completely cheered up, having a better time than she'd had in months. The food was delicious—Cora, New or Old, had surpassed herself—and Maria and Cora were working beautifully as a team. Even Harold, once he was released from Minda, seemed to be having a wonderful time.

So much so that when they had finished the main course, and Cora and Maria were efficiently clearing the table to make way for the salad and cheese, Harold made a great point of catching her eye and giving her a broad, beamish, congratulatory smile. And in the pleasant glow of the moment, she forgot all their differences and smiled back, while he inclined his head toward his empty glass: more wine? She nodded: though everybody was well afloat by then, she saw no point in not keeping up a good thing, not keeping things the way they were. So Harold got up and went to the sideboard where two bottles of Margaux stood unopened (they had already polished off four), and while Maria and Cora slowly began passing salad and cheese in tandem, he carefully worked out the corks. Then, first bottle in hand, he followed Maria and Cora around the table, filling glasses. "I work on Saturdays," Gladys protested feebly, happily watching the wine climb in her glass; "Write down the name of this for me later," said Simon, eagerly lifting his glass to make things easier for Harold; "I was afraid you'd run dry," murmured Sarah, while Peter Wolfe said, "Beautiful burgundy, Hal," and neither wincing nor pointing out that it was a Bordeaux, "Hal" smiled appreciatively, filled Emma's glass with the last of that bottle, and went back to the sideboard for the other.

As he continued up the other side of the table, Emma contentedly settled down to her wine and salad and cheese. Peter Wolfe was talking to Sarah, Desmund was listening, glassyeyed, while Celia Bates de-

scribed the *accouchement* of their cairn terrier. Momentarily free to
give herself over to the pleasure of eating, Emma happily smeared
runny Brie on a biscuit: just like her strength, her healthy old appetite
was coming back.

"I dassn't."

It was the trick of the acoustics, the telephonic tunnel again. Unable to believe her ears, Emma reluctantly lifted her eyes from her
salad, and looked down at the far end of the table where Minda, her
hand clamped over her wine glass, sat swiveled around in her chair
laughing up at Harold, who stood behind her inclining the neck of the
bottle toward her covered glass.

"You what?" Harold said dully, clearly unable to believe his eyes, not
his ears: rooted, he stood stupidly staring down into Minda's unlaced
buccaneer shirt and big, wet, laughing mouth.

"Dassn't have any more wine. It always upsets my tummy when I
mix the grain and the grape."

The idiot phrases washing over him, Harold just stood there goggling, bottle tilted toward the glass, frozen into one of those moments
that seem to last an eternity, but actually last no longer than the batting
of an eye. One of those moments when the world seems to stop. For
Harold, the moment when he fell in love with Minda. Or fell into
something—Minda's brassiere-less cleavage being the least of it.

Split seconds, not long enough for anybody to notice, but, recoiling
as though from a blow, Harold finally straightened up and confusedly
looked around the table, anxiously trying to ascertain if anybody had
seen what had just happened to him. Apparently no one but Minda
had seen—clever Minda, now busily reclaiming Scrim from Jack
Desprez.

And Emma. But Emma, who had seen, was giving the job of spearing a lettuce leaf her full attention by the time Harold's frightened
glance came to her. She could almost feel his relief as his eyes swept
past her. These things, she discovered, were inborn, were brought off
with sheer nervy instinct: skills and talents she never knew she
possessed came rushing to her aid. Her senses, suddenly heightened,
operated on several levels at once, so that while she seemed to be looking at Desmund and listening to him bitterly complain about his last
wife, she was actually observing and listening to what was going on
down the far end of the table. Suddenly gifted with double vision, she
could stare into Desmund's homely face and at the same time "see"
Harold go back and sit down heavily in his chair, set the bottle on the

table without refilling his own glass, and morosely stare down at his loaded salad plate, grimly determined not to look at Minda. Whom she "saw" abandon Scrim and turn to Harold, now that he was back, and whom she heard say in a new furry voice: "I helped you to salad and cheese, Harold."

"Thanks, that was very nice of you," mumbled Harold, glum, almost surly, still determined not to look up at her.

"It's absolutely yummy cheese," persisted Minda, equally determined, cutting up Brie like sirloin with her knife and fork.

Apparently heartened—he couldn't possibly be hooked by anybody who talked like that!—Harold finally gave Minda a quick sidelong glance . . . and it was immediately clear he could be. Hooked. Trapped. Sunk. It was all there on his face.

For one long moment, dispensing with tricky double-vision, Emma openly stared at Harold as he stared at Minda (who now cleverly kept her eyes on her cheese), watching his face take on the sick, bloated look of total infatuation. And lust. Mixed with despair. There was despair—she had to give him that. But that was all she was prepared to give him, and, quickly turning off the battery of her new hyperperceptions, she picked up her wine glass, almost breaking the delicate stem as she gave herself over to a kind of despair of her own. And jealousy. And murderous rage.

Luckily at this point, finding herself forced to talk to Peter Wolfe—whose charm had totally vanished, and whom she felt like violently kicking—a diversion was provided that rescued her from her terrible anger. At least, temporarily. Which was still something to be grateful for: if she'd had time to sit there much longer, she would have given the tablecloth a powerful yank and sent all the dishes crashing to the floor.

Cora, she finally realized, was urgently beckoning through the cracked-open kitchen door. Murmuring apologies to Peter, she got up and went into the kitchen, where she found that Cora had cut herself. Badly—the counter and a stack of plates were splattered with blood. Cora had tightly wound a makeshift tourniquet of paper toweling just above the cut, which was on her upper forearm—a peculiar place to have cut herself. Also peculiar was the fact that the first-aid kit they kept in one of the counter drawers was gone. And more peculiar still was the news that the sight of poor Cora's blood had made Maria sick —so sick she'd gone to collapse on the bed in her room.

Really finding all this more than peculiar, finding it all downright bizarre—why, for instance, had Cora been using a knife at all now, since the carving had been done long ago, and preparations for serving a dessert of chocolate mousse were underway?—she told herself it was no more bizarre than what was going on at the table inside, and, advising Cora to keep the tourniquet tight, slipped unobtrusively through the dining room and went up to their bathroom. Where, just as she'd expected, she found Harold's medicine cabinet well stocked with gauze and tape. This time she received curious glances as she passed back through the dining room, and when she pushed through the swinging door to the kitchen, Harold was close on her heels: "What's wrong, Em? What's going *on*?"

A good question, but she was spared the job of answering since Cora immediately came out with a curiously labored explanation: she had cut herself while slicing more veal for the light supper she and Maria had planned to have before starting on the big job of washing up. Though something in the story didn't ring true—more than something, since a beautifully arranged buffet platter with many leftover slices of veal was sitting on the formica table—she left Harold bandaging Cora with expertise, and went in to Maria, who was lying on her bed, a wrung-out washcloth across her waxen brow. "I very sorry, *señora*," she said quaveringly, after explaining that she always reacted violently to the sight of blood, "but I can help no more with the party tonight. I hope you not getting angry."

Finding this bizarre too—the poor thing seemed badly shaken and frightened, and she doubted that just the sight of Cora's blood could be responsible—she assured her she wasn't angry, and after making certain there was nothing she could do to help, told her to lie still and take it *very* easy, and slipped out. Catching a glimpse of Maria sitting up and frantically crossing herself as she shut the door.

Harold had gone back to the dining room, Cora stood impassively by the sink with a professionally bandaged forearm. Sensing trouble—something mutinous was emanating from this tall tower of a woman—she braced herself and explained that since Maria wasn't well enough to do it, she herself would help with the rest of the clearing and the serving of dessert. Her premonitions had been right: "No sirree, Mrs. Sohier. If you'll stop and remember, I've managed bigger parties than this all by myself. I could have managed this one fine without that girl, and I'll manage fine now. There's no need for you to disturb yourself or your guests—you just go sit back down at that table and enjoy yourself. You leave everything to me."

Echoes, but hardly the Old Cora. But then she was hardly the old Darlin'. "I'm sorry, Cora, but I'm going to help you."

A long and nasty silence. Then a sigh: "As you please, Mrs. Sohier. As you please."

And on this chilling note they began to work together. With Cora growing more remote and forbidding by the minute, with a tense silence sparking between them like static, they cleared the table and set out the mousse for buffet service on the sideboard, managing this smoothly except for one bad moment: after the first flurry of bewilderment among her guests had died down, after offers of help from Celia and Gladys had been firmly declined, Emma was removing Minda's plate and glass half-filled with wine (which she longed to pour over Minda's head), when Minda looked up at her: "It's just sabotage. I *warned* you they're all alike."

"Who's all alike?" From Scrim, ever hanging on Minda's every word.

"Maids. Lousy, hostile maids," Minda answered to the table at large, as Cora came in with a stack of dessert plates and set them on the sideboard. Moving woodenly. Vacant-faced.

That ought to cool the ardor of those two Theoretical Radicals, thought Emma, furiously rushing into the kitchen with Minda's dirty dishes. But she was wrong. Apparently nothing could. They were both hooked, Scrim and his editor. Though Scrim was unaware of having company, a rival, in Harold.

Somehow she managed to get through the dessert course without having to put in much time at the table. In the brief intervals she was forced to sit there, toying with her mousse and talking to Desmund (Sarah was monopolizing Peter Wolfe), she was overwhelmingly aware of Harold at the far end of the table, talking to Gladys (Scrim was monopolizing Minda), fighting a battle with himself, suffering. And by the time dessert was over, and everyone adjourned to the living room for coffee, she had turned to stone. She didn't have to help Cora serve the coffee: looking pale and subdued, Maria had come out of her room by then, in a rapid, if somewhat mysterious, recovery.

In the living room everyone settled into new groupings and pairings —everyone, that is, with the exception of Scrim, who relentlessly followed Minda to the settee, where Simon Bates immediately plopped himself down on Minda's other side. Simon too? wondered Emma, trying to decide where to sit. Then she saw Harold, moving around the room with a trayful of brandy and liqueurs, suddenly pause and sneak a long look at Minda, who was sitting on the settee in what was apparently her favorite pose—sprawled back, legs splayed wide. And as she watched Harold's eyes, worse than Scrim's had been, fasten on Minda's crotch, Emma decided not only where she was going to sit, but also how she was going to get herself through the balance of the evening.

With the highhanded license of a woman who knows she has a longstanding conquest in one man, she corralled Jack Desprez, whom she'd deliberately not paid much attention to before now. She liked Jack—more than liked Jack—and he knew it, but inviting him to the party had been enough of a come-on: if there was one thing she prided herself on, it was never being a tease. Or cruel. "Come talk to me, we haven't had a good talk in ages," she said softly, putting her arm through his and leading him off to one of the corner couches, where she had one minute of doubt as they sank down: You're going to pay for this, old girl. But it only lasted a minute, and turning her back on any other distressing spectacles the middle of the room might offer, she said in a voice, furry like Minda's, "Tell me about everything—the agency, who you've been seeing, *you*." Which he did. Eagerly. Gratefully. And while he did, she sat there waiting hopefully, needfully, impatiently for the furtive touches, the little proddings and grazings of knee and thigh and hand and elbow that had warmed her for years, that had kept her reassured about her attractiveness and desirability—but she waited in vain. The fleeting pats and jostlings, and the accompanying, smoldering glances never came.

Suddenly the talk petered out, and he gave her a long, shrewd look with his acid-blue eyes. "Feel any better now?"

"What?" she said confusedly.

"I said do you feel better now, have you recovered your cool? I'm surprised at you, baby—I thought you learned how to handle all that years ago. Thought you were beyond reacting."

"I don't know what you mean." Prissy indignation.

"I mean your husband's acute case of blue balls. I'll grant you, I've never seen him so . . . ah carried away, but as I said, I thought you learned how to handle that, live with it."

Her eyes maddeningly filling, she stared at his cool Irish face and saw what she had missed: his ten-year-old infatuation was over. Done. Pay for it? Oh, she was beginning to pay for it. Right now. "As I told you over the phone when I called to invite you," she said sharply, "I've just been through a terrible year. A year which affected everything—including my self-confidence."

"I would say so. Also your judgment. What the hell's the *matter* with you, sweetheart? What the fuck do you care if he goes around making an asshole out of himself, acting like some raunchy old goat. If you're determined to stay with him—and God knows why, but you probably are—then at least go out and have some fun yourself. It'll make you feel like a new woman. And high time. All you'd have to do is snap your fingers. I happen to know of five different guys who would just love to get you into the sack."

"Swellies. Don't forget to mail me a list of their names . . . with references of course."

"Sit down, stupid. Sorry, but you're acting stupid. You're acting like a goddamn idiot. Sit back down here and listen. I've got a few things to say to you."

She sat back down. And listened. But he had more than a few things to say:

"For years, and you damned well know it," he began, giving her a devastatingly charming smile, "in fact you more than know it, you've been banking on it—for *years* I've been sitting around waiting for you to give me the signal, waiting for you to let me know the time was ripe. I think the time is finally ripe right now, though you might not even know it yet yourself, but—and I've never seen it fail—but it's too goddamn late. Love, true love, has finally hit old Jack. Hooked. Reformed. And yet. And yet . . ." His eyes, smoldering at last, ran slowly downward from her mouth to her breasts and he burst out laughing: "And yet maybe not comple*te*ly reformed. Maybe it's not too late for you and me after all. Jesus. Going by the . . . vibes, I'd say it wasn't. As I've been trying to tell you for years, sweetheart, I'm a highly talented—*and* well-equipped—chap. I may be fifty-two but I can match any stud in his thirties any time. And I think I could do you a world of good. As for myself, there's nothing worse than an unfulfilled yen: fulfill it, and everything falls into place, old ghosts get laid to rest." He laughed again, intoxicated with himself. "Listen. Meet me late some morning —it could be at some hotel if you're leery about being seen going into my apartment house—and we'll spend the rest of the day fucking our brains out. You could even be home in time to mix the martinis for Old Horny. Of course there's always the possibility we could get seriously hung up, but I think, more likely, it would just be a terrific release for both of us. For me, it would be a sort of settling of old accounts. For you . . . Well, I think it would wipe that lousy year of yours right off the map, would do you more good than a thousand iron injections." More excited laughter. "Come on, sweetheart, don't sit there looking like that. You've needed a talking-to for a long time. You also need what I just proposed. I do too. In fact, I'm beginning to think maybe I'm not as in love as I think, since just talking about all this suddenly has me so . . . hey. Cut that *out*."

"I . . . thought you were my friend."

"Christ. I *am* your friend. The best damned friend you'll ever have. I've just had too many years of hanging around like some prize schnook, hoping you'd change your mind and see the light. My fault, not yours. Come on, sweetie, pull yourself together. You don't want any of *this* crew to see you with all your defenses down. I'm sorry, baby, I guess I piled it on too thick. Only shows how much I still care."

Still keeping her back turned toward the middle of the room, she furtively scrubbed at her cheeks with her hand. She couldn't talk. And he misinterpreted her silence:

"You *know* I'm right, Em baby. I can tell. Come to me and let me prove how right I am. If you're afraid he'll find out, let me assure you that even if he does—and he won't—he'd never leave you. You ought to know that by now. So if that's what's worrying you, forget it. And if you're worried about his leaving you for that sloppy cunt on the settee, forget that too. He'll give her a coupla fast *shtupps*—that is, if he can manage to squeeze himself in, ha ha, between her bouts with old Scrim—and he'll be back, all contrite, asking you to . . . I'll finish later. Here comes Houghton the Hatchet to play Miss Otis Regrets."

Which was exactly right. Coming up to kiss Emma's cheek (and giving her a quick, shrewd look when her lips encountered teary wetness), Sarah said that much as she regretted leaving such a *marvelous* party so early on a Friday night, she had to get up at the crack of dawn and drive to Vermont—to spend the balance of the weekend with one of her authors.

And within minutes, Sarah's departure triggered a general exodus. Within minutes, most of the others got up to go, all of them matching Sarah with elaborate explanations of why they had to leave such a *"marvelous"* party at just a little past eleven on a Friday night.

By twenty past eleven, the only ones left were the Wolfes and Scrim and Jack Desprez. Minda and Scrim sat on the settee, Peter, Emma, Jack and Harold sat on the L-shaped arrangement of couches in the corner. After manfully trying to pass some time in that company, Jack stood up and announced he had to leave too. Determined not to see him to the door, Emma stayed where she was. "I'll see you out, Jack," Harold finally said with great weariness and got up, giving the two on the settee a long and hard look before starting for the door. But not to be put off, Jack came to stand over Emma, and after loudly thanking her for a lovely evening, bent to kiss her good-by. "I'll call you first thing Monday morning," he said softly, slowly drawing his lips along her cheek and briefly burying his nose in her soft light hair—completely ignoring Peter Wolfe, who sat raptly taking all this in from less than a foot away on the corduroy couch cushions.

"Don't bother," she said as he straightened up.

For one second he stood over her, giving her one last stinging look: Ok*ay*, then. So that's it. Bye-bye Emma. And abruptly turning away, finally followed Harold to the door.

"Quite a little girl, aren't you," said Peter Wolfe, then laughed: "And what a swell little group of friends you have."

Frightened, blushing, Emma stared at him. He stared levelly back, giving her a knowing, smirking look which encompassed all—even Minda and Scrim on the settee.

Her fear growing (Minda was right, he *was* a monster), she sat silent until Harold came back from seeing Jack out, sitting down heavily and turning his back on anything distressing that might be happening in the middle of the room—just as she had a while ago. Though nothing actually seemed to be happening, Minda and Scrim were just quietly talking, the implications of what might be happening under all that quiet talk were too much for Emma, and she sat there getting more nervous and upset by the second, trying not to think of what she'd just done to Jack, and what she'd just done to herself: bye-bye Jack. Meanwhile, Harold and Peter kept making labored attempts at small talk, with Peter frequently glancing over at the two on the settee with shining eyes—as if he liked what he saw. Finally, when Emma felt she couldn't stand one more second of this sick situation—and oh it was sick—Scrim got to his feet and loudly announced he had to leave, explaining he had an early plane to catch in the morning.

Which didn't match Harold's earlier story about Scrim's dentist. And though it was just possible that Scrim's dentist had finished working on him that afternoon, Emma saw that the possibility that this was just a covering lie for Peter Wolfe was greater. And saw that Harold saw it too.

Scrim, who could be charming and gracious when required, came to thank her, then said good night to all the others in turn, reserving a particularly perfunctory good-by for Minda. Which fooled no one.

As Scrim went to the front door with Harold, Peter got up and went to his wife, now sitting in chaste solitude on the settee. "Well, Min, we'd better shove off too—we've got to meet the real estate agent up in the country at noon."

Not looking at all put out by this abridgment of her name (which, along with Minna and Minnie, had been declared impermissible years ago), "Min" obediently stood up, and the three of them trailed out to the front hall, where Harold was just closing the door on Scrim.

With icy detachment, Emma watched Harold turn from the door, saw his face fall when he realized Minda was leaving—then saw him quickly try to hide his disappointment by ducking into the closet for their coats. Brace yourself, she thought: This is going to be a real treat.

And so it was:

Something, probably just the simple instinct of self-preservation (no furtive and Inflaming Jack Desprez-type fumblings for *him*), made Harold hand Peter his wife's coat, and once Peter had helped her into it, Minda came toward her gushing in a loud voice, "Absolutely *fantas-tic* party, angel," —adding in a whisper as she kissed the air by her cheek, "My God, what *fun*. I'll call Monday when we can talk." Then off she went to Harold, something Emma particularly wanted to see, while in musical-chairs rotation, Peter came up and, deliberately imitating Jack, gave her a long nasty nuzzling kiss on the cheek. Paralyzed by anger, she fixedly stared past the pink rim of his ear at Minda, who was now going up to Harold, standing puffily like Major Hoople at the door; "Thanks for a lovely evening, Harold. . . . I'm sorry we didn't have more time to talk," Minda said daintily to Harold, while Minda's hus-band hotly whispered in Emma's ear, "What say we have a little drinky-poo sometime." Finally coming to life, Emma pulled roughly away—just in time to see Minda, politely shaking Harold's hand, sud-denly swoop forward in a stagy "impulsive" way to give him a kiss on the cheek . . . and give him a neatly calculated swipe with her big right bobbling breast.

Emma looked at her husband, swollen, apoplectically pink, then at Peter Wolfe, leering, thoroughly pleased with himself. "I'll say good night now, Minda and Peter—there's someone in the kitchen I have to see," she said, and rushed off, leaving Harold the job of seeing them out. And composing himself.

On her way through the dining room, she stopped and took her wallet out of the sideboard drawer, where she'd stuck it after paying the
delivery boy for the ice. The kitchen was spotless; Maria's door was
closed. Cora was sitting at the formica table reading the *Times* again,
fully dressed, clearly long-ready to go. Wondering why she hadn't come
out to say she was ready to leave, Emma paid her, adding a lavish tip
—and wasn't at all surprised, when after thanking her, Cora said it
would probably be the last time, since she didn't think she would be
doing "this sort of work" any more. What surprised her was her reaction: boredom. She couldn't have cared less. And as cool and reserved
as Cora herself, she said she was sorry to hear that, but she quite "understood" (a lie, since she understood nothing, nothing), and silently
accompanied Cora up front.

At the door, Cora paused with her hand on the knob, clearly weighing something, and finally—perhaps just because they were far from
Maria's door, well out of earshot—decided to speak. "I take back what
I said earlier about that Maria-girl, Mrs. Sohier. I'm glad she won't be
staying on with you. She's a good worker, but she's . . . a strange one.
I can get along with most anyone, as you know. But there's something *definitely* wrong with that girl." When Emma merely looked
baffled, she suddenly reached out and grabbed her hand, vigorously
pumping it up and down while giving it an "affectionate" squeeze.
Then, to Emma's increasing horror, as though having shrewdly guessed
at all those earlier thoughts and wanting to make some wry concession
to them, she obligingly turned into Ruby Dandridge for one split second, bobbing her head and flashing a blinding Bojangles smile: "Now
you call me times to times and let me know how y'all are," she said,
giving Emma's hand a last powerful squeeze before opening the door:
"Don't you go and be a stranger now, you *heah?*"

Emma heard. And sick at heart said, "I won't, Cora," turning away
as Cora slipped out the door.

Luckily, she still had several things to do before going to bed. With
even more luck, Harold would be asleep by the time she finally got to
their room.

Returning to the kitchen, she picked up her wallet and considered
Maria's closed door. Whether she was a Strange One or not, Maria deserved a handsome tip too: she'd not only obligingly postponed leaving
for her weekend off until Saturday morning, but had also worked
hard, *very* hard, and on top of it all had undoubtedly forced herself to
get up and work again, sick as she'd felt after that business of Cora

cutting herself. Though giving her the tip momentarily posed a problem—Maria was probably asleep now and would be leaving early, long before they were awake—Emma solved it by sticking a twenty-dollar bill in an old laundry-bill envelope, along with a note that read, "*Muchas gracias* for helping with the party, Emma Sohier," and shoved the envelope through the crack under Maria's door.

Flipping off the fluorescent lights, she trudged up to the living room and started turning off all the lamps in there. As she went to get the last light, a small spotlight over the bar, she stared at the festive jumble of bottles, then poured herself a small snifter of brandy: she hadn't had any brandy earlier—she hadn't been drinking much all evening, in fact—but felt she certainly could use something now. Taking a first large mouthful, she stared over the rim of the glass at the Jack-o-lantern stuck in one of the bookshelves over the bar. In just four days it had begun to wrinkle and cave in on itself. It had also begun to rot, as Harold had said: above the heady fumes of brandy, the fetid stench of decay came wafting to her nostrils. Appropriate, that.

Sipping more slowly, she reviewed the events of the evening, and with the same detachment that had come over her since dessert, asked herself what she felt. The answers: anger. Above all, anger—almost rage. Scorn: he'd looked like such an *idiot* standing over Minda, gaping down into her cleavage like some vaudeville comedian, like Bobby Clark. Shame. For both of them: making himself look like such a total ass, and making her look (if only by implication) such a helpless, vulnerable fool. A touch of fear: what was going to happen now? Where did they go from here? A touch of sadness, by no means grief, that sprang up from a terrible sense of waste, a sense of time and emotions being recklessly squandered and sent down the drain. A weary sort of acceptance and acknowledgment—as if this was something she'd known was going to happen all along.

This last idea really hit her, shook her up out of that detachment at last. Yes. That moment during dinner when Harold had stood over Minda, bottle in hand, eyes devouring her breasts, had the feeling of a *déjà vu*, of something she had already seen. Or had expected to see. Or had wanted to see.

Had she subconsciously been working toward this, planning on its happening all along?

Going still, very still, she considered this. Considered the way she had stayed focused on Minda's negative qualities—her nuisance value, her neuroticism and selfishness and intrusiveness—ignoring, perhaps deliberately, Minda's obvious physical charms and well-known irresistibility to men, particularly certain kinds of men. Could it be that she hadn't really been "putting up" with Minda's annoying presence at all, but had actually been *keeping* her in her life, even drawing her in further—wanting to bring about what had happened tonight? Knowing she could bring it about? Knowing the outcome was inevitable?

Rocking, frightening questions. With implications reaching so far and so deep, she could hardly expect to answer them while standing there, drinking brandy at the bar. If ever.

Flattened, exhausted, she quickly drained the glass, turned off the spotlight and started up the hall, where she stopped, and against her better judgment, went noiselessly into Benjy's room. Moving carefully in the pitchy darkness, she went to his bed and stood looking down at the huddled shape, remembering his pompous little tour of the living room. Strange. Sad. Strange sad little boy. Who was he? she wondered, while he mumbled fitfully in his sleep and rolled away nearer the wall—as if he sensed her standing above him in the darkness, a frightened, unhappy woman, about to reach down and scoop him up in a suffocating maternal stranglehold. She turned and groped for the door: what did she want from him? Who *was* he? Just a boy. A troubled and, like herself, probably unhappy, eleven-year-old boy—not a rock for her to attach herself to like some limpet.

Harold, stripped down only as far as his shirt and shorts and socks, was sitting in the armchair staring bleakly off into space.

Dazed, he watched her come in and go straight to her closet for pajamas, then began guiltily blinking—as though expecting her to ask why he was still sitting there half-undressed. She didn't ask. Just as he didn't ask what she'd been doing all this time: he obviously hadn't even noticed how long she'd been gone.

As she carried her pajamas around to her side of the bed, he stirred and seemed to give himself a shake, mental as well as physical. "Well. How do you think it went."

"Fairly well. I think everybody had a pretty good time. Don't you?"

"I guess. I think it went along at a nice clip for a while, but suddenly ran down toward the end. Ran out of gas."

Perched on the edge of the bed, she slipped off her sheer tights and pants without taking off her long velvet skirt: something warned her not to show any more flesh than was necessary. "I think it went a lot better than that. Some people had a marvelous time." She paused, then laughed: "Particularly Scrim." Ah, the joys of cruelty.

Again he stirred, or really shuddered, this time, and finally stood up and began unbuttoning his shirt. Peeling it off and draping it carefully over the back of the chair, he then heavily sat back down. "She's even worse than I thought she'd be."

She turned and glared: she was to be spared nothing, it seemed. "Who."

"*Who.* Your pal. Your big buddy. Minda. Minda Wolfe."

He was, she finally realized, in the grip of that nice old romantic compulsion to speak The Beloved's—(The *Beloved*)—name. He was also, she saw, in the grip of one of those guilt-inspired self-destructive impulses that made one want to blurt out the incriminating truth ("She's . . . wonderful"), but, nerve suddenly failing, made one come out with its opposite.

Almost smiling—her anger was that terrible—she yanked off the long velvet skirt and reached for her pajama pants. "I really don't understand, Harold. I mean just before dinner you were going on about how she'd saved the day, how she was turning a disaster into a night we'd never forget, and now you're contradicting yourself. I happen to think she behaved beautifully. Scrim was the one who behaved badly. He was disgusting. But aside from Scrim, everyone else seemed to like Minda. Including you, I thought. In fact I was under the impression you and she were really getting along just *swimmingly*."

"I barely talked to her, for Chrissake! We exchanged maybe four words all in all!" he exploded indignantly. Guiltily. "But even that was enough. She's an absolute idiot, a stupid, vulgar, pretentious slut. Poet. Poet, my arse. Running off at the mouth to Scrim about that dumb book of poems she wrote fifty years ago like she'd gotten the Nobel Prize. Christ. I don't understand how she ever got into Berkeley or Radcliffe, much less managed to write a poem. She's a stupid, supercilious *flea*-brain, and I think it's damned demeaning for you to have somebody like that for a friend."

Did she have to *listen* to all this? Have to watch him, so besotted and wild with jealousy about Scrim, completely give himself away?

"Actually, there's no need to get so excited, because I couldn't agree more," she said softly, savoring this totally new sensation—this heady sense of power and excitement that came with being deliberately cruel. "As I explained when I said I'd invited them, I was discharging a final sort of obligation to Minda by asking her here tonight. From this point on I'm going to ease her out of my life. So you don't have to worry about my having any 'demeaning' friends—or about my ever asking her here again."

She could almost hear the moan in his head.

"I'm glad to hear that," he said in a humbled, muffled voice as he bent to tug off his socks. Then he sat up straight and stared at her as she unhooked her brassiere and slipped into her pajama top. "It sounds like you're all back to yourself. It certainly looked that way tonight. It was the first time I've seen you look like you were enjoying yourself in months."

"Oh, I was. Enjoying myself." She stood up, planning a fast escape to the bathroom: a sudden thickening in his voice told her what was going to happen if she didn't.

It happened before she could escape. He came lumbering over to where she stood, an enormous erection poking out his shorts, and gripped her shoulders with hands so hot they scalded her through the thin silk of the pajamas. It's Minda, not you. Don't just *stand* here, she told herself as he fumbled with the buttons of her pajama top, breathing hard through his nose. *Say* something, stupid. Say something that will hit him where he lives, shake him up, get him off you. Tell him to go in the bathroom and whack off while he thinks of Minda. Tell him to go call *up* Minda, and whack off into the phone. Tell him you're not going to be the proxy lay for any slut.

But she didn't say a word. Or move. His lust was contagious. She had never felt anything like it before.

"I'm not . . . fixed up," she gasped, as he ripped open her pajama pants and, shoving them down and forcing her legs apart, jammed into her standing up, gripping her bottom with burning hands.

Cursing, he made a guttural sound, then said something clearer that sounded like "Always . . . abortion now."

"What? *What* did you say?"

He withdrew and stood there shaking, eyes closed. "Get fixed up. Hurry *up*."

And so she did. Despising herself, shaking, as frantic as he, she fixed up in record time.

When she came out she found that he had ripped a sheet off the bed and spread it on the floor, and for one split second something like reason returned: was he that afraid of germs? She stared at him as he stood there, *Sohier erectus*, Aquarian man. "Get down on all fours."

She did at once. It was a position she had never much liked, since she rarely had an orgasm that way, but meek as a mild white cow she got down on all fours and he mounted her like an angry bull.

She had a violent orgasm right away.

But not he. Goaded by her shuddering bovine movements, and by thoughts of Minda (she could feel it with each thrust), he slowly began to move her, almost ride her, down the length of the room. And as, grunting and snorting and panting like the two copulating beasts they were, they moved off the sheet onto the rug, poor Emma had two last lightning thoughts before she was reduced to orgasmic idiocy. One was: Benjy will hear us. The other: It's like Blazes Boylan and Molly Bloom. Then they ran out of floor space, and Harold got her against the far wall, where, head lowered like some docile quivering ewe, she stopped having any thoughts. About Benjy. Or life-and-art. Or anything. At all.

Rx

"Guess what."

"What."

"Go ahead and *guess*."

Harold just called and asked you to spend the day with him in a suite at the Plaza. Or to fly away for a mad week in Rome. "I can't guess, Minda."

"Scrim just called and told me he'd stayed over, just so he could take me to lunch today."

"I thought all those arrangements had been made before he left here Friday night."

". . . what?"

"I said, that's nice, Minda. Ought to be fun. A lot of laughs."

"For God's sake, Emma—what's the matter with you?"

You well may ask. "Nothing, really. Just tired, I guess."

"The party was probably too much for you. But I'm selfish enough to be glad you gave it. I haven't had such fun in years. I was dying to call you from the country to rehash the whole thing in detail, but that damned storm Saturday afternoon knocked out all the telephone lines up there. Life in the country has its drawbacks. I would have called when we got in last night, but nosy Peter was hanging around. . . . He thinks you're absolutely terrific, by the way."

"That's nice. I'm glad. I liked him too. He's very charming and . . . sweet."

"Sweet isn't exactly what *I'd* call him, but he does have a lot of charm and knows how to spread it around."

"He's also damned smart. A lot smarter than you give him credit for being, and I'd be very careful if I were you."

A long simmering pause. Then a nasty laugh. "I know how smart he is, dear girl. And if you're talking about Scrim, there's something you don't understand. He *loved* that, you dingdong. Was thrilled. It's one of his hangups—he loves watching men, particularly when they're rich or famous, make passes at me. I told you he was sick, but then you never believe a word I say. What I'd like to know is what you think I'm going to do with Scrim. I'm just going to have *lunch* with the man, and while I'm at it see if I can get him to help me get some kind of job in publishing."

"I see."

"No. I don't think you do. Jesus, you're a real pain in the ass today. I guess you didn't hear me. I said job. J-O-B. Remember? Just what you've been telling me to get."

"I heard you the first time. And I think it's dandy you want to get a job. But you're picking the wrong time to try for a job in publishing. —They're firing, not hiring people in publishing now. According to Harold."

So then. The name was out. Deliberately brought out—she wanted to see what Minda would do with it.

"Well, that's hardly encouraging. But I'd still like to give it a try. . . . Incidentally, talking about sweet, Harold is *really* sweet, a perfect dear."

"Yes. He is that." Sweet. Just the heavy-handed sort of approach she might have expected. Subtle as a head-on collision.

"And talking about smart, *there's* somebody really smart. I mean we never exchanged more than ten words, but I still got the picture. Got the vibes. Brain waves. I mean."

I'll bet you got them. Only Harold said all you exchanged were *four* words. "Yes. Harold's very smart."

"Well. I can see you're not in any mood to talk. I have to go and wash my hair anyway. No time to run downtown and have it done. —Thank *God* Gunnar will be here when the twins come in at noon from play group. She's an absolute dream, by the way. I'll call you late this afternoon and tell you how it went."

"How what went."

"*Lunch.*"

With the crash of the slammed-down phone still reverberating in her ear, Emma hung up and stared at the drawer-pull she had just garroted with the phone cord again. Then raised her eyes and considered the picture of her *suegra*, sitting in its usual place between the phone and lamp. Then snatched it up and hurled it at the far wall of the room. The chunks of lucite, with Erasmus-Elsie sandwiched in between, bounced off the wall, leaving a small gray mark—and dropped, intact, on the deep-piled rug. And she burst out laughing: just as she'd always known, the old witch was indestructible.

From far away in the kitchen, came the sound of Maria's clattering. Looking pale and subdued, Maria had returned from her weekend a half hour ago, suddenly appearing in the bedroom door to thank her for *"la propina"*—the tip she'd pushed under the door Friday night— afterward lingering to ask: "You have any special plan for the week, *señora?*" And when she'd said she didn't understand, Maria had said: "I mean is next-to-last week I be here, and I wondering if you have any special thing you want me to do, any special plan for the week."

"No, Maria," she'd finally answered. "I have no special plan for the week."

Which was a lie, in a way, since she had one special plan for the week: she was going to wait it out.

Because a week, she had decided, would tell the story. Not only of what might happen between Harold and Minda, but to all of them. The story of what *she* would do, no matter what Harold and Minda did. Having spent the weekend watching Harold—pale, distracted, obviously suffering and struggling—having seen that he wasn't eager for the trouble Minda spelled out, she had found, to her amazement, that she simply didn't care how he resolved it. There was only one as- pect of his resolving it that she did care about, but he at least had enough sense—and possibly decency—not to try and repeat their little Joycean scene of Friday night. Lucky for him, since she would have garroted him, instead of the drawer-pull, with the phone cord had he tried.

The week passed quickly and quietly. One of the things that at least made it *seem* so quiet was that for the first time since May, five days went by without Minda calling: Minda never called to tell her about the "lunch" with Scrim—or anything else. And though this might have been taken as something ominous, something fraught with dark signif- icance, she didn't take it that way: She could tell from Harold's con- dition that nothing had happened . . . yet.

But as quickly as the week passed, and as uneventful as it seemed, it was an important week—with many things going on beneath the placid surface, many things shifting and changing. Irrevocably.

Though she continued to watch Harold, it was from a great distance, and though by the end of the week she saw he had passed through some crisis point, it really didn't matter, since by that time she had already

passed through some crisis point of her own. Her Rough Year had come
to an end. In every way. As early as the middle of the week, she knew,
without the official word from Tepp (whom she was due to see again
on Friday), that she was completely well, and on Thursday called
Knickerbocker House and told them she would be back on Monday.
But more important than that: she was completely restored mentally as
well as physically, was turned back into her old positive-minded self.
Not once during that week did she have a glimmer of an attack,
a thought about falling bodies. (Nor had she had any the week before.)
No dreams or thoughts about Burt. None of that. No more hankering
after lost golden days . . . and lost golden boys. No more brooding about the world's great ugliness—or its imminent ending. And hence
no more fears of falling bodies, no more attacks. Gone. All gone. Over
and done. All that was behind her, and all those weeks, months really,
of fear and depression seemed to have happened to somebody else. And
she'd done it all herself, and finally pulled herself up by the bootstraps
just as she'd promised herself she would, and had made herself accept
things the way they were. Which—with the exception of Harold, and
she felt she could even come to grips with that when the time came—
were not only not as bad as they'd seemed, but were definitely on the
upgrade.

Because the week was full of changes for everybody. Changes that
were subtler, but still unmistakable. Benjy, for instance, went on being solicitous, but in a less forced and suffocating way . . . in a
bumbling sort of way that touched her, moved her deeply. Even better,
the phone began ringing for him early in the week, and on Wednesday
he even went to Oliver Ulrich's after school and stayed for dinner.
But best of all, she didn't see him bring one single new piece of electrical equipment into the house during that week, or see him tinkering
with what was already on the shelves—and she had the feeling that one
day soon she would come in and find the tangles of junk gone from
the shelves, and the neat piles of books and games and records restored
to their rightful places. *"When I was a child, I spake as a child, I understood as a child, I thought as a child; but when I became a man, I put
away childish things."* . . . Or something like that.

There were also subtle changes in Maria. Though she went on being almost unnaturally quiet and subdued throughout the week, there
was nothing jarring or unpleasant in her silences or in just the feeling
of her presence—all that smoldering hostility seemed to have burned
itself off—and by the end of the week Emma even thought she detected

some hopeful new light in the dark eyes. Which of course just might have been due to the fact that she saw the end in sight, knew she had only one more week to get through . . . and then back she'd be going to her *mamá* and little Carlos in Santa Marta. *Gracias a Dios.*

Even the weather passed through some crisis point that week, suddenly switching from the dragging midsummer heat to brisk autumnal cold. Which struck her as being particularly right: looking back, it seemed to her that all the terrible things that had happened in recent months had taken place in a setting of fierce, coruscating sunlight and oppressive heat. And on Friday morning, at the week's end, when she got out of bed and saw the cold gray day outside, she smiled: perfect, a proper ending for that week's long ordeal—and for her Rough Year.

Breakfast, however, was as quiet and uncomfortable as it had been all week long. When Benjy stood up to leave for school, she said it looked like a cold day and told him to wear his warmly interlined hooded poplin jacket, but he shook his head: "I don't really need it, ma. A sweater under my blazer is enough."

"For God's *sake!*" Harold suddenly shouted, slapping down the *Times* he'd been hiding behind—revealing the sick, strained white face they'd had to live with all week long. "You do what your mother tells you to do—and don't be so goddamn fresh. And if I hear one more smartass word out of you, I'll give you the thrashing of your life!"

Slowly Benjy looked from his father to Emma, then back to his father again. "Yes, sir," he said like Roddy McDowall, and turned and trotted from the room.

"How *dare* you take your misery out on that child," she finally whispered.

Strikingly refraining from asking what she meant by "misery," Harold dully glared at her. "Somebody's got to be firm with him. He's been getting away with murder around here. Acting like some goddamn little faggy freak. *Christ.* I'm tired of it. Fed up. It's time he shaped up and started acting like a normal child."

Digging her fingernails into her palms, she stood up, breathing hard. "He's shaped up—no thanks to you. It's a little late to be talking about firmness, since you're just about the most permissive—and disinterested—father a child could have. But he's managed in spite of that. He's perfectly fine and normal. But you're not. And if anybody's been getting away with murder and needs shaping up—it's *you.*"

"What? Just what the hell do you mean?"

But she was already on her way up front, where she passed Benjy just slipping out the door. Wearing his warm jacket as she'd asked. But she kept herself from following him out into the hall to make sure he was all right—and to try and make up for monster Harold with a hug. He would do better if she let him alone. She was learning—fast.

Going into the bathroom, she locked the door and sat down on the edge of the tub. Her teeth were chattering and her whole body was aching and shaking with anger—a kind of aching and shaking she didn't mind. After several minutes, Harold rapped on the door and announced he was leaving—was she all right? She didn't answer. She didn't trust herself to speak.

She waited until she was sure he would be gone, then let herself out. Needing some immediate distraction, she headed for the living-room corner, where she kept a leather folio filled with her Knickerbocker House papers in a bookcase cabinet above one of the couches.

Harold's dispatch case was standing on the floor in front of one of the couches, halfhidden by the end of the glass table.

Harold had brought work home every night that week, undoubtedly a ploy to help keep his mind off Minda, retiring to the living-room corner the minute dinner was over, while she herself retired to their bedroom to read or watch TV. Last night around nine-thirty she'd come out to make sure Benjy was getting ready for bed, and then had gone on to the kitchen for a snack: now that her healthy old appetite was back, she was back to all her old habits. Returning to the bedroom with a loaded tray, she'd caught a glimpse of Harold in the corner—had first seen him stiffen at the clatter of glassware on the tray, then furtively cover something in his lap with a manila envelope. Which she'd thought peculiar, but no more peculiar than the rest of his behavior all that week: she'd hardly thought he'd been sitting there, trying to hide drafts of impassioned love letters to Minda.

Now she stood staring at the dispatch case. OPEN ME, it seemed to say in Lewis Carrolliana, like the plaque above Dr. Hobbema's doorbell. Harold, she swiftly calculated, would be halfway to the office by now; with four other passengers in the private taxi that took him to work, he could hardly ask the driver to turn around so he could come back for the case. He might, of course, send a messenger for it once he got to the office, but that would take at least an hour, if not two.

For one more second she stood there, battling her old weakness. Then lost the battle, as she invariably did nowadays.

She sat down on one of the couches and hauled the dispatch case onto the coffee table, her hands trembling with impatience as she snapped open the latches, giddy with the sick, guilty excitement of the congenital snoop. She hardly knew what she expected to find—again, she didn't think it would be imaginary letters to Minda, his way of letting off steam—but like all inveterate trespassers, she longed to find something particularly private, something especially not intended for prying eyes. Something perhaps even faintly incriminating.

And so she did.

Lying topmost on the pile of things in the case were several Xeroxed copies of the royalty statements Phaedre Press sent its authors twice a year—very boring. Setting them aside on the couch cushions, she considered the next item in the dispatch case—a bulging manila folder marked *Rx* with a red felt-tip pen, the same folder she'd seen in Harold's desk drawer last May. On the day her losing battle with her will power had begun.

As she lifted it out and put it in her lap, she saw that another folder identically marked *Rx* was lying beneath it, but decided the one in her lap looked more promising, being enormously fat and bulging—and turning back the cover, immediately found out why: stuffed inside were layers and layers of old newspaper and magazine clippings, piled in disordered heaps, curling and crackling like dried autumn leaves. With growing uneasiness, she reluctantly dug a hand deep into the heap of clippings, and began sifting through them, occasionally stopping to read at random. Each clipping had a date line written in Harold's hand at the top. And though there wasn't any visible attempt at order, at organizing the clips into any meaningful sequence, she soon saw that they were in a rough sort of chronological order—the ones nearest the top of the pile having date lines as recent as two months ago, while the ones she dredged up from the bottom had date lines that went back as far as six years. Which, in the case of these last, in terms of what they were about, could have been written six hundred years ago, or sixty thousand, could, in effect, have been newsclippings from the Stone Age, scratched with flint on rock: six years had made their "news" that obsolescent.

The "news" on all the clips was more or less about the same unbelievable thing: all the hazards and threats, great or small, to health, and sometimes life itself, in the contemporary world. Some were just news items about the simplest kind of health hazards—the dangerous additives in certain foods, the violations of health codes, the unsanitary conditions in the kitchens of certain New York restaurants (which were listed, and sometimes underlined by Harold)—and had headings like

"FDA Recalls Candy Bars Contaminated by Rodent Hairs" and "EPA Warning on Talcum Powder" and "Limitation on Antibiotics in Feed for Livestock Urged by FDA." Others, more portentous, sometimes almost article length, described every poison or pollutant that had been discovered in the environment during the last six years, and had headings like "Surgeon General's Office Warns Against Use of NTA" and "Plants Called Endangered Along with Rare Animals" and "Environmental Protection Administrator Warns Against Depletion of Earth's Minerals."

Suddenly depleted herself, she actually didn't do more than glance at the headings. Soon she even stopped doing that and, trying to suppress the visions of a glittery-eyed scissor-brandishing Harold, just sifted through a few more crackling handfuls, words like Ecology and Mercury and Crisis and Biodegradable flashing before her eyes, then wearily shut the folder and put it on top of the Xeroxed royalty statements next to her on the couch. After a long, weighing moment, she took the other *Rx* folder out of the brief case and gingerly laid it across her knees: though, unlike the other one, this was very slim and flat, she hardly took that as a promising sign, and feeling like Pandora— there was no telling what she'd let out *this* time—she warily turned back the cover.

Not warily enough.

The first thing she saw was her own name, printed in the Pica-type caps of the old Royal portable they kept in the front closet. "EMMA'S FUO." Typed as a title across the top of a page of blue-lined yellow paper. With a parenthesized message directly beneath: "(Consider the beauty, the sheer poetic irony of their calling it a FUO—FUO being an anagram of UFO, Unidentified Flying Object, both being perfect examples of frightening phenomena our so-called experts can't explain.)"

She read this three times. Slowly. Then read on. Below it, after a large space, there was a subheading, in caps again: "ARGUMENTS FOR S.O.B. TEPP." Then, filling the rest of the page, the ARGUMENTS:

"1. The psychogenic-in-origin factor. Emma's repressed guilt about her mother's death eating (literally) away at her, weakening her physically and lowering her body's defenses, leaving her wide open to #2.

"2. Prevalence of wildly virulent new organisms in the environment, and lack of updated tests sensitive and advanced enough to detect presence of said deadly organisms.

"3. The way Emma could have picked up said organisms. Her eating habits. Her appetite (which genius-Tepp might not know about, with her being so thin). The way she'll eat anything that doesn't move when she's hungry. The way she's always hungry. The kinds of things she finds to eat in those squalid neighborhoods her Knickerbocker House work puts her in. Hot dogs and sauerkraut from some filthy cart with an umbrella *crusty* with pigeon droppings and soot. Hot pretzels and chestnuts from vendors obviously in the advanced stages of syphilis. Tacos or pizzas or chili from some booth in a block of tenements, where dead cockroaches and rat droppings are mixed in with the sawdust on the floor. Rare—never medium or well-done—always almost-raw *rare* hamburgers, which are always eaten at some fleabitten five-and-ten snack bar or some drugstore soda-counter, never an authentic hamburger joint. Egg- or tuna-salad sandwiches oozing old mayonnaise in those short-order "luncheonettes," where they keep the food in those unrefrigerated bins from one day to the next. (Just listing all this makes me sick.)

"4. Emma's running that play group in a church on the Lower East Side last July—where she undoubtedly ate some disgusting snack off a pushcart, which contained the as-yet-unclassified organism causing her FUO, some distant cousin, say, of the amoeba or salmonella, genus unknown.

"5. Afterthought. For what it's worth. Red-herring question for Tepp: *Is cancer catching?*"

Afterthought. For what it's worth. Red-herring question for Emma: Is Harold Sohier for real, or is *he* some as-yet-unclassified organism, genus unknown? she thought as she sat clutching the yellow paper, suddenly noticing the date line written across the upper right-hand corner. A day in early September a month and a half ago, when she'd been in the hospital. A day, she rapidly calculated, just shortly before her terrible depression struck. Suddenly all the mysterious questions Tepp had asked about Harold on the second day of her depression came rushing back; matching the dates, Harold would have presented poor "S.O.B." Tepp with his "arguments" by then. Arguments to what end? To prove that he, Harold Sohier, had come up with the explanation for her FUO, where the "so-called experts" had failed? Poor Tepp. Poor sweet, restrained Martin Tepp. Asking her all those veiled questions about her "relationship" with Harold, even asking Harold's age, no doubt hoping he could hang Harold's extraordinary behavior on The Male Climacteric—which at age thirty-six Harold was too young for (but then, maybe not). Poor Tepp, suspecting that Harold was the cause of her depression. Poor Tepp, trying to spare her, trying not to plunge her even deeper into gloom and depression by even hinting at his suspicions, or hinting at what her eccentric husband was currently up to. And with good reason—since if she'd known that after Harold left her at the hospital, he'd gone home to cut out clippings and type documents like this at the kitchen table, she probably *would* have pinned her depression on him, instead of her crash Required Reading program.

But . . . in the matter of Required Reading, there was still more material in the folder. As long as she'd gone this far, she'd better go all the way and see how bad it was. How much worse could it get?

Next in the folder were several sheets of the creamy 8 x 10 note-pad paper Harold always used for writing reports (and this, as it turned out, was a kind of report), held together by a paper clip. Under the clip was another date line—a mid-April day six years ago. Across the top of the first page Harold had neatly printed a block-lettered title, which read like the rambling, discursive chapter heading in some eighteenth-century novel: SOME COMMON DISEASES, SOME OF THEIR CAUSES AND SOURCES, SOME SIMPLE PRECAUTIONS AND PREVENTATIVE MEASURES TO BE TAKEN. Under this, with a remarkably precise border-indentation of two inches, was a thick column of Harold's tiny, idiosyncratic backhand, the letters formed with the crabbed painstakingness that was always a sign of Harold's being deeply engrossed in his subject. Which, to put it mildly, was the case here, she now found, as squinting in the poor light, she began to read:

(1) *Beef Tapeworm*

Some sources:

a. tartar steak (in spite of your passion for it, an absolute no-no); the head of the worm, which is invisible to the naked eye when embedded in the beef-fibers, is never destroyed by the whirling blades of any meat-grinder; nor, in this case, is it ever destroyed by intense heat, its Nemesis, since the beef is served raw; the ingested head takes the winding trip down to the intestine, where it immediately sinks its hooks into the intestine wall and digs in, settling down to a long (sometimes as long as twenty feet!) and happy life of reproduction *b.* steaks ordered "bleu" or rare hamburgers

Preventative measure: never eat any of aforementioned; when ordering steaks or burgers, insist they be "well done"

(2) *Fish Tapeworm*

Some sources:

a. any kind of raw fish; while one might assume this is a problem applying only to Eskimos, Hawaiians, Scandinavians and certain Orientals, there is a trend among pretentious hostesses to serve only the new or the wildly exotic, and one often finds oneself confronted with a chunk of raw fish (marinated, our hostess proudly informs us, in some "yummy" secret-formula sauce) impaled on a toothpick on the hors d'oeuvre tray; though one might find raw fish on the menus of one's local Eskimo or Japanese or Hawaiian restaurant, it doesn't pose any serious problem where we are concerned

Preventative measure: At a cocktail party, never eat any suspicious-looking canapés without first cross-examining the hostess or waitress or maid

(3) *Hepatitis (infectious)*

Some sources:

a. food handlers; the phrase covers an incredibly wide range of types —starting with top-drawer fancy chefs, and going on through their retinues of captains (like Bruno, who bone the fishes and fowls on a side table in a dazzling display of dexterity), waiters, busboys, dishwashers—working all the way down to people like short-order cooks in luncheonettes; anyone, in short, who handles or tastes (for seasoning, one hopes) the food one is served in public places, or who handles the equipment the food has been cooked in or served on—anyone, to get to the point, who could have "foreign matter" on their unwashed hands or under their fingernails, "foreign matter" being the polite euphemism for what one would imagine

b. shellfish caught in polluted waters; waters where sewage contain . . .

Unable to make out the words—the gray day outside had steadily darkened—Emma reached around and snapped on the spotlight fastened to the bookcase above her, then read on. Holding a hand to her tightening head, she read the rest of Harold's list of "Sources and Preventative Measures" for Infectious Hepatitis, and his lists of "Sources and Preventative Measures" for Trichinosis, Staphylococcal

Gastroenteritis (which turned out to be plain, old-fashioned food poisoning), and Botulism, which having been written long before the Bon Vivant scandal, mostly concerned itself with the home-canned efforts of authors' wives and Celia Bates—whose annual Christmas present of homemade preserves, she now remembered, had been given to the cleaning woman at his request for the last six years. Sometimes groaning, sometimes muttering, sometimes even laughing as she read, she wasn't sure *what* to do when she reached Number Seven on Harold's list, which read: *Common Colds, Flu, Grippe, Strange Viral Infections (particularly in their epidemic form, when they are on the rampage around town).* Wondering if her eyes were playing tricks on her, she read Harold's list of "Sources" for these collective maladies, the Sources running from the air in crowded public places (listed as *a.*) to direct contact with "infected persons" (*b.*), and to all cooking and serving equipment in "public eateries" (*c.*) . . . and to public telephones (*d.*) and money (*e.*). Then she read:

Preventative measures: (for Sources *a., b.,* and even *c.*)—the best and most effective precaution of course would be to stay out of all public places during the height of epidemics; since this is not quite feasible, either in terms of the office itself or the VIPs one is obliged to feed in expensive restaurants, a few rules about restaurant dining during epidemics are necessary: only eat piping hot food (never be timid about sending back lukewarm things); whenever possible, either wipe off cutlery with a napkin, or sterilize it by scorching it with matches or a pocket-lighter when nobody's looking; never, *under any circumstances,* drink out of their glasses or cups; (for Source *d.*)—if for some reason it's necessary to use a public phone, cover the mouthpiece with a Kleenex, then drop it the minute the call is completed and go wash hands with strong soap in the nearest public bathroom; might even be a good idea to keep can of something like Lysol disinfectant spray in brief case during epidemics, which would be perfect for spraying public phones, as well as any number of other possibly contaminated objects, but not our next Source, which poses a real problem (for Source *e.*)—it seems to me that money . . .

The writing dwindled off here, in the middle of the last page.

Glassyeyed, Emma stared at this place where Harold had bogged down years ago—and small wonder, since in order to follow through on any of these "Preventative Measures," he would have had to stop eating and breathing and carrying money—would have had to go live

in some hermetically sealed germ-free room like Proust. Or Howard
Hughes.

That did it. The thought of Harold turned into Howard Hughes,
Harold all togged out in sneakers and white gloves, racing across some
desert in a sealed limousine to have a telephone conversation on a
sterilized telephone—set her off. She burst out laughing, gasping,
wheezing, whooping . . . when a sudden loud clatter stopped her cold.
Wiping her eyes, she turned and saw Maria in the doorway, the
Electrolux at her feet, shopping bag full of cleaning equipment dangling from her hand.

Cleaning day. Friday. Like someone returning from another planet,
she stared at poor Maria—who stood apprehensively blinking at her
sitting there with a lapful of papers, the echoes of her unhinged
laughter still ringing in the air.

Then Maria wet her lips: "I was going to do this room now, *señora*
. . . but if you like, I go somewhere else first."

Good grief. "Would you, Maria? That's awfully nice of you," she
said, trying to cover her embarrassment with a *grande dame* sort of
graciousness. "Why don't you go do Benjy's room—by the time you've
finished, I'll be through in here."

Through with what? said the pale, still faintly-alarmed face, as she
gave the open brief case and littered papers a last look, then picked up
the vacuum and went away.

Completely sobered, Emma sank back on the corduroy cushions and
stared unseeingly at the windows across the room, framing the dark
gray day outside. Poor Harold. Poor poor Harold. What had she called
his hypochondria? A rose? Good God. Here she'd been, upset and
ashamed, chastising herself for her fear of falling bodies and thoughts
about the end of the world—and all the time she'd been living with a
man running so scared, a man so frightened (of what? was the question), he went around spraying telephones with Lysol like some kind of
nut. The only thing was . . . was he so nutty? Though it certainly
looked like it, she wasn't so sure. Wasn't so sure that a lot of the people
one saw walking around, looking perfectly normal, weren't secretly
doing things just as whackily compulsive as this. Things that were
actually a lot like the quirky rituals of superstition—like rapping wood
when a black cat crossed one's path, or clapping hands to one's ears and
chanting "Bunny-bunny-rap-rap" when one drove past a cemetery. The
fetishes of fear.

Maybe. She wasn't sure. But there was one thing she *was* sure about

—so much for the Great Lover, *Sohier erectus*, *homo Aquarius*, the man she'd been convinced was ravening for Minda, struggling in the toils of a passion too big for him to handle, endlessly scheming up ways to get Minda into bed. When all the while there he'd been, a man who —if he really *was* in the least impassioned, and ever got up enough nerve for any of the preliminary skirmishing involved in getting-to-bed, and tried to do something, say, like take Minda out to lunch—would spend all his time checking the waiter's fingernails or wondering if the busboy was syphilitic, and would put his hands under the table to scorch the silverware, not Minda with his burning touch. She felt . . . foolish. And flat. Empty. And sad. Not pitying, just deflatedly sad. The way one felt after finding oneself the butt of a very bad and stupid practical joke. Only there wasn't anything particularly joky about Harold's image. Though his figure, true, suddenly mercilessly lit up, had some of the comic aspects of a plodding Leopold Bloom (as opposed to the Blazes Boylan he'd played the other night)—there was nothing funny about it. Not remotely.

Exhausted, she sat up and glanced at her watch. It was getting late: she had an appointment with Tepp, and she'd better put all this stuff back in the dispatch case just as she'd found it, in case Harold sent a messenger for it. Although she didn't think he would—aside from the royalty statements, there was hardly anything here he'd need in the course of a day's work. Why had he brought it all home in the first place? she wondered, as she began gathering up the sheets she'd unclipped and put next to her on the couch. Maybe just to have a last look at them. Maybe, having come to his senses, having finally seen the complete screwiness and uselessness of all this simple-minded documentation (which had undoubtedly led to the collection of clippings and the purchase of *Merck*), he'd brought it all home with the idea of going through it a last time—before shoving it down the incinerator-chute at the end of the hall. Just like his son had disposed of his sheets. Inadmissible evidence.

Which, if it was true, was an encouraging possibility. But not feeling the least bit encouraged, she slowly began clipping the pages back together, when she suddenly noticed something she'd missed at the bottom of the last page—the page where the problem of disinfecting money had brought him to an impasse. A tiny scrawl, which, unlike the rest of the document which was written in black ink, was written in pencil, very likely the pencil still lying on the glass coffee table. Some comment he'd probably scribbled on the page last night as a sort of final coda, a cryptic remark that wrapped things up.

She bent close to read it—and there it was. Smeared by a sweaty hand. A coda that wrapped things up.

Minda. *Mmmmmminda.*

Like a lovesick schoolboy's doodle.

Like a scream.

A Man of Parts

Halfway to the office in Harry's Taxi, he realized he'd left his dispatch case sitting on the living-room floor, but after one wild, careening moment of panic, he calmed back down: Emma never went poking around in his or anybody else's belongings. Emma never pried or snooped. One of her greatest virtues, and God knows she had many (the more frantic he got about Minda, the more clearly he saw Emma's true worth), was her great respect for other people's privacy. He could send a messenger for the case or just leave it where it was—either way it was safe.

It was of course the terrible row they'd had at breakfast, not really what you'd even call a row, and probably all the more terrible because of that. It had gotten him so upset (what did she *mean* by his "misery"?), he'd not only forgotten the damned case, but forgotten to do what he'd brought it home for in the first place—namely to shove the two folders in it down the incinerator chute on his way out this morning, now that he'd gone through them a final time last night.

Which had constituted another sort of upset, reading all that, seeing how out of his head he'd been for years. *Years.* And not just about his health. Years of struggling and suffering, which had peaked last March with his promotion to the vice presidency—a time when Emma had been too stunned by the news about her mother to notice the state he'd been in, thank God. But all that was over. Having finally come out of it, having just recently picked himself up and dusted himself off, in effect, and having carefully assessed the benefits and rewards of his new position, he had decided to consolidate his gains. Now that he had reached his permanent plateau of achievement, or whatever they called it, now that he was released once and for all from that impossibly demanding and inhibiting old image of himself—Harold Sohier, stellar editor, sober intellectual, political activist manqué—he'd decided he was going to loosen up and live a little. Enjoy himself. In the simplest of ways . . . he'd thought until a week ago. A little conspicuous consumption, now that he was done with being deliberately frugal and understated and modest. A few purchases, a few trips. The obvious sort of things. The sort of things he'd denied himself for years.

And now . . . another way of enjoying himself had entered the picture. One he meant to deny himself with a vengeance. One that was driving him right out of his head again. Making him do things like lash out at that poor kid, who, admittedly, had been getting on his nerves lately, but who still didn't deserve the raw deal he'd gotten this morning. But he was hardly, as the expression went, himself. And besides that, his nerves were so frazzled from lack of sleep, he really wasn't accountable for his actions. For six nights in a row, he had awakened at three or four to a cyclonic siege of lust and despair about Minda, an assault of images and physical sensations so tormenting and humiliating, it had been impossible to get back to sleep. Some last vestiges of sanity and decency had kept him from waking poor Emma and taking it out on her hide any of those nights—just as they'd kept him fighting the craving to call Minda all week long. He felt that if he got through the week without calling her he'd be saved. He wanted to be saved. He thought.

It had been the worst week of his life. He'd been through physical infatuations before (though, granted, none of them had ever had the intensity or high negative-charge of this one), and knew that if they were hopeless, or you didn't intend to do anything about them (same thing), you had to sweat them out, ride them out like a fever. And he'd actually thought he'd been doing pretty well until Tuesday, when Scrim called just before going back to Maine—and then raging jealousy had been added to the list of emotions that had him on the rack. Unaware that his editor was sitting at the other end of the line, distractedly toying with a paper knife he would have gladly plunged into that phthisic chest, Scrim had sniggeringly gone into all the details of his afternoon with Minda the day before. "A fantastic body, as anybody can see," Scrim had said, winding it all up, "and a lot of action, but then . . . nothing. I mean she comes on like gangbusters, but doesn't come. Like all ballbreakers, she's frigid as hell." Guessing that just the reverse was probably true—that like many professional swordsmen Scrim probably had many moments of "then . . . nothing" himself—he'd still been so sick with rage and jealousy that he'd spent the rest of the day wondering how he could pass Scrim on to somebody else at Phaedre Press.

Now, three days later, though he still felt less than sanguine about his relationship with Scrim, he certainly felt more hopeful and sanguine about himself. He was going to make it. He was sure of it. He was going to beat it. The week was up and he'd just about finished with it. One or two more days and it would be completely over, no more than a bad dream.

By the time he reached the office, he decided not to bother sending a messenger for his dispatch case and plunged into a busy morning. At ten forty-two Miss Mayross buzzed him: "I'm sorry to disturb you, Mr. Sohier, but a Mrs. Wolfe is on the phone. I *told* her you were busy, but she said she was a friend of the family, and in*sisted* that I tell you she was on the line. . . . Shall I put her through?"

Sitting immobilized, he finally let out a blast of air—which he hoped Miss Mayross would take for the exasperated sigh of a much put-upon man. "Yes, put her through. If I don't talk to her now, I'll only have to make up for it later. I might as well get it over with."

True. In every way.

A click, and then she was saying in that furry put-on voice, "Harold? It's Minda Wolfe."

"Hullo, Minda. What can I do for you?" he said aptly and swung the mouthpiece of the phone up toward his forehead so that she couldn't hear him gasping for air.

"Well. It's a bit awkward and embarrassing. It's about getting some sort of part-time job in publishing, but it's awfully hard to talk about it on the phone. . . . Could I possibly pop by and talk to you?"

"Like . . . when?"

"What? I can't hear you, Harold. You sound a thousand miles away."

He reluctantly brought the mouthpiece down nearer his lips. "I said like *when* were you thinking of popping by?"

"Well . . . today. This morning. Now, if you could swing it. I could hop in a cab and be there in twenty minutes. It wouldn't take long."

It certainly wouldn't, he thought, and had a lightning-fantasy of letting her have it on his turkey carpet—with the office staff cheering him on. "This morning's an absolute bitch, Minda . . . I'm afraid it's impossible," he finally said, using all the words that were in his head, just rearranging them into a more acceptable sequence.

"Oh." Teeny-voiced.

He shut his eyes and felt himself hopelessly sink, like someone in an elevator with snapped cables, toward the pit. "Actually, it just happens that I'm free for lunch," he lied. "If you like, I could meet you somewhere for lunch around twelve-thirty."

"Oh, I *would* like that, Harold. But I hate to put you to so much trouble. I have a feeling I'm making a pest of myself."

He sat churningly silent.

"Where shall I meet you?"

He gave her the name and address of a restaurant he'd just thought of, one that would be relatively safe.

"Luvverly," said Minda. "Twelve-thirty, then."

With great reluctance he hung up, then suddenly pushed back his chair, leapt up and did a brief but spirited jig across his turkey carpet. Madness. He knew he was mad. Lost. Yet . . . he didn't care. He felt wildly exhilarated . . . and about sixteen years old. He felt renewed. Revitalized. He didn't know where the lunch would lead, or *if* it would lead anywhere, but it didn't matter. What mattered was the way he felt that very moment—which was almost worth anything. And he was finally going to give in and do what everybody else he knew was doing—he was going to live for the moment, seize . . . the day.

Finally calming himself, he buzzed Miss Mayross and gave her the elaborate alibi he'd just worked up for breaking his business lunch date, and for keeping himself covered for at least part of the afternoon: one of the inlays in his teeth had just come out, he explained, taking a leaf from Scrim's book, and he'd just called his dentist since it felt like he had exposed a nerve.

Good old Mayross, not in the least suspicious, was only sympathetic. "I hope it doesn't hurt too much, Mr. Sohier," she said anxiously.

"It hurts like hell, Miss Mayross," he came back, in a statement covering all.

She was late. Though she was just the type to be calculatedly late, this infuriated him all the same. Particularly since he'd purposely arrived at the restaurant twenty minutes early (to give himself time to compose himself and sedate himself with a martini), and all told it just made too long a wait in that dump. Sadly enough, in spite of its new paint job and fake-Provencal decor, the restaurant *had* turned into a terrible dump. Five or six years ago it had been a favorite lunch spot for everybody in publishing, but it had long since been deserted by that fickle mob of agents and editors, and was now taken over by Greenwich matrons in town for a day of shopping and young men who worked in a nearby Design Center. He'd deliberately chosen it because nobody *he* knew was likely to be lunching there—and because he fondly remembered a sparkling Gallic cleanliness, a cozy, intimate atmosphere. But it had obviously fallen on bad times, into bad hands, and as he sat there trying not to gulp down the martini, and trying to ignore the powerful smell of some exterminator's spray that came wafting through the heavy smells of gravy and garlic, he stared morosely at the filthy-looking chefs and scullions working in the glass-enclosed kitchen at the far end of the room, and wondered how he could possibly risk eating *anything* there.

Then there was a sudden stir and a turning of heads and he stopped wondering, stopped thinking—because there she was, walking down the center aisle between the tables, still wearing her sunglasses, long hair streaming, coat open on jouncing breasts.

"Hi," she said breathlessly, effortlessly sliding in next to him on the banquette, as the fawning headwaiter (eyes fastened on her chest) practically dragged the table out into the middle of the room to accommodate her. "How nice to see you," she said breezily, and, neither apologizing for being late (an omission as calculated as the lateness), nor trying for a light kiss on the cheek (another calculated omission), began struggling out of her coat.

He leaned over to help her, his senses reeling at the rich gusts of perfume that came from under the peeled-back coat, and at the way her breasts jutted forward and precisely defined their brassiere-less state as she took her arms from the coat sleeves. Thrown into total confusion, he quickly looked away across the restaurant—and saw two young men from the Design Center sitting opposite them, glaring with outrage at Minda's chest.

He burst out laughing. And that brought him out of it. Brought him back to sanity for a while.

And for a while (after assuring the nettled Minda that he wasn't laughing at *her*), as he grimly kept his eyes off her and sipped at his second martini, and as she demurely sipped at her Kir, they made polite, labored conversation. At first she did most of the talking, telling him what she felt she was equipped to do in publishing (he knew what she was equipped to do, and it wasn't in publishing), then he took over, explaining about the scarcity of jobs, the bleakness of the publishing scene at the moment. And all the time, he kept his eyes focused on things like the smeary glassware, the suspiciously rheumy look of their waiter's face, the ominous color of the *pâté maison* his neighbor was eating, and tried to figure out a way of not eating anything in that pesthole.

They were finally studying their menus, and he had finally worked out a clever way to order but then not eat certain dishes, when Minda suddenly said to the huge, glossy card she was holding in front of her face: "Isn't it time we stopped all this shit?"

"I beg your pardon."

"I waited all week for you to call."

". . . what?"

"I *said* I waited all week for you to call. Why didn't you?"

"I'm afraid I don't know what you're talking about, Minda," he finally managed.

"Oh, come *off* it, Harold. Who are you trying to kid?"

For several seconds he just sat there, paralyzed, fixedly staring straight ahead, not seeing the enormous cockroach crawling up the opposite wall, not hearing their waiter juicily cough all over the basket of rolls he was setting on their table. At last he said: "How many conquests do you need in one week?"

She laughed. "That bastard. So he called you. It figures. The ones who can't make it are always the ones to kiss and tell. I'll bet he even told you I was a lousy lay."

He couldn't speak. Kiss-and-tell.

She laughed again. "I see he did. Well let me tell you—I'm *not* a lousy lay. Far from it. And the same goes for you. I have a feel for that kind of thing, and I could tell right away you were a terrific fuck. Well so am I, and I think we should take advantage of all that. I mean life is too damned short to let opportunities like this slip by. I was sure you got the message and felt exactly the way I did. I could feel it. And I waited and waited, but when you hadn't called by today, I realized you probably never would—and decided to take matters into my own hands."

And with that Minda took matters into her own hands.

"For. God's. Sake. Don't *do* that, Minda."

"Oh luvverly."

"Minda. Are you out of your *mind*? What kind of broad are you, anyway?"

"No, I'm not out of my mind. And the one thing I'm clear about is the kind of broad I am: horny as hell."

"If you don't take your hand away you're going to embarrass both of us."

"So I see," she giggled, not taking her hand away.

Not even trying to disguise his movements, he reached under the table and tore her hand away with a rough, lunging gesture. Across the room the two young men sat gaping at them, their faces a bursting brilliant pink. "*Goddamnit,* Minda," he whispered hoarsely. Picking up his water glass with a shaking hand, he took a deep swallow, as though hoping the water's icy chill would have some effect on the remoter parts of his body. But it didn't. "What I'd like to know," he finally said with great effort, "is how you square this away: what about Emma? My wife. Your big buddy. Your long lost friend."

"Emma *is* my friend and I'm hers," she snapped. "This won't hurt Emma, if that's what you mean."

"I think in one way maybe it already has."

"*What* way." As he sat silent, redfaced, she burst out laughing. "I dare say *that* affected her rather . . . pleasantly."

The bitch. The slutty whore. And yet . . .

"To get back to what I was saying—this won't affect or hurt Emma. Unless, of course, you tell her about it. And I know you wouldn't be that stupid. This is between you and me. This wouldn't hurt anyone and would do us both a world of good. Can't you feel it? Feel how good it would be?"

The awful thing was he could. Sitting inches away, no part of their bodies touching, he could still feel the physical vibrations drawing and tugging between them like a magnet's force-field. It was . . . staggering.

"Harold. Let's get out of here."

"And go where."

"Some hotel or motel. There are thousands of places."

"But we don't have any luggage."

"Oh. Sweet. Jesus. And here I thought you were a man of experience. A man of parts."

Stung, he almost rose to the bait and told her that he was indeed a man of experience—but that in his experience the girls involved had had their own apartments, so these sordid little considerations had never come up. Almost, but he didn't. Something warned him not to give her the satisfaction—or ammunition. "I have an afternoon full of appointments," he finally said, which of course was a lie, since he had already cleared away most of the afternoon's business, paving the way for this business—in the hope it would happen.

"Call your office," she said in the patient voice one would use with a trying child, "and tell your secretary some sort of medical emergency has come up. You don't have to be specific. In fact, the vaguer you are, the more embarrassed she'll be—too embarrassed to ask questions."

"And what if she asks where I can be reached—in case something important comes up in the office."

"Tell her you're going to be on the move—between specialists." Laughter.

"And then what."

"*Then* you'll call some place and make a reservation. For a double room." Giving a little groan, she threw back her head and said to the ceiling: "Good grief. Who'd ever *believe* it."

Which was just the reaction he'd wanted: he was damned if he was going to let her know how he'd already worked out details like this a thousand times in his head this past week—damned if he'd take the initiative. And full responsibility. And blame.

"Come *on* now, Harold. Get the check and pay for these lousy drinks."

He got the check. And paid for the lousy drinks. And did everything else she told him to do: called his office and left a message for Miss Mayross, who luckily was out to lunch, to the effect that complications had arisen with his tooth and he wouldn't be back for the rest of the day; called the motel Minda thought of, and made a reservation for a double room; went to the desk when they reached the motel and signed the fictitious name she'd made up for them, then crossed the lobby and went up in the elevator with her without exchanging one glance or word; opened the door to the room . . . and even before it slammed shut behind them, grabbed her and got her up against the fake grass-cloth wall.

From which point on she didn't try to tell him what to do.

Lights Out

"Why it's Robert! Hello, Robert. How *nice* to see you. It's been so long—much too long," Emma said to the boy who had just rushed past her in the lobby, bring her out of her trance.

The boy, Robert Gorvey, her son's oldest friend, stood by the steps, blushing, alarmed. Then mumbled ". . . finemizoyer," and fled up the steps, out the glass doors, to the safe darkness outside.

Chastened, completely out of her trance, she went and punched the elevator bell.

The trance had been brought on by spending three hours at the movies in the middle of the afternoon, something she never did. She'd passed the theater on her way home from Tepp. Tepp had discharged her, as she'd known he would. "The change from two weeks ago is just *amazing*, Emma. You must have done everything right. Followed my advice and took life easy and pampered yourself. Well, you can pick up where you left off, now—but I'd give it one more week before going back to work. Otherwise, you can resume your normal life. Just come back in a month and let me check your blood—pure routine."

Letting all that lie ("took life easy," "pampered" herself these last two weeks?), deciding not to ask him exactly what had happened when Harold had presented his Arguments for what had caused her FUO (wasn't it obvious?), she thanked Tepp, even kissed him on the cheek, and once outside decided to walk home. She was striding briskly along, considering the comic aspects of Tepp's telling her to pick up where she'd left off and to resume a "normal life" (whatever that was) —when she passed a neighborhood theater, with a marquee announcing "LAUREL AND HARDY FESTIVAL—LOTSA LAFFS," and without a moment's hesitation, bought a ticket and went in. And for the next three hours sat, not thinking, not smiling, not laffing, watching Stan Laurel's every move, watching every expression that crossed his Silly-Putty face. Stan

Laurel was, she realized from the first moment he came shuffling and dipping onto the screen, her spiritual twin. Her *Doppelgänger*—to use the overworked kind of in-voguey word that drove Harold-the-ex-editor up the wall. That sad and infinitely vulnerable rubber face. That forlorn *nebbish* air of gloom and doom. That genius for flapping and bumbling and stumbling and unfailingly doing the absolutely wrong thing. Who else but Emma? Emma herself. The *real* Emma, the one hiding behind the "cool" blond facade everybody saw. The Emma rattling around inside that hollow dummy, that "forceful" and "effective" impostor. Why hadn't she—or anybody else, for that matter—ever seen it before?

Moving like a zombie through the dark streets, she had pondered that all the way home.

Now, getting off at her floor, she decided that at least *one* good thing had happened that day—the reappearance of Robert Gorvey was the positive omen, the sign she'd been waiting for without knowing she'd been waiting: Benjy was going to be all right. From there on in, no matter what happened, no matter how grim things looked for her and Harold, Benjy would be all right. In fact—though certainly with no thanks to herself, or thanks to any of the brilliant revelations she'd had in Hobbema's waiting room—Benjy *was* all right.

Instead of ringing the bell, she let herself in the apartment with her own key, a habit she'd fallen into during the past two weeks. Maybe just because she half hoped she'd catch some member of her household in some strange or compromising act.

For once, a completely appetizing smell filled the little entrance hall, and as she took off her coat, she tried to remember what Maria had said she was going to cook for dinner . . . some Spanish dish? Appetizing or not, she didn't even want to *think* about food, and decided while she hung her coat away, to have a good, stiff drink before even letting anybody know she was home. She needed a stiff drink. As she had so often lately. Her drinking had picked up considerably in the last two weeks.

As she came out of the front closet, voices drifted through the thin wood partitions of the bookcase-divider wall:

"*Arroz con pollo.* Is very good. You will see."

"What's all that yellow cr . . . stuff?"

"*Azafrán.* Saffron I think you call. Is very important to the taste."

In the long silence that followed, she turned on some lamps and, more determined than ever to get the drink, headed for the bar.

The voices from the kitchen resumed, coming even more clearly now.
"What is it you look for in that closet, Benjamin?"
"Saltines."
"Sortines?"
"Saltines. Dry crackers covered with salt."
"I never see such a thing. And I certainly no eat."
"Christ. I didn't say you did."
"You no say. But is what you think. And please—you no take the
name of my *Jesús* in vain. You be *Judío*, the Hebray, and have no right
to call upon my Lord. And why you eating again now, Benjamin? You
and your *amigo* eat up the whole box choco-chip cooky and drink four
cans ganger ale when you come from school—so why you eating again
now? Is no right. I work hard and cook this delicious *pollo*, and when
is time for dinner I sure you no eat it. When I your age I sometime go
whole day without food."
"Tough titty. Maria."
"Taff . . . ??"
"Titty."
"Tafftiddy. What that mean."
"That means too bad. It's too bad you didn't have enough to eat when
you were my age."
As a new and eloquent silence fell, Emma, who had been standing
and staring down into the empty ice bucket, picked it up and rushed
toward the kitchen. Not really for ice—to break that up.
"I tell you something really tafftiddy. Really too bad. My niece,
Engracia, die of the pneumonie when she three. She die because her
madre had no moneys to buy the wander drug, the *penicilina*."
"I agree, Maria. That *is* really tough. I honestly mean it. That's more
than too bad," and making a fast exit on this line, he came barreling
out of the kitchen, almost colliding with Emma in the half-darkness of
the dining room. "Jaysus, you scared me, ma! When'd *you* get home?"
And without waiting for an answer, streaked off to his room.
Maria stood at the stove, carefully lifting pieces of browned chicken
with a pair of tongs from a frying pan, putting them into a large pottery
casserole. As Emma came in, she barely returned her greeting, and
after glancing at the ice bucket, went back to transferring the chicken.
For the first time in a week she was radiating hostility, giving off such
poisonous waves of it Emma had to remind herself there was only one
more week to go.
"Were there any calls while I was out, Maria?" she asked as she car-

ried an ice tray to the sink—just to break the ugly silence; she wasn't interested in any calls.

"Just the *Señor* Soller. He say to tell you he may be late. And when I ask him how late—only because I worry this *pollo* I cooking get ruin, and think maybe not to put in oven so soon—the *señor* get terrible angry and shout he no know, maybe *very* late, and slamming down the phone on me."

As Maria went on to say how "insult" it made her feel to be shouted at, Emma stood holding the tray under the stream of running water to loosen the cubes—while a piercing cold, which had nothing to do with the ice in her hands, penetrated to the very marrow of her bones. This is it. It's happening now. This very minute. They're at it hot and heavy as I stand here—Minda the Whore and the Aquarian Man.

Meanwhile Maria was still going on about the "angry *señor*" and what a terrible "tamper" he had. To drown her out, Emma finally broke cubes into the bucket with a thunderous clatter, then started back to the icebox with the refilled tray.

"I telling you, *señora,* but you not listening, and is important. You the *madre* and should pay attention. The Benjamin be just like his *papá.* He have no manner just like the *papá.* He talk insult to me many time. And he be terrible spoil."

Emma stopped short, making water slosh over the edge of the tray onto the floor. "I beg your pardon . . . what did you say?"

"I say the Benjamin is terrible spoil," answered Maria, calmly ladling bright yellow liquid into the casserole. "He get every little thing he want. He is *muy consentido.* Spoil. I sure that the correck word. I often hear Mrs. Spratt call the terrible *nieta* of her friend spoil. I know what I saying."

Emma finally proceeded to the icebox and put the tray away: tonight. She would tell her to clear out tonight . . . and not just for her weekend in the Bronx. She would pay her for the next week and tell her to pack her things and get the hell *out.* She would tell her as soon as she'd fortified herself with that drink she'd never gotten. And she picked up the filled ice bucket, intending to get the drink without saying anything to Maria before she left the kitchen, but the words came tumbling out. "I can't imagine why you would say such things, Maria, but that's hardly the point. The point is, I don't like anything you said. I don't like your attitude." She made herself stop before putting it more forcibly.

"You no like because is the truth. You never like to hear the truth. I see that for long time now.—Well, is many thing I no like to hear I must listen to in this house. There is many thing I no *like* I must hendure in this house. Many thing. Many thing. Such as all these snix. These snax. Everybody in this crazy house is always eating the snax. And when I cook the wunnerful food, nobody here eat it. Also, the *señor* is just the crazy eater, always afraid I putting the bad thing—maybe he think the poison—in the food, and never say anything nice what I cook. And you. You just no eat at all. And the Benjamin he copy the two you. Is only natural the child copy the parent, but the Benjamin be terrible spoil beside. Is the parent fault too. He get everything he want, that boy. And you the real *madraza*. He say, 'Mama, get the sortine' and you get, he say, 'Mama, get the choco-chip' and you get. But not only the snax—he get every thing he ask. Is terrible no one ever say no to the child, it make for no respeck and much trouble. One these days he get in bad trouble, your Benjamin—he will steal the moneys and buy the drug. Turn into the *tecato*, your Benjamin, you will see. You no even have to wait, he already in trouble your Benjamin. He the real *maricon*. Why he so quiet? Why he have no *amigos*? This terrible boy come visit today be the first *amigo* I ever see, and he just as bad the Benjamin—they take all the snax and go in the room and lock the door and be laughing and laughing, for sure doing the evil thing. But this the only time I see any boy come visit, and he usual sit all alone in the room making the crazies with that *eléctrico* garbage, making that merchine he never let me dust. Is not *normal*, that I tell you. I been around many children, and the Benjamin is not *normal*, I tell you that."

"And I'll tell you something: you'd better clear out. Now. This minute."

". . . *Qúe?*"

"I said get out. You're fired. Dismissed. Pack your things and get out of here fast—*pronto*. While you're packing, I'll write you a check for next week. Which means you'll be getting paid twice for work you won't be doing, since you've already been paid for next week by my mother-in-law."

". . . that old war."

Emma wheeled around at the door. "*What* did you say?"

"I say that old war, your *suegra*—she the liar. Like all of you. You can no treat me like this. I do no wrong thing, I only speak the truth. Is people like you who can no stand the truth—either to speak or to hear. That old war liar, your *suegra*, she tell my aunt Constanza you wunnerful people, nice, refine. She liar. You terrible people, worse I ever met. Now the Spratt *they* wunnerful people, the way refine peoples should be. They treat me like the lady, like the humans being. 'Maria, you absolute wunnerful. There be no one like you, Maria,' the Spratt tell me all the time. And they always asking the news my *madre* and my little Carlos—but nobody *this* house ever ask me news my little Carlos and my *madre* since I come here. Nobody this house interest in anything about me, nobody treat me like the humans being. Everybody this house think only on themself. Selfish. And crazy. And bad. Is bad, is evil in this house, and is miracle I no fall into bad and evil ways living here. But from the time I first come here, I go to the church and make many novena. And I also go to the *adivina*, the spiritist, the fortune-tell, and ask her how to proteck myself the evil in this house, and she give me many secret charm and tell me how to make certain secret spell against the Evil Eye, and is only reason I being able to stay in this terrible house.—That old war, your *suegra*, she tell my aunt Constanza your husband be the very important man. Again she the liar. That be the biggest lie of all. He crazy man. Greedy. Dirty. *Bajo*. He look up my skirt when I on the ladder, or peekaboo down my dress when I serve the peas. And when he no acting crazy about the food, he be eating like the pig. When you still in hospital he eat whole jar the caviar cost $25.00 in the bathroom one night, another night a whole jar olive cost $3.69—I know because I find the hempty jars mark with the price in the bathroom can of garbage next day. If that no be disgusting and *cochino*, then I no know what is. What kind man is that? A man like that be important? *Maria Purisma*, some important that is! How can the Benjamin keep from do the crazies when he have the *papá* like that? Is law the nature and *Dios* that the son follow in the step of the *padre*. And the Benjamin follow his *papá*. While you still in hospital and I alone here at night with those two, I lock my door every night and push the chair against the door and puts the Kleenex in the keyhole so Maria can undress without the crazy *papá* and *muchacho* spying."

All during this speech, Emma had slowly edged back along the sink counter toward the drawer where objects of considerable heft—rolling pins, whetstones, pestles and ricers—were kept. Now she stealthily put her hand behind her back and slipped it into the drawer, blindly groping while she talked. "Maria. If you don't stop all this ranting, and just pack and leave without a fuss, I'm going to call the police." She was going to call the police in any case. Call the police and send Benjy to stay with the Raffertys, some nice neighbors down the hall, until the police had escorted Maria from the house.

"Police. Heff. You make me laugh." And she laughed—a sound that sent chills up Emma's spine and made her clench the hand in the drawer around what felt like the whetstone's handle. "I go. I can no go fast enough from this place. If it haven't be for my Carlos and the worry I make Constanza lose her job, I would be gone long ago, long before you come from hospital. When you first come from hospital, I think maybe you change things here, maybe you make my stay here better. I think you very *graciosa*, very nice, total different from the husband and son, just very weak from be sick. *Ave Maria*, how wrong I be! You as bad as the other two, maybe worse. You. You no think on anybody but yourself. You hanging around all the day doing nothing but the crying and feeling sorry yourself. Ho yes, I see that. Maria never miss the trick. I also see that all this thinking on yourself make you do stupid thing. You buy enough food what feed a family in Santa Marta a month—cheap, lousy food from the super-store except for when the company come, and then you want to put on the big show—and when you and the crazy husband and son no eat, you make me throw the food in the garbage can. You no care. What you care? The whole worl is suffering and changing and dying, but you sits around doing nothing for anybody, sometime crying from feeling sorry yourself, sometime talking on the phone that other *señora* who even worse than you, talking the disgusting thing about the sex and the husbands what they do.—Is no wunner with a *mujer* such as you, the Señor Soller peekaboos down the dress. A stick such as you, no juice, no meat. Is no wunner I never see on your bedsheet the sign that you a lady beloved. Any *muchacha* work the house and make the bed, know from the bedsheet how it be between the husband and wife. And I no mind that. Is beautiful thing when a man love the woman and leave the sign his love on the sheet—it always make me very happy to find. But you. I read your bedsheet like my *adivina* read my palm and tea leaf from my cup. I read the whole story your marry, your life, on your bedsheet, and is sad. Very sad. In true, I feel sorry for you. I have hard life, but is never bad like your life. I have many terrible thing happen to me, but I having much love, *mucho* love. I very lucky, lucky far than you. . . . Wal. Now I finish what you call the runting, now I go. Away from this terrible place. *Si*, I go, I go! I can no go fast enough!" And go she did, first neatly spitting on the floor, then shooting into her room and slamming the door, locking it with a frantic scrabble of the key—as if Emma was the one who was mad and possibly dangerous.

"Good God," whispered Emma. "Good *God*." And finally coming to life with a shudder, rushed up front, deciding as she passed Benjy's closed door to send him to the Raffertys' after she'd called the police: though from all she'd been hearing lately, she gathered it practically had to be murder before the police would come, she felt there was potential murder in the air, and was frightened enough to want to make the try. So frightened she couldn't even remember the police emergency number. Quickly snapping on some lamps, she looked it up in the phone book, and had just picked up the phone and dialed 9, when the lights went out—not just the lamps in the bedroom: the distant glow of the hall and living room lights had been snuffed out too. But maybe it was all in her head, maybe she'd blacked out from sheer strain and fright, she thought as the uncompleted call touched off some automatic device, and a series of loud clicks started coming from the phone at her ear. Then over the clicking she heard the crashing blare of car horns in the street, and a loud thump and muffled swearing as Benjy bumped into something in his dark room.

"Ma?" he called from the blackness of the hallway, as she fumblingly hung up the phone.

"I'm right here in my room, darling," she said, trying to sound matter-of-fact. "Don't be frightened—it's probably just Big Allis. But I need a flashlight. Can you bring me your flashlight, darling . . . I have an urgent call to make."

"*I'm* not frightened.—What kind of urgent call?"

"Benjy. *Please*. Just get me the flashlight and I'll explain later."

As she heard him move cautiously back into his room, she got up and groped her way to one of the windows, pulling up the blind. Blackness. Dense, blottery blackness except for the random, stabbing beams of headlights far down in the street below, and a faint pink glow in the sky above the buildings across the street—which meant the blackout hadn't hit the downtown part of the city. Yet. Shivering, she finally let herself think of Harold, and was wondering where he, and most certainly Minda, were in all that darkness, when Benjy, preceded by a thin wash of light on the rug, came to join her at the window.

"The batteries are pretty shot, ma. I know where I can get hold of some more but it'll take a little while for me to get at them."

"Thanks, darling, this will do for now," she said, grabbing the flashlight, and rushing to the phone.

"What's the big emergency, ma? I mean you just finished saying it was only Big . . ."

A long howling wail from the kitchen drowned him out.

"That's the big emergency," she said, listening with despair to the new sounds—bursts of popping static—coming from the receiver: the phones had blacked out too. She hung up. "It's really not an emergency. Maria's just a bit . . . upset." As the howling from the kitchen grew louder, she stood up and held out the flashlight. "Here, take this, Benjy dear, and go down the hall to the Raffertys. The phone just conked out. If Dr. Rafferty's home, send him back here. But whether he's home or not, you *stay* there."

"Not a chance, ma."

"What?"

A second's silence as the howling suddenly stopped, then a low sobbing began.

"I said not a chance, ma. I'm not leaving you alone with that lunatic."

"Benjamin. You're wasting time and getting me very upset. Maria's not a lunatic. She's just . . . frightened. You can tell from the way she's crying now. As soon as I explain the blackout to her, she'll be all right, she'll calm down. And *I'll* be all right. Go *on* now, Benjamin."

"If you think you'll be all right, then why do you want Dr. Rafferty? Or want me to stay there?—But you're right, we *are* wasting time; c'mon let's *both* go explain about the blackout before she really flips out."

Seeing there was no point in arguing with that stubbornness, seeing that they were, indeed, wasting time, she wearily said, "All right, but let me go first," and off they went. Preceded by the fast-dimming beacon of the flashlight, which made grotesque shadows loom and leap on the surrounding walls, they crept toward the kitchen, the sound of sobbing growing louder with each step. It abruptly broke off with the first thrust of the feeble flashbeam into the kitchen, which seemed to be empty when Emma stepped over the threshold and probingly swept the room with the light. Then at a low moan from the corner, she swung the light that way, and picked out Maria, sitting on the floor, propped against the washing machine: her back against the round glass loading-window, sproddled legs stuck stiffly out in front of her, she sat, tears streaming down her face, the tiny gold crucifix she always wore inside her uniform, pulled out on its chain and held against her moving lips.

"Jesus Christ," whispered Benjy.

"Don't *say* that," Emma whispered fiercely. "Here, take this flashlight, and stay right where you are. Don't you dare move."

Roughly handing him the flashlight, she crossed the room to Maria, who sat, lips soundlessly moving against the tiny gold cross, streaming eyes focused on the floor, completely oblivious to Emma standing above her. "Maria," she called softly. "Maria, it's Mrs. Sohier. Don't be frightened. It's only the electricity. A power failure. There's nothing to be afraid of. Come on now . . . let me help you up."

"No," said Maria, raising her eyes only as far as Emma's knees. "Is the end of the worl. The time has come."

"Come now, don't be silly, Maria. It's only the electric company. Con Ed. Conna Edisona? The . . . *electricictato?* . . . has gone off for a while. It's just Big Allis. They'll soon have it fixed and all the lights will go back on.—Please, Maria, stop crying now and come get up."

"No. Is not the *electricidad*. Is not the Allah. Is not even my *Jesús* or your Jehovah. Is the *diablo* triumphing for sure. Evil. The evil spirits. *Los demonios* has final won. Is the end of the worl. The day of the judgment has come."

"Wrecked. Absolutely wrecked," came a sudden whisper in Emma's ear.

"*Benjy*. I thought I told you to . . ." began Emma, angrily turning on him, but was cut short by the ringing of the phone—a strangely frightening sound in that feebly lit room.

All three of them, Maria included, stared at the instrument on the wall, jangling and clamoring with an ominous, almost human, insistence.

"The phone seems to be working again," Emma heard herself say stupidly, as she stood rooted, reluctant to answer it, thinking: Maybe it's Harold.

"Maybe it's Dad," said Benjy, eerily reading her mind, and went to pick it up. "What?" he said after listening several seconds. "*What?* . . . No. No, she can't. . . . I tell you she can't talk now, for Chrissake!" he roared and hung up.

"That was perfectly disgusting, Benjamin. Who on earth *was* that?" said Emma, warily keeping her eyes on Maria, who had suddenly gone very still. Too still.

"Mrs. Wolfe. *She* was perfectly disgusting, not me. She's all spaced out, just like Mar . . . Listen, ma. As long as the phone's working, I'll go up front and make that little call you were trying to make. I know who you were trying to call now, and I think it's a good idea. I think we could use them. I'll leave you the flashlight and take one of those candlesticks off the sideboard—are there any matches in there?"

"In the top drawer of the sideboard," she answered automatically, too upset by Minda's calling to mind his overbearing manner, or to tell him they didn't need the police: judging from the sounds of sirens out in the street, the police had more important things to do than come quiet a hysterical woman.

Because that's all it was, she realized, listening to Benjy striking matches in the dining room, keeping the flashlight trained on Maria, who sat rigid, glassily staring off into space—obviously in the grip of some sort of hysterical seizure or fit. Hysteria, she knew, could take many forms, but also knew that whatever form it took it had to be handled cautiously, delicately. Perhaps even handled professionally in this case, she thought, uneasily peering at Maria and wondering if she shouldn't send Benjy for Dr. Rafferty the minute he came back: frozen, fixedly staring, Maria looked almost catatonic now—the glazed eyes not even blinking when the phone suddenly started ringing again. Still keeping the flashlight's dim beam turned on Maria, she backed to the phone and picked it up.

"You have got to talk to me!" shouted Minda over what sounded like a click on the line. Benjy picking up in the bedroom? she wondered, but then immediately stopped wondering anything, and gave her full attention to the matter at hand: Here it is. Here we go.

"I don't see why you think I have to talk to you, Minda," she said acidly, stalling, trying to ward it all off a little longer. "There's a blackout going on, and on top of that we have a little . . . emergency going on here."

"Blackout? What blackout? All the lights are on over here.—But never mind that. *I* have a little emergency going on here too, and you'd damned well better listen to what I've got to say."

Staring unseeingly at Maria, she knew she damned well better had. "Make it fast, Minda. Just what *is* it that you've got to say." Form's sake: she knew.

"What I've got to *say* is that I'm in some lousy motel down near the Lincoln Tunnel. I've been here all afternoon. With your husband. Who just this second walked out the door. He was still here in the bathroom when I called before—I wanted to trap him, put him right on the spot—but that rotten brat of yours wouldn't put you on the phone. Probably just as well, since he was in quite a state when he finally came out of the bathroom, and I could see he'd beat me up if I tried to call you again while he was here. So I waited, and he's gone. But we spent the whole afternoon in this room. He acted like some . . . wild animal. And now that he's gotten all that out of his system—exactly the words he used, plus a few other beauts—now that he's had his fun and finished calling me names and finished washing himself clean—he must've stood under the shower twenty minutes—now he's coming home to confess, to tell you about the whole thing. Tell you that I threw myself at him, tell you that I'm a . . ." she broke off in gasping sobs.

Looking across what seemed like miles of checkered linoleum, she saw that Maria was still sitting taut, motionless. "Why are you calling me, Minda? I don't understand."

"I'm calling because you're the only friend I've ever had. And though I'm partly to blame—I *did* call the bastard to ask if he could help me get a job in publishing—he was the one who asked me to lunch. He was the one who acted like a maniac in the restaurant, and halfway through cocktails took my hand and put it on his . . . oh my *God*. The lights just went out!"

"It's only another power failure, Minda. Try to be brave."

"Please, Emma. Don't hang up. Oh God, I'm frightened. I'm *fright*ened, Em."

"What of? The dark? Open the door and call the conquering hero back."

"He's probably stuck in the elevator. And it's not the dark I'm frightened of. It's . . ."

"I don't give a damn *what* it is you're frightened of," she cut in. Then laughed: "The elevator—perfect." And hung up.

The phone immediately began ringing, but stopped after two rings. A second of suspended silence; Maria remained rocklike, transfixed. Then suddenly came to life, clapping a hand to either side of her head, beginning to scream. Completely in the grip of some hysterical seizure now, she sat up stiff as a ramrod, her face a bulging red, and opened her mouth and let out a series of high, mechanical, ludicrously comical shrieks. And dispensing with any thoughts of "delicate handling," having had enough hysteria to last her a lifetime, Emma crossed the kitchen in four long strides and bent down and briskly slapped her on each burning cheek. The screams instantly stopped; Maria sat goggling, open-mouthed. Then a dull, feral rage began seeping across the red face, and Emma braced herself, expecting Maria to leap up snarling and start clawing at her. But the rage suddenly dissolved, and Maria covered her face with her hands and began weeping—a terrible, rending sound that made Emma's skin crawl, made her almost queasy with guilt and pity, but also filled her with relief: the crisis, such as it had been, was obviously past. The clenching pattern of the hysteria was broken.

As she stood wondering what to do next—how to get her to stop that awful crying and how to get her up off that floor—the room strangely lightened and brightened, and she turned to see Benjamin Sohier standing in the doorway, holding a lighted candle aloft like Wee Willie Winkie.

Putting a finger to her lips, she tiptoed over: "She's much better, everything's going to be all right now.—I hope you didn't call the police."

An ironic glance at the weeping Maria: better? Then dryly: "I couldn't call the police—or anybody else. Not even Dr. Rafferty. When I picked up the phone after you hung up on Mrs. Wolfe, there was only this crazy whistling sound, and I . . ." Realizing his slip, he broke off, unflinchingly returning her stare: *Yes* I was on the line—and heard every damned word. Then, briskly, officiously: "At any rate, the phone's out again, but why don't I go down the hall and get Dr. Rafferty myself? Maybe he could give her something to turn her off."

Yes I was on the line. "I think that might be a very good idea," she finally said with a dryness that matched his own. "But before you leave, I'd like to get her some brandy. I think she could use some brandy." *I could use some brandy.* "She's so frightened and upset, I hate to leave her alone . . . would you mind staying with her while I get some brandy from the bar? I mean, you won't be afraid, will you?"

"Of what. Of her?"

She wordlessly brushed past him and started up front with the flickery flashlight that she'd been holding all along. The bathroom and brandy. Those were her needs, in that order. With the fast-failing flashbeam lighting her way, she went into her room and stopped at one of the windows outside the bathroom, drawn by all the noises from the street. What *were* all those sirens? Police cars? Ambulances? Rescue squads? Fire trucks? Had the blackout touched off a wave of violent lootings and muggings and terrible accidents? Shuddering, she stared at the sky above the pale looming shape of the building across the street, all murky blackness now, the downtown glow extinguished. But of course. The lights near the Holland Tunnel had just gone out. For one minute she let herself think about it. First, Benjy: So now he knows about his Dear Dad—and where do we go from here? Then she thought of Harold, suspended high in some elevator shaft, his worst nightmare come true. I hope it drops, she thought, and went into the bathroom.

As she was washing her hands, the flashlight, which she'd stood up-ended on the sink shelf, went out. Not caring, she rushed headlong through the black bedroom, miraculously not bumping into anything, and was passing Benjy's open door when something caught her eye and stopped her in her tracks. A faint glimmery winking. A tiny bluish sparking. Reluctantly moving to the threshold, she peered into the pitchy blackness and gasped: myriad pinpoints of light, faint and blue as starlight, were winking and twinkling from the dark space where the shelves hung above the desk.

Putting a supporting hand on the doorframe, she, Emma Sohier, who as Maria had put it, was Hebray, stood there fighting a wild impulse to drop to her knees and cross herself—just as Maria would have done. Maria who might have been right after all: maybe it *was* the End of the Worl. Maybe it wasn't Con Ed or Big Allis. Or even Allah. Maybe the lights were out all over the world. And the *diablo* or evil spirits or what-ever were triumphing for sure. And this . . . contraption, this infernal machine of her son's, hooked up to no man-made electrical source, had somehow blunderingly tuned into some interstellar communications system in the great void and, converting the warning bleeps into those minuscule blue winks, was relaying the message here into the unheed-ing darkness: PREPARE. THE END IS NEAR. . . . Just as she'd thought in the hospital.

For one more second she stood there, once again seeing herself clutch-ing her son—her son, the Electrical Genius and Prophet—getting him in a maternal stranglehold as the two of them were whisked off together into oblivion or The Great Beyond. Then, making a high moaning sound, she rushed off to the bar, grabbed the first bottle her hand en-countered, and with cat-vision flew without mishap through the dark-ness into the kitchen, which suddenly seemed blindingly alight.

Benjy stood, arms crossed, leaning against the counter, staring at the huddled, quivering shape in the corner with sublime disgust. Which changed to dismay as she flew in pale, wide-eyed.

"Jesus, ma—*now* what?"

"Your . . . machine."

"My what?"

"Your . . . Those shelves above your desk. Go *look* at them."

Blinking—was she serious?—he saw that indeed she was, and took the candlestick from the counter and went out. The counter was the source of the dazzling light: while she'd been gone, he'd taken a batch of candles and stuck them in a line of tall juice glasses, where they lolled crazily to one side, producing the strangely stagy, fluttering, slanted brilliance. Slowly, she looked from the weeping Maria to the bottle in her hand—Harold's best twenty-one-year-old Chivas Regal, not brandy. All to the good. Clattering the neck of the bottle against a tumbler, she poured out a quarter of a glass and quickly tossed it off. At the moment she needed it more than Maria, who would get some straightaway.

Benjy returned. "I don't get it, ma. What about the shelves?"

"Weren't there lights going on and off? Signaling?"

"Signaling?" Assuming one of his more deliberate "owlish" looks, he pointedly focused on the bottle in her hand. "There are lights . . . but what about them?"

"What *about* them is that they're not attached to any outlet. How can they light up if they're not hooked up to anything?"

The galling "owlishness" gave way to dawning comprehension. And squeezing his eyes shut, he doubled over and began laughing. Gasping, wheezing, smacking his thigh.

"Benjamin. Benjamin Sohier. You *stop* that. D'you *hear* me?"

He heard, but only stopped with the greatest difficulty. "I'm sorry, ma," he said, straightening up, taking off his glasses and wiping his eyes with the back of a hand, "but Gorvey and I did a lot of horsing around this afternoon. Gorvey thought all the stuff on the shelves was neat, but said it ought to *do* something. So we spliced a lot of wires together and hooked them up to some batteries and little pen-light bulbs I had. We had a lot of laughs. I went in there before to try and get a few of the batteries free, just after Mrs. Wol . . . just after the phone went out, and I must've accidentally switched it on." With a last shake of the head, he shoved the glasses back on his short pointy nose. "What did you think it was, hey?" Sly. Sly and cool.

Oh no. She stared at this boy, this wizened little personage she had seen herself clutching to her maternal breast as she was delivered up unto oblivion. Well, she was delivered up all right. To at least ten years —but not of oblivion.

His face had slowly turned pink under her stare. "I guess I'll go get Dr. Rafferty now. You sure you'll be all right?"

"Quite."

And as he went through the door with the candlestick, called out after him, "Tell him to bring a sedative."

And now Maria. Poor, neglected Maria. Filling a fresh glass with scotch, she crouched in front of her. "Maria. Maria Nonez. Stop crying now."

The hands came away from a blotched, swollen face. Bloodshot eyes stared blankly.

"Here, Maria. Take some of this." She held the glass to bloodless, faintly chapped lips.

Maria docilely took some of that. The tiniest sip.

"Take some more—it will make you feel better."

Maria took some more—several huge greedy gulps. Then began spluttering and coughing, amber liquid running down her chin. Emma quickly got some Kleenex and wiped it off. "That floor must be cold, Maria—let me help you inside to your bed."

"No bed. I all right. I just upset and fright. And very tired. But I no need the bed. I tired this place, this house, but not the kind tired I need the bed. I start out be very angry and say all those thing to you and getting ready to go from this place, when the light go out and then I get very fright. *Cielos*, how fright! I still very fright, tell you the true. . . . Is the end of the worl, *Señora* Soller?"

Señora Soller was just the right one to ask. "No, Maria. It's just a power failure as I tried to tell you before. The *generador* which makes the *electricidad* is broken—*descompuesta*—but they'll have it fixed soon." She paused, mystified by this sudden return of high school Spanish that had been eluding her for weeks. "If you don't want to lie down on your bed, at least get up off the floor. Here."

Finally accepting her help, Maria let herself be led to one of the chairs at the formica table, sitting down heavily and immediately reaching for the glass of scotch Emma set in front of her. "Where is the Benjamin—where he go?" she asked, taking a deep swig.

"He went down the hall to get a doctor. We were . . . very worried about you."

"I no need the doctor. I fine." More scotch. "This happen very often this blockout?"

"Yes. Very often."

"That no surprise me." And drained the glass in two healthy gulps.

Deciding she had the right idea, Emma went to the counter for the bottle and her own glass. The counter was covered with frozen gobbets and rivulets of wax that had dripped from the listing candles—a strangely pleasing sight. Next to the bottle of Chivas was the casserole filled with browned chicken and vegetables and saffrony liquid and uncooked rice that Maria had left ready for the oven—how long ago? The wall clock had stopped at five fifty-seven. She had no idea how much time had passed since then—it seemed an eternity—but blackout or not, they would be hungry at some point, and with all the food in the icebox spoiling, they had better eat, and eat well, while they could. She was just about to ask Maria how to set the oven, when Maria said:

"The *Señor* Soller—he out in all that dark?"

"Yes, Maria. That's where he is. In the dark." She splashed out more scotch and gulped it down. "Maria, what temperature does the *arroz con pollo* get cooked at? And for how long?"

Maria swiveled around in the chair, blurry-faced, wearing a sweet, saintly smile. ". . . *qué, señora?*"

"The *pollo*. For dinner. *La cena*. Is necessary we eat. How I cook?" Finally hearing herself, she burst out laughing.

Maria joined in, chortling, shaking her head. "Ho, yes. The *pollo*. *La cena*. Put at three-fifty for half the hour.—You think the *Señor* Soller he be here by half the hour?"

"I'm not counting on it, Maria, I'm not banking on it. He may be stuck somewhere because of the blackout." And twirling the thermostat-dial, she shoved the casserole in the oven and, picking up the bottle and glass, went to sit at the table, plonking the bottle down midway between herself and Maria on the white formica. After watching her pour herself more scotch, Maria followed her example, reaching for the bottle and generously refilling her own empty glass, but Emma saw no reason to stop her. The whole situation was beginning to appeal to her: outside, the city lay in darkness and chaos, and there they were, sitting and sopping it up like two boozy old biddies in a Third Avenue bar. Yes. The whole thing had a certain dead-on rightness. Aptness. Only the nagging thought of Benjy intruded, Benjy maybe wandering the hall corridors with his candle like Wee Willie Winkie wandering through the town. But she suddenly remembered: no Wee Willie Winkie he—that Wee personage could take care of himself.

After a few sips, Maria set down her glass; outside of a certain misti-ness to her smiles and facial expressions, the whiskey didn't really seem to affect Maria, marveled Emma, who suddenly realized she couldn't say the same for herself.

"*Señora* Soller, I have a few thing I must explain," Maria said ami-ably. "I say many terrible thing to you before that I be very sorry for now. I like to pologize and try to explain. I be very unhappy this house, *si*, but I no be so angry like I am until the other night. The night the party. *Ave Maria*, but I get angry that night! You want I should tell you why?"

Emma didn't want her to tell her why, Emma didn't want her to tell her *anything*—she'd heard all she ever wanted to hear from Maria—but there seemed to be a breakdown in her synapses, in the hookup between motor impulses and brain. So that, intending to say something deterring, she found herself muzzily smiling and saying, "Yesh, Mia. Why wash that?"

Maria leaned forward, black eyes burning. "You know that old black war cook the party the other night?"

Too late, she set down the glass and pushed it away. "You benny chance speakingbout Coramathu?" Her tongue was like a catcher's mitt.

"*Si*, that who I mean. That war Cora. That war Cora treat me unbelievable that night. I tell myself it no matter, that in two week I be gone from this crazy country, this crazy house, back my own country with my *mamá* and Carlos and my own people who be normal . . . but I no can forget what happen that night, it chew at my inside and make me feel so terrible I can no describe. She treat me like the filthy, the *mugre*, that Cora war. She boss me around and give me order like no one ever do, no even the terrible *Señora* Larrabee, the friend Mrs. Lewis T. Spratt from Wirmington Delaware. Do this, say the Cora. Do this, do that. Wash the ashtray, wash the plate. Dry the glass. Fill the bowl. Hurry up. I no like that, I tell you—I no like that at all. I wunnerful worker and I never mind the work hard, but I only work for one boss at a time. It no have anything to do with her be *moya*, be *negra*, with the black color her skin—but *she* think is that, and when I tell her you my boss and I only take order from you, she get very very angry and excite . . . *Aie*, is terrible thing! And you know what she say, this war? She say, 'I got no interest being your boss, girl, so you better stick the facks!' She then tell me the facks is that you call her up and put her charge the party because she do the party with you before and know the way you like thing—and because she have more the hexperience. She say, 'Just because my skin be black no mean I can't no be smarter than you or have more hexperience than you. Ever since I get here this afternoon you be giving me a pain with your supirra airs. Just because your skin be white no make you better than me. Girl. Under this black skin mine is vein with blood just red as yours. My blood the same color like yours. Cut my vein and the same red blood like yours come spouting out.'—Haiee. I tell you, *Señora* Soller, I no like this speech one little bits. I know how excite these ladies can get, and she very near the knife-rick when she make this speech. 'Maria,' I say myself, 'one little minute and this crazy war going to take the knife out the rick and cut your vein to check the color your blood come spouting out!'—And, *Mariá Purísma*, I soon find out I almost right! But first, because I so very fright you can himagine, I say, 'Señora Matthew, you getting me wrong, I certain no think I be better than you. In fack, I know you better than me in many way, such as the matter the hexperience, and you also the better cook than me by far.' Of course I no really think that, *Señora* Soller, I know I much the better cook, but I very fright and see the need say anything to quiet the war down. And for one little minute I think I success, because she begin the smile. How she smile and smile and show all the tooth, and I be so stupid with fright I now see how strange is this smiling. Then quick like the *relámpago* she grab the big knife she use carve the veal from the knife-rick—and she cut herself, snick, on the arm. And she laughing—*Ay, Virgen!* how she laughing! 'See that?' she say as the blood come dripping all over the plate we have ready to serve the dessert. 'Red,' she say while all the blood dropping from her arm. 'Is red like yours. Not black. Bright and pure and clean and red like yours. You see that, girl?' Of course I see, and I can no tell you how disgusting it be, *Señora* Soller! I always be sick the apparition the blood, and I getting sick then, but I too fright to move because I sure she coming next to cut my vein and see the color *my* blood. But *gracias a Dios* she no do that. She just stay there the disgusting blood dropping the plate and laugh and be so happy with herself she think she teach me the lesson. Then final she stop the laughing and ask where you keeps the Band-Aid, and while she go to the drawer to get I runs in my bathroom and be sick. So sick the knees is collapsing and the walls going around and I no think to lock the door. I so tizzy that when I come out the bathroom and dropping on the bed, it look like the wall with my *Jesús* ready to fall on me —and I decide that is very important sign. I trying to understand what it mean my *Jesús* falling, when in you come, *Señora* Soller, and I see you no really believe I be sick and think I just making with the *temperamento*. While you talking to me, I hear the *Señor* Soller out the kitchen making the fuss over the war Cora. 'Gollies gracious, Cora, what an awful cut—here lets me bandage it, you poors thing!' go the *señor*, make the fuss like no one this house ever make over Maria for sure. And that get me so more angry and upset I think to tell you how that old war cut herself, but I know you will never believe me. So out you go my room, and I still so tizzy I no think to get up and lock the door, and I just lays there hearing you talking the Cora. Then all on a sudden, zup, opens my door and in come the terrible war Cora. When she see my *Jesús* she drap down the knee and do the generflux—she tell me in the afternoon she be Catholic like me—and I think that maybe save me. She have no knife, but when she gets up and stand over the bed, her face is worse the knife. 'Listen,' she say all choking in the throat. 'Now you listen to me, you lousy spic. You gets yourself up offen that bed and you helps me finish this party. There still a heap o work be done and you better come do you share. They no reason you should ruin the party for these folk, no reason Missus Soller should do you work. And speaking of that, you ever tells these folk how I cuts my arm you going be very very sorry. Girl. You do that and I going to tell these people what a war they got working for them—you gots quite a repertation in this building, you little *hispanos* slut. You tell them bout me and I tell them what the back elevator mans tell me when he hear I coming to work a party in the Soller apartment. Some lovely story bout you putting it out for some fella name Joseph work this building —and for bout fifty other Joes beside. All the delivery boy and even the xsterminator too. So iffen you knows what good for you you better gets your *chicano* ass up offen that bed and come and help me, *pranto*, you lousy little spic tramp!' . . . . Yes, is true *Señora* Soller. She really say those thing. *Ay, bendito* to call Maria such thing! *Chicano*, and I tell her I be Colombian. Spic. And slut. And war. And that filth the Joseph, which I soon explain to you, *Señora* Soller.—But that night I decide is too much. All those name make me so angry I gets up and finish the party and say no one more word to that war. And when the work is finish and she finishing changing the clothes in my bathroom, I go in my room and locks the door and I hear her talking with you and final leaving. It is then I lie there in the darkness on my bed, and I deciding on the next morning, the Saturday, I will go no just for the weekend but for final and leave you the note explaining—when hup-zupp, suddenly you pushing the henvelope under my door. So I gets up and opens the henvelope and find the twenty dollar and the note you write me *gracias* for being big help the party . . . and I start the weeping because I see is no right to leave in this way. I tell myself in spite the many bad thing you do, you really very nice and *generosa* and that is only right I finish my time here. I tell myself two week is no such the long time. But I be wrong. Two week is much much the too much. Is too much unhappys and crazy here. Is too much what that terrible war Cora say to me, and is too much what going on in this house, this city, this country—all this for Maria Nonez is too much."

Also for Maria Nonez was too much scotch.

But as she poured herself some more, Emma didn't try to stop her. Emma, having completely and chillingly sobered up during this speech, sat numbly silent, realizing some kind of comment from her was required, but not knowing what it could be. Also realizing that Benjy had been gone too long, she stood up: "I'm terribly sorry about all that, Maria. I certainly never dreamed you were so unhappy with us, or had any *idea* of what was going on with Cora the night of the party . . . but we'll talk about it later. I'm going to look for Benjy. Before I go, just let me say, fast, that the black people in this country have had a horrible time of it for years and years, and they've finally begun to stand up for themselves. Which is a wonderful thing." Nauseated—was she really *saying* all this?—she still went on. "*Anyway*, Maria, all the black people in this country are on edge these days, and Cora is too. I've known her for a long time, and even I found her . . . strange last Friday, but something probably set her off, something that had nothing to do with you or me. Maybe somebody called her a bad name in the subway or treated her insultingly in a store. These things still happen, black people are still being treated badly in this country. The point is, Cora is a fine, intelligent woman, and you really shouldn't call her a whore, you . . ."

"I call her war because that is what she call me! War and spic and *chicano* slut she call me! And my people—in fack all the *hispanos* come this country, no just from Colombia, but from Mexico and Puerto Rico and many other place—all have just as bad a time this country as the black. And get call the name in the subway and other thing worse by far. And please you stay here one more little minute, *Señora* Soller, because I have something to say what is more important than you go look for the Benjamin, who is big boy and can take care hisself. I have to tell you something *really* important. But first I want to say something else: there be many black people in my family, many *trigueños*, but I not be ashame of this, I be proud. I have the cousin Florinda live in Cartagena be blacker than the Cora, but I no tell her that the other night because I see she want to think she have more cause to be angry than anyone else. I see if I tell her about the black people in my family, she only think I lying to try and take something away from her, to try take away her right to be so terrible angry. And *ay bendito*, this is one angry woman! But no matter how angry she be, she have no right to call me the filth name and make the threat to tell about the Joseph she know nothing about. She think *I* have no feeling? She think she the only one who suffer this worl? She think I no know the disgusting thing the men who work this building saying of me . . . and wish to die of this? Do she know that I ready to kill myself for two week now over the evil I do with the Joseph, and the suffer the Joseph put me through?—*Atención, Señora* Soller, *you will please stay and listen!*"

Emma, who had slyly been edging away, froze. And reluctantly stayed and listened.

"It is only justice that you hear me! With the men telling the story, you will hear too—and you must know *Maria's* story. You so concern the Cora feelings, is only right you be concern for Maria too. Is only the justice. . . . Eh, *así*: Yes, I be the bad girl with Joseph the back elevator this building. Yes, I commit the sin and still do the *penitencia* for what the Joseph make me do. But is no use. Joseph is evil and make me evil too, and no matter how many time I go the *confésione* and no matter how many the *penitencia* I do, it never be right again. Never. Mind you, this no happen because I stupid. This happen because Joseph hide his evil behind the lie. Right away he tell me that he love me and will marry me and make me citizer United States and I send for my *mamá* and Carlos and we all live the big apartment in the Bronx. And I believe the Joseph and love him too. Is very *guapo*, the Joseph, a real *macho*, and I believe all he say and think I love and give in the weakness of the flesh. It be six year my husband Felipe die, six year since I be with the man, and I give in the weakness the flesh and commit the mortal sin. Then I find the Joseph lie. Fitzclurence, who work the front door, pull me into the mail room one day, and tell me the truth about the Joseph. He tell me the Joseph already have the wife and four *ninos* out in Flushing. And while I almost fainting from that, Fitzclurence go on to tell me how the Joseph going round boast to all the other men this building—even the *fascista* super—about this 'hot spic piece' he have upstair. Even to the boys deliver the package and grocery he boast this too. At first I want to die, you unnerstand, but I go next to the Joseph to make sure all the Fitzclurence have tell me is true—the Fitzclurence is terrible liar too. But the Joseph final admit all is true, and when I start weeping and trying to hit him, he get very angry and call me name like the Cora and hit *me*—and I final come back this apartment and think only to kill myself. But is mortal sin. Then I think to kill the Joseph, but I no want the sin of *asesinato* on my mortal soul, and if they put me to sit in the prison or in the chair

eléctrico then who would take care my *mamá* and Carlos? Eh? So I go
to my *adivina*, my spiritist, and tell her the whole story. And she give
me many thing—many special root and herb to burn and to even put in
the water for the bath—thing to make the powerful spell and put the
Evil Eye on Joseph. And *ay, Virgen!* it work! How beautiful it work,
Señora Soller! Five day ago the wicked Joseph be carrying the garbage
can from basement up to the street—and hupp-zupp he trip and fall
down all the many stone step coming from the basement, and now is in
hospital with broken arm and hip!"

The Evil Eye. The Evil Eye. Shuddering in spite of herself, she
stared at the laughing Maria, remembering the vile smells and charred
twigs in the ashtray: maybe Maria's *adivina* had put the Evil Eye on
everybody in that house. From all that had recently happened, it would
certainly seem she had.

"I sorry I ask you to stay here and listen all this ugliness, *señora*,"
said Maria, the delighted laughter subsiding, "but I feel is important
you know my part . . . oh. Hal*lo* there, Benjamin! How long you be
standing there? I no see you come in. But is good you come now—
your poor *mamá* just going to look for you, she so worry something happen you walking around alone in the dark."

Emma turned, and yes, there he was. Benjamin Sohier, without Dr.
Rafferty, hands jammed into the pockets of his chinos, solemnly taking
everything in. How long *had* he been there? And how much of the
Maria-and-Joseph story had he heard?

But she was too relieved to see him to care. "I *was* just going to look
for you, Benjy darling—I was beginning to get very worried. Have you
been at the Raffertys' all this time?"

Slowly he looked from her to the flushed Maria to the bottle and two
glasses then back to her again: very worried? Then, hands still rammed
in his pockets, he lounged back against the doorframe with a Rex Har-
rison sort of nonchalance—and, even employing that gentleman's ur-
bane, rapid-fire, pattering style of delivery, said:

"I'm sorry you were worried, but there really wasn't anything to
worry about. No, I wasn't at the Raffertys' all this time. Nobody was
home at the Raffertys'. I rang six other doorbells on this floor, and in
three of the apartments nobody was home. In the other three apartments people came to the door, asked who it was, then told me to go
away. My frigging candle blew out and they must've thought I was
some kind of mugger disguising my voice. At the seventh apartment
some freaked-out old broad named Braithwhaite finally opened the

door. Her place was lit up like Christmas with skeighty-eight candles stuck in fancy candelabra—silver, china, glass, brass. It was wild. When I first walked in I thought I was on the movie set for *Great Expectations*. In fact, I began to think I was *in Great Expectations* with her doing Haversham and me doing Pip. She was just like old Haversham, not at all frightened by the blackout, just lonely and waiting for some unsuspecting sucker like me to walk in and keep her company. Christ. She was all knocked out to see me, and made me sit down on some torn old sofa and brought me this piece of ratty old stale cake she said she'd just baked this afternoon. Then she started yakking about her son—she said I was the spitting image of her son, who she said had been killed in the war. The Spanish-American War, for sure. Had to be. Then she started going on about what was wrong with this city, this country and the whole frigging world. Christ. She was more spaced-out than old Haversham ever was. She said this blackout was only a little dress rehearsal for the real thing—which was coming soon. I would've cleared out right away only she had a portable radio blasting away in one of the other rooms. So I sat there, pretending to eat her lousy cake and in between all her yakking managed to hear bits of the radio news. Seems the whole eastern seaboard is blacked out, and the big-deal experts still haven't figured out where the breakdown is, but they know it's sure as hell more than old Big Allis this time. Anyway, I finally got all the cake choked down and managed to get away by telling her that my poor mother was sick and all alone. I don't think she would have let me go otherwise. I didn't see much point in asking her to come back here—she's about a hundred years old and walks with a cane and certainly wouldn't have been much help for . . . for any sick and frightened mom." Faintly, ever so cynically smiling, he took in Maria, now obviously drunk. "I'm sorry you were worried about me. Funny, since I was worried about *you*."

Funny, thought Emma, bleakly staring: It was the most she'd heard him say at one time for many many months. It was the most she wanted to hear him say for many many months to come.

"Come sit down, Benjamin!" Maria called out affably, now that the stream of words had stopped: all during the time he'd been talking, she had sat vapidly smiling with complete incomprehension, patiently waiting for him to finish. "We are having the very innaresting discussions, you *mamá* and me. Is *bueno*. Very good. And very himportant. Is very himportant peoples should be able talk."

Ignoring her, Benjy turned to Emma: "What's that lousy smell?"

"Oh, the chicken!" cried Emma, and went rushing to the oven which she now saw she had set at *four*-fifty instead of three-fifty. Thanks to her little bout with the Chivas. Yanking out the smoking casserole with potholders, she set it on top of the stove and turned off the oven; the top layer of chicken and rice looked a bit scorched, but otherwise it seemed perfectly edible. "You must be starved, Benjy dear. The kitchen clock stopped and I haven't had time to look at my bedroom clock . . . but I imagine it's close to eight o'clock."

"It's closer to nine. It was eight-thirty when I first got to Braith-whaite's—they announced the time on the radio. But Braithwaite's lousy cake killed my appetite, so I'm not hungry.—Any word from Dad?"

Dahd. He pronounced it Dahd. Something inside Emma congealed like the rivulets of wax on the counter. Slowly, almost majestic, she turned: "No. There hasn't been any word. But I'm sure he's all right. Wherever he is.—Now. If you're not hungry, Benjamin, why don't you take a few candles and go on up to your room and . . ."

"I no hungry either!" Maria announced happily. "So why the Benjamin not sit down with us? Why he should go to his room by hisself? We having the innaresting discussion, and be nice the Benjamin join up. Is himportant the boss and the *criada* be able to talk. Is only way for peoples unnerstand each other. Is real meaning *democracia*. Maybe the Benjamin learn something hear us talk."

The Benjamin has learned quite enough for one day. For one lifetime. "I think that Benjamin might have things he wants to do in his room, Maria," she said loudly, trying to catch her son's eye, but he was too busy watching Maria pour out still more scotch to pay any attention to her. "*Benjy*," she said, even louder, "why don't you go up to your room, as I was about to say, and disconnect a few batteries from that ma . . . from those bulbs you and Robert set up? That way we can have them handy to put in the flashlight if the candles run out. You hear, Benjy? Go on now. I'll stay here and keep Maria company." And as if to graphically prove her point, she went and sat back down at the table with Maria.

Benjy heard. But he stared at Maria, happily swilling scotch, then looked at her angrily, almost accusingly: And leave you alone with that? Then, poker-faced, came to the table and, pulling out a chair, sat down close to Emma with a claiming, proprietary air—too close to suit Emma, who immediately got the drift—and forbearingly crossed his arms.

Lowering her glass, Maria fuzzily beamed at them as they sat chockablock, undoubtedly seeing them through her scotch haze as some classically pretty—and wildly inaccurate—picture of close-knit Mother and Son. "You know, you basic very nice boy, Benjamin. Is not your fault you not so nice sometime. Is same for you, *Señora* Soller. You really can no help the bad way you behave a lot the time. Is your *herencia*. Your heritage. Not just what you herit from your parent, but even more what you herit from this country, from just you living here America. Is way all the peoples living this country be."

As she paused for another sip, Emma wondered why she didn't pass out. Emma was also wondering how to get her to stop drinking and talking and get her into her room without its precipitating another crisis—when Benjy moved his chair still closer to her own and complicitly nudged her thigh with his knobbly knee: Are you digging this? How *about* this?

And though she longed to move her chair away, Emma froze. Was this the beginning of the new order? she wondered, panicking. With Dahd Deposed, that stony statue of authority toppled, was he now going to step up on the pedestal in its place? Was that the way things were going to go? As vistas of an unknown future opened up in front of her, Emma decided she wouldn't try to stop Maria from drinking or talking for anything in the world.

Jouncing down her glass, Maria gave them one last look of soft indulgence—*si*, very pretty, the *madre* and *hijo*—then the eyes hardened: "Long ago, when my aunt Constanza come home to visit in Colombia, she tell stories about some of the Americanos who stay in the Happy Hacienda Motel, and nobody believe her. She tell us that not only do the *yanquis* take everything from motel room that not be nail down or lock with chain—the towel, the sheet, the Bible, the hanger, the lamp, the radio, and would you believe even the television until they learn to chain down—but they sometime make the disgusting thing and leave on the floor like the animal. This I never believe, but one morning when I be in Albuquerque, before I come this job, Constanza find the disgusting thing on floor in one the motel room, and she call me in to see. I go, I see, I final believe, and it make me very sick, because I unnerstand. You know why they do such a thing, some *gringos*, some *yanquis*? They leave such the disgusting thing the middle of the floor just to show what they think the other peoples in the worl. Ah *si*, is absolute true, I swear—it does no good to shake the head. What else you think it mean when one kind of humans leave such a thing for another humans to clean up? It mean, it just a way of saying, 'You be no better than this disgusting thing I making and leaving on the floor.' Is just a way of saying 'I be much better than you by far, I more superior.' Is exactly what that mean. And though I, Maria Nonez, see many strange thing this life and this should no surprise me so much, I tell you I can no unnerstand a people do such a thing. What is that? I ask you. What kind of people doing thing like that? Is possible such people think they educate? Or civilize? Just because such people discover to make the hydro and tomic *bomba* and to send the stronauts off to jump like monkeys around the moon—is any reason for such a people to think they superior the rest the worl? What care I the stronauts go picking at the moon rock when my little niece Engracia die because there be not enough pesos to buy the *penicilina?* What care I the stronauts coming down the moon and falling in ocean and climbing on the boat where immediate *El Presidente* is calling on telephone from Warshington to say, 'Nice work, boys! I congrats!' And when these gringo stronauts riding in parade, all the little peoples like me supposing to stand on the sidewalk and clap the hand and shout like *El Presidente,* 'Well done, boys! Hoorays, Hoorays!' . . . Hoorays what? What care I such idiot thing going on? For why I should cheer? Is same thing when *yanquis* like the stronauts going marching over the little people with the big boot and shotting in the ditch with the gun and throwing the gorsaline and dropping the *bomba*—and all the time is saying is for to keep those little peoples free, to keep the *democracia* and freedom alive in the worl. Ha. Is some big funny that. Freedom for to do what? Freedom for that such a one as I shall go down on the knee to scrub the floor for such a one as you? Or clean up the disgusting thing? Why should that be, I ask you? Someone must explain why some peoples has all the moneys and powers and say-sos in this worl—and little peoples like I and even the war Cora has to do all the hard work. Has to take the order and say, 'Yes, please, you is absolute right,' and kiss the berhine just to get enough moneys for a *nino* like my Carlos to have the shoe and bread and wander drug. Hoo. Haiye. *Cielos,* I no can unnerstand such a thing! In the very truth I can no *stand* such a thing and oftime thinking I can no longer go on. That I should go on in a worl where is such things make absolute no sense. That such a one as I should have to cook and clean for peoples so selfish and unhappy they be blind all their blessing—make no sense at all. Peoples be so stupid with unhappy they no know how enjoy the life, how to *live* the life. Peoples who making a house where is no sunshine, no joy. A house where is no napkin ring. No spoon to eat the grapefruit. No finger-bowl. No laughter or singing. No lace tablecloth. A house where is no love to shine the air. No silver teapot. No glasses cut from crystal. No pride. No feeling for the *gloria* that is the life. . . . *O Dios!* What *is* that? I ask you. *Señora,* the Benjamin, *por favor* to explain . . . that Maria should struggle to exist such a worl . . . is make sense? . . . is right? . . . is fair? . . . is *nice?"*

"You can get up off the floor now, hero—one more slam of the crow-bar and they'll have the door pried wide enough for us to get out."

As a pocket lighter flared, Harold lifted his head (he'd had it hang-ing between his knees) and looked up into the face of his tormenter—a balding, fat, middle-aged man wearing steel-rimmed glasses and a plastic badge that read: "Ordway Morgan, Manager, Eastern Branch."

Eastern Branch of the National Vacuum Cleaner Corporation, Harold had decided during the time he'd been trapped in the motel elevator with Ordway Morgan and a bearded, bushy-haired young man named "Mickey," who had the worst body odor of any human being Harold had ever encountered. A time that had seemed an eternity, but he now saw from his watch it had only been an hour and three quarters that he'd been stranded between the sixth and seventh floors with these two, caught in a situation that was his worst dream come true. And from the moment the elevator had shuddered to a stop and the lights had gone out, he'd been sitting in the fetal position on the elevator floor, head lowered between his knees, arms locked about his legs, not mov-ing or making a sound, totally given over to the monumental task of maintaining self-control. In all ways. His terror was that great.

His two companions, after first trying to draw him into their specu-lations—was it just their elevator or the motel's whole electrical system that had broken down? would somebody come get them if they shouted for help? (and they immediately started bellowing for help)—had fi-nally given up on him and, coming together in some unlikely and un-holy alliance, had begun directing a steady stream of abuse at him, making disparaging remarks that touched on his manhood, his mother, his religion, even keeping it up through the hammering of the crowbar on the door. Not caring (Sticks-and-Stones), feeling that anything was better than losing control (blubbering or even more humiliating pos-sibilities) in front of these two, he'd sat huddled, involved in some spec-ulations of his own—would the cables snap and the elevator fall? would they use up all the air and suffocate before help came?—and he too had finally touched on his religion in a totally mystifying regression: Was he being punished for his afternoon with Minda? Was this, in effect, his lightning bolt? Not once letting himself think directly about Minda —either to wonder if she too was sitting in darkness five floors above, or to review, in any way, those hours they'd spent together—he had sat on the floor, literally holding himself together, not even stirring at the shouts of their rescuers or at the first slammings of the crowbar on the outer sixth floor door to the shaft.

Now Ordway Morgan's lighter went out, giving way to the brighter, flickering light of candles or lanterns down on the sixth floor corridor: with their elevator door pried all the way back, Harold now saw that there was only a space of four feet to escape through—the space left between the floor of the car he sat on and the top of the sixth-floor corridor door. Gripped by fresh terrors, he sat paralyzed while men he couldn't see shouted instructions about jumping through the four-foot aperture, and first Ordway, then Mickey, got down on all fours and dropped out of sight. "*You* in there—come on out!" a voice now bellowed at him, but he didn't budge. As the voice shouted again, giving him more violently specific instructions, he knew he had to do it—they might leave him in there for days otherwise. So, trying not to think of the possibility of the elevator's suddenly moving (and thereupon squashing him flatter than a June bug) while he came through the four-foot aperture, he dragged himself to the door on all fours and finally jumped . . . landing with amazing agility on the carpet of the sixth-floor corridor, coming down smack in the middle of a small clump of onlookers and workmen in coveralls who cheered as he safely touched down.

Unable to believe he was safe, unable to believe the strange scene he had just leaped into, Harold picked himself up with the help of many reaching hands, dusted himself off, and, mumbling thanks, blinked around him. The long motel corridor was like a stage set, glowingly lit by candles and flashbeams and Coleman lamps and lanterns, with people comfortably milling about, casually moving from room to room. With only two exceptions, all the doors on the floor were open, and Harold caught glimpses of rooms cozily lit up with the same flickery glow, where people were sitting about in companionable twosomes and threesomes, or stood talking in small clusters. In a brightly lit room directly across from the elevators, he saw his two tormentors standing with paper cups in hand, animatedly laughing and shaking their heads. "There's sumpn'll make you feel a lot better in there," said what appeared to be the foreman of the group in coveralls, inclining his head toward this room. "You suttinly look like you could use it."

Though he suttinly could have used it—he could have polished off a whole bottle of whatever it was they were offering—he decided against any further encounters with Ordway and Mickey. "Thanks, I'm okay," he lied to the man, who was gathering up his tools and preparing to follow the others—to pry open more elevators, no doubt. "What is it? A fuse in the building blow?"

The man laughed. "Some fuse. The whole town's black out. The whole eastern coast, some say."

So much for his Wrathful Jehovah. And Jehovah's curve-ball pitch on the lightning bolt. "How can I get downstairs?"

"You can't."

"What do you mean I can't. There must be a stairway."

"There is. But you can't use it. It isn't lighted, and they aren't covered for that sort of risk."

Quick as a flash, Harold had out a twenty-dollar bill and was holding it in front of the man's nose. "Think that would cover it?"

Without so much as a blink, the foreman wordlessly pocketed the bill and pointed to a closed door at the end of the corridor. "Here. Better take this." Fishing a flashlight from one of the coverall's bulging pockets, he handed it to Harold and went off in the opposite direction.

Feeling strangely lightheaded and unreal, Harold turned on the flashlight and went down a grim-looking iron stairwell with rough brick walls, his footsteps making a doomy sort of echoing and booming on the metal treads. He foolishly lost count of just how many flights he had come down, but finally reached a landing where a huge red EXIT sign was painted above a padded door, and, heaving the door open, found himself in what appeared to be a rear corridor of the main floor, with red arrows painted along the walls. Following the arrows along a labyrinthine course, he at last came to another door, and, pushing through it, found himself in the middle of another incongruous scene. The large, ugly lobby he and Minda had skulked through hours ago (God only knew how many hours) was now jammed with people either moving confusedly about or sitting on every available surface— couches, chairs, window seats, the floor—sometimes alone, sometimes in small groups that huddled around candles, lanterns and, occasionally, a portable radio. The place had the look of a temporary shelter set up for the first survivors of some disaster—a shipwreck or flood.

He shivered in spite of himself: though he hardly thought there had been a disaster, there was something about the whole thing he didn't like at *all*, and though just a few steps would have brought him nearer one of those portable radios, and would have helped him find out exactly what this was—blackout, brownout, grayout, whatever—his only thought was to get to a phone and see if Benjy and Emma were home safe. Phones, he remembered, usually didn't go out in power failures.

But phones, he now remembered, were nonexistent in that lobby: he'd had to make his covering phone call home from the room upstairs—had had to talk to that damned Maria while Minda lay laughing on the bed, impatiently waiting for him to finish so they could have another go-around.

Shivering again—he was *not* going to let himself think of any of that, think of all the go-arounds there had been—he pushed out through glass revolving doors into the chaos of Eighth Avenue. For a moment he stood blinking, vaguely frightened, taking it all in—the cars inching along with headlights blazing and horns blaring, the cars hopelessly jammed in an intersection without traffic signals, the people groping along the sidewalks, some lighting their way with flashlights and lanterns, some picking their way along in the glare of the headlights, others just standing around in those strange little clusters, getting some kind of comfort and reassurance out of company. Needing only one kind of reassurance himself, he cautiously set out in search of a phone booth, suddenly remembering the foreman's flashlight which he'd shoved into one of his pockets when he'd reached the lobby. As he took it out and flipped it on, he happily laughed: never had twenty bucks bought so much.

He'd gone two blocks when he finally saw a phone booth on the corner. Ducking inside, he put a dime in the slot—and miraculously got a dial tone. With a cold, shaking hand, he dialed his number. And got a busy signal. He hung up and cackled with relief: they were home! they were safe! After a minute he tried again, but the line was still busy. Not quite so jubilant, he hung up again, as it suddenly occurred to him it might be Emma on the phone, Emma calling around to see if she could find out where *he* was, trying to find out if *he* was all right. Though that gave him a bad moment, he reminded himself of the alibi call he'd made, when he'd told Maria he would be quite late, and assured himself that there was no way on earth Emma could find out where he'd been.

After another short wait, he put the dime back in the slot—but instead of the dial tone, got a barrage of violently popping firecracker reports. Rubbing his ear, he hung up, then tried again, this time holding the phone a good distance away. When the explosive crackling came again, he gave up: apparently in *this* blackout the phones had given out.

Still not seriously disheartened, he stepped from the booth into the noisy, swarming dark, and rapidly calculated: he was forty-six—actually fifty-four, counting cross-town boulevards—blocks from home. A long haul. A long way to go. It would take a lot of time, and there were certain hazards, but he would make it. He was sure of it. Nothing—no mugger or errant car or anything else—was going to keep him from it.

And so he purposefully set out, cleaving to the buildings on his left, lighting his way with the foreman's torch, not at all disturbed or frightened by the strange noises, the confusion, the blanketing darkness: he was completely confident that with one gigantic soundless click the lights would go back on again, order would be restored.

And this balming thought soon took over his whole mind, diffusing so that it became his feeling about his whole life and the state of the world—an idea which, in its wording, naggingly reminded him of some song they'd played over and over during World War Two. Something about lights going on. What was it again? How had it gone? Damned peculiar he couldn't remember, since he remembered almost everything else about that awful time, even though he'd been only four or five. Particularly the way that gloomy old Brooklyn apartment had always reverberated with the roar of the radio, either turned on by his mother and father, catching the latest news before they left for work or had just come in from work, or turned on by Alonese, the skinny, teen-aged Negro maid who'd cleaned the apartment and taken care of him while Elsie taught school. Christ, what a lonely, pathetic little bugger he'd been. Afraid of his own shadow. Scared out of his wits by all those blasting news bulletins about raids and invasions and bombings and surrenders—and by the sight of Elsie and his poor old man (who died the month after Hiroshima) huddled, grim and gray faced, around the huge old Stromberg-Carlson. What a relief when he was finally left alone with Alonese, and music came pouring out through the gold-brocade-covered loudspeaker—music that sometimes got Alonese so excited, she would grab up a mop or broom and do a switching Lindy with it all around the room. Thank God for Alonese. How he'd loved her and, maybe just through association, loved all those songs, "Chattanooga-Choo-Choo" and "Praise the Lord and Pass the Ammunition" and "Don't Sit Under the Apple Tree with Anyone Else But Me."—And that song.

Which suddenly came rushing back.

And tremulously smiling, his mind flooded with images of skinny, beloved Alonese and snatches of that song, Harold moved jauntily through the blackness, first softly humming, then singing aloud. Completely unaware of the startled glances shooting at him like flashbeams

through the darkness, off he went, trundling up Eighth Avenue, sometimes singing, sometimes counting down the blocks: ". . . thirty-nine,
thirty-eight, thirty-seven, thirty-six . . . 'When the lights go on again'
. . . thirty-five, thirty-four . . . 'All over the wo-o-o-*orld*' . . .
　. . . thirty-three . . .
　. . . thirty-two . . .
　. . . thirty-one."